THE TEMP

Serena Mackesy's school predicted a dire end for her, so after stints as a teacher, temp, lexicographical proof-reader, barmaid, crossword editor and door-to-door salesperson, she became a journalist. She currently contributes regular columns and features to the *Independent* and also supplies features and travel writing to a variety of national newspapers and journals. She lives in South London, likes airline food, seeing in the dawn, Malta and talking, and dislikes ideologues, tidiness and cheap shoes.

The extract from *Finn Family Moomintroll* by Tove Jansson is reprinted by kind permission of A & C Black (Publishers) Limited.

THE TEMP

Serena Mackesy

ARROW

Published by Arrow Books in 1999

3 5 7 9 10 8 6 4

First published in the United Kingdom in 1999 by Century

Arrow Books Limited
The Random House Group Limited,
20 Vauxhall Bridge Road, London, SWIV 2SA

Random House Australia (Pty) Limited
20 Alfred Street, Milsons Point, Sydney,
New South Wales 2061, Australia

Random House New Zealand Limited
18 Poland Road, Glenfield
Auckland 10, New Zealand

Random House (Pty) Limited
Endulini, 5a Jubilee Road, Parktown 2193, South Africa

The Random House Group Limited Reg. No. 954009

www.randomhouse.co.uk

A CIP catalogue record for this book
is available from the British Library

Papers used by The Random House Group Limited
are natural, recyclable products made from wood grown in
sustainable forests. The manufacturing processes conform to
the environmental regulations of the country of origin

ISBN 0 09 9409879

Typeset in Bembo by MATS, Southend-on-Sea, Essex
Printed and bound in Norway by
AIT Trondheim AS

For my parents, with love, admiration and thanks for coping, and for Hilly Janes, an honourable Aslan

Special thanks to the following people:
Jane Conway-Gordon; my wonderful agent, who has revolutionized my life; Kate Elton, my editor at Arrow, for her light touch, humour and good sense; Hilly Janes, who originally commissioned The Temp as a column, and has always been generous in sharing her skill and wisdom; Charlie Standing, who took time he could ill-afford to coach me in criminal activities; Asif Noorani, King of Fashion, for being an angel, and Brian, Claire, Diana and Stonehouse for ranting and hangovers.

And to all those in offices around the world who unknowingly made their own special contributions: thanks. I couldn't have done it without you.

Chapter One

London, England, The World

PAs: have you ever thought about what might happen while you're soaking up the sun in Ibiza? Have you thought about that interloper who will be sitting in your seat, answering the phone, dealing with the mail, transcribing the letters, organizing the diary, taking minutes, chasing up the corporate caterers, doing all those little chores that make you indispensable? No? Well, you should. No-one's job is safe these days, and the last thing you want is to come back to find that everyone liked The Temp better than they like you.

Don't let it happen. There are steps you can take to make sure it doesn't. All permanent secretaries should have a holiday checklist, and, in case you're unfamiliar with standard procedure, it should read something like this:

• Six weeks before leaving: book resort. Show everyone the brochure, swimming-pool, descriptions of night-life etc. Go on diet to fit into puce polka-dot bikini bought in winter sales. Be seen eating Prêt-à-Manger take-away salads and fat-free yoghurt at desk. Book sessions on a sunbed.

• Month before leaving: start heaving worried sighs about how the office will function without you. Fill time making lists on Post-it notes and racing up and down the back stairs with wodges of paper in your hand. Tell anyone who tries to get you to type anything that you don't have time as you have to get ahead enough to get away. Write big sign saying 'BOOK TEMP!!!', doodle flowers all over it and Sellotape it to your telephone.

• Two weeks before leaving: reorganize the filing system, so that no-one can find anything without your help. File-by-date is a good one, because only you will remember when something came in. Failing that, try something like file-by-colour or file-by-nickname. Talk about how grateful you're going to be to get a rest.

• Three days before departure: ring round the agencies. It's best if you can manage to do this on a Friday afternoon, so that the incoming secretary isn't informed of her assignment until Monday morning but, failing that, as long as you give your own name as the contact and a start time of two hours after the office opens, you will have made sure she gets off to a rocky start. If you have any special skills like shorthand, neglect to inform the agency, but if you work in a formal, power-dressing office, make sure to tell them that the dress code is casual.

• Day before departure: tidy your desk. Leave framed photo of boyfriend, cuddly toy and personal coffee mug (unwashed) out to mark your territory, and lock all stationery, pens, petty cash and directions about standard correspondence layout, into lower desk drawers. Do not hide the key under the begonia by the telephone, as that is the first place she'll look. Most important: take the following and hide them in a filing cabinet on the other side of the office or, even better, on a completely different floor: internal telephone list, telephone and computer instructions, boss's diary. Get bikini wax in lunch-hour. If boss has computerized diary, password-protect it and keep your password secret. If you can also manage to lock away the telephone and the audio-typing equipment, all the better. If possible, inform your colleagues that you're not sure if The Temp speaks English as a first language. Tell colleagues that The Temp is called Tracie unless, of course, her name actually is Tracie. This is a brilliant move, as they will spend the first week wondering why she never reacts when they speak to her, and be convinced of her low IQ. Spend two hours writing a note explaining where the coffee-making facilities are, but if there is a daily essential such as collecting telexes from another part of the building and filing them for urgent attention, keep it quiet. Never, ever leave directions to the loo.

• Day of departure: remember to pack sun-cream. Phone from airport saying, 'Has The Temp arrived yet?' an hour before you told her to come in. Relax in the knowledge that, while you're sucking on a pina colada, some woman you have never met has just walked into hell. And found that her name is Tracie.

Chapter Two

All Grown Up

Having a career, having something you actually *do*, is far more important than I ever thought when I was younger. God knows, I've always wanted to *do* something, but it wasn't until I started doing what I do do that I found out that, in other people's eyes at least, I don't do anything at all. In other people's eyes, I'm an 'Oh'. So are Craig, my flatmate, Matthew, my boyfriend, Donna, my flatmate, and Ben, my landlord. We're all 'Oh's, though there was a time when Ben was a 'Really?'.

You know 'Oh' syndrome. It's when you're at a party and you don't know anyone, or you do, but you haven't seen them for a while. So you take a breath and break the ice, and, within the first five minutes, someone will ask you what you do. And me, I'll say, 'I'm a temp, a temporary secretary, at the moment,' or in Craig and Matt's case, 'I'm signing on,' or in Donna's case, 'I'm a council housing officer,' or Ben's, 'I used to be famous, but now I don't do anything much,' and they, in reply, will go 'Oh.' And something will pass out of their eyes, and after a few minutes you will find yourself being passed on like a parcel. Because a job isn't just what you *do*, is it? It's what you *are*.

Our other flatmate, Tania, who is a 'Really?' herself, suggested to me recently that I'm not an ambitious person.

4

I was insulted at the time, but now it's set me wondering. I mean, I always thought I was ambitious, but ambitious people don't end up typing for a living, do they? It doesn't help if you don't really know where your ambitions lie, just have a formless desire to be successful, to be something. My school wanted us to go to university, as though that would, aside from keeping them up in the league tables, be the magic formula. 'You don't want to end up typing for a living,' they said. So I went to university, got the degree and bingo, here I am typing for a living anyway.

There are six of us in our house, and between us we have notched up five degrees, two careers, one ex-career and one entry into home-ownership, three dope habits, two years on the dole and, so far this year, sixteen jobs, fourteen of them done by me. I don't know if this is a good record or a bad one for a group of early twentysomethings: I suspect it's somewhere in the middle. But all I really know is that for the last year I've had no name. Week on week, month on month, I put on work clothes, trudge up to Stockwell tube and go to another place where I'm known, behind my back, as 'The Temp' and, to my face, as 'Um, hi'.

Ben says I might as well change my name by deed poll. I say he might as well change his face by plastic surgery, as it's the only chance he's got of anyone forgetting his past. He was pretty cross the first time I said this, because, of course, it's true. Washed-up child stars are hampered in adulthood only by their names; washed-up teen stars carry the faces that were once their fortunes with them like the Babycham brand.

Anyway, I digress. I hated temping, absolutely hated it, for the first few months, but I've got used to it now. I decided one morning that as there's very little I can do to influence the situation until one of my trickle of interviews pays off, I might as well shrug off the indifference, the invisibility, the tedium, the insults, and try to find the laughs instead. I am, after all, paying the rent and having Life Experience, and Craig and Matthew are getting precious little Life Experience watching daytime TV day after day. I'm not getting the cash benefits that Tania sees as a baby broker, but at least I don't have 'Went up to the off-licence and bought a can of Red Stripe' or 'Got an eight on *Countdown*' as my anecdote of the day.

So I grin, and I bear it, and I read the women's magazines – 'So you've got the career, you've got the holidays, you've got that just-have-to-have Prada handbag, but why can't you get a man?' – and the books that are supposed to be about me ('Giles or Luke? Penny couldn't decide. All she knew was that being a successful model/editor/advertising executive/film producer/private detective was not proving to be as fulfilling as she had expected . . .' 'What do you do when you've got everything but all you want is love . . . ?') and I flip channels in the evenings, watching thirtysomethings with expensive haircuts pretend to be twentysomethings with high-flying careers as lawyers or doctors or forensic psychologists and think, 'They should be so lucky.' Prada handbag? I'd just like to reach the end of the month without worrying about where the rent comes from. Nights out on the town? All I long for at the moment is a night with the house to myself. Fame and fortune? I'd settle for a boss who knows my name.

But you go on, don't you? Maybe I still believe in fairy-tales, but I have to convince myself that things will come right in the end. Like me, this life I'm leading has to be temporary. I'm not going to live like this for ever. Please, God, let that be the truth.

Chapter Three

Lipstick

Work clothes aren't made for travelling in, and yet we spend two hours a day crammed like anchovies into some of the most cramped travelling conditions in the world. After three wearings, my one good suit, the one my mum bought from Marks and Sparks and replaced the buttons on, fantasizing all the while about the figure I would cut as the BBC, Saatchi's and the greatest names in the publishing world brawled over my services, develops a strange fug of ancient grime, unwashed hair and light sweat from being pressed up against all the other wage-slaves. Dry-cleaning costs the earth: the suit spends a lot of time hanging out of my bedroom window in a vain attempt to air it.

At least hair and skin can go under the shower. After strap-hanging down the Misery Line (it took me six weeks of rush-hour travel to realize that that disembodied voice was exhorting me to mind, not find, the Gap), on yet another double-crowded Thursday night, I am caked and sticky, and on the walk from the tube, down a road that regularly has those yellow police signs appealing for information on robberies, assaults and murders, my hands are slightly slippery with tension. I'm convinced that all I want is a gin and tonic, maybe a nice massage, a friendly greeting. But then, if I really wanted that, I wouldn't have flatmates.

I dump my bag – extra-heavy because of the *A-Z*, book, make-up, pens, notebook, spare clothes in case of spillages and all the other stuff you have to carry with you everywhere if you don't have a desk of your own – just inside the front door, check myself in the mirror and wish I hadn't. Think about going straight down the basement stairs to the kitchen and getting straight into the gin bottle, but decide that I really should be sociable. So I push open the living-room door, because I can hear shrieks from the telly behind it and surmise that this is where the boys are.

Craig and Matthew are lying on the sofa and floor, smoking weed, drinking tea and watching *Jerry Springer*, which they've taped because neither of them got up early enough to watch it at lunch-time. It's half past Ricki, and Craig's still in his dressing-gown. Matt's managed to pull on a sweatshirt and a pair of jogging pants, the statutory uniform of those whose only exercise is to reach for the remote control.

'Hi.' I stand there and wait for a response. Matt and Craig grunt, eyes not moving from the screen. A woman with a white beehive is screaming a series of bleeps in the face of a 20-stone black woman in Lycra leggings and a crop top.

'Hang on,' says Craig, 'I thought they were two different stories.'

'They are,' says Matt. 'But the big one says that the weaselly one with the 'tache has been pestering her in her hotel room and he's supposed to be the one that the beehive has dumped for her brother-in-law.'

'Ah,' says Craig. 'Bet you two cigarettes that the one that played the banjo in *Deliverance* is going to clock weaselly one.'

'No, no. He's the gay one who's just told weasel he fancies him.'

'Ah. Then black woman's going to hit him.'

'Probably.'

My wrists hurt after a long day hunched over a hot keyboard. 'How was your day? Pretty average, really. Eight hours of non-stop typing, and no-one spoke to me. Still, it makes all the difference to come home to such a caring welcome.'

Matt tears his eyes from the screen. 'Huh?'

I shake my head. 'Never mind.' Little weaselly one with the 'tache launches himself at black lady. Matt's eyes swivel back to the screen. Weasel disappears between fat one's breasts; a pummelling fist occasionally appears from among the folds of flesh. 'Hey! Hey!' bleats Jerry, proving that only on television can you be paid obscene amounts for being completely ineffectual. (And, of course, in government or the privatized utilities.)

'He'll suffocate,' says Craig.

'Let him,' I say, stomping off to make a cup of tea.

Tania has been leaving notes again, attached to the fridge by the *Mater Dolorosa* magnet so no-one can miss them. Tania is full of little cutenesses like that: good news gets stuck under the cherub, bad news, tellings-off, grumbles, get the full weeping virgin. '*Whoever keeps nicking my milk and replacing it with full-fat, fuck off and die*,' it says. '*This means you!*' Donna, home already, is in her dressing-gown at the kitchen table, smoking a fag and reading the *Standard*.

'I'm going to have a disagreement with a superior and you're going to find that things get worse before they get better,' she says, scratching her arm. 'Phone bill came.'

I put on the kettle. 'Tea?'

Donna shakes her head, waves an icy glass. 'Gin.'

'Good day?'

'Great. Two people threatened to come back and get

me, and a woman brought her five kids in and burst into tears. They've cut off the electricity at her B and B and she can't get any hot water. And Ben rang to say that he didn't get the part, so can we have the rent ready for tomorrow as otherwise he'll have to go back to the telelab, and then *Caught You Out!* will get him again and it'll be all our faults.' Donna is not looking her usual self these days. Her skin, which normally shines with tones of gold and russet, has turned an ashy shade of grey, and she's started chewing the fingernails that used to change colour every day.

There's a burst of life from the sitting-room upstairs. Matt and Craig are shouting, 'Go on! Go on! Kill him!' I guess I'll have to break the news about the rent to them later and extract the housing benefit from Craig, which is a bit like getting teeth from a parrot. I've been playing bossy mummy to Matt for months now, extracting his rent and hiding it under the bed the moment his dole money comes through.

Donna finishes the rest of her glass. 'Her Majesty won't be pleased.' Reaches for the bottle.

'Well, he'll have to ask her himself. Is there any milk?'

'Well, there's Hers. You'll be able to tell it because it's got TANIA written on it in biro. The boys finished the other one.'

'They've not been shopping today, then?' Donna makes a noise somewhere between a laugh and a snore. 'Sugar?' I ask.

'I've got some hidden in the cupboard where the cleaning stuff lives. They'll never find it there.'

'Smart dolly.'

Donna, new drink in hand, gets up. 'I'm going to drink this in the bath.'

'Mmm. Have a good one.'

'Thanks. See you later,' she says, and then, because Donna always takes time to act on her decisions – it's a standing joke in our household – she slopes over, instead, to the mirror by the foot of the stairs and, grumbling, inspects a spot on her chin. 'God, look at the state of me,' she moans. 'I'm starting to look like my mum. And I'm only twenty-three years old. Oh, that reminds me. I can't come and have lunch with Marina on Saturday. I've got to get my hair done.'

Oh, damn. You can't even move a lunch to fit round Donna getting her hair done. It's a full day's work: unpicking the last lot of cornrows or whatever and sewing in whatever extensions she's decided to have done this time. Thank God it only happens every three months.

'Bugger. I was hoping you'd be able to deflect a few opinions. What are you going to have done?'

Donna fingers the little nubbles on her head. 'I thought I might go long this time. Loads of little plaits like your lot get done on Caribbean holidays. I haven't had it long in ages.'

'Cool. It suits you long.'

Donna smiles, starts fingering her spot again.

I light a fag, flick ash into her ashtray. The kettle boils to a clunk and I open my store cupboard. Though the box is still on the shelf, the tea bags are finished.

A bang, a clatter, and Tania is home from the City. Walks into the kitchen just as Donna starts to leave, going 'haar, gaar' and flicking her hair about. 'I hope nobody's in the bath,' she says. 'I've got a client dinner and I simply *have* to be clean.'

'What?' I ask. 'You have to sleep with them, do you?'

Tania flicks round, eyes popping. 'No, of course not.' Irony rationing was in place when Tania was growing up, and she's never really learned to recognize the stuff. 'But I've been working all day, unlike some people.' Donna and I look at each other, as she obviously means us as well as the boys.

'Well, I was just about to have a soak myself, Tania . . .' Donna starts.

'No,' says Tania, 'you can't. Not until I'm done. I'll be quick. Pleease.'

'Oh, well,' says Donna. Tania clatters upstairs.

''S great,' Craig announces from the doorway. 'There was this huge lesbian, I mean, built like the Channel ferry, and she started clouting this rockabilly that had been shagging her girlfriend, only it turned out that the girlfriend didn't really fancy him at all, but had been sleeping with her dog-breeding partner all along. Are we out of milk again? I don't know where it goes. Anyone mind if I drink this beer? I'll get another one later. Oh, God, is Tania in the bath? Now she'll take all the hot water and I was hoping to have one in a bit. Anyway, then the dog-breeding partner comes on and she turns out to be a man in a dress! With a moustache! So Teddy boy started trying to thump him and Channel Ferry burst into tears. Anyway, I can't stand here gossiping. *Star Trek*: *Deep Space Nine* is about to start.'

He leaves for the sitting-room and Donna switches the kettle on for a cup of coffee. I don't think I've ever seen Donna without something liquid nearby. Upstairs we hear the sound of crashing drawers and slamming doors, and Tania's voice floats down, hurling curses about her. 'Where is it?' she shouts. 'Where the hell IZZIT?'

Donna looks at me and I look at Donna, and Donna sighs, 'Here we go,' and Tania comes banging down the stairs in her Paris Ritz towelling gown (bought, not stolen) and barks, 'Has anybody seen my lipstick?'

★

Tania is in a foul temper, as she seems to be a lot these days and, as usual, the foul temper is about consumer goods. The more money Tania earns, the more clingy she seems to get about her belongings. She crashes round the house, opening cupboard doors and slamming them, looking under tablecloths, shifting chairs, turning out the contents of her handbag all over the kitchen floor, and eyeing me and Donna with a venom that looks set to turn to violence.

'I just don't understand,' she snarls, 'why one of you doesn't just own up. Why can't you just say, "Yes, Tania, it was me who borrowed your Chanel lipstick. I'm sorry I didn't ask before. I'll buy you another one." That's all I want. But instead all I get is people nicking my stuff all day bloody long. My food out of the fridge, my bath oil, my shampoo, my drink, my Dior tights: I know I earn as much as the rest of you put together, but I'm sick of you all thinking I'm some sort of charity shop. I work for my money.'

And so do I, I think. 'Sorry, Tania,' I say, 'but I haven't even clapped eyes on your Chanel lipstick. Or your Dior tights. Is it possible it fell out of your bag last night?'

Another cupboard slams, and the snarl becomes a shriek. 'NOOOO!!!'

'Have you tried your bedroom?' Donna asks.

'OF COURSE I'VE TRIED MY BEDROOM!'

'Sorry. Just asking.'

'I haven't tried *your* bedroom, though,' Tania adds with a snarl.

'Uh-uh.' Donna shakes her head. 'We agreed. Bedrooms are sacrosanct.'

'Oh?' says Tania. 'Got something to hide, then?'

Donna sighs, fixes Tania with a glare and pulls the colour card. 'Give it a rest, Tania. Neither of us has your lipstick.

Why would I steal your lipstick? In case you hadn't noticed, I'm the wrong colour for it. I don't go with shell-pink; it looks like I've spilt nail varnish on my lips. You probably left it in a ladies' lavatory somewhere and some swaps trader is wearing it.'

'And another thing,' Tania abruptly changes the subject. 'If I leave half a bottle of champagne in the fridge, I expect to come back and find half a bottle of champagne in the fridge.'

This one's come out of nowhere. Tania used to be the whiny one at university, the one who mostly got her way by making people feel guilty about how put-upon she was. I suppose she's still doing it, in a way; she still whinges, only now it's at the top of her lungs, and there's an element of boastfulness about it all. She doesn't have a drink any more, she has champagne; she doesn't lose lipstick, she loses Chanel lipstick; she doesn't buy dresses, she goes to Harvey Nick's.

'Fine,' I say, 'sorry. I threw that bottle away because it had been sitting there for three days without a stopper and was totally flat.'

Tania gives me a look that makes it clear that she thinks I'm a complete Neanderthal. 'I don't like the bubbles. No-one drinks the bubbles these days. I leave it in the fridge to lose the bubbles.'

Donna and I catch each other's eye and quickly look away for fear of laughing. 'OK,' Donna keeps her voice even, 'we'll remember that in future.'

Tania goes back to her lipstick. 'What the hell am I going to do? I've got ten minutes and I just know I'll never find it in time. Why do I have to live in this dump? It's impossible. I can't go on like this.'

Ben comes into the kitchen, leans against the door jamb. With all the hysteria, we hadn't heard him get home. 'Well, if you don't like my house, Tania, you can always move out.'

'What?' says Tania, 'I lose my lipstick and the next thing I know I'm being given my notice? I don't believe this.'

'I'm not giving you notice. But you don't seem to like it here much.'

'Well, obviously . . .' Tania trails off. Ben, who perfected a line in devilish looks in his starry years, drops his chin and looks at her from under his raised eyebrows in silence. We all fall quiet for a second, and the sound of Craig's bassline thuds through the house from the attic. *Star Trek* must have been cancelled for snooker or something.

'Well,' says Tania, 'I haven't got time to argue about it now. Maybe it would be nice to have somewhere where I didn't have to guard everything I own from the girls who live there.' She scoops up her handbag (Prada), her key-ring (Asprey) and her fake-croc Filofax and slams out of the front door.

Ben doesn't move until the sound of her heels has clicked efficiently to the corner, then digs in his trouser pocket. 'Well, thank God she's gone.' In his hand is a Chanel lipstick, price label still on.

Donna splutters on her coffee. 'Ben! What the hell are you doing with that?'

Devil turns impish. 'Trying it on, of course. I haven't seen myself in lipstick for years.'

'And?'

'Fabulous, actually. I've not lost my charm. Either of you girls got any foundation you could lend me?'

'You bugger.' Donna waggles a finger. 'She's been blaming us for the last half-hour. Couldn't you have said something?'

'Naah,' says Ben. 'I'm scared stiff of Tania. Now, what do you think? If I drop it casually behind the leg of her dressing-table, will she find it?'

Chapter Four

Green Park

It will be a relief to move on after today. It's wearing enough living with a designer drama queen without having to go to work and face roughly the same tantrums. It's worn me ragged after only five days, and I still have the joy of Marina and her dancing credit card to look forward to tomorrow.

This week I am shared between Melissa and Suzanne. Melissa and Suzanne are partners in a glorified travel agents, which organizes group holidays as rewards for the hundred insurance agents who have persuaded the most teachers to leave their vocational pensions, or for the sharkiest used-car salesmen. It's called incentive travel, and what I do is type up schedules for trips while Melissa and Suzanne ring hoteliers and call them Carlodarling.

The schedules are one long round of sybaritic self-indulgence: '8.30 – 9.00 a.m. Complimentary breakfast in Honolulu Café. 9.30 a.m. Meet in Waikiki Lounge for high achievers' presentation. 11.00 a.m. Cocktail party with MD, Automotive Engine Parts and Sales Director, West Europe. 1.00 p.m. Buffet luncheon, Volcano Grill. 2.30 p.m. Minibus leaves for afternoon's golf at Richie's Country Club. Green fees paid, clubs extra. Partners: afternoon at leisure. 6.30 p.m. Meet for cocktails, Waikiki Lounge.

7.00 p.m. Formal dinner, Palm Beach restaurant. Tuxedos only, please! 9.30 p.m. Rest of evening at leisure.'

Suzanne is all right: she says 'please' sometimes. Melissa is a real horror. Like most people called Melissa, she is American, and her vocabulary is scattered with meaningless business-speak. You hear her on the phone when you're bringing her her herbal tea, and she will be saying, 'I need a bottom line on this, Carlodarling, and I need to know when you will have a window of opportunity to update me on the best way to utilize the figures to maximize roomspace.' I keep looking for the 'The buck stops here' sign on her desk, but it has vanished beneath the heap of Evian sprays and hand-cream. She never looks at you, just waves you away with a flick of her immaculately manicured finger.

My first brush with Melissa was at about half-past nine on Monday morning. She marched from the door to my desk like Joan Crawford in pursuit of a love rival. 'You're The Temp, right?'

'Yes.' I stood up to do the usual 'Hello's.

Her hand whipped from behind her back, and a cup and saucer waved beneath my nose. 'What do you call this?'

It was the cup of coffee I had left on her desk five minutes before. 'Oh. Sorry. Isn't it right? Do you take milk?'

'Decaf!' shouted Melissa. 'Decaf! I only take decaf! Whaddya trina do? Kill me?'

'I'll get you another one.'

'Right.' She marched away.

Trish, the other partner's PA, looked over her computer screen. 'Melissa needs her decaf. She gets a bit tense.'

She does indeed. If workload and noise were in any way related, Melissa would be on 18-hour days. As it is, what she spends most of her time doing is rushing around. It took me three days to realize that, like a lot of busy-sounding people, she actually achieves very little. Suzanne is the one who actually produces things for me to do: most of the chores I get from Melissa involve telephoning: telephoning restaurants for lunch, telephoning restaurants for dinner, telephoning the hairdresser, telephoning the minicab firm to book the car to take her to lunch. My name, by the way, in this office, is a full and formal forename and surname. My surname is 'You!'; my forename is 'Hey!' as in 'Hey! You!'

Yesterday Suzanne took off for Atlanta, Georgia, to supervise a three-day paddle-steamer cruise for air-conditioning salesmen, leaving a 30-page itinerary on Melissa's desk for correction. It came back with changes sketched like spiderwebs with an HB pencil in the margins. I put on my specs, went through them, printed it out.

Five minutes later she was at my desk, face puce. 'When I tell you to change something,' she howled, 'you damn well change it!'

Once I'd landed back in my seat, I went, 'God, I'm sorry, Melissa. What did I miss?'

'This!' On page 17, near the bottom, looking like a fault in the paper, was a single dot, no indication in the text of where it should be. I had missed a full stop. 'I'll do it now. I'm sorry.'

'That agency!' shrieked Melissa. 'Never, ever again! I might as well do it myself. Don't I have enough to do without—' She broke off mid-sentence, stared at her hand, lower lip wobbling. 'Get my manicurist. Now. I need an appointment this afternoon. Tell him it's an emergency.'

Chapter Five

Misery Line

On Fridays, the Northern Line always creeps along at about half a mile an hour, so sod's law would naturally have it that today is the day when I forget to bring a book. Not a good move if you're spending time on public transport. The Poems on the Underground are deliberately chosen for people with a short attention span; William Carlos Williams's plums poem is a gorgeous example of 20th-century pith, but *The Rime of the Ancient Mariner* would be more like it when you have to go all the way up the Misery Line.

It's quite a revolting time to be making the journey, anyway; bang on the middle of the rush hour, in the midst of torrential rain, so that the carriage suppurates with a greyish smog that would have had Carolean Londoners reaching for their posies, and occasionally I am assailed by the urge to check my armpits until I notice that some man has taken his suit jacket off two rows down. After ten minutes' gradual edging towards the seats (you can always tell a true Londoner by their gradual edging), I fling myself onto a shiny patch of someone else's old chewing-gum and start to read the backs of my fellow passengers' newspapers. If you only read the backs of newspapers, you'd think there was an awful lot of sport in the world. Sport, and adultery.

Of course, being rush hour, the train is full of suits. Little shorty skirty suits as seen in a million Hollywood corporate movies, and scratchy grey dry-cleaned-sometime-in-1995 suits as worn by men throughout the century. Shorty skirty suits are mostly dug into books: *Families and How to Survive Them*; *Problem People at Work*; *The Patsy Kensit Diet Book*. Clompy shoes over the aisle is buried in *How to Read a Person like a Book*. Crammed down into my seat, I think: I know how to recognize something that's not in that book: if it's on a train, has its legs splayed in a broad V and is reading a broadsheet newspaper unfolded to its full extent, it's probably a man.

All up the train, the scene is the same: women with elbows tucked in, knees together or legs crossed, managing somehow to avoid tipping over when the train goes round a corner. Which is great, of course, for the leg and bum muscles; women have no need of gyms if they commute regularly. The scratchy suits on either side of me are reading, respectively, *The Times* and the *Torygraph*. Though each seems to feel the need to read both pages four and five at the same time, each also contrives to have his elbows on both arm rests. Left-hand man actually has his elbow over the arm rest, sticking a couple of inches into my seat space.

At Borough, when the train has emptied out a bit with all the land-line people getting off at London Bridge, three brickies get on: roaring drunk, ginger-eyelashed, covered in plaster dust. They slam themselves down in a row, knees bashing familiarly against each other, fingers dangling into their laps. One produces a copy of the *Sport*. All three start leaning over it, straining their dangly dungarees as they grin in astonishment. Ohh, look. A pair of breasts. Bet she'd give me one right here if she copped a look at me. Fwooar. Don't fancy yours much.

They grin, boggle-eyed, up the carriage, and their eyes alight on the air stewardess on the other side of *Times* man from me. She is doing that crowd thing of pretending not to have noticed their arrival. Reads the travel-insurance advert over their heads. Youngest one nudges his mates, gets out a pen, drops it, hunkers down and stares up her skirt. She crosses her legs, shifts her eyes to the anti-ageing-cream poster.

Torygraph man lifts his elbow for a moment from the rest to turn a page. I quickly slip my own into its place. He notices, looks annoyed; I look blank. Another small victory for X-chromosome guerilla tactics. Over the aisle, ginger men are getting worse, egging each other on. Middle one turns another page of the *Sport* and they look in unison from paper to the air hostess's bosom, down at their crotches, back up at her bosom.

She bends to retrieve her overnight bag, setting off a chorus of urk-urks. Pulls a slim volume from the side pocket, fixes each one in turn with a long, cool glance. Opens the book somewhere in the middle and raises it in front of her face so that the title is clearly visible. Ginger men suddenly start to read the Go Blonde in Sunlight ad above her head. I sneak a look at her book. In clinical-looking sans-serif lettering it offers to supply the purchaser with solutions to vaginal thrush. You go, girl.

Chapter Six

Girls' Lunch

Marina, of course, is late. Not like-the-rest-of-us late, you understand: not trapped-in-traffic-on-the-bus late, or phone-call-from-mother late, or couldn't-find-my-keys late, but Something Very Important Came Up late. Because if you're like Marina, and come from a very important family, and know lots of very important people, and do lots of very important things between dandling career choices, then Very Important is the order of the day.

Fortunately, a couple of people are just leaving as I arrive so I'm able, under the nose of a furious-looking woman with a fur coat and hair that looks like it's been combed from the head of a Barbie doll and transplanted into her head, and an armful of those waxed paper bags with the soft string handles that won't ruin your manicure, to nab a pavement table with an excellent view of the King's Road. I order a double espresso and a glass of water, and settle down to watch the skinny chicks wandering around with their midriffs bared in late September in the hope that someone will pop out of Storm and sign them on the spot, the Bromley contingent in their clompy shoes, the women with the giant tinted specs and the pouty mouths, as they make their way through the swing doors of the shops.

The King's Road always fills me with a grinding mix of envy and contempt. Not as much as New Bond Street does, and no way as much as Harvey Nick's, but more, say, than Clapham Junction or Brixton market. Maybe envy and contempt are my primary driving forces; I certainly feel them, both individually and in combination, more than anything apart from hunger. I feel envy and contempt when I'm in chromey bars where the drinks cost £6 a pop, at parties where I hardly know anybody, when I hear about how well my parents' friends' children are doing, when I see someone with a dog and remember that my dog is in Scotland with my parents, when I find a copy of Harpers & Queen and it drops open at Jennifer's Diary, when I read cookery columns and realize that people actually know what to do with kohlrabi. I feel it when I hear about people my age who have already made a million from their car dealership, when yet another celeb gets to go free to another amazing country on the *Holiday* programme, when I meet someone with a title and sometimes, in the night, when I hear someone laughing in the street.

And, most of all, I feel it when Marina arrives half an hour late, tucks a bubble-wrapped package under the table, kisses the air beside my ears and says, 'Sorry. I had to go and pick up a picture.'

'Oh, yes?' I say, 'anything nice?'

Marina pulls one of those 'Yes, but I'm not going to admit to being impressed' faces and says 'OK, I suppose. I think the artist will be worth something in a couple of years. Frightfully cheap at the moment, of course. I bought this for less than a thousand pounds.'

'How nice. What sort of work?'

'Ooh,' says Marina, 'neurotic foundationalism. He used to be a New Realist, and then he went through a phase of painting things with his own faeces, pickling rats and so forth. Now it's all figurative work, frightfully disturbing.'

'Mmm.'

'Do you want to see it?'

'Love to.'

Marina drops her shoulder down to the table, brings the bubble-wrap back up, simultaneously summoning the waitress and demanding a rocket salad and a black coffee. I order a Croque Monsieur because I've never learned the trick of surviving the day on a couple of leaves and a pine kernel.

Marina unpicks the Sellotape from the bubble-wrap and pulls out a canvas eighteen inches long and two feet high, painted an unhealthy shade of khaki. On it is a tiny figure of Marilyn Monroe over that subway grating in *The Seven Year Itch,* obviously cut from a magazine. She has been glued to the centre of a cardboard pizza that looks like it's been cut from the lid of a box.

'Gosh,' I say, because I can't think of anything much else.

'What do you think?' asks Marina.

I know that she'll tell me I don't understand art if I tell her the truth, so I say, 'Has it got a title?'

'*Serving Suggestion,*' she replies.

She starts to wrap it back up as our food comes. My Croque has a French flag on a cocktail stick stuck in the middle: worth a thousand pounds of anybody's money. Marina picks out a single pine kernel with her fork and proceeds to chew it twenty times before she finally allows herself to swallow. I've only ever seen rich people do this. I think it's got something to do with having had their back teeth removed to improve their cheekbones.

The differences between those already on the career ladder and those of us who are still rooting around trying to find something to do began to become plain to me sometime around July. A lot of things became plain after we left university: that there really was a world of difference between me and the rich people, who went straight into flats and houses of their own in Notting Hill and Islington and Pimlico, and me and the aristocracy, who went straight into flats in Kensington or Chelsea, or Georgian mansions full of ancient furniture covered in worn brocade somewhere within easy reach of the House. But it's not so much the material possessions that make the difference: it's the attitude. I've dropped two or three notches down the social ladder in less than a year; God knows if they'll ever let me back up it.

Marina fishes around in her salad and spears a Parmesan shaving. Nibbles the edge, and gets started. 'So how's work?' she asks.

'Crap as ever.' I can't even think of an anecdote.

'Don't tell me,' says Marina, swallows her Parmesan, picks out a sliver of rocket and rests it on her tongue, 'that you're still temping?'

'Yip.'

'How long is it now? Six months?'

'Going on that, yes.'

'And you still haven't got a job?'

'Nope. I've had a couple of interviews, but . . .' but Marina has decided to sort me out, something she's done roughly every six months since I've known her.

'Don't you think,' she says, 'it's time you stopped fooling around and did something serious? You can't live like a student for ever.' And I feel like bursting into tears. Marina has left the country five times in the past year, in the law-school holidays: twice to Greece, once to New York, once to the Caribbean, and once skiing in Klosters. She would have gone to Klosters a second time, only the Spencers were supposed to be there and Marina doesn't approve of the Spencers.

'What do you suggest I do, Marina?'

'Well,' says Marina, 'I'm not sitting around waiting for a break. Why don't you go to law school or something?'

'Paid for by whom?'

Marina bridles. 'I'm paying for it myself.'

Err, yes. From a £30,000-a-year allowance from her family trust. But Marina hates it when you point out that she's rich so, being me, I simply leave it. I haven't seen Marina for a bit; time was when we used to sit up all night talking boys, emotions, social slights, gossip; now it's incomes, who's getting ahead of whom, subtle point-scoring (which Marina always wins) about who is still invited to what. To be honest, I don't have the energy to compete these days.

'So you're just planning to give up, then?' says Marina. 'You're just going to be a secretary?'

'Marina, it's only just over a year since we left university, and Matt and I were travelling for six months of that.'

'So you're a year behind everyone else already.' She drains her Chablis, pulls a mouth like sucking lemons, and I realize that I don't really like her any more, probably never really have. So many friendships turn out to be based on common ground: living next to each other, people you both know, competitiveness, common subjects of study. I shouldn't get so depressed by the fact that half my university friendships have either exploded in my face or fizzled drearily; at least I still have the other half. Misery frightens Marina; I guess if you've never known anything other than money, it's hard to believe that poverty, or struggling, are anything other than signs of moral laxity on the part of the sufferer.

'You've got to settle to something,' Marina informs me. 'If you'd only apply yourself, I'm sure you could have a perfectly respectable career.'

'Thanks, Marina. I'll bear it in mind.'

'No,' she says, 'don't just bear it in mind. Look at me. I was the biggest party-goer last year, and now I'm halfway to being a lawyer.'

'And who are you going to work for next year, Marina?' I say spitefully, because I know perfectly well that she's got a job lined up at her uncle's firm.

Marina doesn't turn a hair. 'I thought I'd go into international shipping,' she says, as though every option has been laid in front of her for the picking. 'So I'm joining Kalamaris and Kalamaris in the autumn.'

'Gosh, that sounds interesting,' I say, though actually it sounds like a living death to me. 'How did you get a job like that?'

Marina gets out her Chanel compact, touches up the browny stuff smeared on her browny lips. 'Just lucky, I guess. Why don't you go to law school? You could probably make a solicitor.'

'I don't have the money.'

Marina makes a sound somewhere between a pish and a posh. 'Everyone can find the money if they're determined enough. You're just not trying. I found the money.'

'Marina,' I enunciate my words very carefully, close to losing my rag altogether, 'I'm not yet earning enough to qualify to pay off my student loan. At this rate, I'll save enough for law school by, ooh, the year 2030, as long as Ben doesn't put the rent up and the charges stay the same in that time.'

27

'Well, borrow it,' she says. 'You shouldn't be so proud. Just ask your parents.' She puts down her fork, her salad half-eaten, pats her stomach to signify that she feels bloated.

I give up. Stare gloomily out at the King's Road, where a woman with a fur coat and two poodles is screaming at a traffic warden for ticketing her open-top Ferrari.

'I can't afford all these tickets!' she shouts. 'Every day, another one! You're driving me to bankruptcy!'

'Oh, well,' says the traffic warden, 'guess you'll have to take taxis like the poor folk, won't you?'

Fur coat squeals, snatches the ticket from his hand and slams into the car, and I feel that rush of pleasure we envy-contemptors get when we see someone with a face-lift looking upset.

'Anyway,' Marina blots her mouth, reaches down to retrieve her wondrous artwork, 'I've got to go. So should you, if we're going to be ready for Georgie Templeton's. What are you wearing, by the way?'

'I – err – nothing.'

'Oh,' says Marina sweetly, 'not invited? You really *are* dropping out, aren't you?'

Chapter Seven

Autograph

'Georgie-bloody-Templeton,' I snarl for about the sixteenth time since Ben decided to take me up to Covent Garden on the razz so that I didn't spend the whole of Sunday going on about Marina and Georgie Templeton. 'I mean, I was never friends with Georgie-bloody-Templeton in the first place. Why on earth would she think that I would want to be asked to Georgie Templeton's party? He never used to ask me to his parties, so why would he start now? The guy's a wazzock. A pompous, self-regarding wazzock. Why would I *want* to go to his party?'

Ben stirs his drink with his straw. 'Honey?'

'What?'

'Shut up.'

'Oh, sorry. I was going on again, wasn't I?'

'Yes.'

We're drinking mojitos at a table in the piazza – a great preparation for Monday's workload – and I'm starting to feel a bit more cheerful when this girl comes up to Ben and says, 'Excuse me, didn't you used to be Ben Cameron?'

No-one in Stockwell even notices Ben: it's when he's in the centre of town, where everyone's celebrity radar is switched on, that he gets grief. And Ben goes, 'Yeah. Still am, as a matter of fact.'

'Ooh,' says the girl, who's around our age, maybe a couple of years younger. 'I thought you were dead.'

Ben takes his own pulse, tells her, 'Nope. Heart's still beating. I'm still alive.'

'Ooh,' she says again, 'can I have your autograph? I used to have ever such a crush on you. You used to be gorgeous.'

Ben takes this sort of thing very calmly; he's been dealing with it for three years now, and I guess he's used to it. This isn't the sort of thing they tell you about when you sign the Faustian pact as a teenager. Actually, I think Ben's still gorgeous, and sometimes, when he's crammed with self-pity, I even tell him so. He's only twenty-four, for heaven's sake, and still has all his hair, even if he isn't the lithe young waif he once was.

'Sure,' says Ben. 'What would you like me to sign?'

She casts around, finds a beer-mat. 'This'll do.' As Ben signs, she starts in on a revamp of his history. 'The Wild Things were the best band ever,' she says. 'Well, now I'm older I realize you were pretty naff, really, but I was devastated when you broke up.'

Ben raises an eyebrow sideways at me. 'Thanks.'

'You were my favourite. Then Jake, then Christian. I didn't like Amir, though—'

'Oh, he's all right,' says Ben. 'I see him all the time.'

'—because he couldn't dance or anything. Are you still addicted to drugs?'

'I never was,' says Ben. 'The papers—'

'So where do you live now? Retired to a house in Kensington? Penthouse in New York? Mansion in Sussex?'

'No,' says Ben. 'I bought a house in South London.'

'What, with all your money?'

'I didn't make all that much money,' says Ben, which is partly true, because a lot went on tax and management and accountants and legal fees, but partly a lie because he pissed a lot of it up the wall. 'Just enough to buy the house, really.'

'So you're not going to buy me a drink, then? Who's this? Your girlfriend?'

'Flatmate.'

'Oh, right,' she says. 'So you can afford to buy her a drink, but you can't buy me one. Typical. Always stick to your own, you lot. What you don't realize is that it's people like me who made you. And now you can't even repay it with a measly little drink.'

'Where do you work?' asks Ben.

'Safeway. The deli counter at Safeway.'

'Oh, well,' says Ben. 'I reckon you owe me a drink, then. It's people like me that keep you in a job. You think you'd have a job if I didn't buy taramasalata? Go on, then. Mine's a pint.'

The people at the tables around us have now noticed that Ben is Ben, and are muttering to each other.

'Go on, Ben. Buy her a drink,' I say. 'As long as she promises to leave us alone.'

'No,' says Ben. 'It's blackmail. I won't do it.'

'I bought all your records,' she says.

'Yeah, and I probably made 15p out of that.'

'I'll buy you a drink, then,' I offer, because these situations make me uncomfortable and Ben's got his stubborn face on.

'And who do you think you are? Lady Bountiful? I don't need you looking down on me just because you're hanging around with celebrities,' says the girl.

'I'm not a celebrity any more.' Ben is glaring at his glass. 'I haven't been a celebrity in three years. Now I'm an ex-celebrity, which means that people like you can come up and be unpleasant to me without the earnings to compensate.'

'Shall we just go?' I ask.

'Any time,' says Ben, picks up his half-drunk mojito and presses it into the girl's hand. 'There you are, love. This one's on me.'

He mutters all the way up to Freud's.

Chapter Eight

Bin Day

At 2 a.m., after Ben and I have been through a skinful, I wake with a raging thirst to remember that it's bin day. I sit up, trying to decide whether to do anything about it. In the dark, Matthew snores gently beside me, curled in foetal position with his bum stuck about a foot across the imaginary line that keeps the sharing of a bed civilized. Bin day. Bugger. In about two hours, they'll do the weekly Lambeth collection, and if I don't get the bags out on the street in time, the garden will be completely uninhabitable by Sunday. It's the third week running that we've all forgotten, and the pile of rotting garbage bags is now waist-high all along the kitchen wall. They prosecute you if you just leave it out on the pavement.

Bugger. It's going to have to be done. I slide back the covers, pull on a dressing-gown, find my shoes, and go down to the kitchen.

Now, this is one of the things about sharing your space with boys: they stuff the bin. They will never believe that enough use has been made of a bin-liner until they've had to take the lid off the bin and the contents have started cascading down the sides. The moonlight disguises the ugliness of the sight of the finest plastic surrounded by propped-up newspapers, empty wine bottles and the big ashtray, which has been left on the top awaiting one of the female of the species replacing the liner.

I decide to leave the light off. Drag the bin out into the middle of the room, start to pull. The bin comes with the liner, lifting off the floor, jammed fast with old pizza boxes. I brace my knees around it, pull again. Get a handful of black plastic for my pains. Bugger. Same every week. Move back to the cooker, jam the bin between the side and my stomach, clamp my knees around the other two sides, try joggling it very, very gently. Nothing. Try again. Another handful of black plastic comes away in my hand.

Switch on light, dig in cupboard for spare liners. Open one up. Fit over top of bin, pull down. Turn bin on side, then flip upside down. Floom. Avalanche. Separate the two, put bottles and papers into new liner, tie up top. Address bin again. Grit teeth and take hold of jam-covered pizza box, pull. Old tin of beans, green stuff growing on edges, tips over and coats my hand. Gulp, grit teeth again. Run hand under tap, go back to liner. Ease it, half-full, from the bin at last.

Drip, drip, drip. Someone's put a liquid container into the bag without emptying it down the sink first. Either that, or that onion and lettuce salad that came with the meat thali on Saturday has finally returned to the sludge whence we all emerged. The bottom of the bin is lined with whitish viscous stuff and little flecks of black. And now the kitchen floor is covered in spots of the same. Another liner off the roll, pop it in. Nearly there.

First two bags out onto the street. Two young boys sit on a wall on the other side of the road, loitering in the classical manner and staring at me in my dressing-gown. I pull it tighter over my breasts, close the front door, find the kitchen keys, go out to sort out the alleyway. There are eight bags, in varying states of decay. The house slumbers on as, like an Untouchable, I creep around the back and rid it of its soil.

Bag five, of course, bursts, as I knew one of them would, and chooses to deposit its contents on the hall carpet, where it can put everyone through the maximum inconvenience. Bugger. More tooth-gritting and jaw-setting: all a bit like my life in general, really. Rubber gloves. New bag. Tea bags, a copy of *Hello!* displaying Charlie Spencer's face liberally smeared with egg, plastic wrappings, bubble-wrap, a half-eaten tin of chili con carne, korma sauce, bits of macaroni cheese, stuff that's had three weeks to lose any semblance of what it once was, a leaking carton of blue-tinged tomato juice, a chicken carcass, half a hamburger and its styrofoam carton, a used condom.

The condom almost makes me smile round the gagging reflex. A condom? One of my flatmates is lying, then: they've done nothing but moan about the sex drought, but someone's obviously scored at some point in the past three weeks. Matt and I went past the condom stage a couple of years ago, and there's an empty Microgynon pack on top of a pair of laddered tights to prove it. The thought of touching a bag full of cold human viscosities, even with a rubber glove on, is more than I can take: I poke it into an old crisp bag with the help of a chewed spare rib, drop it, two-fingered, out of sight.

150,000 cigarette butts still lie on the carpet, soaked in coffee grounds. I'm glad I remembered my shoes. Get out the Hoover and start scraping them up. Gag reflex still working overtime. Donna, in Noddy pyjamas, appears at the top of the stairs, looks at me and the bin-liners, goes back to bed. That's sisterhood. I finish up, put the last bags out of the front door – the boys are still there, still staring.

I guess if they're casing a joint it's not ours any more, anyway.

Lock the kitchen door, sink a shot of Ben's whisky, dab a couple of fingers of Tania's Eau d'Issey under my nostrils to kill the smell, wash my hands about a hundred times. Put a note under the St Sebastian fridge magnet: 'I DO NOT EMPTY THE BINS UNTIL NEW YEAR', sign it, go back to bed.

Matthew has turned into a starfish in my absence, wrist across either side of the bed, legs flopped apart in a yogic position he'd never achieve if he were awake. 'Matt,' I say, 'move over.' Matthew snores.

I say it louder, and he says 'Kiss kiss' without waking up. I take an ankle, straighten his leg, flop it over to the other side. Unhook a hand, get my own under his shoulder-blade, heave.

He wakes up, annoyed. 'There's no need to be so rough.'

Climbing into bed, I say, 'Sorry, but you'd taken over the whole bed.'

'Huh,' says Matt. Curls up, mumbles, 'Where've you been, anyway?'

'I remembered it was bin day. I've been doing the bins.'

He's already almost back down into sleep. 'You shouldn't do that,' he says. 'That's Dad's job.'

Chapter Nine

Belsize Park

Monday morning. I'm in a room. Beyond that, I know very little. I think that the room is attached to an accountant's firm, but you can never trust your agency to have got the details straight. Despite all that sweetie-darling-we'll-give-you-holiday-pay-and-lots-of-attention screed agencies' handouts are filled with, temp controllers are interested in one thing only: commission. They will send anybody anywhere, by lying through their teeth.

Agency forms are full of little boxes: What kind of work? Which areas? Are there types of firm you don't want to work for? The first couple of times I registered with an agency, I was naïve enough to believe that these were read. Well, in a way they are: I'm convinced now that controllers have a game to while away the hours between phone calls: mismatching workers and jobs. 'Hey, Mary. Here's a short-hand secretary who wants creative companies in the centre of town. What do you say we give her the warehouse job with the computer-hardware firm out by the airport?' 'Linda, you're a genius! What about this PA job with the creative director of an advertising firm in Soho?' 'Give that to that guy with the GCSE in electronics.' 'What, the one with the muscles who lives in Hounslow?' 'Yes.' 'Brilliant.'

They can get away with this because a) everyone expects

their temp to be subnormal anyway and b) no-one ever turns down a job twice. If you turn down work, however ill-suited you are, you will be punished by being offered nothing more for three weeks. 'Things are pretty slack at the moment,' Linda will say as you do the weekly round of phone calls. 'Guess you should have taken that part-time filing post in Milton Keynes after all.' Signing on to more than one agency doesn't work either: you end up having ten agencies not offer you any work for three weeks, which is as good for the self-confidence as someone coming up to you in a nightclub and telling you they fancy your friend.

Anyway, I have been in this room, alone, for forty minutes; after half an hour in reception, a hassled-looking woman has led me in here, said, 'I'll send someone to see to you,' and disappeared. I have scoured the room for clues to the nature of this firm, but have drawn a blank. Aside from two desks, three typists' chairs, a computer and a telephone, the room contains a waste-bin full of plastic teacups, some fire regulations and a desk organizer containing two paper-clips.

I poke my head into the corridor. It has that heavy silence you get in school gyms during exams, which suggests that this probably really is an accountant's. I am about to walk down it and ask for help, when the phone rings.

'Hello?' It's not easy knowing what to say when you answer a strange phone.

'Mr Schlumpf,' says a man's crisp voice.

'I'm sorry, who did you want to speak to?'

A heavy sigh. 'Mr Schlumpf.' I cast around hopelessly for a telephone list. 'I'm sorry. Can I transfer you to the switchboard?' I press star zero, race next door into another, equally empty room, which, in place of the desk organizer, contains a phone list. I grab it, run back. The phone is ringing again. The same man.

'Mr Schlumpf,' he says.

'One moment, please.' I scan the S's. No Schlumpf. 'I'm sorry. I can't find a Schlumpf on the list. How do you spell it?' Another sigh.

'M–U–R–D–O–C–H.'

I try the Murdoch extension. Engaged. 'I'm sorry, but Mr Murdoch is engaged.'

'Oh, for God's sake,' says the voice, which obviously has a small ginger moustache attached. 'I'm calling peak rate. What is the hold-up?'

It's my turn to sigh. 'I'm sorry. I'm a temp and I've been left in this room without a phone list. I'm doing what I can.'

'Hah,' he says. 'Typical. Temp. Hah.' He hangs up.

I twiddle my thumbs, look again down the silent corridor. The phone rings.

'Are you The Temp?' says a female voice.

'Yes,' I reply.

'What on earth are you doing on Mr Murdoch's phone?' it says. 'We've been waiting for you for more than an hour.'

Chapter Ten

Chalk Farm

After three days, I have definitely established that this is an accountant's office, and to my relief my stint here only lasts a fortnight. Temping has disadvantages, but the good thing is that if you really hate a place you don't have to stay for long. I'm counting the days. Hours, actually. I haven't been forgiven for waiting in the wrong room for an hour on my first day. Every morning, as I arrive, Kyra looks up, pulls an exaggerated face of surprise and goes, 'Ooh, you haven't got lost, then,' and Fiona goes, 'Good afternoon.' We work on a staggered shift, Kyra and Fiona nine to five and me ten to six, but no-one seems to have told them this. Every day, I laugh politely and pretend that this is the first time I have heard either joke.

I might as well not bother with the niceties, because these are the only words they address to me from one day's end to another, apart from the occasional 'Can you get that?' or 'I'm going to lunch now.' I type in silence, eat lunch in silence, smile when Kyra and Fiona leave, pack up at six and walk to the tube in silence. My tongue would atrophy if I stayed here.

Not that Kyra and Fiona have anything to talk to each other about. They sit back to back and don't communicate at all – just pass bits of paper with comments like 'I think this is yours, actually.' You wouldn't have immediately picked them as friends – Fiona is a straight-faced, straight-haired, strait-laced thirty-year-old Sloane Ranger who wears a lot of navy blue and Kyra is eighteen with a frizzy perm and white shoes – but the wheels of most offices are oiled by the grease of social levelling.

Not here. They both look down on me, obviously, because I am The Temp, but they also despise each other. Fiona looks down on Kyra because she comes from Basildon and goes to the toilet. Kyra looks down on Fiona because Kyra has a fiancé and Fiona doesn't. They do have one thing in common: they are both obsessed by the telephone. I've been audio-typing as much as possible to drown out their voices, but you can't stay plugged into headphones all day.

Maybe it's a case of work expanding to fill the time available. Fiona and Kyra gripe constantly about how overloaded they are, but they each spend three hours on the phone every day. Neither seems capable of carrying out another action while their mouths are in gear; all they can do is lean an elbow on the desk. And they never telephone at the same time.

Kyra will get on the blower to her mum, whom she still lives with, and put in orders for what and when she wants to eat that night. Fiona, meanwhile, will type and look grim. When Kyra hangs up, she will dial immediately.

'Hi, Caro? Me, yah. Ebury Wine Bar? Great,' and she will launch into a fifteen-minute dissertation on the Hugos and Charlies in her world while Kyra rolls her eyes.

When she hangs up, Kyra dials. 'Can I speak to Dean, please? Hello, darling, [this in tones of sugar] it's me. There's no need to be like that. I just wanted to say hello . . .'

Then Fiona: 'Bridge? Fi. Caro says Ebury Wine Bar. Doesn't look like James is coming, though . . .'

Then Kyra: 'Hi? It's me [sigh]. Dean. Yeah. I do love him and everything, but he can be so . . .'

Then Fiona: 'Mum? Me. I thought I'd come down on Saturday this weekend. Mmm. Caledonian Ball.'

And so the day progresses; inanity piled on inanity.

I called Craig the other day to sort out a key drop as he lost his in Brixton, probably at Barney's, and to organize plans for meeting up with this chick he'd developed a crush on.

'You're not going to embarrass me, are you?'

'Don't be silly. We're never embarrassing. What's her name again?' We put in five minutes, had a laugh, sorted out our movements. When I hung up, Fiona and Kyra were squabbling.

'I can't do it,' Fiona was saying. 'I simply haven't the time. Can't you see how much work I've got here?' She paused, then nodded in my direction. 'Why don't you ask – Um – ? She's obviously not busy.'

Chapter Eleven

Sore Finger

'Sometimes I feel like I've disappeared altogether,' I say to Donna on the walk to the take-away. 'I've been counting, and you know how many people have addressed me by my name in the six months I've been doing this temping lark?'

'How many?'

'None. Not one.'

'Try working where I work,' says Donna. 'I couldn't be anonymous if I tried.'

I've not thought about this. 'What do you mean?'

She digs in her coat pocket and produces a melamine badge. 'Donna Brown' it says.

'Christ. You have to wear that?'

'All the time we're in the building. Everybody knows who I am. And it's really scary sometimes, because—'

We push open the door, and are swallowed up by the roar of the telly and clatters and yells from the back kitchen. Donna shows me the whites of her eyes, and we advance to the counter to be shouted at.

The man in the chippy talks – well, shouts over the blare of *Family Fortunes*, actually – a foreign language. *Family Fortunes* seems to be on whatever time of night you go in. And he's first-generation Chinese, so of course he talks a foreign language, but his English is also one of those versions that make you constantly stop halfway through what you thought was a conversation and say, 'I'm sorry. I thought you said something else.' Sometimes it sounds like the backing vocals for an early Elvis record. For instance, when you walk in, he yells: 'Wha-you-wa?' Sometimes you think he's giving you advice, like the 'No have praw, praw bad' a couple of weeks ago, to which I replied, 'Well, why are you selling them?' until I realised that it was actually a piece of menu-availability information.

I get through my order with a simple snarl, but Donna, as usual, gets away with nothing. He listens to her order, grabs a paper menu from the dump bin on the counter, slaps it down in front of her and raises the decibel level.

'Why you come here, every time,' he cries, 'have chip? I make Chinee foo'. Vay good. Wan ton, crispy duck, lemo chicka, Singapore noodor. Every ti', you go spring ro', chip. You wan' chip, you buy kebab.'

Donna thinks for a while, goes, 'Yes, but your chips are much better than his. You cook them properly. His come out of the freezer.'

'Chip gourmet?' he yells. 'You wan' gourmet, try Nancy Lam.' And then he goes off into one of those unintelligible strings of punching vowels: 'Swee sa saw? Kari saw?'

Donna pauses for a second and glances at his daughter, who as usual is buried in a huge hardback with illustrations of cell structures on the front and a title like '*Elements of Proton Engineering*' or '*A Biochemical Primer*'. She's doing five A levels, all in sciences, and wants to specialize in oncology after university. Ben once said, 'What's an onc?' but she didn't think it was very funny. I have a feeling that she doesn't think that many of the people who come into the chippy are up to much. She's probably right. She smiles and waits for Donna to work it out for herself. Finally, Donna tosses her head in understanding, says, 'No, thanks,' and comes over to sit on the Formica-covered MDF bench beside me.

'You see?' she goes. 'You get to disappear into the crowd half the time. I don't even get to be ignored in the chip shop.'

'It's not a chip shop.'

'Well, it is to me. But, look, honestly, would you really rather work somewhere where all your clients are angry and every single one of them knows what your name is? This woman threatened to get my address off the electoral register and come and get me this afternoon.'

'Why? What had you done?'

'I couldn't find her file. Stupid. I'd had it in my hand not more than five minutes before her appointment. Poor cow, you can't blame her. She's been living in a one-bedroom flat with three children for five years, and there's still no sign of her moving up the list.'

'Still, it's hardly your fault, is it?'

'You try telling her that. She was sitting there crying and ranting with this snot-covered two-year-old bawling on her knee, and I got so flustered I slammed my hand in the drawer of the filing cabinet.' Donna shows me where her fingernail has been ripped off a few millimetres into the bed.

'Ow.'

'Don't suppose you'd be able to type with that.'

'Babe, I'd have to. Did she say sorry?'

'Of course not. Said something about me knowing how it felt now. And this afternoon, I had to go round to check this flat where the tenants had moved out. There's supposed to be someone moving in next week, a whole family, and there's no way. The whole place had been stripped: light sockets, cupboards, the lot. They even nicked the kitchen sink. We'd not have known otherwise, only the tenant downstairs was on the phone screaming blue murder about the water coming down his walls. But that wasn't the worst. Jesus, you wouldn't believe it.'

The proprietor re-emerges with a white plastic bag, fixes me with a steely glance and goes, 'For you. Chili praw, fry ri, monk vegetabor.' We start to stand up and he shakes his head fiercely at Donna. 'Not for you. Chip take longer.'

I collect my food and sit down again. 'They'd obviously kept a dog,' says Donna, 'and never walked it. The hall carpet had simply rotted away in some places. Your feet sank in about an inch and stuck whenever you tried to walk. Living-room was the same, where you could see the carpet for Tennants Extra cans. Oh, and the pile of used nappies under the window. I couldn't work out what they were to begin with, 'cos it looked black, but when we got nearer this huge swarm of flies took off from them and started buzzing around.'

'Excuse me,' says an old bloke in a tweed hat on the bench next to us, 'but I'm about to eat my supper, here.'

'Sorry,' says Donna. 'So then I had to ring this guy up and break the news to him that it's going to take at least three weeks just to fumigate the place, and then he'll be moving into a place with concrete floors, and he started going, "I know your name. I'm going to make a complaint about you." Believe me, you don't want people knowing who you are all the time.'

'Why are you doing this job, Dons?'

She shakes her head. 'I don't know. I thought I'd be doing some good in the world. Not just living for myself. I don't know. Or maybe it was the only one I could get. At least the money's regular. And everyone I work with knows who I am as well, and includes me in going out to the pub and stuff.'

I wonder if I'd have liked to go to the pub with any of the people I've been working for in the past few months and decide probably, on balance, that I wouldn't. After all, if they can't be bothered to be nice to the new girl, they're not really the kind of people I want to hang with. But maybe I'm just feeling alienated. You get like that when you're tired and no-one's cast so much as a word that wasn't related directly to the task in hand in your direction in nine hours. I sigh.

'What?' Donna is picking at the skin around her nail.

'Please don't do that,' I say. 'Did you ever think it was going to be like this, then? When we grew up, I mean?'

'Dunno,' says Donna. 'I suppose not. I guess I thought I was going to go into local government and show them what could be done with a bit of organization. I thought it would be tough, but you'd get the rewards of helping people out, maybe get to see the happiness on their faces when things went right.'

We subside into grim silence.

Chip-shop owner comes back out with another white plastic carrier and a bundle of paper. 'You wan' open or close?' he snarls at Donna. She leaps to her feet, heads towards him. 'Closed, please.'

'Sore finger?'

'No, thanks,' says Donna, 'just salt.'

'No,' he says with a toss of the chin, 'I mean you should put plaster on that. It get dirty, could go septic.'

Chapter Twelve

Midnight Fast

'Oh, for God's sake. Do you have to kick me?'

'Sorry. Sorry. I was having that dream again.'

'Oh, right, and you felt the need to share it.'

'Sorry. I was asleep. I didn't know I was moving.'

'Well, stop it. I was asleep too.'

The bedsheets are soaked and I'm still shaking. I've been having this drowning dream for the past two months, and it never gets any better. I long to turn on the light, reassure myself that the room is still there, but know that there will be a row if I do.

Then suddenly I think no, hang on a sec, this isn't right.

'Matthew?'

'What?'

'You used to hug me when I had nightmares.'

'For God's sake.' Instead of me, he hugs the duvet closer around him so that my bum is sticking full out in the night air. 'I've got an interview in the morning. Tania has pulled out all the stops to get this for me. Are you trying to sabotage it or something?'

'No. Sorry.'

'Right.' He bangs his pillow a couple of times, huffs and clamps his arm over the top of the bedclothes.

My body is gradually slowing down. I lie there feeling

uncomfortable for a while, but now we've started, I can't just let it go. I know you wouldn't be able to tell it from looking at us now, but we weren't always like this. We used to talk. A lot. That was the thing people always noticed about us: 'Do you two ever draw breath?' they'd say. 'Don't you get sore throats, the amount you talk?' When we were living together at university, the house we shared with Craig was the one that everyone dropped in on all the time, because they knew it was where there would be noise and chat and someone to sit up all night with.

And now look at us: scarcely a word to swap between us; me and Matt and Craig, sunk so far in our own misery that we can hardly meet each other's eyes. But I look over at Matthew sometimes, remember how I used to want to scrunch my fingers into that hair, kiss his eyelids, how my brother used to take the mick when we rang each other three or four times a day during the vacations just to hear the sound of each other's voices, and wonder how we're going to get it all back when this bad period of our lives is over. Matthew has shrunk into himself since we got back from travelling, watching me with baleful eyes as I get dressed for work each morning, rolling over and pretending to be asleep when I come over to kiss him goodbye. I know I should sympathize, understand that it's hard for him discovering that there are thousands of nicely spoken boys with average degrees and a bit of travelling experience filling up the job market but, you know, it's hard for me, too. And there was a time when, if one of us had a problem, we would talk about it. Now, all we do is turn our backs to each other in bed and pretend to be asleep.

Maybe I ought to go and take a pill, because now I'm wide awake and I need to sleep. I try to ease the duvet back over myself, but he's got it clamped beneath his arm and isn't going to cede any territory. Matthew, what's happened? A year ago, we were sitting on a beach in Micronesia with our backpacks, and making promises about how we were never going to let the world get in the way of us: that no matter how serious the world became, we would always keep time for each other.

It's patently obvious that Matthew is still awake as well: I know his breathing when he's asleep, the in–pause–out, the twitches, and this even, steady rhythm is that of someone pretending. It's no good. I have to talk.

'Matt?'

'Oh, God,' he mumbles, then, 'what?'

'We are all right, aren't we?'

'What do you mean, all right?'

'You know – us.'

'Look.' Matthew sits up in the dark. 'Stop this. I'm sorry I didn't make a fuss of you when you had a nightmare, but you don't have to make every nightmare into a drama for everyone else. I have an interview in the morning. It's really important. This is the first real break I've had and I can't afford to not be on form. I need to sleep. What I don't need is you accusing me of things in the middle of the night.'

'I wasn't accusing you of—'

'Shut up. No. Go to sleep.'

He lies down again, turns his back on me. Thumps his pillow again, pulls it over to his side of the bed and falls silent.

I lie there, arms folded, staring at the ceiling until the sound of Tania's alarm clock next door lets us know that it's six o'clock.

Chapter Thirteen

Fulham Broadway

Pete, chief designer, saunters over to the desk of Susie, quantity surveyor, puts a hand on the surface and says, 'Hi, there,' while gazing at a point in the far distance.

'Hi,' says Susie, and stares down at her desk.

'Urr,' says Pete, 'have you got a copy of that feasibility report lurking around? I thought I ought to make a copy of it, maybe.'

A couple of tiny points of colour dot the tips of Susie's cheekbones. 'Yes,' she says, 'hold on.'

She dips down into her filing drawer and Pete glances briefly at her back. Snaps his eyes upward when she resurfaces.

'Here we are,' she says, holding out a bound document, 'I'll need it back, though.' For a moment she continues to hold one side while he grips the other, and their eyes lock. A tiny, secret smile passes between them.

'Of course,' he says. 'I'll bring it back in a second.'

It couldn't be much more obvious that Susie and Pete are having an affair if they were to flop over the desktop and start pawing at each other's bits. No-one has said anything to me (sometimes people like to use the temp as the office confessional, as they know she will move on and no harm will be done), but a few days observing her has left me in no doubt. Of course, a high proportion of people meet their partner through work these days, so a relationship going on in the office is hardly unusual. But it's funny how controlled people manage to be, on the whole, about sticking to the proprieties. Tania had been at her job for six weeks before she realized that two of the people she worked with were actually married, and to each other.

It's not the things that people do that give them away: it's the things they don't. Anglo-Saxon society requires that anyone who wants to establish trust, or co-operation – a fairly basic thing in colleagues – will attempt to meet eyes every ten seconds or so. Pete and Susie virtually never exchange glances, though their eyes are constantly following each other's backs. They never tell each other jokes or swap information that's not strictly related to the job in hand. They rarely leaven what they are saying with a smile, but talk, instead, very seriously, very wide-eyed. Lunch-time comes and they will always leave and return within five minutes of each other, though never at the same time. And Pete needs to learn to dial Susie's full direct-line number, not her extension: there is no greater give-away to an office affair than when a phone makes that single ring of the internal line and the person who picks it up goes all pretty and giggly when they answer.

As Pete scratches his head by the photocopier, I can see Susie watching his backside slyly out of the corner of her eye. Pete has a nice bum, even in a cheap suit, and I've occasionally cheered up the odd dull moment admiring it myself. But Susie fiddles with her pen for a full thirty seconds while her pupils point sideways before sighing and pulling her piece of paper back into the fray.

He comes back to her desk. 'I'm sorry to bother you,' he says, 'but I can't work out how it works. You couldn't—'

Susie has gained her feet before he finishes the request. 'Sure,' she says, and they cross the floor in step, hands swinging exactly in time. Looking at the control panel, she leans onto her forearms and rests one foot up on its toes, staring down, hair dropping into her eyes. Seconds later, Pete has assumed the same position, only he looks at her face rather than the display. He says something quiet, and she gives him a foxy little 'aren't we naughty' smile.

Susie punches a couple of keys, hits the start button. They stay there, ostensibly making sure everything's working OK, but facing each other, arms crossed casually over their stomachs, chatting. Susie reaches over and picks some imaginary fluff off his shoulder, two fingers, flicks it away, and he doesn't even look down to see what it is. When she walks back to her seat, the dimples either side of her mouth are about an inch deep.

Chapter Fourteen

Caught You Out!

Craig hasn't worked a day since we graduated. With his first-class degree he was expecting to get headhunted to commission films for Channel Four, or be offered a professorship at Cambridge, or at the very least be sought out by Saatchi's for his fantastic creative mind, and has been waiting by the telephone in the living-room ever since. He goes up to the offy to buy Red Stripe every day, to the DSS to sign on once a week and to see someone called Barney in Brixton once a fortnight, but otherwise we have the constant pleasure of his company. He's such a permanent fixture that most of the time it's like the sofa has suddenly said something when he speaks. But every now and again you feel his presence with a vengeance.

Like tonight. Tonight he's sitting in front of the telly going, 'I don't believe it. Why did he do it? I mean, what does he think he's doing? You wouldn't catch me going along with this however desperate I got.' Ben's gone down the Surprise, partly because he doesn't want to listen to Craig carrying on, and partly because it's the one pub in London where they don't have a telly. You can't blame him. I don't suppose many people want to be near a telly when they're on *Caught You Out!*

'I can't believe this,' mutters Craig, and we go, 'Shut up, Craig.'

'Well, I'm only *saying.*'

'We heard you the first time.' I throw a cushion from the corner of the room, which he catches and slots in behind his head with all the others.

The theme tune plonkety-plonks to an end and Lenny London, professional game-show host, what they now call 'veteran game-show host', a man with a silvery-white bouffant wig that makes him look like the logo on a Mr Whippy van, a reputation for extreme fondness for small children and a wardrobe of shiny suits, bounces on, claps his hands a couple of times, does his trademark tap-dancer's whirl and comes to a halt, hands outstretched to a studio audience consisting of toothless crones bussed in from maximum-security twilight homes.

'Welcome! Welcome! Welcome!' he cries, and the audience participates with the standard response of 'And welcome to you, Lenny!'

Lenny turns to tonight's celebrity panel and we all start to cringe. Tonight's line-up consists of Diana Pepper, the blonde one with the hot pants and push-up bra out of the Seventies sitcom *We Don't Do That on Mondays*, Brian Donaghey, keep-fit guru to the stars, Bhangra star Shady Noo, noted for his hit *Bhangra in the House*, which reached No. 17 in the charts four years ago, former MP and Talk Radio presenter Charlie Harris, Leslie Breeks, former wife of the Arsenal midfielder Rodney, who now presides over her own digital-TV chat show, *Leslie!* and, up on the top right, looking ill-fitted to the set with his black T-shirt and shaven head, Ben, former A-lister tasting the fruits of life on the B list.

'But why's he doing this?' Craig splutters.

'You know perfectly well why,' snarls Tania. 'Because he had very little alternative and at least this way he gets to see some money.'

'Well, I wouldn't sink this low, even for money. I'd leave the country.'

'With what, exactly?' Tania growls. Craig curls his lip.

Diana Pepper still has the magnificent bosom she had at twenty-one; she jiggles it to emphasize her thoughts, which reduces the audience to tears of laughter just as it did twenty-odd years ago. She, along with Leslie, seems to be totally unconcerned about her appearance on the show. Then again, so does Ben. There's nothing foreshadowing the three-week bender he went on immediately afterwards, a misery binge where I found him crashed out on the living-room floor with a full glass of whisky in his hand six times and had hell's own job, given that he's got five inches and fifty pounds on me, to drag him up to bed. A binge in which he disappeared altogether for three days in the middle, turning up in the end at the Holiday Inn in Leeds.

It hasn't been like this since the black days after Christian died: the band, their wholesome image blown to smithereens in one fell swoop by a gay-sex-and-drugs-death-scandal, disappeared in a welter of suit and counter-suit, and I spent nights at university lying awake fretting. Ben used to turn up on the doorstep of the house we shared with Craig periodically that year, miserably pissed or evilly hung-over, and the boys would haul him bodily up the stairs and tuck him up with a spliff or a coffee and a sigh of familiarity. Ben's my mate, but Matthew's been better to him than most people. Christ, his family, sitting in the executive home he bought them on the outskirts of Banchory, refused to have him in the house for fear that they'd be bothered by the *News of the World*. That's why

Ben's put up with the lack of rent, the sulkiness, the unchanging presence of Matt and Craig under his roof, without a murmur of discontent.

But on screen, he's the consummate showbiz professional. He smiles, he laughs, he touches Diana Pepper on the arm like he fancies her (which, of course, he did when he was a kid. I remember him getting his first crush on her at the age of seven when they repeated the sitcom on Sunday afternoons). You would never know that, like all the guests on this top-rating show, he's been got there by dint of blackmail.

Caught You Out! is a sort of combination of *Where Are They Now*, *Candid Camera* and *Surprise Surprise!* with little of the feelgood factor of any. It's showbiz's revenge on itself, a chance to see the fallen mighty go splat on their faces. What they do is this: the show's researchers (and members of the public, encouraged by the £1,000 reward on offer) find out about former celebs who have been reduced to demeaning jobs to make a living. Then they set up an embarrassing situation, secretly film them, burst in and shout '*Caught You Out!*' And the ex-celebs have little alternative but to show themselves to be good sports, play along and slap Lenny matily on the shoulder: this is prime-time telly, after all, and the film will be shown with or without their co-operation. That, and the £2,000 appearance fee, which few of the victims can afford to pass up, is why Lenny London manages an almost 100 per cent hit-rate on getting the subjects to turn up to the studio to laugh at themselves. Fun, eh?

So Ben rocks with laughter as it turns out that Diana Pepper is now hand modelling at the Ideal Home Exhibition, that Brian Donaghey owns a juice bar on the Holloway Road (how we laughed when they asked for bison juice!) and that Shady Noo has gone back to university to train as a doctor just in time for *Caught You Out!* to plant a live cadaver on his dissection table! Ben smiles good-naturedly as Lenny asks him if he still dances, agrees when Lenny says that boy bands aren't what they used to be and, when the music starts up to signify the first ad break, gives a broad grin and waves.

'What time's your second interview tomorrow, Matthew?' asks Tania.

Matt taps out his cigarette end into Craig's empty beer can. 'Eight fifteen.'

Tania looks pleased. 'Oh, right. They're seeing you after trading's started, then.'

'Does that mean anything?' I ask.

'Mmm. If they're going to take the time out during work hours, then they must be really interested.'

'Well,' says Matthew, 'I did think I got on well with them.'

'Oh, yes, you did. Sebastian Faulkner was on the phone this morning asking me what sort of money you'd be thinking of. Said he thought you were very bright.'

'It's very sweet of you to do this.' Donna unwraps her legs, re-wraps them in the opposite direction.

'Well, you know.' Tania looks coy, ruffles Matthew's hair. He pushes back against the palm of her hand like a cat. 'If you can't help your friends out, who can you help?'

'Fab,' says Donna, 'so is there any chance you could put us two up for anything, then?'

Tania recoils. 'Ah, well, um, you've got a vocation, Donna. And anyway, you wouldn't like it in the City.'

'Wouldn't I? Why not?'

'Well, you're –' it's quite obvious that Tania's trying not to say the B word '– so different from all the people there.

You take life so seriously. And besides, I've always seen you as one of those caring sorts of people. Surely what you want to do is help people?'

Donna shrugs. 'Helping people isn't all it's cracked up to be. And what about her?' She gestures to me. 'I'm sure she'd fit in beautifully. Talks proper and everything.'

Tania laughs that tinkly laugh she always does when she's uncomfortable. 'Ooh, well, but she's not qualified.'

'Tania,' I say, 'Matthew and I both read Psychology. What's the difference?'

'Yes, but—' Tania fishes for her bottle, remembers it's empty and twiddles her glass instead. 'Well, Matthew's a leader. I see you more in support roles.'

'How come?'

'Well, look what you're doing now.'

'So hang on. I've been temping for a few months so that's what I've become?'

'Well,' Tania smiles a smile of pure patronage, 'sometimes people fall into the thing that suits their personality best. Look at me. I didn't think of myself as a city type at all . . .'

'Oh,' says Donna. 'We did.'

Tania ignores this.

'So how come,' asks Donna, 'you've spotted this leadership potential in Matthew? Surely if your old mate here is going to be typecast as a secretary, Matthew should be typecast as someone who sits around playing Scrabble with Craig?'

Matthew picks up the remote, slaps up the volume. As the titles fade away we see a close-up of Ben's face, side-on, in the grainy texture of a hidden camera, telephonist's headphones clamped to his ears, microphone across his lips.

'Ben Cameron has swapped the stage microphone,' says a voiceover by Lenny, 'for another sort of microphone altogether. Nowadays, Ben makes ends meet by working in a call centre, servicing telephone-banking account holders. In fact, you could say he's no longer in a position to call us, now he's waiting for us to call him!'

A whoop from the audience. Hilarious. Look at the fallen star. Watch him twinkle now. Wait for the hoax. Point, laugh, and remember that you, too, could make a tidy sum just by shopping someone you used to envy. 'Oh, Ben,' chortles Lenny London, 'you don't get much screaming now, do you? Apart from angry customers, that is.'

'No, Lenny,' says Ben, 'but you hear people screaming as they run away from you all the time, don't you?'

Collapse. The camera returns to dwelling on Ben's call-centre nightmare, just in time to catch the call where the hoaxer rings up to complain that he dosen't like the bank's latest advertising jingle and asks Ben to sing him some others to see if any of them are more memorable.

I stand up. I don't want to see any more of this. I know what the punchline's going to be, anyway: the people's paedophile will burst in with his entourage just as Ben is finally persuaded to do a creditable rendition of the Bodyform wail. The others sit, transfixed, while Ben obligingly hums to keep the customer happy. I think it's better if I go and keep my poor old mate company.

I go down the Wandsworth Road, past the boarded-up shops and the pie-and-mash shop to the Surprise, where I find Ben in the back room, furiously playing pinball. I touch him on the shoulder and he glances at me.

'Is it over?'

'Yes. Do you want a drink?'

He nods. 'Snakebite.' I buy him a pint of lager, bring it back, stand there and watch him slam the hell out of the buttons.

'So?'

'Well.'

I don't really have a lot to say. Ben bashes the machine too hard, the tilt bell rings and the game is over. He takes his pint of lager and sups on it without a word about snakebite.

'Want a game?'

'Not really. You'll just get angry with me for being crap.'

'No I won't.'

'You will, Ben, in the mood you're in.'

His shoulders slump. 'Can you blame me?'

I shake my head. 'Of course not. Shall we go outside?' He nods. We settle under the pergola, the air strong with honeysuckle and the smell of dogshit in Larkhall Park. Neither of us says anything much for the first drink, then Ben goes in and buys another round, and we sit elbow to elbow staring at the wall.

'I suppose,' he says glumly, 'the others are having a good laugh.'

'No. I don't think so. I think they sympathize.'

'I only did it for the money,' he says. 'It's either that or a call centre.' After five years' touring, three court cases and a major bender, Ben has little to show for his years of fame apart from a Georgian house in a less than salubrious area, a rapidly decaying jeep and a mum in a bungalow.

'Yeah, sure,' I say. 'And it keeps your profile up in some way, even if it's not the way you'd like.'

He pulls a face, sups his pint. 'Christ,' he says, 'how did it ever come to this?'

Chapter Fifteen

How Did it Come to This?

Once you've been famous, you never quite stop being famous. Some people try: join closed religious orders, change their names, go backpacking round countries where they've not been heard of, have babies and never leave their houses again except for the school run, but it never really works. No-one ever makes that clear before you sign up. There's loads of discussion about how difficult it is to be Madonna now, but no-one said to her while she was still doing the New York nightclub circuit, 'Look, Madonna, it's not just a decade or two. It's the rest of your life. Every time you have an operation for piles, break a bone, have a row over service in a restaurant, buy tampons, go out without make-up, get married, get divorced, have any ill fortune at all, it'll be all over the papers. Nothing will ever be entirely your own again; there will always be the chance that there's no news one summer and the Sundays will go big on how you've let yourself go. When you reach your deathbed, there will still be people out there chasing the details of your last revolting cough, the deterioration of your mind, the details of your will, because everyone wants that reassurance that, however charmed your life has been, however much you have escaped the daily grind of factory life and shagging in alleyways on a Saturday night, you will still arrive at the same degradation in the end. People *want* famous people to be miserable. It makes them feel better.' No, that sort of thing you only find out once the pact is signed and the dogs have been unleashed.

Ben was sixteen years old when he became famous. And who would say no at sixteen years old? Sixteen, and looking at the world through lipstick-stained tour-bus windows; sixteen and able to get any amount of sex you want, as long as you accept there's the possibility that your every premature ejaculation is going to be known to the rest of the world on Sunday; sixteen and watching girls not much younger than you pee themselves on arena floors because they think they've met your eye; sixteen and getting your coke for free. That's got to have an effect on you, however level-headed you start off.

I knew Ben when he was the boy who burped next to me in the back row at junior school. I hit him with a toy tractor. He burst into tears, then hit me back. We both got put in the corridor, and, after ten minutes of glaring, caused havoc in the cloakrooms and became best friends. I know boys and girls aren't supposed to be best friends, but we didn't have much option: Ben was the biggest show-off in the school and I was the biggest tomboy, and no-one else really wanted to be best friends with us. They may have been educating their womenfolk while the English were still refusing them property of their own, but the Scots still don't appreciate a tomboy.

That was at the village school. My parents sent me away to learn to talk like a lady at the age of twelve, and Ben's sent him to Banchory comprehensive and had him feeding sheep out on the hillsides when he got home after dark. I think they all expected us to drift apart, to learn over the years to hang around with our own class – my brother, after all, had spent a fair amount of time damming burns with Tom, Ben's older brother, in their childhood, but they had got down to friendly waves out of car windows by the time they were eighteen – but somehow it didn't work out like that. Ben was always waiting for me to get back from school, I was always waiting to sneak out and go into town with him. Ben didn't like feeding sheep, and he didn't want to settle down with someone called Kirstie, buy a clapped-out Cortina and wait to be resettled in a council flat. He started bunking school and busking in the shopping centre, and spent the money he made on drama lessons and singing lessons. His dad was afraid he was a poof and his mum was afraid of what the neighbours would say. They soon shut up when he built them Bonnyview, their dream bungalow with the vista of Morven and sent them to Disneyworld for Christmas.

Look: Ben didn't have any option. He wasn't going to be a doctor, a lawyer, a landowner, an officer. All he had was a certain devilish look and a childish competitive urge. But he never forgot me: whatever he got up to, however arrogant, and uppity, and spoiled and greedy he became, he never let go of our friendship. I spent my sixth-form holidays in hotel rooms and dressing-rooms, beating Ben at cards, playing stupid chicken games with knives and cigarette lighters, being elbowed out of the way by older, more determined women. God, it was great having a friend who was famous: everyone at school wanted to know me, everyone at university asked me to things in the hope that I'd get them asked to better things: if it was that good for me, think how good it was for Ben. And when you're sixteen, you don't think it will ever end.

Everybody wants to be famous when they're sixteen, don't they? Someone comes up to you at a club you've sneaked into by pretending to be eighteen, and goes, 'OK, so you're good-looking and you can dance: can you sing? Because if you can we'll take you out of school, away from a future of YTS builders' courses and boring, boring white-shirt-and-tie photocopying and we'll pay you hundreds of thousands of pounds, everyone will want to know you and you'll get laid more in a year than everyone else you know will be in a lifetime. Probably put together.' What was he supposed to say? 'No, thank you. I want to work night shifts in an abattoir and come home to a flat that smells of chip fat because we couldn't afford to replace the carpet after the last tenants left'?

It wasn't a choice: not really. I don't think he would have made any other choice even if someone had said, right then, 'And the pay-off is that the whole world will be waiting for your life to go wrong. By the time you're twenty-three you'll be going to auditions and having people ask, "Didn't you used to be Ben out of the Wild Things?" and wondering whatever happened to your miserable, fucked-up career. You'll get six good years and spend the rest of your life being gloated over.' No-one had ever expected much from Ben's future. He was a small-life person, someone who was meant to leave school with no qualifications and spend his life doing manual labour while his wife cleaned the houses of people like my parents and his children looked forward to more of the same. If someone gave you that choice, what would you do?

Chapter Sixteen

Covent Garden

If working has taught me one thing, it's that men don't really care about cars at all. Those weekends spent lying on a skateboard underneath some rusting Cortina are just an excuse to get away from women. Because if, as men claim, they like machines and are better at them than women, how come everybody who has ever worked in an office knows that if the photocopier is broken the only person who can mend it is a woman?

Think about it. Think about all those times you have been heading across the open plan, clutching some big cheese's 500-page autobiography, which they want reproduced in quadruplicate, complete with folded-in A3 illustrations, in now minus ten minutes. The copier will be standing there, innocently, in a corner, screened off by portable walls. And then you will see something that makes your heart sink. Walking towards you, in a suit, is a man. Carrying a single sheet of A4. He will roll his eyes at the ceiling tiles as he passes, and you know what he's going to say next: 'It's broken.' And then, if he's Mark, he'll go and find Susie to help him mend it, as I've seen him do three times already this week.

'It's broken.' The only phrase men use in offices more than 'it's broken' is 'I've told you not to call me at work.'

You stick your tongue out at his back as he strides off, hunter–gatherer-like, to jam up the machine on the next floor down, and approach your target with sinking heart.

Usually, 'broken' means that the 'out of paper' light is illuminated. That's on an old-fashioned copier. For the last ten years, copiers have had digital instruction pads on the front, which will read something like 'Out of paper. Open paper drawer and refill', beside a line drawing covered in arrows showing where the drawer is. Why is it that, despite the fact that one of the requirements for an office job is basic reading skills, all men become illiterate when faced with instruction manuals? It must be another aspect of that X-Y chromosome thing that, because the scientists doing the study were men, has never been investigated.

They trust us to sort things out, and we usually do. Do you ever grab the man who is walking away and say, 'It's just run out of paper. I'll show you how to fill it up'? No. You sigh, hunker down, pull open the drawer, break open another ream of A4, slam the drawer shut and wait for ten minutes for it to warm up because it's been standing idle for an hour as a stream of men have walked in, seen a red light, screamed and walked out.

There are times, of course, when the photocopier actually is broken. You can usually tell, because the display will read something like 'Completely kaput. Call engineer immediately as liable to explode'. In this case, there will also always be a man to tell you about it. You know the conversation. 'I wouldn't bother with that. It's been broken for three days/a week/three months.' 'Ah. Has anyone reported it?' 'Dunno. I wouldn't know who to report it to.' At this point, resist the temptation to say, 'Well, I know who to report it to and I'm only the Temp'. Say, 'I'll see what I can do,' call the number on the label stuck prominently on the lid and go and replace the paper in another machine.

The thing is, these rules don't apply only to photo-copiers, they apply to all office machinery: printers, faxes, coffee machines, telephones. If you see a man near a piece of machinery you plan to use, avoid it. The kitchen, when it's not stinking of pot noodle, will always echo with the thump-thump-thump of a bloke trying to get a second can of Coke for free. When a fax beeps and says 'paper jam', the masculine instinct, instead of pulling the piece of paper out and trying again, is to leave it dangling and walk away shrugging. If a man uses a printer (sorry: joke) and it runs out of paper, he will only put in the precise number of sheets he needs to finish his own job. Trust me: you can sometimes actually watch them counting. And to think they still earn a third more than we do.

Chapter Seventeen

Charidee

I wonder about Marina sometimes. Sometimes I think that, despite her protestations, despite the fact that she's always telling people how fond of me she is, mostly as a preamble to telling them what I'm doing wrong with my life, Marina isn't a friend of mine at all. Sometimes I have a feeling that she has, in fact, secretly sworn to be my enemy for life and is merely pretending to be a friend the better to exact her tortures.

'Come to the Music Therapy for Kosovars ball,' she trills. 'I'm taking a party. All in a good cause. I've got loads of people you used to know coming.' She says this pointedly. 'Bring everyone. Tickets only eighty quid a head including buffet. Come to Uncle Giorgos's for a drink before at eight. And do try to dress for a party, not a barn dance.'

Eighty quid: the price of a gramme and a half of coke for an evening in some aircraft hangar with a load of toffs. I scrabble around for excuses, as I'd as soon spend the evening licking soap, but when Matthew finds out that I've been keeping it from him, he has a tantrum and insists we go. 'Look,' he says, 'now I've got my new job I'm going to have to start circulating.'

'Yes,' says Tania, 'and anyway, it'll be such enormous fun.'

'Fun?' I squeak. 'What makes you think it'll be fun? This

will be as much fun as a night out with Norman Tebbit.'

'Ooh, come on,' Tania chirps, '*champagne*.'

'Champagne gives me dyspepsia.'

'Dancing.'

'Dancing to old Spandau Ballet records and being trodden on by people who learned their sense of rhythm on the hunting field.'

'And it's a chance to dress up,' says Tania, at which I pull a face, because when Tania means dressing up she means doing yourself out to look like you've been designed to hide the spare bog roll in a lavatory in Croydon, and anyway, I always trip over long dresses.

'Well, why don't you two go, anyway? It doesn't mean I have to.'

'Don't be silly,' Tania says, 'Marina's your friend. You have to come if we're going.'

'I can't afford it.'

Matthew rolls his eyes with all the affected boredom of one who has been earning for a week, and offers to pay for me, which is an effective stymie out of left field: Matthew hasn't paid for anything in six months, and I'm hard pressed to refuse the opportunity when it comes up. I stutter for a bit.

'Can't you just give me the money and I'll spend it on something I really want?'

'No.' He looks pained, and his hair flops over his face in that persuasive way of his. 'Look, I want to give you something. Can't you just accept a present?'

'And besides,' says Tania, 'it's for Charidee.'

'I'll give half of it to Save the Children, OK?'

'But look,' Tania waves the leaflet under my nose, 'Save the Children don't do this. Music is a lifeline for these people. It will help them get over the trauma of what's happened to them.'

'Do you know how much rice I could buy wholesale for eighty pounds? I could buy some and drop it off at the local charity shop.'

'Yerr,' laughs Tania, 'like any of it will get to them. At least we know where the money's going if we do it this way.'

'Mmm,' Craig pipes up, finally deciding to get involved. 'Forty quid on booze, ten on food, ten on entertainment, fifteen on venue hire . . .'

'Well, I'll buy you a ticket anyway,' Matthew closes the conversation firmly. 'And I'd really appreciate it if you'd just come and stop spoiling everyone else's fun.'

So I put on a dress, and Matthew puts on his new dinner jacket with a discreet flash of Rolex Oyster (500 baht on a beach last year), and Donna wears lime-green crushed velvet because she can get away with it, and Tania goes to Harvey Nicks and spends £800 on something that looks suspiciously like it's held together with herring bones, and Ben makes an effort to shave, and Craig refuses point blank to come on the grounds that he doesn't approve of things like that and wants to watch *Casualty*. And Donna calls a minicab and we set off for Hyde Park Gardens.

We pitch up at half past eight on the dot, Tania having taken us on a circuitous route involving Lambeth Bridge, Horseferry Road and a lot of reversing. Tania likes to take charge in taxis. I am the kind of tube bore who takes pride in knowing where to stand on a platform to get out opposite the exit at Tottenham Court Road, but Tania likes to prove that she has the Knowledge by leaning over the front seat, enunciating clearly in case the Gambian doctor driving us doesn't understand what she's saying, and getting hopelessly lost somewhere between Buckingham

Palace and Mayfair. I've got lost with Tania in Mayfair on the way from Stockwell to Fulham.

But finally we find our way out of Mayfair and into Bayswater, clatter up to the front door and mill about uneasily in Marina's uncle's netball court of a front hall while a woman in a white pinny takes our coats and holds them at arm's length, all apart from Tania's, which she clutches to her bosom like a long-lost friend. I'm still feeling a bit queasy from the combined stench of Tania's scent, the driver's panicky sweat and the odour of three pine-tree-shaped air deodorizers dangling from the rear-view mirror, but I smile gamely as we pass into the drawing-room, which is the size of the whole first floor of our house.

The evening starts badly. As I scoop a glass off a passing tray, I collide with Marina's cousin Chloe (pronounced, in the Greek fashion, Cloy, with a sort of throat-clearing noise at the front). She is wearing something made out of tinfoil and safety pins and smoking a pink Sobranie. I don't like Chloe much. It's not the unfortunate underbite that makes her look like she's trying to fish a bit of mutton out from between her incisors. It's not the unfortunate tendency to believe that lashings of Diorissima are the way to cover body odour. There's just a smug Chloe-ness about her that has always made me want to stick a pin in her and see what oozes out.

Chloe tuts at me and refuses a canapé. I grab one – a pizza the size of a 50p piece with a shred of anchovy, a caper and half an olive embedded in the mozzarella – smile coldly at her and move on. Tania stops beside her and, with shrieks of recognition, they exchange kisses. I think: that's it. No-one's going to be able to get near Tania for the rest of the night.

'I hear you've got engaged!' cries Tania.

'Yes,' replies Chloe in her bored, exhausted voice.

'Congratulations! Tell me all about him!'

'Well,' says Chloe, 'he's my second cousin, Dmitri.' She adds a surname we all associate with major tenant disputes in the Westminster area.

Tania practically claps her hands. 'But how romantic! Is it one of those childhood romances? Did you grow up together?'

'Well, no,' says Chloe, 'he's forty-three.'

'An older man! How marvellous! Can I see the ring?'

Chloe extends her finger, where a rock the size of Gibraltar nestles among the hairs on her knuckles.

'How gorgeous!' coos Tania. 'Lucky you! I'm so jealous!'

Chloe becomes almost animated for a moment. 'So you're still not engaged yourself, then?'

'Oh, noooo,' says Tania, cupping her chin with her hand, 'just a poor old career girl looking for love. You'll have to give me a few tips.'

'Jesus,' Ben mutters, and we leave them to it. Ben grabs a miniature hamburger speared with a tinsel-covered cocktail stick from a passing plate, holds it out in his palm and says, 'Where did she get these, then? The Saatchi Gallery?' Matthew seems to have melted off into the crowd already. Donna grabs another set of glasses from a passing waitress, and we take to a wall to watch.

I soon recognize some of the people I'm supposed to have known at university. They stand – no, sorry: they lounge – by one of the fireplaces, a group of floppy-haired fellas who only ever talked to each other and were always getting their faces into Harpers & Queen at each other's 21st-birthday parties. Matthew has materialized beside them, trying out his new persona as Master of the Universe.

73

'Who are those guys?' asks Donna, who went to the University of the South Bank and didn't have to deal with this nonsense.

'Marina's posh friends,' I reply. 'The tall one with the marcel wave is Hugh Farquhar.'

'Huge Fucker?' cries Donna. 'You can't call somebody something like that!'

'No, not Fucker, Farquhar.'

'Oh, Faakhaa. And the one with no chin and a bulge in his forehead?'

'Tom Lowenthal. Known as Tedium. And the one that looks like he's been skinned alive, that's Trojan Parsley.'

'What?'

'Well, Cholmondeley, but everyone knows him as Parsley.'

'Why?'

'Cholmondeley, Bumley, Arseley, Parsley.'

'Ah. They all look like they've been squashed by a hay-baler.'

'You'd look like that too if your ancestors had been marrying their cousins for the last thirty generations.'

'Is it mandatory,' asks Ben, 'to have no chin if you're going to be an aristocrat? Do they actually get them taken out at birth?'

'Well, they don't have a lot of use for their jaws. They live on nursery food and never open their mouths when they talk.'

'Oh,' Ben nods. 'So they've evolved that way.'

'But what happens when they laugh?' Donna drains her glass, snatches another.

'Huge Fucker is laughing now,' I tell her.

'Oh, right. I thought he'd sneezed.'

'No. That's a laugh. They teach them that at Eton.'

'God,' says Donna, 'I wish they'd taught us that at

Streatham High. It must be really useful at funerals and that.'

'. . . Klosters,' says a girl with immaculate white high-lights and rock-hard breasts next to me, 'but of course, he would say that, wouldn't he?'

'I heard,' replies a portly chap with a German accent and the eye-glint of someone who likes to spend his weekends thrashing things, 'that they made their money in meat wholesaling.'

'No!' cries highlights. 'Worse! Car dealerships! And his father's family owned a school!' They laugh so much, they have to prop each other up.

We catch sight of Marina on the other side of the room. She raises an eyebrow and comes over.

'Thanks for coming,' she says. 'How are you? I hear Matthew's got a job.'

'Mmm.'

'What's he doing?'

'He's a bond trader.'

Donna tugs my bracelet and says, 'While they're out of earshot, I have to ask. What exactly *is* a bond trader?'

I give her a patronizing look. 'Why, it's someone who trades bonds, of course, Ms Brown.'

'Oh, well, that's as clear as mud. And what is a bond?'

'Um, it's a financial thingy.'

'So Matthew trades financial thingies?'

'Yes.'

'Like, buys them and sells them?'

'Well, yes, once they've taught him how to do it. At the moment he's assisting someone else who buys and sells them and learning what they do.'

'And what do they do?'

German guy takes the opportunity to intrude, looking down at Donna like a big cat eyeing its prey. 'A bond,' he says, 'is a piece of paper representing a debt. It pays an annual return, and that is what the traders are trading.' He clicks his heels together and offers a hand. 'Klaus von Schleswig-Wittgenstein,' he says, or something like that, anyway, 'from Austria. And you are?'

Donna shakes the hand. 'Donna Brown. Brixton and Barbados. Nice to meet you.'

'Ah, Barbados! And you know my good friends the Hunter-Bowles?'

'Well,' says Donna, 'we're mostly based here these days. I don't go back much.'

'*Ja*,' says Klaus, 'I know. Is difficult to find the time these days. And your friends?'

I introduce myself, and Ben says 'Ben Cameron,' and pumps the pink.

'Ah! I know you!' Klaus continues to hold Ben's hand, and stares deeply into his eyes. 'You are an actor, no?'

'No, not really.' Ben eventually manages to get his hand back by dint of some hard tugging.

'But I have seen you on the television. Recently.'

'Well, you might have.' Ben starts to colour.

'Now what was the programme? I'll remember in a moment—'

'So what do you do, Klaus?' I attempt to change the subject.

'Oh, you know, the usual,' he replies. The usual what? The usual bus-driving? The usual running a greengrocers? The usual teaching in a primary school? 'But I am certain I have seen your friend recently on the television. It was something early in the evening. Don't remind me. I do so love to guess . . .'

'So if you do the usual in the daytime,' asks Donna, 'what do you do for fun?'

Klaus chokes on a tiny blini topped with sour cream and caviare. 'What do I—' hack hack, search for handkerchief, tears streaming down face. Whatever Klaus gets up to for fun, we probably don't want to be joining in. While we bang him on the back Ben scoots off and joins Tania, who is working the room with the ferocity of one who feels she has minutes left to live. Her voice rises above the hubbub: ' . . . flat in Fulham. I've almost completed, actually . . . flatmates . . . fed up . . . grows apart in the end . . . Yes, well Matthew's at Fleming-Rothschild International Swiss and Chartered . . . this old thing? I just threw on the first thing that came to hand . . . yummy, aren't they? Have you tried the cherry tomatoes stuffed with crabmeat? . . . Oh, you *are* sweet . . .'

Over by the fireplace, Matthew gestures towards her, then towards me and Donna. The Hughs glance impassively, then one of them lights a cigarette and hands a silver-plated case to the others. Matthew, it turns out, is one of these others already; he lights up, puffs at the ceiling.

'Do you ever feel at all,' asks Donna by my side, 'as though you've fallen through a hole in the wainscot?'

'Oh, God, all the time. What was that that Tania was saying about a flat?'

Donna shakes her head. 'I don't know. I know she was going on about it after she lost her lipstick, but I didn't know she was actually doing something about it.'

'No. Nor did I.'

'Doesn't surprise me,' says Donna. 'She's probably deliberately keeping it quiet so we can all be shocked and hurt when she announces she's moving out.'

'Will you be shocked and hurt, Donna?'

'Dreadfully. I'll probably cry myself to sleep.'

'Me, too.'

Marina starts ushering people towards the front door. It's time to retrieve our coats from whatever cellar the maid has thrown them in, and do our bit for Charidee.

'And Marina is friends with all these people?' asks Donna.

'She knows them. They know her. I think that's how it works.'

Klaus has fled from Donna's dangerous questions, and is locked in conversation with a woman whose surgeon has either made a terrible mistake or was under orders to make her look like her pet Gila monster. Her eyebrows have crept so far up her forehead that they resemble antennae.

Donna sighs, helps herself to a Parmesan crisp with a blob of wasabi and some sea-urchin roe, empties her glass. 'Well, at least I'm getting to see how the other half live.'

I accept a miniaturised hot-dog on which a yellow zigzag has been piped in French's American mustard. 'You ain't seen nothing yet, love.'

Ben squeezes past Klaus and the dragon on his way to the door. Gila monster nudges Klaus, whispers something. Klaus's face lights up like Christmas. 'Of course!' he cries. Grabs Ben by the elbow, claps him on the back. '*Caught You Out!*'

Chapter Eighteen

Charing Cross

'Notice to all models: Please note that Accounts is ONLY open to models on THURSDAYS. If you need to go through your account and/or need money you must come into the accounts department on THURSDAY. If you are unable to attend in person you may telephone on THURSDAYS and we can send a cheque in the post if there is an emergency. Please make sure you plan your finances at least one week in advance. Calls can ONLY be accepted on THURSDAYS and you must ensure you have sufficient funds to last until the following Thursday.'

This sign is pinned up everywhere: inside the doors of the loos; behind the reception desk, on the door of the fabled accounts department, above the books, Sellotaped to the sides of computer terminals, lining the wall above the low, armless sofas in the waiting area. It slightly undermines the 'our models are members of our family' line that the bookers try to punt all the time. Mind you, families tend to deal in a roughly similar fashion with children's pocket money, so there's an element of truth in the claim. After all, they can always get a paper round if they don't like it.

Some places are a world apart, and a model agency more like a separate universe. I'm working in reception, which means picking up phone calls as they come through and punting them on to the relevant bookers, and looking people up and down as they come in off Bond Street, making them feel tiny before allowing them to get a word in. I learned the latter work-essential from Monique before she left for her holiday. Monique is a past mistress of the art; if she had walked in among the Hughs at Marina's on Saturday night, they would have embraced her as one of their own without thinking. Face completely impassive, she can run her eyes from head to feet and back again and make the action last a full five seconds. Then she says "nelpyou?' with such utter disdain that the object of her stare will take another five seconds to clear his or her throat before replying.

We get roughly five new girls a day through reception clutching their portfolios, and it's my job to put them off. Every magazine carries a story about the miraculous rise to fame of a girl from Croydon who dropped into an agency on her way to her supermarket job, but the facts are harsher. The bookers are safely tucked away behind a stripped-brick wall covered in poster-sized shots of their most famous clients, and the talent scouts, such as they are, spend more time scouring the shows for talent to poach from other agencies than lurking in Next or What She Wants. Most people who fancy a modelling career get no further than someone like me, whose arbitrary judgement will decide whether they are seen or not.

But I have to do this, because the people I work for are monsters. Monsters. I've come across unfeeling, ruthless people before, but these are full-on gorgons. Obviously, working in a business that takes schoolgirls and turns them into Lolitas must deaden your finer feelings, but the way these people talk gives me goosebumps. They walk past the reception desk going, 'Well, it's not my fault she can't get work. She's covered in flab. She must weigh nine stone,' and their colleagues go 'Ugh, thunderthighs.' Sophie Dahl may be an icon, but if anyone else has the temerity to outgrow size ten they turn into blimps, pigs, cows, Dawns. When I put calls through from models they growl 'Oh, God,' and then switch on the phoniest sugar-voices when the unfortunate fourteen-year-old comes on the line: 'Hello, darling. How are yooooouuuu?' I thought my own controllers were ghastly. At least they're not judging me on my waistline.

I don't know why anybody would want to be a model. It's the most degrading job, trailing from go-see to go-see while middle-aged men comment on the state of your rear end as though you're not there. The big-eyed girls on the sofas, to whom I bring cups of weak, milkless, sugarless tea, seem so enervated they can scarcely speak. And though they say please and thank you readily enough, they can rarely raise a smile. The Jewish Mother in me quails at the sight of them. I want to wrap them in thick jumpers and shout, 'Eat! You must eat! You'll fade away to nothing!' But I don't. I just go back behind my desk, where I occasionally duck my head down and pop another bacon crisp into my mouth.

All day a parade of skinny teens passes my desk, hands too big on wrists that look as though they would snap if you twisted them even slightly. Little voices issue from schoolgirls who have had too much of one sort of experience (undressing in front of strangers, staying in hotels, being offered champagne by middle-aged boys with permanent snuffles), and not enough of the others (clubbing together to buy chips, schoolday curfews, being told to go upstairs and wash that muck off your face).

All this experience doesn't seem to have done a whole

lot of rounding out, personality-wise, for these girls: you learn a lot more about life from mistakes made caravanning in Newquay than from being driven from airport to hotel to studio. I meet eighteen-year-olds who are bored – *bored* – with Milan, Paris, New York, talk about them in the way that their contemporaries talk about Salford. And yet, despite this globetrotting, this exposure to the freedom of the airways, most of them are perpetually skint. They may get their expenses paid on trips, but the real, concrete money is less easily come by. Half of them are up to their ears in debt, what with advances, haircuts, the ever-escalating cost of Paris lips.

Everything here is about image; everyone here spends almost all their disposable income on the outer trappings of success: clothes, make-up, light but glowing suntans, hoovering out their body fat. And the monsters, the women who spend their lives on the phone smarming designers, editors, catalogue-putters-together, are as obsessed as the ones who have to go in front of the camera.

I read the other day that, while one in five people believe they have a food intolerance, less than a tenth of those people actually do. Well, they all work here. Everyone here has a line of pill bottles next to her computer screen: vitamins, minerals, ginseng, green stuff, wheat grass, blue stuff, evening primrose, fish oils, purple stuff, B complex, orange stuff. The sound of speakerphones dialling 14-figure numbers is regularly punctuated by the rattle of supplements and the glug of the water cooler. Despite the fact that everyone here has a mobile phone, they all seem afraid to leave their desks in search of lunch in case they miss that vital Versace call that never comes. So one of my duties is to forsake the reception at twelve every day to go to the supermarket. I have a list as long as my arm, prepared by Monique, listing the dos and don'ts of feeding a roomful of bookers. And it's one heck of a task because, while everyone has a fad, no-one shares their fad with any of the others. Linzi lives on wholemeal bread, cream cheese and lettuce; the cheese I buy by the tub every three days, and she gets through one lettuce every two. Kim has three pieces of fruit at each meal, which must be different every time; my Filofax is full of little notes: 'grapes/tangerines/melon', 'kiwi/apples/dates'. I bought her strawberries once, and she practically threw them at me because they give her a rash. Bibi is yeast-intolerant; Richard doesn't chow on gluten (I tried one of his puffed rice cakes and it tasted exactly like the expanded polystyrene it resembles); Jane is fat-free; Mandy is eating for her blood type, which means meat (finding organic cooked meats is a bit like finding an MSG-free pot noodle) but no grains or pulses; Dee doesn't do dairy. The daily shop takes an hour, and I visit every aisle in the superstore to cull a single carrier bag of food. It puts a whole new complexion on the phrase hunter-gatherer.

And when they're not cooing at clients ('Hello, Giovanni, my favourite man, how are you?') they sit around swapping symptoms. Fragments of conversation drift round the screen to amuse me and edify the waiting teens: 'One bite and I swelled up like a balloon . . .' ' . . . covered in scales . . .' ' . . . martyr to irritable-bowel syndrome . . .' And I can see the teens drinking it all in, developing neuroses of their own. I think it's God's punishment for pushy parents: indulge in hubris over Lolita's looks, and what you get is a droopy stick who spurns the family dinner with the words, 'I can't eat any of that. I'll just have a spoonful of peas and a pear.' God knows, I always wanted to be pretty: I'm grateful now that everyone laughed at the thought of me as Face of '91.

Chapter Nineteen

Big Break

I can't believe that it's only six weeks since I booked Matthew in for a haircut, and went up to Chelsea to scour the charity shops for a posh shirt, and Ben lent him an Armani suit that he'd kept from a video shoot when he was sixteen (Ben's grown out of it and Matthew has just grown into it), which we calmed down by replacing the buttons with a set of anti-fashion ones from John Lewis, and Tania trained him in the right vocabulary, and Craig and he spent the weekend going through their old A-level economics textbooks to remind themselves of the difference between Free Trade and Open Markets, and we packed him off for his interview with Fleming-Rothschild International Swiss and Chartered. Six weeks is all, but you'd think he's been there a lifetime.

I can't quite get over it. Matthew has gone in this short time from hippy to stiff; drinks Famous Grouse when he comes in in the evening, says things like 'Footsie dropped five points and all the signs are that the Hang Seng's about to turn bear,' plays squash, shaves. Spends the evenings down in the kitchen with Tania sharing jokes like 'Bought in at 187? Ha-ha-ha!' which they find hilarious and the rest of us find impenetrable. Matthew, who a year ago was searching his rucksack to see if he had enough change for a bowl of nasi goreng while ranting about the tourists in the compound behind us, now says things like 'I think Aman resorts would be a good bet for the millennium.' And then he pauses, looks at me, and says, 'Of course, you're not going to be able to afford it.'

So now we scarcely see each other, except at weekends. Matthew sees more of Tania than of me these days: they get up together at six, whisper their way round the house eating toast and power cereals, leave their bowls and plates in the sink and set off into town side by side like an old couple, in their suits, Tania in her elegant camel-coloured overcoat. He got a loan for a thousand pounds and bought three suits the day he got his contract; now he looks the part in charcoal, grey, and charcoal-with-a-pinstripe. Tania seems to buy a new outfit every couple of weeks or so; the bathroom bin is always lined with Harvey Nicks bags.

I drift back to sleep for an hour and a bit after he goes, then leap from my bed in a manic panic the moment I hear the bathroom door slam behind Donna. Run around, half in, half out of my tights, persuade Donna to let me in to pee while she's brushing her teeth, brush my hair while I'm squatting, glug a mug of water by the kitchen sink, then Donna and I walk up to the tube together while sneaking our first nicotine of the day. Three little couples: me and Donna, Matthew and Tania, and Craig and Ben dysfunctionally ignoring each other and doing nothing about the housework.

I tried calling Matthew at lunch-time the first few days, just to see how he was getting on, but after the second day he was always out. He has always complained that I change my office phone too much for contact in the daytime, but doesn't seem to have the time to try and track me down. I think sometimes about getting a mobile, but then the normal phone bill comes in, or the heel falls off my shoe, or someone gets tickets to Glastonbury and the phone seems to have a lower priority. So sometimes I call Ben for a natter, because it can get lonely if you've no-one to talk to at work all day, but most times I sit at my desk with a sandwich and the *Independent*, or go for a walk and look at all the people who know where they are scurrying in and out of shops.

So it goes for the Masters of the Universe: they talk about the hours they put in, seem to get some testosterone boost from showing off about it, but when you need to track them down at lunch-time, the last place you will find them is at their desks. Same in the evening. Matthew never gets home before nine, nor does Tania, but if you call either of them after five thirty, they're long gone. Come home smelling of six-quid-a-glass wine bars, saying things like 'Thanks, but we had some sushi on the way home,' take off for bed around ten o'clock. Ten o'clock, for God's sake, like a pair of forty-year-olds.

And there are other things. Matthew has taken to hanging his clothes up before bed, and gets his shirts taken away for laundering once a week. Tania hangs her suits up in the shower to get the wrinkles out, just like in the women's magazines. No-one in the women's magazines says anything about making sure you don't use up all the hot water while you're doing it. On Sunday nights, when the rest of us are playing poker or bitching about the *Antiques Greedshow*, Matthew gets out a plastic bag full of brushes and cleans his shoes. He's bought two pairs of brogues, one black, one brown, and he brings them over to the table sometimes to show us the shine he's buffed up. 'Very nice, Matthew,' said Ben once, 'perhaps you'd like to polish my specs now?' Matthew just looked at him and walked away.

On Saturdays, Matthew and Tania read the *FT*. On Sundays they read *Sunday Business*. There's a copy of *The Economist* next to the loo, which I know he reads for that half-hour a day that men seem to mysteriously need to spend locked in. The other day he dragged me into Harrods and spent 45 minutes trying to choose between a shirt with a thin red stripe and a shirt with a thin green stripe. In the end I made him buy them both, or we'd never have got out of there. There was a time when Matthew liked to drop into Harrods to laugh at those weird Joan Rivers lookalikes with the concrete bobs in the Circle restaurant. Now he goes into Harrods because they have the best range of red braces. No wonder I'm confused.

And another thing: our house has suddenly turned into an electronic hell. Matthew must spend his life in House of Gadgets, because he imports a new one almost daily. There's the key-ring that bleeps when you whistle (or talk, or put the kettle down too forcefully on the kitchen top); the mobile that plays 'Colonel Bogey' instead of ringing; the minidisc; the bottle-opener-cum-nail-clipper-cum-nosehair-trimmer in the black leather carry-case. A while ago, he bought a Filofax and spent the weekend transferring his phone numbers from address book into the bit marked 'addresses'. Now he has a Psion organizer, and spent a whole weekend transferring his numbers into it.

'Look,' he said, 'I can tell what time it is in Jakarta at the press of a button.'

'Why do you want to know what time it is in Jakarta?'

'In case I need to call there, obviously.'

'Who do you want to call in Jakarta?'

'Look,' he said, 'it doesn't have to be Jakarta, OK? It was only an example. It could be Nairobi. Do you have to be so literal?'

Um, yeah, actually: I know for a fact that he doesn't know anyone in Nairobi, either. When he started showing me how he could do spreadsheets on the train, I fell asleep.

Another thing about the Psion: it bleeps whenever he has to remember something in his diary. Bleeps to remind him to take a pill, bleeps to remind him to have lunch, bleeps to remind him to call his mum, probably bleeps to remind him to take a shit, for all I know. But the other day it was our anniversary: three years since we hit on each other on the stairs in a house in Sheffield and woke up the next day an item. I waited all day, but it never bleeped once.

Chapter Twenty

Peace Pagoda

'How long is it since you had a girlfriend, Ben?' Donna sits down on the steps of the Peace Pagoda, fake Police specs reflecting the azure of the sky. It's one of those rare winter days when the sun suddenly shines with a vigour it rarely manages at the height of summer, and we've decided to walk round Battersea Park and make the most of the air being this clean. Donna's wearing flared leggings and a big inflatable coat covered in printed hibiscus. She looks like a sofa with legs, but neither of us tells her that.

Ben squints up at the golden Buddha above our heads. As usual, he has forgotten his sunglasses and is in a grump because his green eyes don't deal too well with bright sunlight. 'Have you ever noticed,' he says, 'that this is the only monument anywhere in this city apart from the Albert Memorial that doesn't have graffiti on it? Why do you think that is?'

'No-one's going to fool with the might of Ken Livingstone,' Donna sucks on her straw. 'And don't change the subject.'

'Well, how long is it since you had a boyfriend, for that matter?'

Donna cackles. 'I don't think I'd know what to do with one if I got one, love. Answer the question, Ben.'

'Depends what you mean by girlfriend.'

Donna shakes her head. 'Well you must have had loads of girlfriends when you were a pop star 'n' that.'

I open the can of Coke I've been carrying in my coat pocket and take a slug. 'Don't be silly, Donna. They were so busy they didn't have time for girlfriends.'

'Mmm.' Ben stops squinting and smiles at her. 'But we always hoped we'd find a nice girl one day to have a real relationship with.'

An old lady with a black hat and a small dog approaches. The dog looks from a distance like a Jack Russell, but proves on closer inspection to be a white Scottie with alopecia. It trots across the gravel to the foot of the pagoda and lifts its leg while its mistress accosts us. 'I hope you're not going to leave that can behind you when you go,' she says. 'Disgusting, I call it.' The land around the Peace Pagoda is scattered with bits of paper, old hamburger wrappers, Oasis bottles. If it weren't such a nice place to sit, with its view of the embankment, the Victorian wedding cakes of Albert and Chelsea bridges and the power station, you'd seriously think twice before sitting down. But once you've been there a while, you start to tune out the litter.

Ben looks solemnly at her and assures her that we have every intention of clearing up after ourselves. The dog has made its way over to some railings, where it squats, cross-eyed with concentration, and evacuates its bowels.

'You say that now,' says the old lady, 'but I know you young people. So interested in the next thing you forget all about the mess you leave behind you.'

'No, really,' I say, 'we promise we're going to take it away. There's a rubbish bin over there, look.'

'Well,' she turns, calls to the mutt, which is investigating its own droppings, tail stiff with excitement, 'mind you do.

This park is for everyone, you know.' And on she passes, looking for the next group of walkers to accost.

'Bitch,' snarls Ben. 'How dare she?'

'She's lonely,' Donna says. 'Wants someone to talk to. Anyway, you have to be nice to the twirlies. It's bad luck otherwise.'

'Twirlies? What's a twirly?'

'Don't you know what a twirly is?'

'No, Donna. I wouldn't be asking you if I did.'

'It's what my brother calls them. Old ladies. They all call them that on the buses.' Donna's brother spent four years driving the 19 across town before he went to college to train as a social worker. Now he's a probation officer in Brixton. If the Brown family resigned, Lambeth council would probably collapse: her mum is a psychiatric social worker dealing with child abuse, her dad is one of the few accountants who kept their jobs when Heather Rabatts took over and her sister, Marnie, teaches remedial English.

'Why do they call them that?'

'Well, you know how they all wake up at six in the morning and spend the next three and a half hours pacing up and down until it's time to go off to the supermarket to get cat food the moment their old girls' cards come into action?'

'Mmm?'

'Well, Rodney says that at 9.28 every morning, they're all there at every bus stop, all the old ladies, with their shopping bags on wheels, waving their old girls' cards and going, 'Am I twirly?''

'Actually,' says Ben, 'I've not really had a girlfriend.'

'Apart from Kirstie Campbell,' I remind him.

'Kirstie Campbell was at school.'

'You went out with her, though.'

'Yeah, I suppose I did. You can't really call fourteen-year-old sex a relationship, though, can you?'

'I should think Kirstie does. Anyway, relationships aren't all they're cracked up to be.'

'Oh, yeah,' says Donna. 'You can say that from the luxury of being in one. And how many girls have you slept with, Ben?'

Ben thinks for a long, long time. 'I don't know. A lot. Around one every other night for four years.'

'What, is that showing-off, or truth?'

'Truth. How many men have you slept with?'

'Um.' She rolls her eyes, counts on her fingers. 'Boys, nineteen. Men, five.'

Blimey. And I thought I'd done OK with six. 'And how many men have *you* slept with?' Donna asks.

Ben smiles. 'Three.'

'Three?' Donna squeaks and sits up. 'Are you serious? I was only joking. You've slept with men? Three men? When?'

'Well, you know,' says Ben, which we don't.

'Why?'

'I dunno. Because they were there?'

'And did you like it?'

'Yeah, it was OK.'

Donna thinks. 'You mean, like, penetrative?'

Ben pulls a face. 'Nosy. You never know when to stop, do you?'

'So, like, were they fans?'

'Sort of. We didn't really sleep with fans much. Too dangerous. And most of them were too young, anyway.'

'Well, I'm jiggered.' Donna delves in her pocket and brings out a Mars bar. Tears off the top of the wrapper and carelessly flicks it away over the grass.

'So don't you want a girlfriend, then?' I ask.

'I don't know. Maybe. I don't think I'm very good material for your average chick at the moment. I'm not exactly Mr Moneybags.'

'Ben, do you really think that every woman is after men for what they can give her financially?'

Ben shrugs.

'You don't, do you?'

'Let's face it. I couldn't move for them when I was doing well, and I rarely see them for dust now. I'm lucky if I get offers from some toxic waste in Stringfellows these days.'

We all sit back, thinking. I'm thinking: God, poor old Ben. Is there anything good that's come out of those years? He's got no money, no self-respect, and now he doesn't even like women all that much. Ben's probably thinking: Christ, why did I say all that? Now they think I'm really sad. Donna sorts it all out by saying, 'Well, I'd give you one, Ben. And I wouldn't even charge you.'

'Would you, love?' He almost looks grateful for a moment.

'Yeah, well,' says Donna, 'I'm that desperate, I'd shag a warthog.'

Ben gets to his knees and flings himself on her, starts tickling her as she lies pinioned, arms and legs waving in the air like an upturned beetle, shrieking at the sun as the Buddhas smile benignly and radiate peace over the world.

Chapter Twenty-one

Chancery Lane

Have you ever read *Finn Family Moomintroll*? There's a character in this fine children's book called the Groke. The Groke is one of those characters that sticks in your memory, shapes ever so slightly your view of the world in adulthood. Here, in case you don't remember, is the moment the Groke first appears:

'She sat motionless on the sandy path at the bottom of the steps and stared at them with round, expressionless eyes. She was not particularly big and didn't look dangerous, either, but you felt that she was terribly evil and would wait forever. Nobody plucked up enough courage to attack. She sat there for a while, and then slid away into the darkness. But where she was sitting, the ground had been frozen!'

The point about this is that everybody, but everybody, has met at least one Groke in their lives: people who make the air around them go cold, whose primary driving force is a frozen self-interest that alienates them from the rest of humanity. I've worked for a Groke, as a matter of fact: a man whose management strategy was to sack as many people as possible and make the lives of those who remained hellish, in the hope that they would resign. You always knew when he was approaching because the place fell silent as he passed through it and the temperature dropped. He was a big cheese, this man: a big cheese in small packaging, one of those little people who can make others feel two feet high. I once travelled 23 floors with him in a lift. Not a word was exchanged between us, but he stared at me, expressionless, from the moment I pressed the 'doors close' button to the moment I hauled myself up and clambered over the lintel to exit.

If you think about it, every office is peopled by characters out of children's books. That, of course, is the secret of a successful children's book: to find a character trait and exaggerate it to monstrous proportions. And children's books are, after all, intended as tools to equip us for the harsh realities of the adult world. Look around you, and you will find that everyone you know has probably been written up already by Tolkien, Nesbit, C. S. Lewis et al. Here are a few examples:

Gollum (*The Hobbit*): similar to a Groke, only less powerful. Inhabits dark corners, often Finance or Accounts, grumbling, asking impossible questions and waiting to pounce viciously on the unwary.

The White Witch (*The Lion, the Witch and the Wardrobe*): a woman of a certain age, who has fought her way up when the system was much tougher on women, developing an icy carapace and a belief that she must rule with a rod of iron. Great clothes, no sense of humour.

Scarecrow, Tin Man, Cowardly Lion (*The Wizard of Oz*): these usually travel in threes, performing junior management jobs. One has no brains, one has no heart, one has no courage. The Tin Man usually turns, in time, into a Groke; or shuffles off, full of resentment, to become a Gollum.

Noddy: the yes-man

Aslan (*Narnia*): the good boss, rarely reaches the pinnacle of management because he/she is more of a co-operator than a backstabber. The person everyone turns to for advice because he/she is the only true competent in the place. Constantly fighting off attacks by White Witches, Gollums, Grokes etc.

Mrs Doasyouwouldbedoneby (*The Water Babies*): the office mother, male or female; spends time trying to smooth over the worst of office politics and get people to be nice to each other. Believes in fairness and is permanently disappointed, harbouring secret fantasy of possessing the powers of Mrs Bedonebyasyoudid.

Any one of the Famous Five: graduate trainee, hideously enthusiastic. Cycles to work, brings tomato sandwiches and ginger beer to consume at desk.

Artful Dodger: ace salesman, no taste in clothes.

Willy Wonka: crazed personnel officer who latches on to every employment fad and inflicts endless personality tests on potential employees.

Little Lord Fauntleroy: has read two self-help books and regales colleagues with small homilies on how to run their lives. Everyone wants to hit him.

The Nice Old Gentleman (*The Railway Children*): patrician boss of the old school: believes in responsibility towards his retainers, loyalty and lunch.

The Little Match Girl: extra thin, lank hair, believes herself to be terribly put-upon. Goes all droopy when asked to do anything.

Cruella de Vil: divorcee: fingernails, designer clothes, rock-hard hairdo. Works as troubleshooter. Often to be seen drinking champagne in wine bars with senior management.

Postman Pat: delivers the mail. Usually has a lengthy excuse about overturned milk floats for why it's two days late.

Teletubbies: genial types with lovely round tummies from lunch-times eating Tubby Toast in the local greasy spoon and early evenings gulping pints in local pub.

Cinderella: only got her job because her shoes fitted, but somehow no-one seems to resent her. Probably because she represents the fact that promotion can be secured by anyone, given a little luck.

Prince Charming: the office dish, and boy, does he know it. Consistent butt of Teletubby ribaldry.

Shoemakers' elves: IT people. Perform miracles that no-one understands. People only believe they exist when something goes wrong.

Barbie: usually starts as a secretary. Rarely stays one for long.

Chapter Twenty-two

Trouble in Fairyland

Donna and I come in from the shops, and there's a row going on. 'Oh bugger,' says Donna, 'it's your boyfriend again.'

'Don't call him my boyfriend,' I say.

'Oh, yes? What, then?' asks Donna. 'What exactly do you want me to call him, then?'

I think. 'We live together. Does that make him a partner?'

'Partner?' says Donna, 'Partner, schmartner. Partner is one of those words coined by people who've obviously never had one or, if they did, are hopelessly naïve about the division of labour. Matthew is not your partner. He's the bloke who leaves his trolleys out for you to wash and occasionally has a burst of sharing your viscosities when he can get up the energy after a hard day scratching his stomach. He is not your partner. Nor is he your other half, your lover, your flatmate or your spouse. You may live with him, but he's your boyfriend. And at the moment he's having one hell of a row with your landlord, which isn't a good idea considering you're both a month behind with the rent.'

'Oh, God. Do you think I ought to go in there and stop it?'

'Humph,' says Donna, 'if you want to, I suppose.' She

pauses. 'I think I'd just try listening, if I were you.' And then she throws me a look.

Ben, who after years of training has a mighty decibel level, is shouting, and Matthew is, occasionally, protesting. 'You're the most selfish person I've ever met!' thunders Ben. 'I can't believe you'd do something like this! You're only living here because you're going out with my best friend, and I won't fucking put up with it! I swear, if you don't sort it out, I'll get her to sort it out for you. I swear.'

'No,' says Matthew, sounding sulky, 'no, don't do that. Look, I'll—'

'Don't even *think* about that. Just because I'm another guy doesn't mean I'm going to cover up for every sneaky, lazy, dirty thing you do. I won't! You can fucking well face the consequences of what you do and not hide behind everyone else any longer . . .'

'Blimey,' I say, 'what the hell's he done?' But Donna has already walked off down the stairs to the kitchen.

I decide not to interrupt for the time being, and follow her. As I come down the stairs, I hear her talking to someone. ' . . . proud of yourself . . .' she says. I pull the door open, and Tania is huddled over the sink, scrubbing away at an omelette pan, with Donna leaning against the draining-board beside her, arms crossed. They both look up, and Tania lets out a gay little laugh. 'Yes, I am rather. I worked bloody hard for this bonus and I deserve it. I know you're underpaid in local government, but that doesn't mean I should put up with it where I work.'

'Hi, Tania,' I say, 'you're home early.'

'Mmm,' she says. 'We got our half-year bonuses today and I came home at lunchtime to celebrate.'

She is looking flushed, and a bit pale underneath. 'Are you OK? You're looking a bit odd.'

'Oh, no no no . . .' She brings her sudsy hands up to her black Alice band and rearranges it on her Nicky-Clarke-cut hair. 'Well, I did think I might be coming down with something, but I feel OK now, just slightly shaky.'

'I'm sorry. Why on earth are you doing the washing-up? It's that bloody boyfriend of mine's left that, isn't it?'

'Oh,' says Tania, 'I don't mind. Someone's got to keep this place clean and the rest of you don't seem to care two hoots about the state . . .'

'Bollocks,' says Donna. 'I really object to that, Tania. You can be such a sanctimonious cow.'

Christ. Everyone seems to be in a foul temper today. 'Is this what those two are rowing about upstairs?' I try to change the subject before I have to leave the house to get away from the shouting.

'I don't think so,' says Donna. 'Perhaps you know what they're rowing about, Tania?'

'Are they?' says Tania. 'I didn't hear. I've been down here all the time.'

'All what time, Tania?' Donna is obviously in a needling mood.

'All the— Oh, never mind. I'm going upstairs.'

'Back to bed?'

Tania glares at Donna. 'No.' She slams out of the room, and, a few seconds later, the front door bangs.

'What was that all about?'

'Oh,' Donna shakes her head, curls a lip. 'I just don't like her much. I think she's sneaky.'

I laugh. 'Donna, she was always sneaky, don't you remember?'

'Mmm, but not like this. She's – I just don't trust her, that's all, and you shouldn't either.'

'Donna,' I say, in one of those speeches that you always

know afterwards was asking for trouble, 'I've known Tania since she was eighteen years old and sleeping with people to get party invitations. I know what sort of animal she is. Yes, she's sneaky, yes she'd sell her grandmother for a step up on the career ladder, yes, she has no scruples about trying to take whatever she thinks should be hers. But she has got some morals, and one of them is not doing the dirty on her friends. She wouldn't do the dirty on you, she wouldn't do the dirty on me, she wouldn't do the dirty on Matthew. Ben she might, because they've not known each other very long, but believe me, you have nothing to worry about. And besides, she's doing brilliantly. What on earth could we have that she would want that she can't just go out and buy?'

Donna stays silent, and raises her eyebrows.

'Give it a rest, Dons. It's bad enough those two going at it upstairs without you trying to start a guerilla skirmish down here.'

'OK,' says Donna. 'Whatever you say.'

Clomp, clomp, clomp: the door opens and Matthew bursts in, closely followed by Ben, who is going, 'You can't just pretend that everything's normal. You've got to . . .' until he catches sight of me and dries up. There's no attempt at Tania's bright, businesslike demeanour; he simply shuffles his feet and glares at Matthew, who is staring at the floor.

'I didn't hear you come in,' says Matt. 'When did you get in?'

'What's going on?' I say, because even I can't be blind for ever.

The three of them cast around for something to look at: anything, it seems, apart from me. Matthew looks at Donna, Donna picks at the omelette pan, still sitting in the sink, and Ben looks at Matthew as though an enormous bubo has just popped open on his cheek.

I feel faintly sick. Secrets always make me feel sick, ever since I found out why my parents had been so vague about how the cat had died when I was eight. 'You'd better tell me,' I hear myself say, 'because I know you're all up to something now.'

'No,' Ben says into the silence, 'not all of us.'

I look at Matthew. 'You, then.'

Silence. Matthew clears his throat, Donna starts slapping the draining board. 'Go on,' says Ben. 'Tell her. If you don't, I will.'

Matthew just continues to stand there, glaring at the warm-feel vinyl flooring. I'm having a little trouble with my larynx, but eventually I manage to stutter: 'OK, then. Tell me.'

Ben takes a breath, and the world caves in.

Chapter Twenty-three

Secrets

Each of us colonizes a corner of the kitchen, probably in order to be as far away from the others as we can. Ben and Donna are staring at Matthew and I'm staring, well, everywhere. I think everyone's expecting me to cry, but I don't generally cry much, and then it's usually when I'm watching something like *It's a Wonderful Life*, not when someone's stuck their hand through my ribcage and ripped my heart out.

'Well,' I say eventually, 'no wonder she's been taking such an interest in your career.' Two spots of colour appear on the points of Matthew's cheekbones and he looks even more sheepish than he looked while Ben was talking.

'So how long has this been going on for, then?'

Matthew doesn't answer.

'What? A month? A couple of months? Since Tania moved in? Since we moved in?'

Matthew looks around as though in search of an escape route and, finding all exits blocked, eventually grunts, 'I'm sorry.'

'Yeah, right. That sorts everything out then, doesn't it?' Ben growls.

'And when were you going to tell me?'

Again, silence. Matthew is completely puce by now, and

scratches behind his ear violently, something he always does when he's thinking.

'Don't try and make something up. Tell me the truth.'

'You bastard,' says Ben, 'you weren't going to tell her at all, were you? You were just going to move out and let her work it out for herself.'

'Move out?'

The front door clunks, and Tania comes hesitantly down the stairs. Peers round the door, comes a little way into the room, but not so far as to cut off her avenue of escape. I can't even bring myself to look at her; there's something sour lurking at the back of my throat and I think it might come bursting out if I glance in her direction.

'So you're moving out with *her*, then?'

Matthew nods, gouges at the back of his neck as though trying to rid himself of some nasty parasite before it makes it all the way to his eyes.

Tania speaks. 'I've bought a flat –' She stops, then starts agains. 'I'm sorry. It's not as if either of us meant this to happen.'

'What? Me finding out?'

'No.' She waves a hand around as though doing so will somehow explain what she's talking about. 'All this,' she finishes lamely.

'Fuck off, you silly, silly cow,' I snarl, and feel the momentary satisfaction of at least getting to say what I've wanted to say every time she has had a tantrum in the last three months.

Tania gasps, then says, 'It just happened. Matthew fell in love with me and I fell in love with him. We couldn't help it.'

'God, Tania. Even *junkies* don't use that piece of self-justification any more.'

Matthew clears his throat. 'I'm as much to blame for this as Tania. Don't think this happened without my co-operation.'

'No. You're perfectly capable of betraying people all by yourself,' snaps Donna.

I feel a rush of suspicion. 'So you two knew about this, then?'

Ben and Donna look uncomfortable. Not as uncomfortable as Tania and Matthew, but still guilty.

'And how long have you been keeping this secret from me, then?'

'No, babe,' Donna says, 'it's not like that.'

'Well, it bloody feels like it. How long have you known?'

'I found out today,' Ben says. 'I'm sorry. I'm slow at these things. Or maybe they've just been good at hiding it.'

'And you?'

Donna gulps. 'I – well, I got suspicious a while ago. Tania was looking so smug. Then again, she always looks smug.' This she aims at Tania, who jerks her chin in offence. 'But she kept looking smug when you walked into the room, and I guessed something was up. I'm sorry.'

'And you didn't tell me?'

'I didn't know what to do. I thought you'd blame me or something, especially if I'd got it wrong.'

'I don't believe you.'

'Well, I hate you,' she suddenly yells at Matthew.

This is too bloody much. I haven't shouted, or shed a tear, or done anything dramatic yet. The least she could do is leave me that.

'That's great, Donna. Turn it into your drama, why don't you? In case you hadn't bloody noticed, I'm the one who's been lied to by everyone around here.'

Donna subsides. Ben says, very softly, 'I don't think we're

the ones you should be blaming for lying, sweets.' We stand around listening to the ticking of the clock, and I put my hand on my solar plexus to quell the queasiness. I feel a lot of things I didn't know you felt in these situations: sick, empty, like my skin's on fire and, most of all, frightened.

'Look,' says Tania, 'you have to face reality. Matthew's grown out of you. He's moved on, got a career, and you're still living like a student, thinking about little things and going nowhere. He doesn't want to carry someone else. He wants someone with some ambition, someone who's going to be able to keep up with him, and that someone just happens to be me.'

Which is about the best thing she could have said. This loosens me up, allows me to feel something, even if it is only white-hot anger. I pick up the mug lying beside me on the worktop – a Liberty mug that Tania bought for some phenomenal price in the sales – hurl it at her head, and shout – I'm rather proud of this later – 'Get out of here or I'll flay you alive, you supercilious no-brain yuppie!' and she turns on her heel and flees.

My rage snaps off as quickly as it came on, and I find myself crouching in the doorway, rubbing my face and picking up the shards one by one. Donna unpeels herself from the sink, gets the dustpan and brush from the hook on the wall and crouches beside me. She looks up into my face, and I'm surprised to see that she's in tears.

We finish our task and stand up. Donna finds an old copy of *Sunday* magazine and wraps the pieces in it before putting them in the dustbin. I don't really know what to do next. Ben starts to come towards me. I can tell he wants to touch me and I can't bear that. He puts a hand out and I shrug it off. 'Don't.'

'Look—'

'No, just don't.' I grab my jacket from the back of the chair.

'Honey,' says Donna.

'No.' I start to rub my face again, and I can tell they all think I'm about to weep. I'm not. It's just that there are some lizards crawling around underneath my skin and I have to scratch. Matthew is still slumped there against the fridge, and I want to hit him.

I don't want to be here any more. Matthew and I have been together three years, and I never thought once about how it would feel to lose him. 'I'm going out,' I say. Ben and Donna make to follow me as I run up the stairs, but I slam the door in their faces, bolt through the front door and race towards the tube.

It's getting dark already, and there's nowhere to go in Stockwell after dark where you can be alone. When I get round the corner, I slow to a walk. Everything seems to be happening in slow motion. You know that dream you have sometimes, the one where your legs don't seem to work? I feel like that now, only it's real life. My feet drag along the pavement as I make my way up Lansdowne Way. A couple of people cross the road when they see me coming; I must look seriously unhinged.

What do I do? I mean, what the hell do I do? This wasn't how the plan went. We were going to be so splendid, the two of us: make money, get famous, be respected by our peers, have one of those huge, messy houses full of kids and dogs and an overflowing larder ready to entertain the hundreds of people who would want to drop by. And now there's nothing, there's no more me and Matthew. There's Tania and Matthew, and me watching all my assumptions drain away like water through my fingers. I mean, what do I do now?

A hand on my shoulder. I break from my reverie, and look up to find Craig grinning down at me. 'I thought you were ignoring me or something,' he says. 'Where are you off to? I've just been to see Barney in Brixton and . . .' He trails off as I stare blankly at him, frowns and tightens his grip. 'Sweetheart,' he says, 'what's wrong? What's happened?'

'Oh, Craig.' My chest opens up and I swallow in a huge gulp of air as I feel my face crumple. Craig reaches out to me and pulls me into his arms as the tears begin to come.

Chapter Twenty-four

Bank

And this is the bugger of it: temps don't have lives, and any sign that they do is an insult to the employer. The rest of you, with your salaries and colleagues, your end-year bonuses, and paid holidays, are allowed off-days; when something happens in your household, those who work with you will tip each other the wink, tell each other to go easy on you, tiptoe around your grief or your stress or your anger until the healing process has had time to start working. Not so people like me. If you find your temp in floods at her desk, or prone to drifting off into fugues, or exhausted from lying awake all night worrying, she is nothing other than a shirker, a drip, a wet, maybe a bit emotionally unstable. Treat her with the contempt she deserves: you're not supposed to bring your private life to the workplace, after all, and any signs of weakness are a slap in the face of professionalism.

So Matthew, now that he has a new image, wants a life partner who fits it. He wants a girlfriend who looks elegant in little skirty suits, has a haircut every month, never wears tights with ladders because she always has a spare pair of 10 deniers tucked in her executive shoulder-bag. He wants someone whose confidence isn't at an all-time low, someone who's got spare cash to spend on champagne.

And he didn't even have to leave the house to find one. There are loads of girls in Bally heels floating around the City, confidently laying their gold cards down on polished wooden bars, fondling discreet gold earrings; all he had to do was take his pick. So he picked my so-called friend.

And of course, as it is with men, it's all my fault. Whatever stage you're at in life, the roving eye of the male is always the fault of the female he's involved with. 'You're not the woman I married,' 'You've let yourself go', 'You're more interested in the kids than you are in me.' Matthew has fallen back on that old standard, 'We don't seem to have anything in common any more.' Christ knows, we had enough in common last year while he was signing on and failing interviews, and the only money for going out came from the fruits of my typing.

But you see, I deserve what I get, because I'm an embarrassment. Matthew can't go to parties with his new friends and introduce his girlfriend, the temporary secretary, to their babylegs ski-bum consorts. 'You're so negative,' he says. 'I deserve to be with someone who's got a positive outlook on life. Someone who's going places.' And strangely, I'm the one who's going places in the short term: Matthew and Tania are staying put for the next week and I'm staying with Marina, because Tania knows her rights and, having paid her rent until the end of this week, refuses to move out until she can take possession of her double-power-shower, Colefax and Fowler, Lots Rd-auction-furnished Fulham bloody yuppie love-nest.

Slept like a log last night, much to my surprise, in the crisp linen sheets on Marina's spare bed, and got up this morning feeling like someone had attached lead weights to my wrists and ankles. And the double bugger of it is that I'm working in the City and have to spend the whole week staring at women in Alice bands and thinking about how they are all, with their confidence, their arrogance, their ready cash, responsible for my situation. Had a bath in Marina's marble bathroom, scrubbing myself with a loofah to get the feeling of dirt out. Half an hour with a flannel over my face, ten minutes painting out the streaks, half an hour late for work.

Lucy (I'll believe in the classless society when City executives are called Kylie) snarls at me when I arrive: 'You're late.'

'I'm sorry.' I hang my head, which aches from the pressure in my sinuses. Lucy is hardly older than me, but a world away: straight from uni onto a training scheme, first bonus at twenty-two. 'You're supposed to be here at nine o'clock,' she persists.

'I know. I'm sorry.' I sit down, hoping to plug into earphones for the day.

Lucy says, 'Don't think you can write down eight hours on your time sheet.'

'I wasn't going to.'

'Well, don't.' She stalks off on her Bruno Maglis.

Today is not a good day. I'm way off beam, lose a couple of calls in the phone system, fill letters with basic spelling mistakes that take hours to correct. Matthew says I've become boring, and it's probably true. I don't actually find his talk of mergers and deals particularly stimulating, but at least his new girl has something more to say than 'Typed some letters and answered the phone today.'

On the other side of the screen, Lucy tells a client about the minibreak she's taking this weekend. 'Yah,' she says, 'country house hotel outside Bath. He's going to spend the day shooting and I'm heading straight for the spa. Mmm? Pretty good, actually. £300 each all-in for the weekend.

Mmm. I'll let you know what it was like.' This weekend I'm going to the launderette and probably avoiding a party on Saturday in case Matthew's there.

She reappears to check up on me just as I'm blowing my nose. 'Cold?' she says.

I reach out for some sympathy. 'No, I—'

'Never mind,' interrupts Lucy. 'There's a chemist in Liverpool Street. Buy some Nurofen cold and flu. That'll sort it. Oh, and can you make me a reservation for four at le Caprice on Thursday at eight? If they're full, Quaglino's will do.' She stalks off again, looks back as she reaches the screen that hides hoi polloi like me from the rest of them, to be brought out only when we are of use. 'By the way,' she says, 'your mascara's running.'

Chapter Twenty-five

Told You So

Marina rests her cigarette in the ashtray while she gets down the gin glasses. There is one thing you can say for Marina, and that's that she always has a full complement of drink in the house, even if you do have to go through a series of homilies to get to it. And I really need a drink.

'So.' Marina opens the ice compartment of her American-style walk-in fridge-freezer, wraps some ice in a tea towel and bashes it with a rolling-pin. Selects a lime from the fruit bowl, cuts it in quarters, squeezes one quarter into the bottom of each glass, wipes it round the rim, discards it into the chrome pedal bin. Puts half the crushed ice into the glasses, drops in the other lime quarters, tops them with the rest of the ice. With Marina, everything has to be just so. But then again, a Marina gin and tonic is one of those things guaranteed to set you back on the road to well-being.

'Why do you think it happened?'

'God,' I snitch a fag from her packet. 'I don't know.'

'Well,' says Marina, 'I suppose I've been a bit worried for a while now, but I didn't like to say anything.'

Here it comes. I arrived so late last night that she didn't get a chance to lecture me, but now Marina is going to tell me all the things I did wrong, so that I don't repeat the mistake, of course. But she is also pouring roughly an eighth of a bottle of gin over the ice in each of the highballs. I vacillate between getting out while my self-esteem is relatively intact and getting my mouth round the icy, oily firewater that steams gently in the glasses, and the gin wins out. That, and the need for a bed for a few nights.

'The thing is,' says Marina, 'you have been letting yourself go a bit lately, haven't you?'

I gulp. 'Have I?'

'Well, yes.' Marina goes back into the fridge for a couple of those little glass bottles they do tonic water in in pubs. She won't do big bottles like you get in the supermarket, because the fizz goes off them. 'I mean, when did you last have a decent haircut?'

I think. 'Oh, yeah. I was going to get my hair done, but the phone bill came in and I had to pay both of our shares as Matthew didn't have any money.'

'Look,' says Marina, 'that's another thing. A man doesn't want to be emasculated by a woman who takes charge all the time, especially as you seem to spend so much time thinking about money. Look at me. I never go on about money, do I?'

Well, no, I think, but then, you've got plenty of it.

'Matthew's been having a very hard time,' continues Marina. 'It's not easy being jobless, you know, and you really haven't helped.'

'How haven't I helped, Marina?'

'You never seemed to have time to listen to him. And when he did try to talk to you about his situation, all you'd suggest was little dead-end jobs like you're doing.'

'Yes, well someone had to . . .'

Finally, she hands me my drink, and I sink a third in one gulp. It is completely delicious: a drink like you see in 1930s films full of silver-plated cocktail shakers.

'The thing is,' she says, 'if a woman neglects her man, she can hardly be surprised if he looks elsewhere. And let's face it, Tania is a much more attractive prospect.'

'Thanks.'

'No, really. She's got ambition, she's got a good job, she looks after herself. You come home at night and all you have to talk about is paper-clips. Tania comes home and talks about million-pound deals. Matthew's got ambitions himself, you know.'

'So have I.'

'Oh, yes. Evidently.'

The gin, fortunately, is working very fast, mostly because I haven't eaten anything since lunch-time yesterday. After spending yesterday evening throwing up in the upstairs loo while everybody else slammed doors, I wasn't terribly hungry by the time I got to Marina's.

'I have tried to warn you,' says Marina. 'Haven't I tried to warn you?'

'I suppose so,' I say sulkily.

'Well,' says Marina, 'now it's happened. I suppose they'll be moving to Fulham together?'

'I suppose so. I don't really care, to be honest. They can jump off Chelsea Bridge together, for all I care.'

'Well, it's very inconvenient. I do hate it when these things blow up. Suddenly everyone has to walk on eggshells about who to ask to what.'

'I'm so sorry to put you out, Marina,' I say with all the sarcasm I can muster. As usual, it goes straight over her head.

'I dare say we'll cope,' she says. 'How long do you want to stay?'

'Well, Tania's rent runs out at the end of the week. I suppose Matthew will go then, too.'

'A week?' She looks shocked.

'Yes.'

'Can't they find anywhere to go before then?'

'I'm sorry, Marina.' I suddenly find myself close to tears. Matthew's behaved like a shit, and I'm a burden to everyone. 'I can always go and stay with someone else.' And a big, fat tear rolls out of my left eye, and there's nothing I can do about it. It plops onto the counter and I wipe it away with my sleeve.

'No,' says Marina, 'don't be silly.' Suddenly she's concerned, even reaches out and pats me on the arm, a gesture I've never seen her offer another woman. 'That wasn't what I meant. Not at all. You're welcome to stay here as long as you like. It was just that I couldn't believe that they'd be so barefaced. Sorry. I probably seem unsympathetic. I don't mean to be. I just can't believe they've got the nerve.'

'Tania's big on her rights.'

'Yes, well,' says Marina, and reaches into the icebox once again, 'she always was a cow. Does she still divide bills down to exact pence?'

'Oh, yes.' I finish my gin and push my glass in her direction. 'And she takes the service off in restaurants if the staff don't kiss her arse hard enough.'

'When I lived with her,' says Marina, 'she had a special loo roll that she'd bring from her bedroom to the bathroom every time she went.' Bash bash bash on the ice, slash-squeeze on the limes.

'Still does that. And she puts hairs across the lids of food cartons so she can tell if anyone's used them.'

'And the thing with the tea bags?'

I nod.

Gin hits rocks, rocks crackle. 'Hah,' says Marina. 'They deserve each other. D'you want a sandwich?'

Chapter Twenty-six

Oxford Circus

For a change, Tracie at the agency's policy of placing people in jobs for which they're unsuitably qualified has paid dividends; she has sent me to spend the week as a pool typist in a huge insurance company in the West End. Normally, I'd be spitting feathers at this point, as the pay is crap, but at the moment, while my mind is still fudged with misery, it's about all I can cope with. I sit all day at an anonymous desk and type up the dullest letters about the dullest minutiae of small claims and pension enquiries, dictated by random voices into micro-cassette recorders, and it suits me down to the ground.

The thing about typing is that it has a wonderful meditative quality once you get good at it. Zen and the art of yogic stenography. I am such a proficient typist now — 80 words a minute audio at my last test — that I do it without thinking. I hear a word and it flies from the tips of my fingers with no thought process intervening to slow me up. And while I'm typing, I'm free to let my mind drift, to think about the world, its injustices and how to deal with them. But at the same time it's a task that demands enough skill, enough awareness of what you're doing, that your mind can never drift so far away that misery takes over. I can pass whole days now without the thought of tears: an efficient, placid automaton. The strange thing is that the moment I start to think about what I'm doing, I can't do it at all. My fingers turn into sausages and a jumble of mixed letters with no obvious pattern appears on the screen. Go figure.

So I'm sitting there in my pleasant daze, when Lindsey turns up for a visit. She enters the floor from reception at about three o'clock, make-up covering the bags under her eyes, large coat covering the bags in her newly maternal body, pushchair, baby. And the place goes mad. There is a sort of collective gasp, then half my companions leap from their seats going, 'Whooo! Izza BAY-beee! Izza wickle BAY-bee!'

'BAY-beee! Wuzza wuzza wuzza! Hello sweee-tie! Can I hooold her? Ba-ba-ba-ba. Woooeee! Ickle-ickle!' I've never heard so many people revert to gurgles in such a short space of time. Well, I have – whenever a baby enters the room, as a matter of fact, and, of course, in a few rave clubs – but it's still a shock. Women who would otherwise be seen as upstanding, sane and reliable members of society blow raspberries, jig the tiny hand up and down, cross their eyes and puff out their cheeks, heap smacking kisses on the air. In the middle, the object of their attention sits impassive.

Babies: can't live with them, society says you can't eat them, but they bring out the most extreme levels of human behaviour. Down on the ground are the childless-but-want-them women, going 'Aaah' and 'Isn't he gorgeous' (no-one can tell a baby's sex these days) and working at its straps to free it for passing round. Above them tower the parents, lofty in their greater knowledge. No other situation lowers colleagues' inhibitions so: Lindsey is cheerfully talking about the state of her genitals and everyone else is sharing their own tales of stitches, piles and blood, of nipple shields and expressing-pumps.

Not everyone, of course. As I said, only half the office rose from their seats. The rest seem to have developed uniform neck trouble, sitting stiffly with their backs to the action, pretending that nothing is happening at all. Occasionally they catch each other's eyes and grimace, but never cast an eye in the direction of the cries of 'Ohh! Look! He blew a bubble!' and 'My turn! Let me hold him!' I don't mind babies: I know they're a fact of life, but find it hard to show an interest in creatures that communicate by farting. But this is an anthropological situation that might make for a Ph.D. thesis.

I head for the water cooler, craning my ears to catch the best of it, and find two others already there. Nursing her paper cone, Maria says, 'I do wish people wouldn't bring babies into offices. It's not the place.'

'Yugh,' says Nuala, twenty-three, ambitious and protecting herself from the baby trap by aversion therapy, 'I hate babies. Can't stand 'em.' The group around the pushchair is breaking up, those who've been billing and cooing as a matter of form returning to their desks, only the truly besotted remaining.

Office Romeo passes. You can tell he's the office Romeo, because he's got a floppy fringe and always perches on edges of desks rather than standing in his own space. Nuala, who is protecting herself from the office-Romeo trap as well, pulls a face at his back. 'Just watch John,' she says. 'I bet he'll try and hold it to show what a sensitive guy he is.'

John, true enough, pats his hair and enters the scrum. 'This yours, Linds?' he says. 'Ooh!!' he cries. 'Izza BAY-bee! Isn't he lovely? Can I hold him? I love holding babies.'

Takes baby and clutches it to his chest. Sniffs close to its hair and declares that the scent of milk and baby powder is the best in the world. Smiles around the assembled, dropping his head to one side. 'How do I look?' he says. 'Think I'd make a good father?' He puts on a reflective face for the ladies. 'I'd love one of these,' he says. 'I just can't seem to find the right mother.'

Baby raises itself in my estimation by throwing up all over his jacket.

Chapter Twenty-seven

Sleepless in South London

So now it's just the four of us, sad failures, sitting around in front of *Casualty* and eating pizza, each lost in our own misery. Matthew and Tania moved out a week ago and I came back, and none of us has left the house since except, where appropriate, to go to work: Craig is skint, Donna is depressed, Ben hates the world and I haven't been getting enough sleep to do anything other than work, eat, slump.

The day I get back Ben follows me up the stairs and catches me sitting on the bed in Matthew's and my room, dismally staring around at the empty bookshelves, the empty drawers and the clean bits on the walls where his Verve poster and his one picture (oddly enough, a hunting print) used to hang.

'How's it going?' he asks.

'He's taken all the pillows,' I reply.

'Bastard,' says Ben.

'Never mind,' I find it in me to grin at him, 'it could be worse. He could have left me the Manchester United duvet cover.'

Ben sits down on the bed beside me, puts an arm round my shoulders. 'I was thinking,' he says. 'What about if you move into my room?'

I'm startled for a moment, until I realize that he's offering to move out.

'Why?' Ben's room is lovely; far nicer than ours – sorry, mine – facing the morning sun and extending across the whole of the front of the house.

'Well, I was thinking about it,' he says, 'and I thought you probably wouldn't want to sleep in here any more. And then I thought, well, she can have Tania's room which is much nicer (Tania's is on the top floor, over Ben's and is similarly large, though with a sloping ceiling), but then I thought you probably wouldn't want to be there either, what with memories and that. So I've taken over Tania's room. It suits me anyway, being in the top of the house. That way I don't have to listen to anybody else's noise. And you can take over mine, and then you won't have to move out.'

'I wasn't planning to move out, Ben.'

He squeezes my shoulders a bit harder, looks into my eyes. 'Good. We don't want you to. We need you here.'

Darling Ben. Just when you feel the world is peopled by bastards, he thinks of something.

So now I'm on Ben's futon, which we decided was too much like hard work to move upstairs, with clean new bedclothes and pillows that don't bear the slightest trace of Matthew. And I can't sleep. Out back, everything was relatively peaceful, but here you're never sure if you're going to be woken up by one of the thousand fifteen-year-old Fords that seem to be *de rigueur* in this neighbourhood, or the screams of someone being mugged. On a Friday and Saturday the screams come at double the rate, but most of those are screams of joy from people falling out of the Swan at two in the morning with their ears ringing so they can't hear how loud they are.

And the thing is, I could probably get used to the noises over the course of time, but I can't sleep anyway. Because though in the daytime I can convince myself that I hate Matthew, that it's good riddance to bad rubbish, that I don't want someone who values his mobile phone over his record collection and especially don't want someone who would even think of touching Tania with the longest, most algae-covered bargepole, at night I have to face the fact that I miss him. I thought maybe a new bed in a new room would make it easier, feel like a new start, but all I am aware of is this great gaping hole beside me. Funny, isn't it? You spend the whole time while you're locked in a relationship believing that you would get a decent night's sleep if only you had full access to the duvet/could stretch out properly without encountering a starfished leg/weren't always being kept awake by snoring, and the moment you get your desire, you can't sleep because you feel so alone.

The fact is, human beings weren't meant to sleep alone: that's why we give children teddy bears and furry dogs and garish fluffy dinosaurs to share their slumbers with. That's why old ladies have cats. That's why, after a night of tossing and turning, I've brought one of my pillows down under the duvet with me to give me something to wrap my arms and legs around when the loneliness gets too much. It's not Matthew, but at least it's something solid that, after a few minutes, soaks up some of my body heat and reflects it back as though it, too, were alive.

But still I can't sleep. I roll from side to side, kick my feet out into the spaces around me, I sigh, I close my eyes and count sheep, name the girls in my class at school, count backwards from 10,000. I've even tried reading Proust, which is usually guaranteed to send me off soundly in minutes – I'm still on page 137 of *Swann's Way*, stuck in the middle of that endless bloody hawthorn bush, after nearly two years – but still I find myself staring glassy-eyed at the ceiling at three in the morning and thinking, 'What went wrong? Why do I deserve this? Isn't life shitty enough already without being betrayed, thoughtlessly, by the one person I'm supposed to be able to rely on?' And at about three, despite myself, I start to think about what *they* might be up to; burning thoughts of the things he's saying to her, the things she's saying to him, their justifications for chucking me away like I'm some old piece of clothing neither of them has any use for any more. And then – I can't help it – I make myself sick by thinking about them doing sex in their strident yuppie fashion, Tania ordering Matthew about and Matthew going, 'Oh yeah, give it to me,' or some other awful cocaine-fuelled cliché, the thought of Tania's sweat mingling where my sweat used to mingle, Tania putting condoms on – I never did really get the hang of that – in that brisk, efficient fashion of hers. So then my skin prickles with rage, and disgust, and self-hatred, and by the time I see them, curled up together spoonwise as Matthew always liked to do, my hair is salty with tears of self-pity and I know that yet again I won't fall asleep until well after daylight, will see that the clock is maybe an hour off getting-up time before I plunge down at last into complete exhaustion.

On the third night I give up between the conversations and the sex and decide I might as well get up, make a cup of tea, write a letter, watch some repeats of 1970s American cop series on the telly. So I roll over, find my dressing-gown (green silk embossed with soppy dragons: $97HK last year) and go downstairs. Tiptoe through the darkened corridors so as not to disturb the others and start down the stairs to the basement. A crack of light shows under the kitchen door and, as I approach, I hear voices: Donna cackling, Ben chuckling, Craig going, 'Oh, you bastards,' and the slap–slap–slap of cards on the table.

They look up as I come in, and Donna says, 'At last. Welcome to the land of the damned.' Craig reaches behind him and pulls the spare fold-up chair to the table for me.

'What's going on here?'

'Pinochle,' Ben explains, though given that it was me that taught them the game, I would have thought that this much I could work out for myself.

'Yeah, obviously. But why are you all playing it at three in the morning?'

Donna laughs. 'We always play it when we can't sleep. Didn't you know? This is what single people do.'

'Really?' I sit down and Ben, who is dealing, automatically cuts me in.

Craig shakes his head. 'That's the thing about settling down too young. There's all sort of things you never find out about.'

I look at my cards. One three, one jack and nothing else of any merit at all. 'Are we playing this for money, by the way?'

'Penny a point,' says Ben.

'And you do this all the time?'

'Naah,' Donna turns over a six of diamonds, pulls a card, 'only when we can't sleep. Which is about three times a week.'

'Sometimes four,' Craig corrects her, putting down an eight of diamonds, which means that I miss my first go altogether.

Ben follows it with an eight of spades. 'Two, sometimes. But it averages out at about three.'

'How come I didn't know about this?'

'That's what I mean about settling down too young.'

Craig reverses the order of play with a jack and I sit back to await my turn. 'Couples always stay in their rooms once they've gone to bed. Welcome to insomnia.'

'Thanks. I was thinking about having a cup of tea.'

'Don't be silly,' Ben says, 'tea will keep you awake.'

'I don't think I'm going to sleep any more tonight anyway.'

'Well, the pot's there. And don't look at my cards.'

'As if I would.'

'I've known you sixteen years,' he says, 'I know you would.'

By the time I've sat down, the play has finally come back to me. Ben has put down a three. I laugh, slap down my three on top. Craig follows it with another. Donna does the same. I'm pointing at Ben and laughing, when he puts a fifth on top.

'No! Wait a minute! How can that be?'

'Two packs,' says Donna. 'We always play with two packs. Pick up fifteen.'

'No, you bastards!'

Everyone shakes their heads and Donna says something about sore losers. I pick up; my hand is so full now that I can scarcely hold it. Craig takes one of Donna's Lucky Strikes, lights it and puts down a six of hearts.

'So why can't you sleep?' I ask Donna.

'Work. I always get wound up if I've had a bad day, and it's the end of the month this week, when everyone comes in to see how their points are doing. I just hate it when I have to spend a week being sworn at.'

'And you?' I ask Craig.

'Dunno. I've just got out of the habit of sleeping. Nothing to get up for. At least this way I don't have to get up till after Richard and Judy.'

'I haven't really slept at night at all since I was sixteen,' says Ben. 'I was always whacked out after performing, or whacked out on speed, or stewing because someone had said something that had pissed me off or nervous because we had to do something the next day. It gets to be a habit after a while. That's why I sleep so much in the afternoon.'

'And now,' says Donna to me, 'you're lying awake thinking about that lowlife scumbag ex of yours and you've joined the club.'

'He's not a lowlife scumbag, he's a filthy lowlife scumbag.'

'Filthy lowlife yuppie scumbag,' says Craig.

'Fifty lowlife spotty-arsed yuppie scumbag,' says Donna.

'Pinochle.' Ben lays down his second-last card.

'How can you be pinochle?' I cry, almost dropping my half-pack of cards. 'We've only just started!'

'Dinnae fash yersel',' Donna says, which makes both Ben and Craig flash her that look that only Professional Scotsmen have mastered. When it gets to her turn, she slaps down a three and Ben picks up.

'Look,' I say, 'you guys, we've got to get a grip. This house is falling apart and all we do is play cards.'

'I know,' says Donna, 'pinochle. But it's better than lying awake separately crying ourselves to sleep. I mean, what are we going to do? The world's against us at the moment, and there's no point fighting it, man.'

'No, bugger it,' I say, 'I'm not taking that line. I'm bloody well going to fight it. By the time the month's out, I'm going to have a job. I'm determined. You just see if I don't.'

Chapter Twenty-eight

Knight in Shining Armour

And after the first burst of self-pity, Matthew's defection has the same effect on me as a red rag to a bull, or, if not a red rag to a bull, at least the same effect as martyrdom to an early Christian. If Matthew doesn't want me as a failure, I'm damn well going to not want him as a success. I spend nights tarting up my CV, ringing ads in the Media *Guardian* with a red ballpoint and racking my brains about what I'm going to do next. It's all very well being determined, but getting a job is actually a time-consuming process, and I've left myself with very little time to consume. Who would have guessed that my knight in shining armour would gallop into the ring so suddenly, and so unexpectedly?

The Thursday before Christmas, Donna and I go to a fabulously boring drinks party in Shepherd's Bush given by the Respectables, who got married straight out of university, went into Respectable jobs, bought their house on a double mortgage, and plan to build up their capital until she's thirty, when they will have two, or perhaps three, kids before her eggs start to go off. And they'll probably manage it, too: you know how there are some people in the world for whom everything seems to fall out exactly according to the five-year plans, ten-year plans, life plans, they have laid out? Who seem to have managed to get the chaos of the universe under control sometime before GCSEs and maintain order right up until one of them dies a year after retiring on a healthy pension? Janey and Paddy Respectable are like that. It's not that I resent it or anything. No, really. Trust me: I'm a secretary.

So we're standing around in our Respectable Drinks Party gear and though we've made a real effort, we still manage to be out of place. I suddenly remember that ordered people also have knowledge of how to do things that I've never really mastered, like iron, and remember to replace buttons, and have their hair cut in sensible styles that require the minimum of maintenance in order to look clean and tidy, and clean their shoes every Sunday night instead of getting in a video and ordering a pizza and nursing the remains of their Friday-night hangovers, and remember to send out their Christmas party invitations a month in advance so no-one can claim a prior engagement. I mean, we both look clean, but Donna's plaits look very extreme among all these shiny bobs, and I'm the only person, possibly for the first time in my life, wearing black. Janey's been to Marks and Sparks and raided the party-food section, and Paddy's bought in a case of Chardonnay and a case of claret from the discount wine warehouse. Discount wine warehouse! See what I mean? I've never in my life had more than two bottles in the house at one time, and they never lasted more than a night when I did. Paddy and Janey have even remembered to mull theirs, so most of the alcohol boils away and there's no danger of anyone making a fool of themself.

I decide that, if I'm going to look weird, I might as well try to make an impression as helpful, and grab a platter full of Mediterranean bruschetta slices and mini won tons with dipping sauce as Janey produces them from the oven, and use them as cover to work the room. Which is how I bump into Martin.

I haven't seen Martin in five years. Martin is a friend of my brother's – well, not a friend, really, but they used to belong to the same drinking-and-showing-off club at Durham – and three years older than me. I've read things about Martin, because he has turned out to be something of a wunderkind. When he was a year or so younger than me, he set up his own specialist-magazine publishing house which now produces a range of in-house magazines for a variety of huge companies, as well as niche publications like *Fish-Fryers' Monthly, Ditch-Diggers' Gazette* and *The Morticians' Journal*. He currently employs thirty people, has a fully paid-for house in Notting Hill and a pair of diamond-studded cuff-links, which he fiddles with. A lot.

Martin hasn't so much changed as got more himself. As I remember, he was never someone who suffered from self-doubt but the air of prosperous confidence about him now is almost overwhelming. I remind him about who I am, and we get chatting. He asks me about my brother and I tell him about the school in Zambia, at which he nods in surprise and says something about never having had him down as a charity worker. Well, I say, I don't suppose he had you down as a nascent media magnate, at which he laughs his booming laugh and shoves three won tons into his mouth in one swoop.

So I think, well, there's no harm in chatting him up a bit, and ask how he had the nerve to go out on his own at such a young age.

He fiddles with his cuff-links, says, 'Well, it never occurred to me to do anything else.'

'Well,' I say, 'I really admire you. I wish I had your guts.'

Then he asks me what I'm up to. So I tell him. Ham it

up a bit. 'Look,' I say, 'it's not as if I mind, and I get to do some really interesting things, but it's not what I want to do for ever.'

Martin snaffles up a couple of bruschettas, looks down at me sidewise. I think the flattery's worked. 'But you were bright once,' he says. 'Surely you can do better for yourself than that?'

And I say, 'Well, I'm sure I could. The problem is getting anyone to give me the chance in the first place.'

Martin reaches into his breast pocket, under the spotted handkerchief. Produces a stiff, watermarked business card with a gold edge. 'I'm sure we can find something for a bright girl like you,' he says. 'Why don't you drop round and see me?'

'Really?'

'Yes. I don't see why not. At least we can fit you out with a skill,' he says.

Ooh, Matthew, I think, you're going to have to eat your hat now.

'OK,' I say, throwing caution to the wind. OK, so everyone's always issuing warnings about contracts and working for friends and so forth, but gift horses don't come along every day, and it's churlish to check their teeth.

I tuck his card into my bra and beam at him, 'When shall I turn up?'

Chapter Twenty-nine

Canary Wharf

The years roll round and the workies stay the same. Work experience is a great idea: students can gloss their CVs, employers get free slave labour. It's a fantastic idea. Unless you are one of the people who has to work with them.

Students divide into two types: those whose parents support them, who get to cite 'work experience at Warburg's' when entering the milk round, and those who pay for their existence during the vacation, many of whom learn to type and spend their breaks toiling over a hot keyboard. From this situation comes one of life's great ironies: that those with real work experience have little or nothing to decorate their CVs with, while those with none can look employable at twenty-one.

I have two weeks to fill before my appointment with Martin and my future, so I carry on holding the fort, answering the phone and observing what's going on. Outside the next-door glass cage, which belongs to the head of Marketing, two people are sharing a desk. One is called Mary; sitting beside her is Annabel. Mary is a temp; Annabel, who got here the week before I did, is a workie.

The difference between them couldn't be more marked. Mary, who has been here a week, types, answers the phone without making the person at the other end hang up, understands the computer network, has made friends with the post room. Annabel only says hello to those she perceives to be her superiors, hasn't mastered the 'sort' function on the copier and can watch a phone ring for five minutes before reluctantly picking it up and mumbling 'hello'.

Annabel is reading English at Exeter. Everybody knows this, because she wastes no time in telling them. During one of those information-dissemination sessions in the loo, Mary informed me that she was going to hit her if she told her one more time.

'Do you know what she did?' she asked, leaning against the wall by the roller towel. I was sitting on the sink and we were sharing a cigarette, fanning the smoke away from the sprinkler and towards the air-conditioning outlet.

'Uh-uh.'

'She came up to me this morning with this fax. Said, "Can you send this to Lagos? It's in Portugal." So I said, "It's probably for Nigeria, actually." "Lagos," she said, "is in Portugal." "Well," I said, "given that Lagos is a village on the Algarve and we're doing a major push on Africa I think this is probably for the city in Nigeria." So she marched into the boss's office, came back a minute later and tried to hand me the fax. Goes, "You're right. It is for Nigeria." I'd spent the time with my nose in the code book, so I go, "OK. The code's 00234 1." You should have seen her face when she realized I expected her to send it herself. I shouldn't have bothered, of course. She buggered it up, tried to get some bloke to fix it and I ended up spending twenty minutes sorting the mess out.'

I rolled my eyes.

'I think,' said Mary, 'that when she discovered she wasn't going to be planning the company's advertising strategy for the next decade she went into a sulk. She doesn't seem to do anything much all day apart from sit on her arse phoning her friends to tell them how impressed everyone is with her.'

Today is Annabel's last day, and she is in a chirpy mood. She has finally started talking to Mary. Talking at, actually. She is off to her parents' house in Lanzarote for the rest of the Christmas vacation, and looking forward to it.

'It's lovely there,' she says. 'There's a lemon grove below the house and a wonderful view of the sea. We've had it ever since I was little.'

'What next?' asks Mary.

'Oh, well, obviously I have to do finals next year,' says Annabel. 'Urrgh.' She grimaces. 'I'm dreading them. Then I'm going to go into PR or something like that. Something fun that will make use of my social skills. What about you?'

Mary glances up from her screen, where she is inputting a memo about qualitative research. 'Oh, well, finals this year as well,' she says. 'And if I get a First, I'll be doing a Ph.D. in particle physics.'

Chapter Thirty

Brixton

So now it's Monday two weeks and, dressed up in my professional-creative best (funky trouser suit from Camden Lock, see-through silk vest from a catalogue discreetly showing underneath the jacket, not-too-chunky black boots) and warm with the glow of having sacked my tormentors at the agency, I climb the stairs to Martin's offices in Brixton. For the first time in weeks, I've slept the night through with only a couple of breaks in the middle to think about Matthew and how he's going to feel about me when I'm an editorial director flying around the world meeting interesting people and he's stuck behind a computer screen waiting for his time to bluster with the chaps in the Bung Hole, and I'm ready to face whatever challenges Martin has to throw at me. I've got the education, I've got the determination, and now I've got the break. Life starts here, dammit; I'm going to make everything I can of the opportunity.

Martin's offices are up a set of worn concrete stairs in a studio building up a side road opposite Brixton station, on the fifth floor. There is a lift, but five minutes waiting for a sign of it convinces me that either someone's left the grille open on a higher floor or it doesn't work, so I jog my way up on foot. Five floors. Once upon a time I could have done that in a blink, but nine months in a typist's chair has slashed my fitness levels; I have to walk the last two floors, hauling myself up by the banister like an old person.

Panting, I push open the door from the stairs to find a grimy little lobby with worn cream lino flecked with red spots and a buzzer attached to an internal door. I press it. Wait. Press again.

A voice picks up and says, irritatedly, 'Yes?'

I give my name.

'What do you want?' says the voice.

'I've come to start work,' I say. 'Martin offered me a job a couple of weeks ago . . . ?'

A pause.

'Nevvereardovyer,' says the voice, then buzzes me in.

Beyond the door lies a large, undecorated room with brick pillars that looks like it might have had something to do with sweatshops at some point in the past. Certainly, minimum wage was invented for the people who used to work in a place like this. Under the windows, a score of people are attached to their telephones by headphone cords. Three people – a rake-thin man in a leather jacket and two angry-looking women in thick woolly tights and Doc Martens – sit ferociously in a knot in a thick fug of cigarette smoke hanging over a computer screen, and glance up as I come in. They must be the design team. They look creative, just like I do. They look terrifying too, but I'm sure I'll like them when I get to know them. They might like me, as well, once they find out I can smoke and wear leather with the best of them.

'Yes?' says the woman with the black hair and the garnet stud in her upper lip that looks from a distance like a nasty herpetic lesion.

'Hi,' I say. 'Is Martin around?'

'Not at the moment,' says a blonde woman with two perfect triangles of acne across her cheeks.

'Well, he is,' says leather guy, whose mop of cherubic curls hangs over a face that is grey and lined like his jacket, 'but he's tied up. Can we help you?'

'Um, well, yes, probably. Martin offered me a job a couple of weeks ago and told me to start today.'

Blonde woman rolls her eyes. 'He's always doing that,' she says. 'Look, he won't be long. Why don't you sit over there on the sofa and wait?' And with that, they turn back to their screen and give me no more thought.

I slump on a sofa whose bottom has fallen out and which has been covered with a throw that I noticed retailing at £5.99 on the pavement by the tube. The three Creatives stab their fingers at the computer screen, going, 'Well, if we do it in Wob we'll have to have the standfirst in Swiss itals,' and, 'Yes, but you can't have the standfirst in Swiss itals unless the byline's in Swiss bold,' and I think, 'Ooh, at last, a proper editorial office.' It may be low on glamour, and the windows have obviously been waiting for a wash since sometime around when Chamberlain was voted out of office, but these people are doing the kind of thing I want to be doing, and I'm going to be one of them.

Off to my left, a door opens and a woman emerges, backwards, shouting. 'If you think you can get away with this, you're wrong!' she cries. 'I'm suing and I'm bloody well going to win!'

And in her wake comes Martin, smiling and rubbing his cuff-links. 'You'll find, Daphne, that you haven't got a leg to stand on. We don't have a contract.'

'We'll see!' she shouts.

'Indeed we will,' he says. She wheels on one heel, stalks past me and slams the door.

Martin smirks, scratches the back of his head and looks around. He begins to retreat into his room, and I say 'Martin?'

He stops, peers at me suspiciously, then smiles. 'Hello,' he says. 'What are you doing here?'

I lose my nerve. 'You told me to come and see you today, remember?'

'Did I? Oh, yes, at Paddy's party. Yes, I did say something about that, didn't I?' He stands looking down at me for a few moments, as if contemplating his next move, then says 'Well, come in.' He leads me through the door and into a comfortable room with a leather chesterfield, coffee-table, ashtrays and a computer. Goes over to the phone and switches off the answering machine. Sits on the chesterfield, crosses an ankle over a knee and gestures to me to take the chair by the coffee-table. Puts his hands behind his head, elbows out, looks at me. 'So,' he says. 'What can I do for you?'

He shifts slightly, grips the ankle on the knee with one hand and looks at me with a combination of smugness and curiosity. This is not what I expected. Sitting very upright in my chair, I try very hard not to wring my hands.

'Um, well,' I say, 'remember at Paddy and Jane's party, we were talking about what I was doing for a living and you said you could find something for me?'

Martin looks blank. 'Did I? Sorry. I don't remember.'

'Oh.'

The silence stretches out from moments to seconds and from seconds to almost a minute. I have a feeling that I'm being toyed with, that he knows what's going to happen next and is spinning the moment out for his pleasure. Finally he puts his hands back behind his head and says, 'So what sort of work were you looking for, Laura?'

Bugger. He doesn't even remember my name. I correct him, and say, 'Well, I've been a temp PA for the last year or so. I was hoping for some sort of editorial assistant job or something . . .'

I trail off, because he's already shaking his head. 'No can do. We haven't got anything like that going at the moment. I'd love to get an assistant, but our budgets don't run to luxuries like that.'

The phone rings. ''Scuse me,' says Martin, leaps over the coffee-table. 'Hello?' he says. 'Ah, John. Yes. Has she? Well, tough. We don't have any contracts, and she was useless. Never met her targets. No, I'll tell you what. You get back to her lawyer and tell them we'll be suing her for libel if she tries.' He puts the phone down, comes back, twiddling his cuff-links. Today they are white enamel, with 'HOT' on one side and 'COLD' on the other. 'Tell you what,' he sits down again, knees apart, elbows on them, hands clasped in the middle: every inch, in his braces and shirtsleeves, the thrusting young media magnate. I've never noticed before, but Martin has hair sprouting from his ears. He raises his eyebrows and looks me searchingly in the face. 'Have you ever thought about going into advertising?'

Have I ever. Wouldn't everyone like to sit around surrounded by potted palms, having long lunches and making up puns over a couple of bottles of Pouilly Fumé? 'Well, of course I've thought about it,' I say. 'Do you know someone . . . ?'

'We might give you a try-out here,' he says. 'As it happens, we've got a vacancy on our advertising team. Obviously you'll have to start from the bottom, do at least a month's training, but the sky's the limit if you do well.'

'So what do I have to do?'

'Come on,' he leaps dynamically to his feet, 'I'll

introduce you to Ivana,' and strides out of the room.

I follow him out into the big room and over towards the large group of people plugged into headphones by the window. 'This,' Martin does an expansive gesture over their heads, then his hand flicks straight back to his cuff, 'is our advertising team. Hello, guys.'

'Hello, Martin,' they chorus. Voices drift around, going, 'Good morning, can I speak to Jane Riverdale, please? Oh, doesn't she? Well, who's replaced her, please?' and a terrifying Amazon stalks up and down, up and down behind them in a Calvin Klein knock-off and Stuart Weitzmann spike heels.

'Gutt morning, Martin,' she says. She has thin, thin lips painted a dark scarlet, Valkyrie-blonde hair, smooth and shiny, slicked back against the sides of her head and gripped into a chignon. 'Vot ken ve do for you today?'

'Ivana,' says Martin, 'this is Laura. She wants to join your team.'

Ivana looks at me, starting with the very top of my head, working down to my feet, and back up to my eyes. The lips, completely straight and clamped as though trying to keep her teeth from escaping, develop a small upwards curl on the left-hand side. She gives me her hand. It feels like gripping a small lizard: warm, dry and at the same time slippery. 'Gutt morning, Laura,' she says. 'Velcome to our team. Heff you zzold etverdisink before?'

'No.'

Ivana blinks a couple of times, then gives Martin a long look. 'She hess no eggzberience.'

'No, Ivana,' says Martin. 'That's why I thought we'd give her a trial period. Her brother's an old college mate of mine; thought we could give her some training, at least, and get her on her way.' Somewhere to my left someone snorts, but I'm not sure if they're clearing their nose or sneezing.

'Ah,' says Ivana, and the other side of her mouth curls up. 'A trial. OK. Ve go vit dat.'

'You'll explain how it all works, won't you?' says Martin, slaps me on the arm and disappears.

Ivana produces a sheaf of paper. 'These are ze rules,' she says. 'You vill stick to ze script, you vill be punctual, you vill meet your targets. Here is your desk, here is your telephone, here are your leads. You vill learn ze script, and zen you vill call ze vorst number on ze list. Gutt luck.' Then she falls, once again, to stalking up and down behind my fellow workers.

Chapter Thirty-one

Electric Avenue

Telephone advertising sales being essentially a job in which you recite a script over and over again, it's hardly surprising that the majority of people who are any good at it are out-of-work actors. Whenever Ivana stops cracking the whip for a minute (and the whip is only barely metaphorical: a couple of times she's clouted someone round the head, suddenly and without warning, with a rolled-up periodical), and stalks off to the mysteries of Martin's office, my colleagues all revert to type, start gossiping, telling anecdotes against themselves, referring to Joan Plowright in those rather pitying tones as 'Dear Dotty' and rolling their eyes a lot.

'I was in an adaptation of Kafka at the Almeida once,' says Gary, whose bony body and feverish vitamin-poor complexion are somehow ill-suited to the drawn-out vowels that issue from his mouth, 'and I swear one of the characters was based on Ivana.' As Ivana looks nothing like a beetle, I assume he's talking about *The Trial*. Euan refers to Ivana as Goneril; Lucia and Daniel call her 'The Scottish One', which after about a day's thinking I finally interpret as Lady Macbeth. They all hate her, but it's with a campy, admiring sort of loathing. Me, I just hate her in a deep, probably racist, certainly murderous kind of way. Working for Ivana is like being back at school, only there are no break-times and no moments of bunking off to the chip shop to relieve the horror.

I'm selling adspace for *Fireman's Trousers* (a quarterly aimed at safety officers) and *Muckspreader Monthly*, a free sheet which finds its way directly into the heart of the farming community, or that's what it says on my script, anyway. Every day I am handed a list of names and contact numbers, and have to ring through them all by five o'clock. We are supposed to stick rigidly to the script, but, as it was written by Ivana and is full of strange Germanicisms like 'So, you will see the advantages that with us placing the advertisement brings, no?' it's not easy. I realized about halfway through my first successful connection (itself about a fifth of the way down my list) that the person at the other end thought that I was stark, staring bonkers, and have been adjusting the script accordingly ever since.

The script also assumes that everything will go according to plan. I once stuck my hand up and asked what we did if the interview went another way, and Ivana simply said, 'If the interview goes anozzer vay thed is because you are not followink ze scribt correctly.' So, despite the fact that the list was compiled somewhere back in the Stone Age and hardly any of the people listed are still working at the firms involved, we are supposed to plough ahead regardless. It's OK when there's a switchboard, but more often than not, when you're calling a tiny firm that makes double-knit asbestos jockstraps for the specialist market, the conversation goes something like this:

'Ah [the 'ah' is specified], good morning. May I speak to Shaughnah O'Connell, please?'

'She left here two years ago.'

'Ah, well, could I have the name of the person who replaced her, please?'

'John Marks.'

'Thank you. Could I speak to him, please?'

'Sorry. He left three months ago.'

'Ah. And who replaced him?'

'Me.'

By which time the script has already long since been left behind. My companions have, of course, had endless lessons in improv at their respective drama colleges, and seem to find it relatively easy to adjust without straying too far from the original idea, but it's been a big learning process for me.

After the first week, without so much as a nibble of interest from my lists, I was on the verge of giving up. It was only the thought of going home and announcing my return to the typing pool that kept me from taking off my headphones, laying them down on the desk, pulling on my coat and scooting down those stairs. And besides: I hate to think that anything can defeat me. I may not have the best of taste in men, but I'm a fighter. So I sat and listened to Marius and Ralph and Rupert and Leanda as their warm voices cooed: 'So that's a quarter-page with box in the 'Faces of the Moment' spread for the April issue? Fine. I'll put that in writing and get the contract to you tomorrow,' steeled myself and followed their lead.

It was worth staying. I don't know if you've ever felt the joyous rush of triumph against the odds, but I finally sold my first ad in *Muckspreader* on Tuesday last, and it was easily as big a thrill as anything you can get leaning over the cistern of a chrome-bar lavatory cubicle. Putting the phone down, I very nearly whooped, but caught it in time to make a strangled gasp instead. Gary bashed me on the shoulder, nearly dislocating it, and Lucia embossed my cheeks with bright red long-last lipstick.

'Yes!' cried Daniel. 'Champagne in the Fridge Bar!'

I sat back, thinking about the fruits of 10 per cent on a £500 ad and how rosy life would look once I got up to half a dozen a day like the others.

Ivana emerged from her headphones at the end desk. Stalked over. 'Vot do you sink you are doing?' she said.

'Congratulate her, Ivana,' said Gary. 'She just sold her first ad!'

Ivana remained silent, then her lips spread grimly out to the side in that death-mask smile. 'Ah, yes,' she said. 'Zo I hert. Ent I say again, vot do you sink you vere doing?'

'What do you mean?'

'I vas listenink on ze pardy line,' said Ivana. 'And you expressly dizobeyt my orders.'

'How do you mean?'

'I heff tolt you ent tolt you,' said Ivana. 'And yet you bersist. You vill follow ze scribt. Zere is no room for you here if you do not follow ze scribt.'

Chapter Thirty-two
I'm Making Up A-List

I can't sleep. Life without sleep, after a while, gets seriously strange. I don't have trouble getting up in the morning, because, even if I've not gone to bed until four, or lain awake until dawn, my eyes open around six-thirty and there's no way in hell I'll ever get back off after that. So I tend to get up and wander around, make three or four cups of coffee because, even though I'm wakeful, I never feel like my brain has caught up. By the time I'm ready to go off to Brixton – Donna and I walk together: a fifteen-minute walk up the Stockwell Road, then we kiss goodbye outside the tube and I peel off to the right – I've got through six or seven cigarettes already and the day hasn't officially even begun. My head feels like it's full of that wadding you get round boilers until I'm on my sixth coffee, when I finally reach a state of artificial awakeness that I can just about maintain by keeping it topped up with another injection every half-hour or so.

So I'm still awake at one in the morning when Donna comes in from seeing Marina and, after stomping around the house, comes into the sitting-room and finds me.

'How's it going?' I ask, though I've seen her in the last six hours so it's a pretty redundant question. 'How was your evening?'

Donna lets out a noise that sounds amazingly like something Bruce Lee would say just before kicking in the face a giant Samoan bodyguard armed with a Kalashnikov and a machete. 'Waaah!' she cries. 'Haai–yah!'

I nod. 'Not so good, then?'

'Wooo–hah!' howls Donna. 'I've never been so angry in my life. I don't *belieeeeve* it. Dah!'

'What happened, Donnabella?'

She sits down, flumph, and crosses her arms, fists bunched. 'Your friend Marina,' Donna always distances herself from people she's cross with like this, 'is the most outrageous snob I've ever met. Putting people in boxes like that. Who does she think she is? I mean, I said, and who are you to decide who goes on which list anyway? And once they're on the list, do they get to move ever, or is that it? Stuck for life like they're *Hindu* or something?'

'You're talking backwards,' I say. 'What are you on about?'

'Well,' says Donna, 'you know how everyone goes on about not having boyfriends or not getting laid? Well, I make this joke, right, about how long it's been, and Marina launches off into one of her theory sessions and – ooh, wah–hai–oowh.'

'What?'

'Well, like, she goes, "Well, I've realized what's wrong," right? And she goes, "I suddenly realize why so many relationships are doomed to failure and why so many people aren't managing to start relationships. It's because they're not meeting the people who are suited to them in the first place." So I go, "Too right, Marina. I keep saying that myself." I mean, when did you last meet anyone new who you'd do anything other than spit on?'

'Not much lately,' I say.

'So anyway, she gets all enthusiastic, and you won't believe what she says.'

'What?'

'You know how she looks all pleased with herself when she's got a theory? Sticks her chin in the air and proclaims to the world like she's some sort of bloody messiah or something? Well, she's sitting there and talking like she's found out the secret of living, and she goes, "It's all to do with the A-list and the B-list, you see."' Donna does a creditable impression of Marina's accent: a bit of posh, a bit of Eurotrash, the singsong of someone who knows that their place in the world merits them being listened to.

'The what?'

'That's what I said. So Marina goes, "Well, I've realized that I can divide the people I know into A-listers and B-listers, and what I've been doing wrong is mixing them all up together rather than helping them to mix with each other." And I go, "And what is this A-list and B-list? Is this like streaming at school or something?" and she goes, "I suppose it is, sort of, only more sophisticated." And I go, "What do you mean, more sophisticated?" and she goes, "Well, it's not just done on how well you do in exams any more. We're out in the real world now. Other factors have to be taken into account, too." And I go, "Factors like what, Marina?" and she goes, "Well, loads of factors. Like how much money someone's got, and how much they're likely to earn, and what they do for a living, and their social-success factor, and who they know already. You can't mix up someone from a council house and someone who's running a multinational company and expect anything. Their aspirations are just too far apart. It stands to reason."'

I think about this for a moment. 'Which means you're on the B-list, presumably.'

'Well, of course, that's what I said. But she just gets this sort of Mona Lisa smile and looks mysterious. So I say, "What about things like spiritual growth or niceness? Don't they count for anything?" and she goes, "There are nice people on both lists. It's not about niceness, it's about achievement and ambition." And I go, "But Marina, that's simply not fair. Who are you to decide who's got ambitions and who's going to achieve later on?" and she just goes, "Life isn't fair, Donna. There will always be people who do more than others. The point is to match them up so that everyone gets to meet a selection of people on their own level. They've got a far better chance of meeting their match that way." So I go, "So what you're saying is that you want to create a two-level society where the rich people always marry the other rich people and the rest of us can just keep on sinking?" And she goes, "This isn't one of your political discussion groups here, Donna. I'm simply talking sense about what people want out of life." I mean, can you believe it? So I go, "And have you started writing these lists yet?" And she goes, "Of course. They're on my computer at work." And I go, "So do people move between them? Like, what if one of your millionaires goes bankrupt?" And Marina says, "Yes, of course it's possible to move between the lists. Tania's done it, for instance. But naturally it will always be easier to slip down to the B-list than move up to the A. And anyway, if we were just to be honest and admitted that these things matter, it would give loads of B-listers something to work towards." '

She falls silent, and we both reflect on our positions in life. I don't even need to ask which list I'm on.

'Oh, well,' I say eventually, 'at least this means we'll never have to look at the Hughs again.'

'Sod that,' says Donna, 'what are we going to do?'

'Do?'

'I can't stay on a B-list. I can't.'

'You shouldn't listen to Marina. She's silly. She gets these ideas in her head and gets all excited about them and never thinks about how it sounds to other people. You know what she's like.'

'What she's like,' says Donna, 'is a cow. No, she's a shark.'

'No. Tania's a shark. Marina is a sheep. She probably read something in *Tatler* and now she believes it's true. It'll be the cabbala next month. Just wait.'

'So you're not insulted?'

'Of course I'm bloody insulted. D'you think I want someone like Marina patronizing me for the rest of my life?'

'A-list,' says Donna, with the venom of one who sees herself condemned to B-dom.

I pick at the frayed bit on the arm of the sofa.

'We've got to do something,' says Donna.

'What, about Marina? Ignore her. She'll get another enthusiasm soon.'

'No.' She heaves a sigh. 'We've got to do something. We've got to start moving up or our lives are over.'

Chapter Thirty-three

Sell! Sell! Sell!

Well, you never know: at this rate, though doubtless Marina would see my occupation as very *déclassé*, my income should be nudging into the upper Bs within months. I never thought of sales as a career option, let alone telesales, but it turns out that I'm not half bad at it. Two weeks since my first ad, and I've sold another twenty. Gary, Daniel and Lucia turn over five or six a day each, but I've only just started, and I know that some people couldn't sell space if it was on the side of the Millennium Dome, so I'm optimistic.

At a commission rate of 10 per cent, I've already earned the best part of £600 in the last two weeks. OK, so that's peanuts compared with what my compadres are turning over for themselves, but my hit rate is getting higher and every day I get further through each call before my victim says, 'Ah, you're trying to sell me advertising. I don't want any. Really. Thanks,' and hangs up.

This is partly because I've been watching the others, and picking up tips. Ivana may believe that the job is a matter of reciting the script until one of the fishies bites, but there is a lot more to it than that. You have to have a personality. Not your own, not the frail little ego which could get bruised when someone goes, 'I'm sick of you lot bothering me. Bugger off,' but a made-up one, one far enough from the reality of yourself that it can't be destroyed because it doesn't exist, a telephonic individual that draws the listener into believing that they're conspiring with you, or getting one over on you, instead of being conspired against.

Gary is brilliant. Gary's one of those skinny, slightly spotty, pale-faced creatures who would look good in a Danny Boyle movie (he did actually have a walk-on in *Trainspotting* that had become extra-ing by the time they reached the final cut), but he manages to make everyone he speaks to believe that he is gorgeous, and that not only is he gorgeous but that they, male or female, will be in with a chance if they buy a quarter-page with illustration. Lucia has the innocent-Sloane-sharing-unmissable-opportunity act off pat. Daniel does the 'I'm hating doing this as much as you hate being cold-called, so let's just do some business so we can get off the phone' routine. Each individual routine works brilliantly: Daniel once sold twelve ads in a single day across five publications; it was champagne all the way in Bar Humbug that night, I can tell you.

The course of my first week's worth of calls made it obvious that I sounded a bit too much of a smart-arse, and the victim could spot me coming. So I decided that the best policy was to dumb it all down, play the idiot. And that's what I do. I sound so dumb these days, in fact, that no-one, not even Ben, would believe I could be wily. So dumb that the recipients of my calls believe that they are getting the better of me. My brother has a friend who works in the City who has been getting away with this – and offloading unwanted shares on arrogant males just before the markets plummet – for years. Everyone calls her Thicktoria, but her bonuses have gone through the roof year on year. Playing dumb has its disadvantages, of course. I have to put up with a lot of people patronizing me, but it's not as if they didn't used to do that in my old line of work. Besides, it fattens them up nicely for the kill, and I just keep thinking of the rewards at the end of the month.

The only fly in the ointment, apart from the fact that Martin hasn't acknowledged my existence since I arrived, is Ivana. Working for Ivana is like having a part in *The Great Escape*. Once we've tunnelled to liberty, I will spend the rest of my life listening for a voice hissing 'Gutt luck' and a hand clamping down on my shoulder. It's not just me. As she stalks up and down the trenches, you see people shrink and duck in fear: if ever there was a Groke, Ivana is one. Even if you are completely immersed in a call, oblivious to what's going on in the outside world and don't hear the crisp click of her heels, you always know that she has stopped behind you because the hairs on the back of your neck stand up. Horripilation: God's way of telling you there's a German in the room.

'You sink you are gutt,' she barks in her daily pep talk, 'but you are not gutt, you are bett. Ent if you sink ze invective scheme' (by which I think she means the incentive scheme), 'pays out to losers, you vill be wrong. You vill do es I say because zere iss no room for losers here.'

She's the demon boss. Ivana has a pair of headphones hidden beneath the sleek blonde shell of hair that sticks to the sides of her head, never a strand out of place, as though it were made of plastic, and you can never tell if she's got them plugged in until you're in the middle of a sticky sell and a voice suddenly barks, 'Close, now. Demnit, do I heff to do zis myzzelf?' Ten days ago Gus stalked out after she brought a ruler down, thwack, on the back of his hand as he fiddled with his cigarette lighter. She tells Lucia off about her clothes every day.

'You ken not vork looking like zis,' she says, 'vot vill the clients sink?'

'But, Ivana,' says Lucia, 'it's a telephone job.'

Ivana does the smirk and double head-flick of the zealot. 'You sink zey can't tell how you are dressed? Id gums oud in your breezink.'

But Ivana is my route to riches, the price I have to pay for my place on the A-list, so I'll put up with it. Because when my head clears, or when I'm trying to get off to sleep at night, all I can think about is money. Well, money and Matthew, but mostly money, as Matthew moving out cost a lot in replacing all the things we'd shared, like bedclothes and bookshelves and reading lights. And this turnover from weekly wages to monthly pay would be a serious problem if Ben weren't a benevolent landlord. But if my earnings keep on escalating for another week, I should have made enough to pay him next month's rent, and last month's, and my share of the phone bill, and even put a couple of hundred into my overdraft. The bank will see a large single deposit, and assume me to be a proper member of society with borrowing rights, collateral, maybe a cheque-guarantee card. In a couple of months I can buy the shoes, the bag and the lipstick. In a couple of months I'll be able to go to a party in a dress by Ghost and bring a bottle of fizz with me. I'll bump into my perfidious lover and give him the Look. The Look that says, 'See? And you had no faith.' The look that says 'I'm OK without you, sonny. I've got bigger fish to fry.' The Look that says, 'Broke my heart? Believe me, sweets, I have no heart to break.' I can't wait.

Chapter Thirty-four

A House Built upon Sand

Payday. I wake up singing after almost six hours' straight sleep. I've dreamt of sandy beaches, palm trees, dinners with my friends, where no-one has a row and we split the bill equally. In the shower I rinse the last of the shampoo out of the bottle with a bit of water, automatically think, 'Damn, more expense,' and immediately my brain responds with: 'Who cares? As of today you can buy all the shampoo, conditioner, skin glop you want. There's no more eking out mascara with drops of mineral water, no more diluting nail varnish with remover, no more reusing tea bags, no more dabs of nail varnish over the ladders in my stockings and hoping no-one notices.' And I sing even louder: 'What a Wonderful World', with Louis Armstrong throat gurgles. When I emerge Ben is on the landing, grinning from ear to ear.

'You're in a good mood.'

I clap him on both arms, pinch his cheek. 'Sure am, honey. And I intend on staying that way.'

Ben rubs behind one ear, says, 'Good. Well, good. I'm glad to hear it,' and disappears into the bathroom with a copy of *Private Eye*. He's obviously going to be some time.

It's a lovely sunny day, and the walk from Stockwell to Brixton seems almost jolly. Brixton Road is buzzing with market shoppers brought out by the sun, pausing to listen to the hellfire preacher on an upturned milk crate on the pavement, shrugging, wide-handed, at the guy in dreadlocks who's been tapping everyone he passes for a quid ever since I can remember this area. I search in my pocket and give him the pound I would have spent on public transport, go into work with a glow of careless generosity.

Everyone's there on time, as they have been on payday in every office I've ever been in. No-one alludes to this, of course; that would be very much Not The Thing. For once Ivana's not prowling behind us, but I can see a tight-tied silhouette behind the frosted glass of Martin's office door and assume she's in with him. We wait, make calls, anticipate that moment when the tear-tape on the side of the envelope comes apart and the money is truly ours.

At half past twelve Ivana emerges from Martin's office, clutching a handful of envelopes. Goes across to editorial, still hunched over their layouts, almost receives smiles. Comes to us, grinning grimly.

'Pay,' she says. Everyone sits up like it's the first they've heard of it. She circles the desk. 'Karry,' she says, 'Loochia. Tomasz. Tenyell. Marrie.' She pauses beside me, fixes my eye with hers, and her smirk gets a little wider. Then she walks past and hands an envelope to Euan.

And this is when I discover that Martin keeps his outfit profitable by ripping off his staff. Not all of them, obviously: just the ones who show up with tattoos reading 'Desperate. Sucker. Bleed me dry.' Never, ever trust someone you think is a friend in business. By the time you find out the truth, it'll be too late.

No pay packet. I hope for a moment that there's been some mistake, that maybe mine's at the bottom of the pile because I'm the new girl. But Ivana reaches the end of the row opposite me, and is standing with her hands resting on her elbows, smiling tightly as everyone opens up. Cold all over, I stick my hand up and say, 'Ivana, how about me?' and the tight little smile turns into the largest grin I've ever seen crossing her face.

'Vot do you mean, ek-zectly?' she says.

'I was wondering where my pay was,' I pipe in a tiny little voice.

She pauses, frowns slightly, rolling her eyes to heaven to simulate an attempt at recall. 'Egg-scuse me?' Her voice is lilting with pleasure. 'Vot pay?'

Something big and phlegmy has blocked my throat. 'The pay for the month I've been working here?' I squeak.

'No,' says Ivana, and it feels like being played with by a very sadistic cat, 'I done unnerstent.'

'I've sold 31 slots. That should be over £1,000 in commission.'

Ivana looks puzzled, fakes leaping back in amazement, smiles. 'Aah, no, no, no, no, no,' she says, 'I sink you are mistaken, Amy.' She still hasn't got my name straight.

'How do you mean, mistaken? The space is filled and paid for.'

'Bud Amy,' says Ivana, 'you are here as a trainee. You are here do learn. And I heff to zay, I done sink you heff learned very vell. Ze scribt . . .'

'No,' I say, flinging myself to my feet. My so-called co-workers have all dipped their heads and are concentrating fiercely on the morning's phone lists. 'You can't be serious. I sold those ads fair and square.'

Ivana gives me the look that chills. 'Ve heff given you a chance here, Amy,' she says. 'You came asking for helb, and ve heff given you helb. Is zis how you are going to rebay us?'

I rush across the scuffed floor to Martin's office, bash on the glass panel. A voice goes, 'Come in,' and I burst through the door. Martin is in his leather director's chair behind his leather-topped director's desk, feet up on the blotting-pad. 'Ah, Laura,' he says. 'What can I do for you?' He fiddles with his cuff-links. Today, I notice, they are little silver skulls and crossbones. He steeples his fingers, presses them to his lips, looks at me.

'There's been a mistake, Martin,' I stutter.

'Mistake?' enquires Martin. 'How so?'

'The 31 ads I've sold for you. I haven't been paid for them.'

'Paid?' says Martin, and sits so far back in his chair I think it's going to tip over. 'How so, paid?'

No. This can't be happening. 'Commission,' I say.

Martin laughs gaily. 'Commission? You want us to pay you commission? But Laura, we never pay commission to trainees. I'm doing you a favour here. In fact, the way I see it, *you* ought to be paying *us*.'

'*What*?'

'Well,' he tips forward, takes a cigar from the box on his desk, clips the end off with a silver clipper I've seen selling for £85 in Asprey, lights it. 'Well –' he says as he sucks, 'the – way – I see it – is that –' he sits back, blows a smoke-ring at the ceiling, 'you've had a damn good training here. You are beginning to have a skill you didn't have a month ago, and we've let you have access to our phones, our desk space, our lists, and Ivana's expertise for absolutely nothing. I must say, I think you're being very ungrateful.'

'You've got to be kidding.'

'Kidding? Far from it. You told me you didn't have a job, didn't you?'

'Yes.'

'And I told you we didn't have anything here, didn't I?'

'Yes.'

'Well.'

'I thought . . .' I fight for words. Then, pathetically, 'I thought we were friends.'

'Friends?' says Martin. 'Friends? You're some little person I bumped into at a cocktail party and did a favour for. I don't believe this. This is the last time I— get out.' He rises from behind the desk, bears down on me, and I find myself backing towards the door, the scene I witnessed when I first came here rising in my memory.

'You can't do this!' I shout as he propels me from his office. 'You can't! I earned that money fair and square! I'll bloody well sue you if I have to.'

'Sue away, Laura,' he says. 'And if you can show your lawyer a copy of our contract, you might have a leg to stand on.'

Chapter Thirty-five

The Long Arm of the Law

My lawyer (Marina, on her mobile, between classes) tells me that what Martin says is true, and I don't have even a toe-hold in the law.

'So you started doing a job without getting a contract?' she says. 'Why did you do that?'

'Well, it all happened in a rush. I mean, one minute I was talking to him in his office and he was telling me that they didn't have anything, and the next minute he was introducing me to the rest of the advertising salespeople and I was being given a pair of headphones.'

'And he never used the words "Give you a job," or 'Work on the same commission as everyone else,' at any point?'

I think back. 'Well, no. He said he would help me out.'

Marina pauses. 'Mm, sorry, but that could be construed about fifty different ways. So you haven't even got a verbal contract, as far as I can see. What on earth were you doing, taking a job under those conditions?'

'I thought,' and I find myself melting back into tears. I've cried all the way on the walk home. My throat's sore from retching and I feel like all the muscles in my tummy are sprained. 'I thought he was a friend.'

'Some friend,' says Marina.

I start snivelling. 'I don't know what I'm going to do. I don't. What the hell *am* I going to do?'

Marina's voice has softened at the other end of the phone. 'I'm really sorry, sweetheart,' she says. 'I think all you can do is get back on to your agency first thing and wash your hands of the whole sorry episode.'

I snivel some more, then say, 'Well, if you think so . . .'

'Look, don't take this the wrong way,' Marina sounds slightly uncertain, but ploughs ahead, 'but are you going to be in trouble over this? Financial, I mean?'

'I don't know. Yes. I haven't got a bean and I already owe Ben last month's rent.'

'Well, can I lend you something? I'm sorry. I don't want to offend you, but if it'll help you out . . .'

This makes me cry some more. I cry for about a minute, then gather myself together and reply. 'No, Marina. Thank you. It's really kind, but I've got to get out of this hole myself somehow. I'm sorry to dump all this on you.'

'Don't be silly,' she hisses, 'I'm your friend, you idiot. Now, are you sure I can't help? I know you want to sort it out yourself, but sometimes . . .'

'No.' I'm beginning to feel a bit better. There's nothing like an act of kindness to make you feel like there might be something worth living for. 'Thanks. You're sweet.'

'OK,' she sounds doubtful. 'But the offer still stands. Look, I'm sorry, but I have to go to a class now. Take care of yourself.'

'Yeah,' I sniff. 'Thanks, Marina. 'Bye.'

''Bye.'

I hang up and look around the hall, contemplating the prospect of starting all over again.

Chapter Thirty-six

Blood Everywhere

Fortunately Tracie sees the funny side and, instead of inflicting the usual six-weeks'-filing punishment, says she'll see what she can do to get me back into a PA job as quickly as possible. Which obviously won't be until Monday unless some poor cow somewhere goes under a bus and her boss can't look things up in his own diary. I call the bank, explain what's happened and crawl for an extension to my overdraft, and come away with an earful of homilies about living within one's means.

And the stupid thing is, I can't stop crying. I can't stop asking God why he sees fit to rain all this shit on my head when he gives Tania everything without any demands for recompense. And when God doesn't answer, doesn't even say something like, 'It's a test, my daughter, to prepare you for the road ahead,' all I can do is take to my bed, pull the duvet over my head, and cry, and sleep, and cry, and sleep. I've got no money. I can't afford to eat, or smoke, or pay the rent. I can't afford to pay the heating bill, or the phone bill, or the electricity bill. The council tax is due in three days, and though it's only another forty quid, it's forty quid I don't have. I need money, God, quickly. Please help me, God. And God, as usual, doesn't answer.

On the evening of the third day Ben comes into my room

without knocking, plumps down on the futon, pulls back the duvet and says, 'Come on. Get up. Let's go to the pub.'

Blearily I mutter, 'I can't afford to go to the pub,' and he says, 'I think I can stand you a couple of lagers.'

'I don't want to go out,' I say.

'You may not want to go out,' he replies, 'but you can't stay in bed for ever, you'll get ill.'

'Remind me to say that to you next time *you* get depressed,' I murmur resentfully, and he grunts something about doing what he says, not what he does, throws the duvet into a corner of the room and manhandles me into a sitting position.

'Get dressed.'

'I am dressed.'

'No,' he speaks patiently, as to a child, 'you can't go out in the clothes you've been sleeping in for the last three days. Put on some clean ones. And brush your hair. You look like a dandelion.'

Grumbling, I shrug on three jumpers and a coat and we go out into the dark Stockwell night.

It's cold and it's smoggy: spring has failed to materialize. I refuse to go to the Surprise, because I don't want to run the risk of bumping into anyone we know. So on we trudge down the Wandsworth Road, looking disconsolately through tobacco-smeared windows in the hope of finding somewhere where we won't catch something from the glasses. The queue outside the chip shop goes halfway down the block, a mean line of tattie-fed no-hopers looking forward to their weekly treat of saturated fat and carbonated sugar drinks. Three old drunks, all scabs and pink-eye, quarrel on the bench by a bus stop over a bottle of VP sherry. And I'm thinking, 'This is how I'm going to end up. I'll be sharing a cardboard box with a bottle of Thunderbird this time next year.'

Ben goes, 'Cheer up, love. It could be worse,' and I go, 'How, exactly?' and, as if on cue, the heavens open. We start to run. It's one of those downpours that's like someone chucking a bucket of water from a window: so violent and certain of its purpose that we pass out of the pool of light under one street lamp without being able to see the one ahead.

'This is great,' I'm thinking, 'thanks, God. You've made me miserable and now you want to drown me.'

Ben suddenly stops, reaches out, grabs my hand, nearly dislocating my shoulder, and pulls me in through a door. I trip, bang into the back of him, come to a stop and, wiping the water from my eyes, gasp. We're in a pub that none of us has ever gone into before because it looks so frightening. It's called the Port Head, an odd name as we're almost a mile from the river, but everyone in the locality refers to it as the Putrid. Dripping quietly onto a hairless doormat, I gaze around in awe.

That Old Pub smell shrinks my sinuses: a combination of spilt beer, unwiped ashtray and rotting carpet. As my eyes adjust to the gloom – an altogether different, less welcoming gloom than that of the rainstorm outside – I take in our surroundings. Axminster on the floor, worn 'tapestry' on the settles, ancient pinball machine in one corner and dozens and dozens of faded towelling beer-mats nailed to the walls. And around the bar a crowd, all male, all bearded, some tattooed, mostly silent, some offering advice, and all oblivious to us.

We approach, and see that the focus of attention is a scraggy-looking woman in mules and pedal-pushers be-hind the bar. She stands behind the pumps, staring at her hand, which is wrapped in a glass-cloth.

'Hold it up above your head, girl,' says a man in a brown leather jacket and grey trousers whose pockets stick out like butterflies where his belly strains down upon the waistband.

'If I hold it above my head,' she says, 'I faint. You saw what happened last time.'

'Well, can't you find a plaster?' says a man with a spiderweb tattooed on the back of his neck.

She sighs, her shoulders heaving up and down with the effort. 'It's across the whole palm, stupid, and there's blood everywhere. A plaster won't stay on more than ten seconds.'

She catches my eye as we approach. 'Sorry,' she says, 'I'm afraid I'm not serving at the moment.'

'Are you OK?'

She grimaces. 'I was cutting a lemon and the knife slipped,' she says.

'Hah, lemon,' says one of the blokes in the crowd, helpfully.

'Shut up, Mike,' she says. 'I've called John and an ambulance. You'll get your drink in twenty minutes.'

'Twenty minutes?' says Mike. 'I've got an empty glass here.'

'Well, I can't do nothing about it,' she says. 'I can't pull a bloody beer pump with one hand, can I?'

A light-bulb goes on in my head. You know how it happens. One minute you're standing around with your jaw hanging like an ape, the next you're taking control. 'I used to work in a bar,' I say. 'Would you like me to take over while you wait?'

She looks astonished, then relieved. 'Would you?'

'Go on,' says another voice. 'We're dying here, Glenda.'

She steps forward, lifts the flap on the bar, and I slip

through. Mike wants a pint of lager. I pick up a cleanish glass, approach the pump, flip the top. It's so long since I did this – I only used to do it in the village pub in the school holidays, illegally – that the first pint I pour comes out all froth.

'Tip it,' says Glenda, and it all comes flooding back. I start off a pint of Guinness, pour two bitters and a perfect pint of the fizzy stuff with just a smear of froth on the top, go back and flip off the tap on the Guinness just as it reaches the top. Even remember to draw a little heart in the head with the last trickle. Glenda nods approvingly, starts showing me how to work the till.

And so God gives me my break. Causes someone else serious injury to do it, but at least he gives me my break. By the time the fabled John arrives, forty minutes later and just after the ambulance has left, I'm running up and down behind the bar with my biggest smile on, Ben is propped on a stool with a free drink and a packet of pork scratchings, and all the punters are saying, 'Give us our usual, love,' as though I've been there all my life.

Chapter Thirty-seven

Tottenham Court Road

'Good morning, Carol,' says Jenny, 'how are you today?'

'Fine, thanks,' says Carol without looking up.

'Good,' says Jenny mechanically, and, beaming, moves on. 'Good morning, Bob,' she says. 'How are you today?'

Bob looks up. 'Well, thanks, Jenny. How are you?'

'Very well, thank you. Very well,' says Jenny. 'And how are the children?'

'Fine, thanks. Robert's almost over his chickenpox.'

'I'm so glad,' says Jenny, finding a Kleenex in her pocket and wiping a smear of coffee from the desktop by his phone. 'Don't want to let it dry,' she smiles, 'then it'll take twice as long to get clean, won't it?'

And she moves on. 'Good morning, Harriet. How are you today?'

'I'm very well, thanks, Jenny. And how are you?'

'I'm very well, thank you. How did the debrief go yesterday?'

'Yes, fine. I think the client was pleased.'

'Oh, good. Now,' the voice lowers to a confiding level, 'I hope you won't be offended, but I couldn't help noticing that you seemed to be having a few problems keeping your correspondence in order. So I've brought you this.' She hands Harriet a concertina file, gaily decorated with flowered wallpaper. 'I love these things,' she says. 'My life changed since I discovered how easy it was just to slip everything away under the date every month. See if it helps. I'm sure it will.' And, before Harriet can respond, she glides away, the smile fixed ear to ear.

Jenny scares me. I'm convinced that beneath that smiling exterior lurks the Stepford Sec. Perhaps it is her boss who should be giving me the creeps, because obviously someone has kidnapped a woman and replaced her with a smiling, super-efficient, uncomplaining automaton, and the most likely suspect has to be him. Instead of a real human being who has headaches, off-days, lunch-breaks, forgetful moments, calls their insurance company in working hours, can't spell 'stationery', folds letters so that only the bottom half of the address shows in a window envelope, he has opted for an employee who, while personifying perfection in the secretarial field, shows no vestige of either an emotional core or an interest in any subject other than his needs. Jenny's every sentence contains an up-note, like someone trying to sell you cat food: 'I'm *really* well, thank you.' 'Can I *do* anything for you?' 'How are *you* today?' Everything in Jenny's world comes with a positive adjective: fresh cups of coffee, nice cups of tea, delicious sandwiches, marvellous word-processing programme. Jenny soothes her boss's skittish nature by never dressing to suggest she might have ambitions higher up the ladder, doesn't shame him by wearing trousers to greet clients, never does bizarre things with her hair. A conservative sort of bloke, he greets her appearance each day in pleasant floral prints, top-and-skirt combos, Alice bands, maybe a small frill around the neck, with, 'Gosh, you look nice today, Jenny,' and Jenny simpers her thanks.

Jenny on the phone: '*Good* morning,' she trills, 'Mr *Blake's* office. Can I *help* you?' Jenny on the hour: 'Would you like a cup of *tea*, Mr Blake?' Jenny loves to spend time hovering over the fax machine making sure that every page of a document has gone through without a hitch, has filled Blake's office with pot-plants, is always on hand with a paper coaster, has — I've seen it — a change of shirt for her boss, still in its Cellophane, in her bottom drawer. It's not natural. Not even Nanette Newman is like this. The other day, as I groaned my way to the filing cabinets with a pile of paper, she smiled sweetly and said, 'I like to do ten minutes of filing at the end of every day. That way, it doesn't build up.' I was hard-pressed not to clock her with the hole-punch.

One evening, while waiting for the rush hour to die down, I bump into Jenny in Paperchase, in the birthday section. She is picking through the painfully tasteful silver and gold decorations, examining each curly bow minutely for faults, face blank with concentration. On my approach, the smile blinks on: teeth, cheekbones, no lights in the eyes.

'Someone's birthday coming up?' I ask feebly.

'Oh, no, I mean yes,' replies Jenny, 'these are for the Blakes.'

'The Blakes?'

'Yes. It's Tiffany's, their youngest daughter's, thirteenth on Tuesday. Mrs Blake —' she looks shy and confiding at the honour of employing the first name — '*Sheila* — was afraid she wouldn't have time to make it special, so I offered to do the decorations for them.'

Startled, I say, 'But, Jenny, surely you don't have to give up your evenings . . .'

'Oh, no,' says Jenny, 'it's not like that. It's a pleasure. Mr Blake is more than a boss, he's a friend. I never knew how nice working could be until I started working for him. My last place was terrible. Messy. Disorganized. Everyone thinking about themselves. I started picking up their habits, coming in late, dressing in any old thing. I had no idea how miserable I was until I stopped. I owe a great deal to Mr Blake. If it wasn't for him . . .' She trails off, eyes gazing at the far side of the shop, mouth slightly open. Then, suddenly, the sunny smile comes back, the head flicks upright and, calling a tinkling farewell over her shoulder, she marches off home to plug herself into an electric socket and recharge her batteries.

Chapter Thirty-eight

Café Society

Glenda, the barmaid at the Putrid, now has a septic hand and she won't be able to work for three weeks. So where I was unemployed a week ago, I am now someone with two jobs. After my sterling performance during the emergency period when twenty South London builders suddenly found themselves without lager on a Wednesday night, it was inevitable that John the landlord would offer me a temporary job filling in for her.

'You did all right there, girl,' he says on the phone two days after the event. 'How d'you fancy doing it longer-term?' And I jump at the chance. OK, so I'll be exhausted, but it's not like I sleep anyway, and I feel truly blessed to have a chance to crawl out from my hole.

John pays me £25 a shift, cash in hand at the end of the evening, plus the statutory meal – a choice of steak pie and chips, gammon and chips, sausage, beans and chips or egg and chips. For an extra pound I can have the scampi and chips, but he says it's too dear to just hand out. To be honest, I'd rather take the cash and live on bar snacks, but since I read the statistic about the thirteen different samples of men's urine found in the bowl of pub peanuts by the Health and Safety people, I've been less keen: the fellas I serve of an evening, while genial enough, don't look as though hygiene is at the top of their list of priorities. And as it is, I'm pretty grateful: with such a substantial evening input, I don't need to eat in the daytime, and I can live off that £175 while my respectable earnings go straight into the bottomless pit of my bank account. And if you're working seven nights a week in a pub, your extracurricular expenditure drops to almost zero. I've turned recently into one of those people who picks up penny pieces in the street. Sometimes I find myself going through the change in my purse, under the bed, at the bottom of my bag, piling it up into 10p heaps to see if I can make a pound. I caught myself doing it on the bus the other day; I wouldn't have thought about it if I hadn't caught the eye of a teenage boy in baseball cap, baggies and trainers you could have nursed a newborn in, and seen the light of unadulterated contempt that shone from his eyes as he watched me trickle tuppences through my fingers.

So now I'm a double temp: in the morning I put on my suit and haul ass into the City, to answer phones and pretend to be doing real shorthand when I'm actually writing like the wind and hoping like hell that I can remember what my boss was on about for long enough to annotate the scrawl on my spiral-bound pad.

At 5.30, I run to the loo, change into big earrings and eyeliner – not so classy I frighten the clientele, not so sexy I cause trouble – and race to the Putrid. When I fling myself in through the door, Mike, Graham, Barry and the lads look round, grin and cry, 'Let me through! I'm a barmaid!' It's a joke that could be said to have a shelf life, but they never tire of it. And it's nice, after a day dealing with the indifference of the professional classes, to come somewhere where I'm greeted, if not with respect, at least with a touch of affection.

What with washing up and wiping down surfaces, emptying ashtrays and refilling the optics for the next day, I rarely get out of work before midnight. Averaging six hours' sleep a night has made my vision go blurry, with flashes, sometimes, of iridescence like that on the flanks of a lightly rotting trout. I haven't had a chance to do any washing, and will be knickerless (long skirts only) by Thursday. Better not tell the lads that: I'll never hear the end of it.

And yet, strangely, I'm enjoying myself. There's a grim humour in pub life, and my assorted clientele of brickies and hardware salesmen are a grimly humorous lot. They are all male. I think, apart from Glenda, that I am the first woman to set foot through these doors since last Christmas.

Well, not entirely. I keep forgetting the one touch of oestrogen that joins us each evening as I'm surreptitiously running my fingers through my hair and dipping them into over-fizzy pints of lager, where the grease will kill the head. It's not surprising, for no-one, as far as I can see, has ever spoken to her. She comes in with her husband, and has one drink. Every night, the same routine: they walk in at 7.30 sharp, by which time Mike is on his fourth pint. He has a big beard, she has a curly perm. She sits in the far corner by the door, and he lumbers over to the bar.

Mike goes, 'Evening, guv,' every evening, and every evening he ignores him.

Then he says to me in the slowest, most plodding West Country drawl, 'A point of lager and loime and a zzzlimloine bidder lemon please.'

Same order every night, no sign that he recognizes any of his fellow punters or the person serving him. And it's hell waiting for him to put in his order. I know what it's going to be, I know I can't start pouring till he's given it, and, I swear, it takes him five minutes to say the single sentence. Then Mike says, same every night, 'Nice talking to you, mate,' he ignores him and lumbers back to the corner seat. Then they sit, sipping, in silence, staring vaguely at points six inches above each other's heads. And when they finish, they stand up and disappear off to their mysterious existence.

Chapter Thirty-nine

Literally Yours

Donna is perched on a bar stool eating cheese and onion crisps and allowing Mike and Barry to buy her drinks: she has recently developed a taste for Snowballs, and the Putrid is probably the only pub left in London where they still stock them, though each bottle must be a zillion years old if the film of greasy dust that coats them is anything to go by. I try to give them a quick rinse under the tap before I open them, but it doesn't always work and sometimes the Snowball comes out looking more like a Slushball. Donna doesn't seem to mind, though.

Donna's going on and I'm trying to both listen and serve. Mike has a prodigious thirst, and can sink a pint of lager at roughly the rate at which I can pour one out.

'So he says that it could be the start of the end of all our problems,' she says. 'We need a change of attitude, girl, that's what we need.'

Mike, passing his glass over the bar, says, 'Nothing wrong with your attitude, darling,' and she giggles, tosses her plaits over her shoulder.

'So how exactly do we get this change of attitude, then?' I ask. 'Do they sit there and tell us how to organize our lives? Give us interview tips? Are there people there who might be good contacts?' I pass Mike his glass back, and he gulps half of it by the simple expedient of wrapping his entire mouth round the rim and biting down. Damn, why didn't I think of that?

'No,' says Donna, 'it's sort of working on yourself from the inside out. Luke says that you can only begin to change the world by changing yourself, or something like that. Anyway, you know how together Luke is, and he says it's all down to this course. I think we ought to give it a try.'

Donna has met Luke once, at a party, and has been mightily impressed.

'Sounds like a load of old cobblers to me,' says Mike, hands me back his glass.

'No, it's not, honest.' Donna isn't going to be dissuaded.

'So how much does this cost, Donna?'

'I think it's just under £400 for the weekend. That's Friday, Saturday and Sunday.'

'FOUR HUNDRED POUNDS? Where do you think I'm going to get that from?'

'Yeah, yeah, yeah.' Donna jiggles about in her seat. 'But, like, you'll be able to afford it again soon.'

'Look, it's out of the question, I owe Ben two months' rent, the bank's about to prosecute me and anyway, I'd rather go to Ibiza or something with that sort of money.'

'It'll be great, though,' says Donna. 'Don't you want to get your life on track?'

'Well, of course I do.'

'And if you get your life on track, you'll be able to afford any number of weeks in Ibiza, won't you?'

'Well, yes, I suppose.'

'OK, that's settled.' She hands me her glass for another Snowball. 'If you get a windfall or something, or once you're sorted out, we'll go.'

I'm about to protest, but from the corner of my eye, I can

see Beardman approaching and start grinding my teeth instead.

'Sounds a laugh,' I say absently. As I'm not going to be sorted for at least three months, there's not much point in fighting. Beardman's Mrs, with her tight curly perm and her leatherette car coat, has settled on the bench by the door and is watching us with hunted eyes.

'Evening, guv,' says Mike, grins and buries his nose in his lager. Beardman arrives.

'Hello,' I say. 'What can I get you?' I've tried every possible way of circumventing his next sentence but, as it's probably the only thing he says to anyone all day, or maybe because it takes such an effort of will to speak to a relative stranger like me in the first place, nothing is going to stop him getting the full sentence out. I've tried, 'Hi there, the usual?' and even, 'Hello, pint of lager and lime and a slimline bitter lemon, is it?' but all I've had in return is, 'Thaat's roight. A point of laager and loime and a zzlimloine bidder lemon, please.' It's enough to drive a girl to distraction.

'OK, great,' says Donna, 'I'll book it for the end of April, then.' I grimace, because I wasn't expecting her to take me so literally, but then again I've been suffering a bit from literalness all week. Or perhaps it's just that double-shift tiredness has changed my delivery so that people can't tell I'm joking. In the City, Graham, who is the head of unit in the small merchant bank where I'm working at the moment, suffers from both a humour bypass and an empire-building complex. That, I think, is why he won't use his dictaphone, but requires me to come in and sit by his desk with a pad on my knee pretending to take dictation. On Thursday I was spread-sheeting for Malcolm, who had to get some proposal about a potential plastics investment in by lunch-time, when Graham rang.

'Are you busy?' he said.

'Very. I'm just doing my nails,' I said.

'Oh,' he said. 'Can you come in? I've got some letters.'

'Sure,' I said, 'I'll be through in ten minutes. I've just got something urgent to finish up.'

Eight minutes later I arrived at his desk with my Berol Speediwrite and my Niceday spiral-bound to find him sitting with his fingers clasped over a pursed mouth, specs glittering.

'Hello,' I said, fishing a chair from another desk and settling on it. Waited, pen poised expectantly. Started scribbling as he started talking, stopped quite quickly as I realized that he was addressing me rather than a client.

'How are your nails?' he said.

Thinking that we were still sharing my rather feeble joke, I waved my gnawed stubs at him and said, 'Lovely.'

Graham stood up. Started pacing up and down. His colleagues, my other bosses, dropped their pens, raised their heads from their knuckles, put their phone receivers to their chests and started watching. 'I don't expect,' he said, his voice rising a decibel with each syllable, 'to ask for your attention only to be told that you're doing your manicure on the firm's time. You are paid to work and I WILL NOT HAVE IT!'

I dropped my pen, scrabbled around to retrieve it and stuttered 'But, Graham, I was—'

'NO EXCUSES!' shouted Graham, and the people behind the glass screen with the map of the world on the wall came out to look. 'If you want to spend your time doing beauty treatments, train as a beautician.'

'Graham, I was joking.'

'Joking?' His head snapped back like a velociraptor and he eyed me sideways.

'Yes.'

'How joking?'

'You asked me if I was busy and instead of saying that I was I told you I was doing my nails. It was a joke.'

He sat down. 'How is that funny?'

'Um, well it wasn't a very good joke. It was just one of those off-the-cuff things you say.' And instantly regret, I thought.

'Well,' said Graham, 'I don't call that much of a joke myself. I'd be grateful if you'd confine your jokes to outside office hours in future. Now. Are you ready to take some dictation?'

'Of course I am,' I said meekly. 'Sorry.'

Beardman begins his sentence with a couple of throat-clearings and some 'Arr-urr' noises. The bar falls silent in anticipation of the order emerging from among the tufts. I catch Mike's eye and can't resist a small tease.

'Don't tell me,' I say, 'it's a Kahlua and green chartreuse and a Baileys chaser, isn't it?'

Beardman stops, looks suspiciously at me, clears his throat again and says, 'No. A point of laager and loime and a zzlimloine bidder lemon, please.' Then he makes a tutting noise, turns to Mike and says, 'I don't know. You'd have thought I'd have been coming 'ere long enough for 'er to at least know thaad.'

Chapter Forty

Cleaning Up

Work-sleep-work-work-sleep, work-work-sleep work-work-sleep work-work-sleep . . . my life has taken on the rhythm of a waltz with little of the bounce. To bed, to tube, to office, to tube, to bus, to pub, to bed: and on Sundays, in the daytime, I go to the launderette, wander the halls of the Vauxhall Sainsbury's in search of nutritious fast food (and buy beans and sausages in a tin), try to take a walk so that I get to see some natural light. My skin is slug-white from neon striplights, and I think I've lost the power of natural conversation. But Glenda is on the mend and thinks she'll be able to come back next week, and I have, at least, stabilized my finances. By working through lunch every day, and coming into the office two Saturdays in a row (where, fortunately, they have a backlog of filing owing to the fact that they didn't hire a temp until three weeks after they needed one), I've cleared nearly £300 a week after the Chancellor's had his cut and I've contributed to a pension that I'll probably never see, and it's all gone straight into my bank account, and John's put nearly £700 into my hand over my time behind the bar.

Ben comes in on my final Friday with Donna in tow and they take up pole position behind the beer pumps. Ben has an unnerving glitter in his eye as he watches me squeeze

Fairy antibacterial liquid through a greying J–cloth and wipe it around the surfaces.

'What's up, boy?' I hand him his pint of snakebite and Donna her Snowball. John's had to go down the cash and carry to stock up with the things; I only hope he sells them before they get out of date once the Putrid's function as our house meeting-place is over.

'We're celebrating.'

'Uh-huh. Why?' There's a sticky patch where the lemon dish usually stands. I start to scratch at it, then go and find the Jif-with-bleach and give it a good spray.

Ben does a Mike: opens his gullet and simply pours half a pint of snakebite directly into his stomach. 'I've got a part.'

'Ben! No!'

He nods.

'What in?' There's a smudge on the side of his glass that looks suspiciously like engine oil. It must have not come off in the glass-washer. I make a note to give it a good scrub when he's finished. Content myself, in the meantime, with washing the ashtrays rather than giving them the usual quick wipe with an old vest dampened with washing-up water.

Ben puts down his glass, pushes it towards me. 'New Britfilm. *Chasing Nancy*, it's called.'

'Yeah?'

I pour lager on top of the cider, blench as it clouds and forms lumps. Hand it back. 'Who's directing?'

'Young bloke. Marty O'Byrne. Won one of those Channel Four scholarships last year with that short about the coppers trapped in a lift in the middle of a shoot-out. You remember.'

'Yeah, I do. So what's it about?'

'It's a Britfilm,' he says, 'what do you think it's about?'

'Ah, right. A group of marginalized but witty youths pulling off a heist on some people who are pulling off a heist and getting ripped off at the end by Keith Allen?'

Ben nods. 'I'm the Scottish psycho.'

'Christ. So Harry came through in the end, then.' Harry is Ben's agent. Has an office in Ladbroke Grove and an accent he bought off the peg in Oxford Street.

'Pah,' says Ben, 'Harry's history.'

'Since when?'

'Yesterday. You went straight to bed when you got in so I never got the chance to tell you.'

'Why?'

'He's a wanker.'

'Well, he's always been a wanker. So why now?'

I realize that Ben's already had a few drinks.

'No, he's a real wanker.'

My eye lights on the top shelf behind the bar, where the clock is, and a collection of ceramic donkeys from John's holidays in Spain. It's covered in a layer of something that must have come off a gas cooker, though everything here is run on the electric; some of the donkeys, though I know he likes the brown ones, are greenish-grey. I can't help it. I drag a stool in through the hatch in the bar, get up onto it, taking the Flash squirter and a new J-cloth from the shelves under the taps, and start to scrub.

'What happened?'

'Well,' says Ben, 'I found out in the *Stage* that the auditions for this thing were going on today, and I thought, hang on, Harry hasn't said a thing about it. So I went up to Ladbroke Grove yesterday afternoon and dropped in to see him. He's sitting there smoking a cigar, goes, "Ben, dear boy, what a delight to see you. I've just been talking about you." So I go, "Oh, yeah, what about?" and he goes, "We've got a prospect that I think you'll be very excited about." So I say, "What, this part in *Chasing Nancy*?" and he looks completely blank. Completely. And he goes, "I don't know what you're talking about, dear boy. No, this is a real televisual opportunity that should be right up your street. The production houses are very excited, I can tell you."'

'Really?' I've got all the donkeys into the sink now, straw sombreros lined up on the counter, and have covered them in soapy water. Climb back up on the stool to employ some serious elbow grease.

'So I go, "Yeah, what?" and he says, "Presenting, dear boy." And I go, really? What sort of presenting? And he says, well, the perfect market for you. And I'm beginning to get a bit worried about this, but I go, OK, what, chat show? Documentaries? And he says, "No, no. Nothing like that. Children's TV." So I go, "What, Saturday morning slot or something?" and he says, "No. A game show." And I'm, like, what sort of game show? What exactly have you in mind? And he puts out his cigar and says, all triumphant, like, "It's right up your street. Pop trivia. Hilarious format. Trivia, obstacle races, inflatable comic character called Mr Windy. Contestants answer pop questions while bouncing on a bouncy castle. It's bound to be a huge hit."'

'Ben!' I say.

Mike, who's been eyeing Ben for a while, says, 'Bouncy castle?'

'That's what *I* said. I said, "What have I been taking all these acting lessons for, Harry? I thought you understood that I want to act, not stooge a blow-up doll," and he said, "That's not where I see you, dear boy. Light entertainment's the thing. It's where you come from, after all, and what the audience associates you with." And then he goes,

"You don't want to rock the boat too much, you know. You might just fall out." And then he laughs.'

'So then you sacked him.' The donkeys are coming out of the sink with big streaks of clean on them, blackening the J-cloth as I wipe them down.

'I said, "Harry," I said, "I think it's you and I that have had the falling out." And I— Look, what on earth are you doing? All you've done in the last week is clean. I can't find anything in the kitchen any more.'

I look down at the drying-up cloth in my hand and think, Christ, this is serious. I'm so tired I'm taking on other people's personalities, and the personality I'm taking on is Graham's.

Two weeks of Graham, and I've realized that there is more to the geezer than initially meets the eye. I thought at first that it was just that he doesn't have a sense of humour. Actually, there's a lot more there: there is something seriously wrong beneath that spotless suit.

I should have noticed it immediately, given that his first move after shaking my hand on the first day was to take a Wet One from the mega box in the shadow of the box files and wipe down his palm with it before dropping it, two-fingered, into the bin. I'm so used to odd reactions from new bosses that I just thought it was a new, imaginative way of making me feel unwelcome. It wasn't until I'd watched him surreptitiously do the same thing to three clients in a row that I started realizing that this was something of a psychosis, not merely a weird way of pulling rank.

Graham, it seems, is terrified of germs. Now, we're all a little nervous of what we can pick up in offices. They're not hygienic places, especially with air-conditioning carrying every cold virus breathed out by someone in the lift to every desk on the 15th floor. I mean, if the Queen can have legionnaire's disease in the ventilation system at Buck House, what hope is there for her subjects? What with everyone's habit of nicking other people's pens and then putting them in their mouths, it's surprising that any of us is still alive.

But that doesn't explain why Graham's box of Wet Ones are not, as I discovered when hunting through the box files for a copy of last month's board-meeting minutes, Wet Ones at all, but a mega box of sterile wipes. He employs them constantly. He must get through a box every couple of weeks: more than the average surgical unit. First thing in the morning, first thing after lunch and last thing at night, Graham wipes down his entire desk with a wad of the things, paying special attention to the crevices around the drawer handles. Graham is the Michael Jackson of merchant banking.

But it's not just that. He uses them for everything: wiping down pens, pencils, staplers, the keyboard of his computer, his fingers after he's handled a piece of paper. Once a week, a dignified young black woman in an apron and rubber gloves, who doesn't seem to speak a word of English apart from 'Excuse me,' comes round the office with a squirty bottle of something vaguely pine-scented and wipes over the earphones and mouthpieces of the telephones. I find this vaguely comforting. I don't know if you've ever looked at the little holes on a telephone mouthpiece, but it's quite a disturbing sight: slightly mushroomy, slightly cheesy. It's nice that someone is getting the fungi before they get us. Graham, however, isn't contented with this. When she's there, he shrinks back from his desk. When she's gone, he gets out his wipes and carefully covers every square centimetre that she's already been over. And as he does it, his Adam's apple bobs as though he's trying to stop himself being sick.

The thing is, the habit is catching. I've never really looked at my environment in such detail before, thought about where everything might have been. The pub must occasionally pass Health and Safety inspections, I guess, but I suddenly find myself washing my hands thoroughly each time one of my builder clients emerges from the loo and hands me his glass for refilling, and I have to stop myself from doing the same every time I handle change. In the office, following Graham's lead, I have started checking the coffee-cups as they come out of the machine in case some foreign body has attached itself to the outside.

Ben is still looking at me. I put down the drying-up cloth, gulping, and say, 'Sorry. I've got a bit of a hygiene thing at the moment. I'll stop.'

'Good,' says Ben. 'I can't cope with all this cleanliness. It's doing my head in. It's not like you're usually Miss Prim on that front.'

'I know. My boss obviously thinks so, too.'

'What, Graham the nutter?' asks Donna. 'What's he done now?'

'I think he thinks I'm some sort of night-soil porter.' And I tell her how, this morning, he arrived on tiptoe, and his skin was positively green. 'Good morning, Graham,' I said. He didn't answer, as he seemed to be concentrating on standing on one foot while undoing the laces on the other with the tip of a paper-knife. Then he slipped it off, still using the knife, and waved it, sole first, at me, so I saw what was on the bottom. 'Oh,' I said, eyeing it. Strangulated syllables emerged from the very front of Graham's mouth, as though he was afraid to open his airways too wide. 'Can you,' he said, 'deal with this?'

'Eeugh, Jesus,' says Donna. 'I think it's time to move on.'

'Don't worry,' I say, 'I called the agency this morning. So what happened then, Ben?'

'Well, I was up all night last night, as you can imagine. I was so angry, I actually went out for a walk at two in the morning looking for muggers to beat up. Luckily there weren't any.' He grimaces, giggles. 'I couldn't fight a mosquito with its arms tied behind its back. So anyway, I got up first thing this morning and just went down to where they were holding the auditions, and I walked in – I strode in, actually. You should have seen me stride – and went straight over to the director. He's a funny wee chap, you know: middle class as they come, but he's got this Cockney accent that keeps slipping. You know, sort of "Yah, actually, orlright, geezer, stroike a loight, how do you do?" and he dyes his hair black. So I went up to him, and said, "I want to play your Scottish psycho," and he started back and said, "Didn't you used to be Ben—" and I said, "Yeah, you got a problem with that?" and he went, "No, actually, orlright geezer" – I think he was scared stupid, to be honest – and the next thing I knew I was reading the script and they were all sitting back with big smiles on their faces and going, "We had no idea you could be this frightening. What sort of money are you thinking about?" And here we are. I'm officially a scary nutter and you'd all best give me some respect.'

'And what is the money like?' asks Donna.

'It's a Britfilm, isn't it?' Ben sneers.

Which reminds me.

'Which reminds me,' I say, and dig in my handbag for the window envelope I half-inched from work this afternoon when I got back from the bank. Hand it to him.

'What's this?' He studies it, frowning.

'It's the rent. I'm really sorry it's taken me so long to get it together, but it's all there now.'

Ben pushes it back over the counter. 'Don't be silly,' he says.

'But I owe it you, Ben.'

He shakes his head. 'You don't owe me anything.'

'Yes I do.'

'You don't,' he says. 'Really.'

'Don't be ridiculous. I owe you two months.'

'But Marina sorted that,' he says. 'Didn't you know?'

'What do you mean?'

'Well, she came over and gave it to me three weeks ago. Said something about feeling awful about your situation and wanting to do something to help out. Didn't she tell you?'

Marina. All the horrible things I've said about her, and she turns out to be the sturdiest brick of the lot. I almost burst into tears on the spot.

'I—' I stutter.

Donna has sat up, is grinning broadly. 'Well, if that's not a sign from God, I don't know what is,' she says. 'You know what this means, don't you?'

Chapter Forty-one

The Search for Self

Polly stares deep into my eyes. 'I am angry with you,' she says, 'because we never got on, even when I was little. I am angry with you because when all my friends were going on holidays abroad, you always took us to the Lake District. I am angry with you because you never worked and made us feel guilty because we were the focus of your world. You've always ignored me when you weren't finding fault with me. You dress badly and you made my dad's life miserable with your whining. I am angry with you because you gave me your saggy body and your thin hair. I am angry with you because you never liked my friends . . .' By now she is puce with rage, and her face is covered in tears. I, meanwhile, am trying desperately to keep my eyes on hers and not look round the room to see what everyone else is up to, even though I can hear whoops, sobbing, swearing, even shouting. And the phrase that has been going through my head for the last 36 hours is repeating itself more loudly and clearly: 'Oh, bugger.'

At last Jomo shouts 'Stop!' and Polly sits back, puts her hand up for Kleenex and crushes my hand in hers as she wipes herself down. 'Thank you,' she sobs, 'thank you.' I pat her hand and smile wearily at her, scrabbling around inside my head for things to say now my turn's coming up. I really can't think of anything. Mum and I had loads of rows eight, ten years ago, but I can't think what they were about. Incompetence with blusher, probably, or the cost of photo-love-story magazines. What? What can I say?

'OK,' shouts Jomo, 'partner B. Remember, no-one's going to be shocked or hurt by anything you say, so just let it all out. Two minutes from now.' Polly leans forward, takes my hand in hers and gazes deep, deep into my eyes. People are already starting to sob in the background, and I haven't got a word out yet.

'Um,' I say, and think, well, that's ten seconds out of the way. Two minutes has never seemed so long. This self-development stuff is hard work, I can tell you. Let no-one tell you differently. I've given a group of six people a potted self-critique of myself, spent a full five minutes staring at a flower and another minute describing it in excruciating detail, tried meditating by concentrating on the feel of the blood in my veins, shared my snap judgements on everyone at my lunch table, found my Chi and rediscovered the inner child through play. Surely that's enough for now?

Polly nods vigorously at me, dying to take the burden of my relationship with my mother on her shoulders. I've got to think of something. 'I'm angry with you because . . . ' I say, then lose it again. I am seriously pissed off that I'm going along with this. Inspiration. 'Because you never taught me to say no.' Um, shit, it must be nearly a minute now, surely?

'Eighty seconds left,' shouts Jomo, as if to increase the torture. Polly has a look of disbelieving sympathy on her face; I can tell she wants to hug me for being so inhibited.

God, I've got to think of something. Oh, damn it; no-one's going to know if I make it up, are they? 'I'm angry with you because no-one in our household was allowed to discuss their feelings. I'm angry with you for – God, what? – giving my puppy away because you didn't want a dog in the house.' Good one. Yes. Polly's eyes have misted with sympathy. 'I'm angry with you for preferring my brother.' Well, she preferred him over my cousins, anyway. I'm getting into the swing of this now. 'I'm angry with you for never acknowledging my sexuality.' Polly's fingers twitch in mine. To tell the truth, I'm grateful that I never had to have one of those excruciating discussions about contraception. I bet my mum is, too.

I cast around wildly, my eyes flicking away from Polly's, as Jomo shouts out that there are forty seconds left. Maybe I could do some tears; that'll waste a bit of time. When in doubt, cry: Tania's always known that trick. I blink, gulp, manage a sniff, and Polly's grip on my hands starts to cut off my circulation. 'I'm angry with you because . . .' I say very very slowly as a stalling mechanism, then decide to go for it. 'I don't think I'm ever going to live up to your expectations. You don't like my friends –' well, she doesn't like Marina or Tania, and she thinks Matthew's a scumbag, so there's no lie there '– you don't like where I live – ' well, not many people want their daughter living at the far end of mugger's alley '– and you don't like what I do for a living. You never accept me as *me*!' Yesssss! Polly's expression is a heady mix of empathy and triumph. 'I can't do anything right. I'll never be what you expect and I feel guilty all the time.'

Finally I manage to squeeze a tear from the corner of my eye, and Polly's grip begins to turn my fingernails white. 'I just—' Bugger. That's it. Barrel scraped and thoroughly checked underneath. I pretend to be overcome with emotion, gulp and look down at my knees. Actually, if this keeps up any longer, I probably will burst into tears.

'OK. Time's up. Hug your partner and congratulate yourselves for being so honest.'

Polly folds me in her arms and I squeeze her back. This is the easy bit. 'You're very brave,' says Polly. 'I can tell you've never said any of those things before.'

'So are you,' I reply, and it flits across my mind that perhaps we have both been making everything up, perhaps the whole room is full of people inventing stories because they are too cowardly to refuse to play.

We move away from each other and rejoin the crowd, who are forming fireman's lifts with the plastic bucket chairs lined up by the wall. This is the bit I like best so far: good, simple co-operative exercise with no repercussions. Well, anything is pleasurable once you've listened to a total stranger tell you about the time they masturbated with a deodorant bottle.

On the other side of the room, Donna looks quite small and frail, and I can tell that she's been crying again. She smiles and waves at me and I wave back. I settle down next to a balding man in a blue pinstripe jacket with white stains around the pockets. God knows what he's been up to.

'Isn't this amazing?' he asks.

I concur. 'Amazing.' Truly amazing. A unique experience; one never to be repeated. I hope. I have no idea what time it is, as watches are banned in the sharing room, but I could really do with lunch. My stomach was grumbling so loudly before the last exercise that I feared I might be about to come in for a lecture on passive aggression.

'So,' says Jomo, 'what have we learned?' A hundred hands shoot into the air; there's nothing so keen as the middle classes in full cry in pursuit of their neuroses. 'That I can talk about things I've never told anybody,' says a girl with pink dreadlocks and a pierced nose.

'Very good, thank you,' says Jomo, for the 180th time this morning. 'Anyone else?'

A man in an Adidas T-shirt stands up, still visibly shaking from his experience: 'That my mother is the source of everything that's wrong with me,' he says.

'Very good, thank you,' Jomo says again. The number of waving hands has shrunk by half. 'Anyone else?'

I think about sticking my hand up and confessing that I've been making things up, but the thought of that sea of faces all turned to me with a mixture of shock, disappointment and – oh, God – sympathy is more daunting than keeping the secret for the rest of my life. I sit on the urge while Jomo explains.

'What it shows us,' he says, 'is that everyone has problems with their mother. And principally, it shows us that *all the problems are the same*.' The room sighs with relief and settles back. A problem shared, after all, is a problem you can be proud of. I realize that one of the helpers is watching me from the side of the room, that I'm still sitting forward with a frown on my face. Drop back, compose my features. In the world of self-development, invisibility is key.

My stomach makes a grelching sound so loud I think they'll hear it in reception. It's got to be lunch-time soon.

Jomo is one of those people who has been blessed with the sort of piercingly clear blue eyes that give the impression they can see straight through to your soul. They zap like lasers around the room, resting on faces with an intensity that is both frightening and oddly comforting. 'Believe in me,' they say, 'and I will show you the secrets of the world.' Actually, all they say is, 'I am blue and my owner has learned to control his blinking,' because eyes, despite claims to the contrary, are remarkably undemonstrative organs. But if you're searching for the secrets of your soul, you'll believe that a dog can talk if the right person tells you.

Jomo is wearing a big green cotton-knit sweater and loose cotton trousers. Jomo has bobbed hair, but not so bobbed that people over forty distrust him. Jomo talks with the conglomerate accent of one much practised in addressing an international audience: basically English, with a bit of Scandiwegian, a bit of mid-Atlantic, some East European gutturals and a touch of Australasian. The International Forum for Human Happiness has branches in London, Melbourne, Stockholm, Berlin and Atlanta, Georgia. Jomo will presumably be shortening his vowels once again when they open up in Johannesburg.

'So, people,' says Jomo as my stomach howls for comfort, 'we've done great work this morning. I think we're getting somewhere at last. This afternoon we're going to be working on our inhibitions some more. In the meantime, I want you to get five good hugs before you leave. Then go away and make a list of ten things you want to change about yourself. And remember. Don't have lunch with your friends. Eat with someone you've not met before and would never choose to have lunch with under normal circumstances. It's only by breaking the mould that we can learn. Be back here in an hour and a half, have a good break.'

After nine months on the temping circuit, I'm not used to having lunch with people. I've not spent this much unrelieved time in company since school. I decide to duck out quietly as five different people bear down on me from different corners to drag me away. Yesterday I spent an hour listening to a woman with a tight perm and tighter jaw muscles informing me that she could tell that I was bottling up a lot of anger because I smoked. Today I could do with half a pack of Bensons in peace, maybe down by the river, maybe in preparation for high-tailing it out of Newbury.

Pinstripe jacket turns to me. 'Well,' he says, 'how about lunch?'

'Never in a million years,' screams every cell in my body, 'not if you threaten to burn my grandmother!' and I meekly nod and go in search of my coat, and get crushed to the bosom of two angry young men, a grandmother, an actress and a scary Persian.

Pinstripe's name, it turns out, is Carey, 'as in George,' he says. We wander the streets trying to find a suitable wine bar until, to my surprise, we find ourselves agreeing that the only thing we really want in the world is greasy-spoon chips. The Little Nook café, where the chairs are made of anti-suicide green plastic and bolted to rigid iron bars, looks more inviting than a night in Mash. Through the windows of the wholefood café across the road, eating bits of grass and cardboard, I can see at least ten faces I recognize from the Forum. Carey orders sausage and chips, I order beans and chips. We slurp greedily on mugs of stewed tea with five sugars and study each other uncertainly.

Carey must be fifteen years older than me, has big brown eyes and the voice of one whose forebears long since mastered the universe, and has disguised his receding hair-line with a Number One cut. I get out my baccy. I've taken to roll-ups since I realized that I could save £15 a week by smoking them, which constitutes a seriously good holiday.

Carey says, 'Ooh, can I blag one of those? I'm dying for a cig and I didn't manage to get to a shop this morning.' And I think, OK, so he hasn't got a stick up his bum after all, and hand over the baggie.

In silence we roll up, prod tobacco back into the ends
th a matchstick, pass the lighter from hand to hand, sit
ck and sigh with pleasure. 'I know it's killing me,' says
Carey, 'but there are moments when there is nothing in the
world you need more than a cigarette.' We gaze out of the
window at our fellow Life Students as they pause outside
the wholefood restaurant and agree that a lunch of seed-
pods and expanded polystyrene is just the ticket.

'So,' says Carey after a minute or so has elapsed, 'I
suppose we have to do the right thing and discuss why we
wouldn't ever go to lunch together.'

'I suppose,' I reply. 'You asked me. You start.'

'Oh, look, it's nothing bad. It's just that you look so
unfazed by this whole thing, and I can never think of things
to say to people like you. You look like you've never been
thrown by anything in your life. And that makes me
uncomfortable.'

Blow me. And I thought poker faces were meant to be
a virtue. 'So,' says Carey, 'why wouldn't you go out to lunch
with me?'

'Christ. Because you wouldn't ask me. I've worked for
dozens of men like you over the last year, and at lunch-time
you always, without exception, go off to lunch together
and leave me at my desk with a sandwich.'

'What do you do?'

'I'm a temp secretary. I go around offices and type letters
for people who don't want to know I exist.'

'Bloody hell,' he says, 'I thought you probably worked in
the media somewhere. You've got that Soho cocktail bar
look about you. What do you think I do, then?'

'You work in the City, don't you? Probably not a dealer
or trader, you're not flash enough. A stockbroker or an
analyst.'

Carey bellows with laughter. 'That's the jacket, isn't it? I put it on because I thought it was anonymous. It was my father's. He taught in a prep school. That's why it's got stains.'

'So what *do* you do?'

'I design computer software. I make games to help spotty adolescents not have to go out and make friends.'

'You're an anorak?'

'Yes. I even own one.'

'I thought everyone here was in the professions, or counsellors or installation artists or something,' I say.

'Ooh, no, they do loads of things. The woman who spent the whole of yesterday lunch-time saying that she could tell that I was a bully is an anaesthetist.'

'Was that the one with the leather jacket? Looks like she got too close to a gas fire?'

'Yeah. You've met her, then?'

'Yes. She's a helper-out. Got frightfully cross with me because I couldn't think of any sex things I was ashamed of yesterday afternoon.'

Carey shakes his head, miming astonishment. 'I never realized that wanking was such a shameful secret before. I thought it was something everyone did, like picking their nose.'

'Mmm, or biting their toenails.'

Carey stops dead, decides I'm joking and carries on. 'So why are you a temp, then? Commitment phobia, or saving-up-to-go-round-the-world?'

'Naah.' My chips arrive. I scrape the plug of brown gunge from the top of the squeezy bottle off with the tine of my fork and squirt sauce all over the table. 'It's a can't-get-a-job thing.'

'Why?' Carey makes with the vinegar. 'What's wrong with you?'

Offended, I say, 'What do you mean by that?'

'Well. You don't look like a psycho and you're obviously educated. What's wrong with you that no-one's given you a job?'

'It's not that easy. There's a recession.'

Carey shrugs. 'I know all about recessions. I graduated into the early years of Thatcher. There wasn't much going then, either. I was a hospital orderly for six months before I got a break.'

'I've been temping for nearly a year.'

'So why,' he asks, 'do you think that is?'

I don't really want to talk about it.

'I don't really want to talk about it,' I say.

'Fair enough,' he concurs, and we both take to looking around us again. Over the road, a woman with stringy aubergine hair and one of those Hindu-wedding combined ear-and-nose-rings comes out of the wholefood restaurant and wipes Soya Pie with Dandelion Stalks off the specials board.

Carey breaks the silence first. 'So look. Can I ask you something?'

'Sure. What?'

He blushes, slices off a chunk of sausage and chews it while he works up his nerve. 'It's a bit awkward. I just – well, I don't know how to say this really, but is it just me that feels like most of the people here have crawled up their own arses and died?'

I'm in the middle of taking a ladylike sip from my tea. It goes all over the table, the window, the napkin dispenser, my chips, the sauce bottles and Carey's pinstriped lapels. He laughs, grabs a couple of napkins and mops himself down. 'No, but really?'

Eventually, I start to breathe again. 'I couldn't have put

it better myself. Not died, maybe. Just found out that they really like the stuff they've found up there.'

'I knew a girl once,' he says, 'someone I worked with. She went for an intestinal lavage and so many old pill cases came out that she started going weekly. She used to tell us all about what they'd found in her bucket every time she went.'

'What happened? That must be terribly bad for you.'

'I don't know. She moved to Sleaford in the end. It's in Lincolnshire.'

'Well, obviously. If you're in to colonic irrigation, you might as well move to somewhere that sounds like a by-product.'

He laughs, looks out at the window as three people tie the belts of their macs round tummies full of stone grit and papyrus. 'So you're not getting revelations, then? Light-bulbs not going on in your head? No quiet revolution in your world view?' Carey quotes the glossy brochure full of happy, smiling, multicultural success stories and order forms for books and boxed-cassette sets that we received after Donna sent off for information on how to sign up for the first part of the rest of our lives.

'No. I've been having a slight increase in my levels of paranoia and a major drop in my hydration levels.'

'And I'm dying for a drink.'

'Me, too.'

We eye each other for a moment, say 'No' in the same breath.

'Have you done anything like this before?'

I was sent for group counselling by school once when I got caught slapping Rebecca Parrott for being a snotty bitch who thought that her elocution lessons had lent some gravitas to her whingeing, but I think that probably doesn't count. Besides, Rebecca Parrott is still a snotty bitch, and I would still slap her if I got the chance. 'Not really. How about you?'

'Virgin.'

I wipe my last chip around my plate, eat it as slowly as I can. This is the part of the weekend that I have enjoyed most, so far. 'Do you think it's worth going on to the end?'

Carey nods. 'Definitely.'

'I'm not sure. I think I might cut and run back to London before the afternoon session gets going.'

'No. Don't do that.'

'Why not?'

'Look,' says Carey, 'I hate to give you the parental lecture, but if there's one thing I've learned in life it's that there's no regret more powerful than not seeing things through to the end. I know that this is just a bingo-card-of-life experience and probably won't change anything much, but not doing it is another nail in your own coffin. You'll spend the rest of your life wondering if there was something to learn that you missed out on by wimping out.'

'Surely there must be a less ghastly way?'

'Undoubtedly. But you know something?' Carey gets a pair of horn-rimmed spectacles out of his pocket, starts polishing them with another napkin. I wait. 'You want a career, don't you?'

'Yes, of course.'

'Well, listen. Everything you're doing at the moment is temporary, and the longer you do it the longer the state of temporariness becomes permanent. I look at you and I see you thinking about flunking out of this because it makes you uncomfortable, maybe presses a few buttons you don't want pressed, and you know what I think? I think you've stopped applying for jobs because it's safer than making yourself vulnerable to rejection. You're bright, you're pretty and you've got all the social skills, and you're hampering yourself by not seeing the things you start through to the end. That's why you ought to finish it. Sorry if I'm being a bit previous, but I've seen too much of this in the people who got left behind from my generation.'

Wow. I don't really know what to say. This is the sort of speech that usually has me snarling with rage, but for some reason I just sit there and take it from Carey. He finishes rubbing his specs, puts them on the bridge of his nose and grins. 'And I've got to finish because I'm a tosser who's got no friends and I need all the help I can get. Now. We've got ten minutes to work out ten things wrong with us. How far have you got?'

'Well, I've started,' I say sulkily, 'but I haven't finished.' And then I realize what I've just said and am forced to smile.

'Phew,' says Carey, 'so I'm forgiven. Now, go on, give us a fag and we'll polish it off in no time.'

Chapter Forty-two

The First Day of the
Rest of Your Life

Of course, after another fifty-odd good hugs, it turns out that I'm OK, You're OK and so is everyone else with the possible exception of Adolf Hitler, who would no doubt have turned out OK if he'd had the opportunity to work on himself. And after fifty-odd good hugs, I'm still a temp secretary with no career prospects and an ex-boyfriend who wants the stereo, but at least I know where my Chi is, so things must have got better. Plus I've got a flatmate who seems intent on flinging her arms and legs round every walking kaftan she meets and, thank you God, a lift home. Carey, it turns out, drives a convertible Triumph Vitesse that's over thirty years old, and, as the sealing round just about everything has perished with age, the wind whistles round the windows and doors and fills the car. He doesn't have just an anorak on the back seat, but three chunky jumpers and four pairs of gloves, which he insists we put on.

'Why,' says Donna, 'don't you get a car that doesn't have holes in?'

'I've wanted a Vitesse since I was six years old,' he says, as though this suffices as explanation. I know, as long as I live, that I won't come to fully understand men. I mean, I wanted a pony of my own and a collection of Weebles at the age of six, but it doesn't mean I want them now. I pull a Fair Isle over my head, put my coat over the top, tuck my scarf in round my neck and settle into the front passenger seat. The padding has long since compacted, and the metal bars of the frame are all too evident to my spine. And for this a man can long for thirty years.

'If you're going to want to smoke,' says Carey, 'you'd better roll a few now. Your hands are going to be too cold to do anything much in about twenty minutes.'

Donna sits diagonally behind us, her knees digging into my back, and we head for the motorway. I roll feverishly as the breeze rises to a roar and the roar rises to the sound of the Atlantic ocean beating on the rocks of the west coast of Portugal. It's years since I was last in a car without music playing, but I guess there wouldn't be much point in trying in this one.

Nobody says anything much for the first forty miles, each of us wrapped in our own little world. I feel completely drained after three days and two nights of assault on my brain. And that's on top of lying awake in a sleeping bag on a living-room floor, rehearsing in my head speeches that, surprise, surprise, never got used. My neck and shoulder muscles are rigid, and when I press them they yelp. Not that I've been stressed or anything. Sitting knee to knee with strangers playing the vocabulary-response game ('candle' 'sex' 'mud' 'sex' 'mother' 'sex' 'sex' 'money') is something I do every day of the week, let me tell you. The lights on the motorway flick past as I smoke, faces looming behind windows and lost behind us. Though the air on my face is freezing, I'm pleasantly warm wrapped in my layers, knees against the dashboard, the roar of the engine fading into the back of my consciousness. I lean my head against the window and stare at the white lines rushing towards me. And before I know it, my eyes are closed and I'm dreaming that I'm in the ice hotel in Finland and Ben has got inside my sleeping-bag so we can keep each other warm.

'Cold,' says Ben, and I say, 'Not now you're here.' And he puts his arms round me, snuggles in closer. And as he does, I realize that the smell of Ben, a warm, haybarn smell with musky overtones, so familiar that I've hardly noticed it lately, is my favourite smell in the world, that lying with my nose pressed against the side of his neck is my favourite place. So I tell him so, and he says 'I know,' and I say 'Mmm' and slip one of my legs between his, which makes me feel a bit fruity, so I press up closer, at which he smiles and puts his hand on my breast. Somewhere in the next room, Donna is holding forth. 'It's not going to stay like this,' she says. 'I mean, I know life has a way of jolting people out of situations, but I'm not going to sit around and wait for that to happen any more.' Meanwhile Ben is stroking my face with icy fingers and kissing me, very very gently, on the lips, and I'm enjoying it enormously.

And then he goes, 'So what are you going to do?' and I open my eyes and realize that it's not Ben any longer, but Carey, and I open my eyes properly and stare dazedly out through the windscreen, then over at my two companions. I wonder if I look as guilty as I feel: wonder if they know I've just been having an erotic dream about my best friend. A road sign for Heathrow Terminal Four flashes out of the darkness: I must have been asleep for an hour or so, not a few minutes. God, I hope I didn't make any noises. Donna is yelling over the howl of the engine, which seems to find 75 miles an hour an unbearable burden to carry.

'That's why it's been such a great weekend. I've had so much time to think about stuff.' She twiddles a plait. 'You know how you get into that state where you're just generally miserable and you can't see what the details are any more? Well, I think I've got an idea now. You know all that mother stuff?'

Carey pulls a wry face. 'Well,' says Donna, 'I spent all this time listening to other people go on about their stuff, and then I realized that I don't actually have much stuff to go on about.'

'Mmm,' says Carey, and I get the feeling that the reverse might have happened to him.

'But you know what?' Donna continues. 'What I really hate is my job. It drains my energy, it depresses me, it turns me into a person I don't like being.'

'What sort of person is that?' asks Carey mildly.

'A small-time civil servant, man,' she says, and does that sucky thing with her teeth. 'I wasn't meant to be one of those. I used to spend my time in nightclubs, I used to sing, I used to be fun, and now I sit behind a desk and go, 'No, you can't have a house, you've not been waiting long enough.'

'So,' says Carey again, 'what are you gong to do about it?'

Donna slaps the back of the seat. 'I'm going in tomorrow and resigning.'

'Donna!' I shout.

'Don't start.'

'And *then* what are you going to do?'

'I don't know,' she shouts, 'but I don't really care either. I can get a job in a shop or something while I think. Work up the West End, at least be around people who are there for pleasure, not torture. That doesn't matter so much, as long as I'm not doing what I'm doing now.'

'Donna, you're the only person in our house who *has* a job.'

'So that's a reason? You all get by one way or another. I will too.'

Carey breaks in. 'I think it's great. I wish I'd wasted less of my life doing the right thing before I started being what I wanted.'

'Thanks,' says Donna. 'At least someone's supporting me.'

'What did you used to be?' I ask at the same time.

'An accountant,' says Carey, 'in the City. Suits, sandwiches and champagne after work. I'm much happier now.'

We reach the Hammersmith flyover and turn down the Fulham Palace Road. 'Where shall I drop you?' asks Carey. 'Parsons Green do you?'

'God, I'm working up here tomorrow.' The grim London reality bites back with the mention of the name. 'I might as well go and kip down under the arches and save the tube fare. And babe,' I look back at Donna, 'I don't not support you. I think you're great.'

'Good,' says Donna. 'I think you're great too, even if you can't dance.'

Fulham is revoltingly crowded. The Pitcher and Piano is full of women with the kind of haircuts people get when they're depressed, chatting up men in yellow pullovers.

'Ever been in there?' I ask Carey.

'Yes. I go in every time I go to a fireplace shop and upgrade my mantelpieces, cheeky monkey. I suppose you go all the time, look for a nice clean chap to make your future with.'

'No.'

'So where do you like to go, then?'

'I'm not bothered. I like to experiment.'

'Oh, OK,' he says. 'So do you fancy going to some experiment with me sometime?'

Caught off guard, I gulp, while Donna sits back in her seat and grins.

'OK,' I say, 'sure.'

'Good,' he says, digs in his top pocket and hands me a card. Thinking that maybe I can get out of it this way, I apologize for not having a pen.

'Doesn't matter. I've got a perfect memory for numbers.' Meekly, I tell him as he pulls up outside the tube.

'Well,' says Donna as we take the stairs two at a time, 'I didn't know you'd got into the older man.'

'Shove it,' I reply, and she laughs up the empty platform.

Chapter Forty-three

Parsons Green

You get so dazed doing little but type all day that you have to have the odd displacement activity or you turn into one of those crazed, burbling people you see queuing to get into Planet Hollywood. So, to keep up with Donna's new-found drive, I've decided to dedicate myself to academic study. I am working on two theses at the moment: the one outlined below will, I hope, win me the Nobel Prize for medicine.

Well, OK, not the Nobel Prize, but a pat on the back, at least, for my contribution to the well-being of the nation. For, as we all know, the Government is concerned about levels of obesity in the population and our general levels of unfitness. This is, of course, directly related to the amount of television each of us consumes in a week, but, as the entire advertising industry depends on television and people watching it, and the entire Government depends on the advertising industry, it has been deemed appropriate to refer to this factor as 'increasingly sedentary lifestyles'. Thus our office-bound lives are being blamed for our ills and, unless we can turn things around, we are in increasing danger of becoming like the Chinese, forced to take part in dawn robotics in paved-over open spaces.

But wait! Before you waste hundreds of pounds on

membership of a gym that you will attend five times in the first week, then pull something, have to spend three weeks recuperating and somehow never find the time to go again, look at the exercise opportunities about you! While it's possible to pass an entire day at work without doing more than walk to and from the lift, your office can be your own home-gym opportunity. For your health and that of the nation, we present the *Temporary Guide to Office Gymnastics*:

• File, but inefficiently. Place all papers on the floor, close drawers after each paper has found its home. And bend! And lift! And bend! And lift!

• Remember that it is essential to drink at least two litres of water per day. By doing so with only the help of tiny paper cones, you can add almost a quarter of a mile to your daily walking schedule simply going from desk to cooler.

• Shouting at underlings is excellent aerobic exercise.

• Run everywhere. This exercise has the added advantage of making you look important!

• Do your own photocopying. Clearing paper jams is terrific for thigh and bum muscles; swearing forcibly every time a light comes on exercises lung-power; when things are going right, you can practise the ancient t'ai chi exercise of Standing Still Staring into Space while Drumming Fingers.

• Encourage an office policy of meanness with stationery. Allow the key to the stationery stores to only one person, preferably the one who has to be away from their desk most often. Searching in your own and, afterwards, your colleagues' bottom drawers for Post-it notes, pencils, compliments slips, etc. stretches back muscles, thigh muscles and arm muscles and acts as an excellent warm-up for going in search of the stationery supervisor.

- Remember: thinking burns calories. If your day-to-day tasks don't require thinking, take it up. You'll be svelte in no time.
- Tummy tucks: get under your desk to fiddle with wiring to computer, telephone, fax, modem, lighting, etc. Lie on back, feet flat on the ground, knees in the air. And up!
- Institute a smoking ban. Then take up smoking in order to afford yourself the opportunity to take a walk down to the front steps every hour on the hour. This is a particularly effective exercise, as not only does it allow you to catch up on gossip/network with your superiors, but it is an ideal opportunity to get a breath of fresh air.
- Several hours playing Solitaire/Minesweeper/Tetris on screen each day builds strength in index finger and thumb.
- Volunteer to take responsibility for watering the office plants. Walking about the place with a watering-can is excellent low-impact muscle-building.
- Have an affair. That time spent locked around each other in cramped environments like the stationery cupboard will help maintain flexibility in your joints.
- Pen-chewing builds a sturdy jaw.
- Try this change of position every ten minutes: feet-on-desk, feet-off-desk; if performed with straight legs at all times, this will tighten those tummy muscles and give you a six-pack like Ulrika out of *Gladiators*.
- Swivelling in chairs is good for your balance. If your chair has arms, raise yourself from the seat using them from time to time; relieves aching backs. Exercise calf muscles by walking over to your colleague's desk without removing your bum from your seat.
- Commute by public transport during rush hour.

Standing up in a moving confined space for an hour or more at a go is the equivalent of a full week with electrodes strapped to your abs.

• If all else fails, neglect to meet your deadlines. You will spend so much time running away from your boss that you will burn off an extra Mars bar every afternoon.

Chapter Forty-four

Ealing Broadway

Funnily enough, I've gone from grumbling about the fact that the house is never empty to worrying about burglars. Fortunately, because Ben's film is a Britfilm, all the locations are in Docklands, where up-and-coming directors like to make their mark. So though he's been out of the house for the last four weeks, he still comes home at night – chauffeur-driven, no less – and I get the feel of him about the place even though we see each other rarely. He's rushed in and out of the bathroom and been picked up before my alarm goes off. Donna, good as her word, resigned on the Monday after we got back from the seminar, and is now working in Sandro's, a haughty handbag shop – it calls itself a purveyor of fine luggage – on Bond Street. And even Craig has finally shifted himself, and is lecturing part-time down in Brighton, where they seem to need loads of part-time lecturers. And me, I'm back where I always was, though I decided, after Carey's lecture, that I was at least going to stop resenting my position and make the best of it that I could. In the meantime I'm ploughing ahead with my second thesis, which I have a sneaking feeling might make the basis of a million-selling airport book. I call it *The Secret Life of Desks*.

You learn a lot about people from their desks. In the alien

world of the office, the desk is a little extension of home, a place on which you can stamp your identity. People rely on these mementos of their individuality to give them the sense of security essential to handling stress, keeping their tempers, generally getting through the day. If a man's home is his castle, then his desk is, at the very least, the bathing hut he rents down by the seaside in case he ever has a chance to get away for the weekend. I think about this a lot, because I am one of those people who don't have a desk to call their own.

Seems to me that firms who want to stamp their corporate identity on their employees by imposing rules about these things are not only run by people who are in serious need of counselling, but are making a big mistake. I've come across countless clean-desk policies, where nothing unrelated to the job in hand is allowed on a surface, and everything has to be tidied away at the end of the day. I've come across a dreadful thing called Hot Desking, where no-one has a place to call home, a place to keep their bits of paper, their pens, pencils, novelty mouse mats: it's meant, or so I hear, to keep people on their toes, keep them flexible; what it actually does is ensure that no-one ever answers a telephone ringing beside them because they can practically guarantee that it won't be *for* them. If you have ever had trouble getting through to an individual at a company, don't blame the individual, blame the management: the person you're looking for is probably sitting somewhere in the post room because it's the only free table space in the building. I've come across rules only allowing people to use corporate stationery, rules about hanging coats in designated areas, rules about personal phone calls, even rules about eating and drinking *in situ*, but the clean-desk policy has to be the most pernicious of all the experimental work practices of the Nineties.

For a start, an observant manager could learn far more about his employees by allowing them free rein over their desks. Sometimes I get the impression that everyone believes their desk to be shielded by a force field that induces negative hallucinations on the outside world. A negative hallucination is one in which you fail to see something that is there: you have probably had them zillions of times looking for your house keys. If your desk is your castle, then it's the place where you show your true personality. The outside of the desk is like the outside of your house, and maybe the living-room; it's where the stuff for show is kept, our Freudian self-expression.

Hence the photographs of toothless children scattered across the country. Have you ever noticed how many more photos of children than of partners there are on desks? Is this simply a reflection of the single-parent Nineties, or something deeper? I think maybe that our love for children is something we feel able to display more readily to the outside world than the dark complexity of adult relationships. And maybe, while our children are automatically beautiful to us, our partners are a reflection, not only of our taste but, given that the majority of people cleave to those of roughly similar attractiveness, our pulling power. You may love your man to death, but do you want to subject his astigmatism and his taste in nylon shirts to the gaze of strangers? Partners live in wallets and drawers, the bedrooms of the desk.

Matching, black-moulded-plastic desk-organizer and pen pot? 'I see myself as an innovator but actually I buy things from catalogues.' Potted plant? 'I have an eye for beauty and care about my environment.' Dead potted plant? 'I've lost interest in being here.' Magnetic desk ornament? 'No-one knows what to buy me for Christmas.'

Huge pile of seemingly random bits of paper? 'I am, oddly enough, a control freak, and want to make sure that any absence on my part causes serious problems for anyone trying to fill my shoes.' (This can also mean that the office produces too much paper.) Everything labelled and regimented in its proper place? 'I am afraid that I lack control and have to be seen to impose it lest everything collapses around me.' Cute/quirky toy? 'I do have a life outside here, you know.' I've still not sussed out what rubber-band balls (and remember that the person who makes a rubber-band ball gets very angry when anyone takes one of its components to use as a rubber band) or twelve-foot strings of paper-clips mean, but I'm working on it.

But remember this: while the exterior of your domain gives one lot of messages about you, the interior says much, much more. If your desk is your home, then I, out of the necessity of hunting phone lists, computer instructions and so forth, am a burglar. In the same way that burglars constantly enter houses with the key from the back-door lintel, I almost invariably let myself into your desk by up-ending the pen-holder on top. Ninety per cent of keys hidden in women's pen-holders, even in those of the thoroughly post-menopausal, are neatly lodged under a single tampon. Which, given men's squeamishness about such matters, is a brilliant way of stopping them fishing in your drawers.

For if your desk is your home and the exterior is the living-room, then the interior is the bedroom and bathroom combined, the places where we are seen in our awful nakedness. While most people, however chaotic, can contrive to keep their public room, if not tidy, at least quickly mendable in case of unexpected visits from the vicar, the bedroom is where the true personality shows through. You rarely, after all, see discarded underwear on living-room floors.

I feel a twinge every time I have to pick the lock on a desk to get at the contents. You know how people talk when they've been burgled: 'It's not so much the money, it's the thought of some stranger going through my stuff. I feel as though I've been violated.' Every time a drawer slides open under my hand I invade a space that should be sacrosanct. I get a twinge, yes, but it's usually followed by the adrenaline rush of discovery. You know so little about what you have walked into when you arrive to take someone's place, and, because temps often find that their colleagues' attitudes to them are affected by their attitude to the person the temp is replacing, it's worth being prepared.

You can't always tell, of course. Loads of make-up in the top drawer doesn't necessarily mean that the owner goes out a lot. It could as easily mean that the office is the only social life she has. I once came across a pile of cosmetics, heavy on the sky-blue creme eye-shadow, in a man's desk, and am still unsure what to make of it, but then I spent a whole week in January hugging the knowledge that the PA who was off with flu had a black rubber mask with zipper mouth in her bottom drawer, only to find that the staff Christmas party had been a fancy-dress bash in the London Dungeon.

But these dark, secret places behind the Post-it notes hold life stories. Take Tina, whom I met for about an hour on Friday when she showed me the basics of her job: twenty-six, draped in jumpers, slightly reddened skin and those pale eyelashes that make the owner look permanently tearful. Tina had a cold, which she dealt with

with the help of a Kleenex stuffed into her cuff. The outside of Tina's desk is a model of secretarial efficiency: box files neatly propped between Perspex book-ends, a pen pot in which all the pens still have their tops, audio wires held down beneath a plastic strip, the first Roladex I've ever seen which still has its lid, pink-haired gonk Blu-Tacked to the top of the computer, flower-patterned mouse mat.

But, oh, the life beneath the surface. In these dentally conscious days, about 50 per cent of top drawers contain a toothbrush. Tina's contains toothbrush, mouthwash, three half-used tubes of Clorets, deodorant, bottle of antiseptic handwash, handi-wipes, four unopened pocket-packs of tissues, bottle of Clearasil, bottle of eyedrops, bottles of vitamin B-complex, vitamin C, calcium, ginseng, cod-liver oil, iron and extra-strong multivitamins, giant-sized tub of E45 cream. Tucked safely in a leather pouch is a diptych of a nervous-looking young man in an anorak.

The middle drawer gets a bit weirder: it often seems to hold that the lower the drawer, the more bizarre the contents. Tina's middle drawer contains one three-pack of 30-denier tights, American Tan, and a shoebox. In the shoebox is a collection of small change. I counted the coins in the lunch-hour, and they came to nearly £17. Perhaps she's saving for a treat. And later, I dipped down to open the bottom drawer, that really deep one made for hanging files, and started back in amazement. It was completely full of chocolate wrappers: Kit Kats, Lion Bars, Double Deckers, Toffee Crunches, Snickers, Mars bars, Fruit and Nut, Minstrels, Revels, not folded neatly as is her way, but crammed in as though the eater had done it in a hurry to hide her shame. There were so many they burst from the drawer and tried to make a break for freedom. And hidden at the back, a large-size bottle of senna tablets. Looking at them, I felt more than ever like a burglar, or a tabloid journalist, intruding on a secret misery and revealing it, if only for a moment, to the world's damnation. I slammed the drawer to and went back to my typing, wondering if my guilt showed on my face.

Chapter Forty-five

Can I Help You?

Fortunately, you never stay in Ealing for long; firms in Ealing always think they can get away with getting someone in for half the time that the person they're replacing is off for. So before I really have time to polish the *Secret Life*, Tracie has sent me to Soho, which gives me the opportunity to take lunch for a change, and drop in to see Donna in her handbag shop. It's nice when you get a job in the West End, as there is some point in bothering with lunch. I've practically given up doing lunch anywhere else, as there are few experiences more enervating than wandering through unfamiliar streets looking for somewhere to grab a meal. When I'm older, I'm going to set up a business producing employee-orientation packages for companies: something that says all the important stuff that no-one ever remembers, like who is what, what the company does (you'd be amazed how many permanent employees are vague about this when you get into the basements of large firms), how the computer and telephone systems work, where the loos are, who has first-aid skills, and which way to turn out of the building to find the shops. Because you can guarantee one thing about leaving a building in an area you don't know: whichever way you need to go, it's the opposite of the one that looks most likely.

Sandro's Bespoke Luggage is about halfway down New Bond Street, past the shops at the Oxford Street end where all the black kids go to buy Versace shirts with wads of cash on a Saturday, and before the bit where you can buy a Louis XVI armoire if you've got £65,000 in your pocket. Sandro's windows are almost entirely painted over, save for three letter-box-sized apertures which, if you look through them, open onto white-painted wooden boxes in which single handbags – brown in one, black in the other and a mulberry-coloured bandbox in the third – rest. There are no price labels. If you need to ask the price, you shouldn't be shopping at Sandro's. Someone invented this idea in the greedy, show-off 1980s – probably someone in retail, fed up with Old Money's habit of checking their outgoings at all opportunities – and some people still believe in it today.

I press the doorbell and, either because Donna's on door duty or because I'm looking, at least from a distance, pretty smart, gain admission. The interior is dark, and lit in pools by halogen spots playing over the burnished leather of the holy bags. My eyes adjusting gradually to the gloom, I see three figures behind a counter, two of them looking at me balefully as they descry that they're not going to be walking off with a big commission, and Donna, who is standing behind them, smiling secretly at me. I smile back, but in that polite, 'I don't know you' way. Walk over to a pyramid of purses and start examining them as Donna's colleagues register their opinion.

Donna approaches. 'Can I help you, madam?'

'Yes,' I say in my most strident tones, 'I was looking for something that will take all my credit cards. I've been looking for weeks now, and I can't find anything with more than six card slots in it. Do you have anything?'

'Ooh,' says Donna, 'let's see if we can help.' She starts to sort through the pile, flipping one over accidentally so that I see its price label. £54.00. I almost turn into my mother, shrieking, 'Fifty-four pounds for a *purse*?' but suppress the urge for her sake.

'Lunch?' hisses Donna.

'You got time?'

'Give me five minutes.' She raises her voice a decibel or two. 'How about this one, madam? As you can see, it has a fold-out section for credit cards.'

I take the proffered goods, read the label. £82.00. 'Yes, but it still only takes eight. Haven't you got *anything* else? Where?' I whisper immediately after.

'Have you thought about our personal organizers? Round the corner, by that place with the bogus Polish aristocrat's name where Marina buys her skin cream. They have plenty of space for business cards, which I'm sure would do just as well for credit cards.'

'No.' I start to back away towards the door. 'Thank you anyway, but I wanted a purse. A purse, not a Filofax.'

'Certainly,' says Donna. 'Have a good day.'

'Thank you,' I fling over my shoulder, and start, also, to thank the woman who has stalked forward to open the door for me.

She stops me in my tracks by growling imperiously, 'Were you ever intending to buy anything when you came in here?'

'What?' I start to protest, realize she's being deliberately offensive, and say, 'Well, I was, until I saw that all you stock is overpriced tourist tat,' and scarper.

Five minutes later, Donna finds me among the Countess's patent anti-wrinkle creams and we repair to the sandwich shop.

'Ooh, you've got a cheek on you,' she says.

'I have? I've never had anyone be so rude to me in my life. Are they always like that?'

'Oh, no. They can grovel like jackals if they smell money coming in. You should have seen them all over Princess Diana's stepmum the other morning. If she'd had boots on they'd've been licking the dirt off them.'

'What did she buy?'

'Nothing. Thing is, I think that people who work in places like Sandro's get to feel after a while that they have somehow got glamour by association or something. Mmm. I think I'm going to have peanut butter and bacon. I feel like a treat.'

I let this pass. 'So they feel that because they sell things to posh people, they're posh too?'

'I think so. Something like that. Jackie, our manageress, actually talks about half the celebs in the papers by their first names because she's sold them money belts.'

'And you prefer this to your old job?'

Donna nods enthusiastically. 'Loads. It's hilarious. I'm getting all the copy I could ever need for my book, you know. *Retail Anthropology: How to Intimidate the Shopper* by Donna Brown. You should see them all hanging around behind the desk sizing people up when they come in. I'm amazed they sell anything at all, except, of course, that lots of people have such low self-esteem they wouldn't dream of buying things from anywhere that *didn't* make them feel like worms. And honestly, you get really interesting people coming in.'

'Yeah, but it's not like you get to talk to any of them properly or anything.'

'On the contrary,' she collects her greaseproof bag from the counter, hands over the money, and we go to the little Formica bar hanging off the wall to eat. 'I got asked out on a date today.'

'What? Who by?'

'Mark Henley.'

'Who?'

She hands me a business card. Crichton, Francis and Fraser, Chartered Accountants. Mark Henley, Personal Taxation Consultant, it says.

'An accountant?'

'He's more than that.' Donna bites into her sandwich, chews and rolls her eyes with pleasure. 'He does the stuff for loads of famous people. And he's really good-looking. Dresses like a dream.'

'Donna, you're not going to go out with some bloke who picked you up in a shop?'

'Yes,' she says. 'I think I will. He was really funny and flirty, and he spent more than £500 on luggage, so he's obviously not doing badly. Anyway, I think I ought to. I swore after the Forum that I'd say yes to new experiences that came my way. We're always writing people off because of what they do, and I think it's a really bad habit.

'Anyway,' she continues, 'you're a fine one to talk, going out three times in the last month with some old bloke you picked up at a conference.'

'Oh, now, look,' I protest, but Donna smirks like the cow she is. 'No, look, this is a completely different thing. Carey and I are friends and I've learned a lot from knowing him.'

Donna smirks again.

'No, seriously, Donna.'

'He seems very keen for a friend. Always turning up with bottles of stuff and leaving messages for you.'

'Well, yes. I found it disconcerting myself to start with, but honestly, it's not like that: he's just the sort of person who decides he likes someone and doesn't have any inhibitions about showing it. Anyway, there's one big difference. I don't fancy Carey and never could. You, meanwhile, have evil intent written all over your face.'

'Well, not on the first date,' she says, then laughs. 'I've given up doing that. But I wouldn't be a bit surprised if something weren't to come of this. He's really – ooh,' she does a little shimmy on her bar stool.

Mark Henley. Doesn't sound like my sort of name. Sounds a bit like some oily bloke from Epping. But then, Donna's right about my record for rejecting people for pathetic reasons. I'm the worst culprit of the lot. I once turned down a date with the sweetest guy you could ever meet purely because he had one of those voices that sound like adenoids.

'So when are you going?'

'Thursday next week. He says he's going to take me out on the town and we're going to do the works,' she says proudly.

'Eeugh. He'll probably make you go to Stringfellows and everything.'

She slaps me on the wrist. 'You are such a snob you'll end up living all by yourself with a cat in a one-room flat in Chelsea.'

'Hey, aren't we supposed to be going to that launch thing with Ben on Thursday?'

Donna sighs. 'I think Ben will let me off. This is the first time any of us has been out on a Big Date in all the time we've been living together.'

She dabs her lips with a paper napkin, screws it up and puts it in the ashtray just to annoy me. 'I can't wait, I tell you. I bet you anything Mark Henley's going to have a big influence on my life.'

Chapter Forty-six

Under Cover

After our third night in the fleshpots of Old Compton Street, I go round to Carey's for dinner. 'There probably won't be many of us,' he says, 'and I'm crap at balancing tables, but it should be fun. There are a couple of people I know you'll like. Come between eight and nine.'

So on a Monday night I pull on my cleavage, brush out my hair, paint my lips an alluring fuchsia and find that I am, in fact, the only woman in a roomful of men. And one of them is Byron.

Fortunately, he doesn't recognize me. Women look different in and out of work and no-one notices temps anyway, but I recognize him immediately despite the fact that his hair is gelled, his voice has softened and he's wearing a torso-hugging lumberjack shirt with no sleeves. Blimey. You never would have guessed it at work.

Byron smiles, bypasses the handshake and kisses me on both cheeks, presses a drink into my hand – he's obviously at ease in Carey's house, a long-term fixture – and makes some appreciative comment about my dress. 'Carey's been going on about you ever since he went navel-gazing,' he says. 'It's lovely to meet you at last.'

I am stunned speechless. I worked for two weeks for Byron and I don't think we exchanged more than fifty words. He would slouch into my room, plop things in the in-tray and mumble thanks when I brought them back. His colleagues were much more communicative, and even learned my name before the time was up. It wasn't a bad place to work, but Byron displayed all the symptoms of a major attitude problem. In fact I had him down for a major tosser, an example of why it's so wrong that testosterone rules the world.

So here is my eye-opener. In the office Byron was the hyper-lad, talking more about sport than anyone else, spending less time on his appearance than anyone else, loaded up with more gadgetry than anyone else, more prone to 'I told you not to call me at work' calls than anyone else. I remember him clearly, in fact, because he annoyed me so much. I was convinced that his demeanour toward me was related to one-of-the-boys-ishness. Women are always getting wound up by a certain kind of man's refusal to see them as individuals, and Byron gave the impression of being exactly the type to talk about breasts while standing at a pub urinal. Now it turns out that he's one of a completely different type of boy.

'So how do you know Carey?' I ask.

'We met down the Two Brewers about four years ago.' He laughs. 'Carey spilt beer down my back. Still swears it was an accident.' Carey grins and looks sheepish, brings out a bowl of cheese and onion Pringles and something yoghurty. 'Anyway,' continues Byron, 'he bought me a drink to say sorry and we've been friends ever since.'

The doorbell rings and someone called Darryl puts in an appearance, waving flowers and kisses about the room. Sweeps me into his arms along with everyone else, spots Byron. We mill around, rearranging ourselves on the sofas and freshening drinks. Once everyone's settled, in the lull before Carey has to go and fiddle with bits of rocket in the kitchen, Darryl says, 'So, Byron, how's the new job, then? Looks like it's suiting you.'

It's true, as well; Byron has lost at least a stone since last I saw him, and is as brown as a berry. He treats us to a sunny grin. 'Oh, God,' he says, 'it's wonderful. And such a relief.'

'I bet,' says Darryl.

'What do you mean?' I ask. Byron sips his drink.

'I had this really awkward situation in the last place,' he informs me, 'nobody knew I was gay.'

You're telling me, I think. 'D'you mean there would have been a problem?'

'D'you know, that's the stupid thing,' says Byron. 'I have absolutely no idea. It could have been perfectly all right for all I know, but after I failed to grasp the nettle in the first few months, it just got to be a pattern, and before I knew it, I was too scared to let on. I mean, everyone else there was straight, and you just don't know.'

Darryl huffs. 'Well, you should have just told them, shouldn't you?'

Carey says, 'Come on, Darryl, you know it's more complicated than that,' and Darryl, who works in hotels, launches into a rant about everyone who stays in the closet making it more difficult for everyone else.

'Look,' says Byron, 'I know we've disagreed on this before, but you've got to remember that half the people in the hotel industry are queer, so it's hardly comparable, and anyway I'm not as shameless as you. I turned up there as just another man in a suit and you know how straight guys are when they think they're in straight company, however liberal they are on the surface. A couple of backs-to-the-wall gags and I just couldn't go through with it. You know what the Professions are like. They still don't promote women because they think they'll have babies, and they still don't promote us because they think we're hysterics. I didn't make the rules, Darryl.'

'Yeah,' says Darryl, 'but that doesn't mean that the rules shouldn't be broken if they're unfair rules. So because you're too scared to challenge a load of bigots, you spent five years behaving like a schizophrenic and driving the rest of us bananas. When I think of all those stand-up-and-beg cocktail parties you used to have where we were all under orders to behave in case any of your colleagues found out . . .'

'Yes, well,' says Byron, 'it's sorted now. You can stop going on about it, though I don't suppose many of the people I work with will quite know what to do when they're confronted with a screaming old queen like you all done up in make-up and banging on about poppers.'

'So what did you do about the new job?' I ask.

'Oh,' says Byron, settling back, 'I decided to tell them upfront in my interview. I was terrified, of course, but I just took a deep breath and told them about the work I do at the Lighthouse and how I have to be available for that. And then I said that I did it because I felt that I ought to put something back into my community, and let it sink in. And you know what? There was a little pause, and then they said, "OK, that's fine. We always try to help our employees if they're trying to make a contribution to the world outside work." In fact someone actually came and talked to me about putting the Lighthouse on their list of charitable donations this year. You'd never believe it, would you? Mind you, there's probably dozens of closet queens hidden under those suits, paying people to spank them at weekends. Anyway,' he turns to me and changes the subject, 'tell me about yourself. I'm sure I've seen you somewhere before, but I can't think where.'

Chapter Forty-seven

No Biz Like Showbiz

'Oh, Lord,' says Ben as we peer through the smart basement gloom, 'same old face-lifts.'

Craig's already moaning because the only free drink at the bar seems to be vodka and Red Bull. 'They won't even give them me in separate glasses,' he says. I ask him if the red wine is also part of the charge bar. 'Oh, sorry,' he says, 'I forgot about the red wine.'

'Thanks, mate.'

I almost feel jealous of Donna, off on her Big Date with her flirty accountant. She was on top form as she left the house this evening in her red spray-on dress, all rolling eyes and giggles. In contrast, not a person near me has yet cracked a smile; everyone is concentrating on sucking in their cheekbones in case someone famous should stand near them. Of course, they won't. Famous people send their non-famous friends to the bar for them. Famous people sit in roped-off alcoves and get whatever drink they fancy brought to them free on a tray. Famous people don't brace themselves against counters swimming with spilled drink and try to catch someone's eye. Famous people don't get ignored by female barstaff in favour of a bloke in a shiny suit who arrived a minute ago. Ben doesn't have automatic behind-rope status these days; the world of celebrity closes its doors fast and hard behind the fallen. Everyone is haunted by the spectre of Afterwards, and they don't want to look it full in the face. But the news that he's making a film has leaked out, and, just in case, someone's sent him an invitation to attend with hoi polloi.

Craig and I are Ben's little acolytes at this glamorous showbiz party to celebrate another successful year of the People's Awards. 400 of the industry's finest A&R men, PRs, hacks (you can spot them by their black leather jackets and glum expressions), gossips, liggers and hangers-on, leering around to see themselves mixing with stardom, ex-stardom, hopeful stardom and invented stardom. Ghastly, but us hangers-on can't let down our ex-stars. And anyway, it's free. And on top of that, however much I try to pretend I'm not a sad person, I get a sneering, creepy pleasure from sitting there feeling superior in my silent typing corner listening to other people talk about their nights out at TGI Friday. Maybe this is why everybody here goes to parties like this. I can't believe they do it for pleasure.

The three of us spread out into the banks of people queuing. Ben is looking down impassively at a young woman in bright red lipstick who is telling him something. He nods, then shakes his head, then grins, then frowns. She's recognized him then, he's not in a band any more, he was her favourite Thing and she had thought he was either dead or in rehab. The bloke next to me slides his arms through a gap and heaves himself forward, bouncing me backwards a couple of inches at the same time. Bugger. You can't afford to miss a trick.

Then, over the bobbing heads, I spot that the bar is actually square, and that on a dais at what I thought was the back a single man is receiving an armful of drinks. Everyone around me is too intent on staring blankly into the air and composing their features to see beyond the ends of their noses. That's what you get for wearing plain glass specs instead of getting your eyes checked. I start to back up, trip over the bottom of the steps, cannon into three fiftysomething men in bomber jackets and tinted glasses. They flick their pony-tails and ignore me.

On the steps, I recognize Bad Attitude, this year's shaven-headed rapper boys. They wear inflatable anoraks, dark glasses and those trainers with lights built in, like your nephew wears, and are snarling at a man with a tape recorder.

'It's not a question,' says a youth with a medallion that looks like it's been nicked from a bathroom accessories shop, 'of whether we won or lost. The fans know the troof, and we don't care what some fucking *old man* –' he glares at the men in bomber jackets ' – tink.' I wonder what his mum would think of his diction. Guess she probably accepts it, because she knows that to be a pop star you've got to not talk proper.

'What are you working on now?' asks the tape recorder.

'Dub remix of "Downtown". An old Sixties track done by some chick. Givin' it a contemporary feel, mashin' it up hard. 'Cos it's, like, you can't just stay wiv how somefin' was 'cos it's, like, a *classic*, kna'am sane?' I attempt to squeeze past. One of the boyz, clutching the tea cosy on his head, frowns over his shoulder. I do one of those little jiggly apologetic grins you see women doing when someone carves them up in traffic, and he turns back, satisfied.

On the top platform I slot my elbows in beside those of a chisel-handsome chap in a dark suit and yellow tie. We roll our eyes at each other.

'Tell you what,' I say, 'why don't we team up? First one to catch an eye orders for both?'

He wobbles his head, agrees. 'Hell, isn't it?'

'Mmm.' I'm dividing my time between trying to catch Ben's eye, trying to catch Craig's eye, peering into the gloom in the background to see if there's anyone I know here, and trying to assume the sort of friendly drag-queen look that can draw the attention of a group of gay waiters.

'I don't know why I come to these things,' continues suitman. 'They're always dreadful. Full of people on the lam, ordering four drinks each in case the freebies run out.'

'Mmm.' Craig finally meets my eye, slaps his forehead and fights his way towards us.

'People in London are so greedy,' says the suit. 'Don't seem to understand that if they over-order it runs out faster. What are you doing here? In the business?'

Oh, God, a party bore. He's going to tell me how to cope, now. 'Er, no,' I say. 'Came with a mate.'

'Of course,' he continues, 'you never get to meet the *big* names. They're all off at private do's or walled off in the VIP bit.'

'Mmm.' Ben is at the front now, is leaning on the bar, forearms stretched ahead of him. A barman glances up, our eyes meet, I waggle my eyebrows. He holds up a finger. That's either one minute, or fuck off. I guess I'll find out which. He opens two cans and runs them along a row of glasses, spilling most of the contents on the bar.

Craig arrives. Gets attention within seconds, and gathers three glasses of red to his chest. Backs off and sits down on a highly carved wooden bench draped with coats. Winks at me. Starts drinking.

My barman approaches. Smiles at me, maybe because I'm the first person all evening to do the same to him.
'What can I get you?'

I look at my companion.

'Eight vodka and Red Bulls, four beers,' he says, then to me, 'I've got a couple of friends over there.'

'And three red wines,' I call as the barman rushes off.

Down in the main body of the club, round the dance floor where tiny girls in khakis and stage-school make-up practise their dance-class moves – two to the right, two to the left; right hand up, left hand up; shimmy right and *smile* – we wander through gaggles of people who converse by shouting into each other's ears, nodding and shouting into the next ear in line. This, of course, is how London gossip starts: someone says, 'I really like this track,' and it comes out, eight people later, as 'George Michael smokes crack.' Curtains hang across cushioned alcoves where little knots of people feel each other's implants and scrape the tiny tables with their credit cards.

We bump into Amir, the one who used to pull the sincere faces and pat his chest in the Wild Things. Amir is now a manager, putting more teenage boys on the road to ruin. 'Hey,' he says, clasping Ben by the forearm. Ruffles my hair, which he has done, irritatingly, since I was fifteen years old. 'How's it going?'

'Yeah, OK,' says Ben.

'Working?'

'Some,' says Ben, and the two of them share a quick silence for what used to be.

'Saw you on *Caught You Out!* the other night,' says Amir.

'Oh, aye?' says Ben.

'Sorry,' says Amir.

'Doesn't matter,' says Ben. 'It's money, isn't it? Anyway, I'm doing a film now. It's got two footballers in it.'

'Great,' shouts Amir, though he's obviously not really listening. 'Where are you sitting?'

'We've only just got here.'

'Oh, right.' Amir pauses for a moment, glances round in search of someone more useful. Behind me, a woman's voice is going, '. . . had the whole lot sucked out, my dear. Put some in his cheekbones, some in his forehead and the rest is pumping up his biceps.'

It's Candice Murray, universal unlucky star. Candice has left a trail of dead men behind her, and is featured constantly, bewitching in black, in *Hello!*, chronicling her recovery from her latest tragedy. 'Ben Cameron!' she cries, pats him on the shoulder, which coincidentally means that she can get her shoulder between him and me. 'What's happened to you? I thought you'd left the country until I saw you on *Caught You Out!* the other night!'

Craig and I are edged out, as always happens when show-biz gets together. You're of them, or you're on the edge admiring: there's no middle ground. Craig puts down his first glass, starts on his second. I follow suit. Amir shuffles a bit, says, 'What are you up to these days?' and, when I tell him, glazes faster than an Everest salesman. 'Oh,' he says.

I sink my second drink in one. From the corner of my eye, I can see Ben doing the same as Candice Murray says, 'Why don't you get yourself a fiancé, dear? Lots of careers have been saved by a nice juicy link-up. I'm sure there's a Corr still available.' Ben shakes his head, tries to smile. Amir has sloped off; I can just see the back of his head, slipping behind a curtain and into a thick cloud of fragrant smoke.

I smile gamely at the white anorak and velvet hat standing next to me. He looks alarmed, edges closer to the group of white anoraks he came with. Craig clashes his final drink against mine. We lock elbows, and slam them down in a couple of gulps. It's going to be a long night.

★

234

4 a.m., and we're lying on top of each other in the living-room. Ben's on the brown spirits and Craig is spliffing up. Me, I'm helping them out with both.

'Shouldn't you go to bed?' Ben says, pouring me a couple of inches of Lagavullen. 'Aren't you working tomorrow?'

'Naah,' I say, 'fuck it. Who cares? I'm having fun now.' I passed the point of no return at around midnight; frenzy set in sometime around an hour ago. Now, the only thing I can think about is more drink.

'Water?' Ben waves a bottle at me. I shake my head, then take it from him and drink half of it down in a couple of gulps.

Craig hisses, then says in a teeny tiny voice, 'Ben?'

'Mmm?'

'Why do you want to hang with those people?'

'They're the people I know,' says Ben. 'They're the people I've hung with since I was sixteen.'

'But most of them won't even give you the time of day now.'

'Yes,' he says, 'but one day they'll want to again, and then I can refuse to talk to them.'

The front door closes quietly. 'Donna?' I call.

Steps pause outside the living-room door. 'Yes?'

'How'd it go?'

'Yes,' she says softly, 'OK.'

'Want a nightcap?'

'No. No thanks. I think I'm going to have a shower and go to bed.'

'OK. Night.'

'Night.'

'Well,' says Ben, 'she's been out long enough.'

'Urk, urk,' says Craig, 'he could at least have made her breakfast.'

I kick him.

'You know what?' says Ben, drains his glass and takes a sharp tug on Craig's spliff. 'I'm really looking forward to it.'

'What?'

'Looking right in that Murray bitch's face and turning away. I can't wait.'

The shower starts up upstairs.

'Ben,' says Craig, 'do you really think it's ever going to happen? I mean, seriously, haven't you had your fifteen minutes? I know you're in this film and everything, but it's small potatoes, isn't it? And they're only using you for the novelty value.'

'Have you ever thought that they might actually have cast me for my acting?'

'Look, man,' Craig replies, 'you used to be in a boy band. I know you were the Slightly Dangerous Bad Boy, but you were still in a boy band. That's what you'll always be now. You might as well go and train for something else while you can still pay for it.'

'No!' Ben snaps back. 'There isn't anything else I *could* do. Don't you understand? This is what I am now. I'm not going to be a retrospective in the Sunday papers. They showed me all that stuff, told me it was all mine, and they can't take it back. Do you understand?'

'Yes, but Ben, maybe you're just going to be trying and never getting anywhere. It could happen. In a few years you'll be a fortysomething, still hanging around on the fringes of showbiz, doing panto, looking pathetic.'

Ben sloshes more whisky into his glass, gollops it into his mouth. 'Thanks mate. It's the support of my friends that gets me through. So I should give up, huh? I should be grateful, go and buy a pub in Stafford and line the walls with gold discs? Go home and be a local celebrity, open fêtes and wait for the journalists to do the anniversaries? I'm twenty-three, for God's sake. Are you like everyone else, wanting me to slink off quietly now you can't boast about knowing me?'

He's on a roll now; the same roll he gets on every time he gets on the whisky. 'I'm the first person in my family to do anything,' he says. 'Anything. Tenant farmers, mechanics, gamekeepers and me. I can't forget about all that. When I was seventeen I could have any girl I wanted, drive any car I wanted, walk into any restaurant and get a seat, walk past the guest list at any nightclub. I had room service. I couldn't open my curtains in case I caused a riot in the street. Christ, my *mum* couldn't open the curtains in case she caused a riot in the street. Shops opened specially for me. Candice effing Murray used to *beg* for a chat. And you want me to forget about that? Walk away?'

He pauses. Takes another drink. Stares into the air. 'No way,' he says. 'No way.'

Craig, when drunk, is one of those folk who simply can't let a thing ride, has to worry away at it like a pug with a piece of manky old sheepskin. 'All I was saying was that I think—' he starts.

Ben swings his feet down from the sofa, stabs a finger through the air so that it stops, menacingly, an inch from Craig's face. 'I doon't wannae knoo fit ye thank!' he roars. 'Git yeersel' a job and than ye can have an opunion!'

I haven't heard him this broad since the last time he had his brother to stay and they argued about whether Ben had been the family favourite. Craig leans back, waving his palms across each other. 'All right, all right, man,' he croaks, 'there's no need to stain your britches. I was just expressing a legitimate—'

'Craig,' I say.

Craig's chin shoots up in the air. 'Well, Miss Typing Pool. You're hardly a—'

Ben slaps a thigh, stands unsteadily up. 'Ach, God, I'm gon'ae bed. I don't need to listen to this. Who needs muso parties to bring them down when they've got their friends, eh?' He departs, thumps up the stairs to his bedroom full of used underpants.

'Well,' says Craig, 'I'm just—'

'No, Craig.' I wobble to my feet. Somehow, in the course of this brief row, it seems to have become 4.30. I never understand how this happens, but it always does with whisky. 'I'm going to bed too. I've got to work in the *typing pool* tomorrow.'

'Woooh, touchy,' says Craig.

At which I very nearly slap him. Instead, I say, 'Well, it's better than just sitting around on my arse smoking dope all day,' and he says, 'Is that some sort of criticism?' and I say, 'Yes, it bloody is.'

So Craig says, 'What exactly do you mean?'

And I reply, 'Well, look, you're hardly doing yourself a lot of favours, are you?'

'What, and you are?'

'Well, at least I'm doing *something*.'

'It's all right for you,' says Craig. 'You're a girl. You can type.'

'Typing's not a gender ability, Craig. We've been through this a million times. You could type if you would only arse yourself.'

'I don't see,' he huffs, 'why I should do any old crappy job just in order to get money. I've got a degree.'

I can hear my voice rising to a shriek. 'And so have I, stupid. But I'm not blagging off the State, getting me to pay

238

for your upkeep, because I think I'm to grand to do anything less than edit the *Guardian*.'

'Hark at little Miss Thatcher.'

'No. Sod it, Craig. You've had a bloody good education paid for by the State. You should be able to work.'

'Yeah, right. Carting bits of old crap around hospitals, emptying bins, waiting tables. That's a great use for my education.'

'Well, it's a better use for it than the use you're making for it at the moment.'

'God,' he growls. 'I never thought the day would come when I heard you of all people talking like this. What would you like to do? Bring back the poorhouses? Shoot everyone who's been signing on for more than three months at a time? Sterilize single mothers? Tell you what, I've got a joining form for the Conservative party upstairs. Perhaps you'd like to take it? The party needs people like you.'

'Oh, go stuff yourself, Craig.'

He grins. I stumble in a rage up to my bedroom, fall out of my clothes, then have to go all the way down to the basement for a pee, as Donna seems still to be in the bathroom. While I'm in the kitchen, I scrape the mould off a lump of cheese that's probably been sitting in the fridge since Tania moved out, and toast it on a lump of fossilized bread. Take it to bed with me, in the absolute certainty that it will mean the difference between me and a hangover.

Chapter Forty-eight

Old Street

7 a.m.: Oh God, oh God. Oh God, oh God, oh God. Oh, no, oh God. I set the radio to the Country and Western station in the throes of my frenzy last night, and now Shania Twain is telling me that I'm still the one she runs to, the one that she belongs to. Which is not the news I want to hear after two and a half hours' sleep and a skinful of whisky. No, no, God, please, no. Not this again, not when I have a new job to go to.

I obviously didn't scrape the mould off that cheese too well, as it has formed a thick coat over the roof of my mouth and surface of my tongue. I seem to have lost the use of my limbs, panic for a moment, trying to remember if I had any falls last night, realize that my body has been pinned down while I slept by an army of Lilliputians. Decide to give up the fight. Think that if, maybe, I allow my mind to wander free for a couple of minutes, I will find an answer. Drift back into partial coma.

8 a.m.: Eyes spring open, feet hit floor. One of those sour headaches, like someone running their fingernails down a blackboard, grips the back of my skull, while someone thumps between my eyes with a rubber hammer. Go to bathroom, hammer on door, find out Donna's in there.

Obviously didn't get clean enough last night. Consider coffee, realize I've got 45 minutes to get across town. Scream at Donna, consider ditching bath, but remember that alcohol has a habit of seeping out through your pores after a heavy one. I can't go into a new workplace smelling of meths. Besides, the only way to get the mysterious black stuff out from where it's encrusted the underside of my fingernails is to wash my hair. Scream at Donna again.

8.30: No tights. Not entirely true. There are five pairs, but each has a large hole in the left calf from the corner of square metal bin under the desk at my last place of work. Maybe I can get away with a trouser suit. Maybe not. Crotches of both pairs of decent trousers smell decidedly manky. Oh, God . . . run to loo, crumple over it for a couple of minutes. Brush teeth again. Drink down two glasses of water, three ibuprofen. Back into room, pull on suit, button rips off shirt. Ohgodohgod.

8.40: Run to tube. Convinced that someone is following me with a hatchet, and the only reason I don't see him is because he ducks behind hedges when I look back. There is a high-pitched whine in my ears: sounds like a combination of radio static and Kylie Minogue singing 'Lucky Lucky Lucky'. My stomach cartwheels. Long for a sausage sandwich, but turning up to a new job and immediately pitching into breakfast is black mark central.

8.50: Newsagent has run out of tights. They don't even stock novelty ones with patterns on. Run down escalator, fling self at closing doors, miss. Conductor smiles and waves as train pulls out. Lean against the platform wall, hunched into the curve, and swipe on foundation with the aid of my handbag mirror. Skin has developed a Teflon sheen; all attempts at making coverage stick are hopeless. Try dabbing. Develop a strange mottled complexion. Hope the neon strip lights are exaggerating it, and it'll be better in daylight.

8.56 Train pulls in, full. Straphang to Bank, face pressed into the armpit of a charcoal pinstripe jacket that is obviously some way past its annual brush with the dry-cleaner. Elbow an old lady out of the way to snatch a seat for the last two stops. Hurried attempts at finishing make-up: blusher, mascara, lippy. Know that eyeliner is out of the question on a moving train, as tried it once before and ended up with a face like a Lowry painting. Draw on lips, have to wipe them off again after the carriage lurches and leaves me looking like Divine. Compromise by blotting insides of lips and smacking them together. The final effect is far from perfect, but at least I don't look like I've escaped from a morgue.

9.10: Shop in station only has American Tan tights. Who wears American Tan? Americans? Almost cry, buy them anyway. Run down City Road, catch heel in grating, tear chunk out of knee.

9.15: Ring on buzzer, burst through into tiny, white-painted reception containing MDF desk, three chairs, posters and kindly-looking matron. Kindly-looking matron proves that looks can deceive when she snarls, 'You're late,' and clamps lips together.

'I'm sorry,' I say, 'I had a bit of an accident.' Point to my knee, which is black and crusty with odd juicy red bits.

'My God,' she says. 'Haven't you got any tights?' I

brandish my American Tans and she says 'Well, they're hardly going to cover that.'

'I'm sorry,' I say again. 'I'll get some better ones at lunchtime. I had to buy something in a hurry, and that was all they had in the tube station.'

'In my day,' she says, 'one carried a spare pair in one's handbag.'

I apologize again. This day isn't going well.

My stomach lurches, and rumbles conspicuously. There's a silence while she eyes me. Then, 'I'll show you the switchboard,' she says, in a 'and call the agency' voice.

She gets up, brushes past me, sniffs and looks suspicious. Damn, I should have made Donna get out of that shower. I am led into a windowless room where a digital switchboard and a pair of headphones await. 'You know how this works, do you?'

'Of course. It's not difficult. Is the database up to date?' There is no list, as usual. What, after all, would a switchboard employee do with a staff list?

'Of course,' she snarls. I cough. She flips her head away, then throws me a look of disgusted comprehension. Now I know she's going to call the agency. But frankly, if I get through this day alive, I don't really care what happens. All I can think of is the extra ibuprofen in my handbag. The phone goes.

She stands and watches as I take my seat, strap on the headphones, hit return and say in my sweetest voice, 'Good morning, Alcohol Information Group. How can I help you?'

Chapter Forty-nine

Answer Phone

Someone goes under a train at Kennington, and my train gets turfed out and sent to the surface at Borough. Borough, for God's sake. No-one ever goes under a train at an out-of-the-way station, one that won't also bring the entire system grinding to a halt. Tube-train suicides always involve an element of revenge. I guess, if you're unhappy enough to off yourself, you're already convinced that everyone hates you. A few hundred thousand more won't matter.

My hangover is still pretty fierce after eight hours at the switchboard, and I find it hard to work up sympathy, even think about the fact that there is a real person on those tracks, someone driven so far by life that they would rather be mangled than go on, maybe some poor sod who set off for town and a bit of shopping this morning and had no idea that the rush-hour crowds would be their downfall. All I think is, 'God, how can anyone be so selfish,' and start to trudge streetwards at Borough, my hatchet-wielding companion dodging from platform to tunnel and never letting himself get quite into my field of vision.

It takes over two hours to get home. I stop off at the pizza place and buy an extra-large American Hot in the hope that a burst of chilli-carbohydrate might do me some good. Craig's supposed to be going home for the weekend.

Hopefully everyone else will have gone out. The only thing I want to do is lie about and stuff myself in front of the *Comedy Zone*, maybe fall asleep in front of some stalk-and-slash late-nighter where some chick puts on a T-shirt and knickers to investigate noises in the cellar and spends the next hour trying to stuff both fists into her mouth.

The house is plunged in darkness, and the answerphone blinks across the hall. I put the pizza in the living-room, go down to the kitchen, dig out a plate and a can of Coke. Craig has a jar of flaked chilli for when his mouth gets so anaesthetised by skunk that he starts to feel like he's dehydrating and ends up throwing up. I don't know why anyone would want to smoke so much that they do that to themselves, but he swears that a couple of pinches of *gundillas* crunched in the mouth sorts it out. I pop them in my coat pocket.

Play the answerphone. My mum on about something she's seen in the paper about an organization that sorts out your CV and shows graduates how to present themselves as employable. I've been having quite a few calls like this from her lately. Marina trying to get us to buy tickets for some charity thing to buy Nintendos for Sierra Leonean children: dinner, dancing, raffle, auction, free champagne, £80 a head and 20 per cent of proceeds to the charity. People still want Ben to do these things because it makes a press release. Donna's shop wondering why she's late.

Ben emerges from the shadows in the stairway, trackie bottoms and bare chest, the legendary six-pack rippling. It's one of those things about Ben that really annoys me. I have a hangover, and I look like Whistler's mother. Ben's hangovers just make him look more beautiful, in a blitzed, cheekbony way. I wish he would cover himself up a bit, though; I've never been able to feel as sisterly towards him since that fruity dream in Carey's car.

'Hi,' he mumbles, 'what time is it?'

I check my watch. 'Eight o'clock.'

'God,' he says, 'I've been asleep all day, Why didn't anyone wake me?'

'Sorry. I went to work. I've only just got in.'

He scratches the back of his head, making stubbly, scree-scree sounds. 'I feel like death. How much did we drink last night?'

I shake my head. Hand him the can of Coke, which he pops and downs in one. 'Is there any food?'

Well, I was never realistically going to get through a 15-inch deep pan all alone. 'Yeah. Pizza in the living-room.'

'Urr,' he says. 'Any messages?'

'Not for you yet. Hang on a sec.' I press the button and the machine continues to play.

The shop again. 'Donna? It's Jackie here again, it's lunch-time and we're still wondering where you are. Can you give us a call, please?' Beep. Then, huffily, 'Donna? It's Jackie here. I have to say, I'm seriously pissed off with you. It's five o'clock. I haven't had a break. You could at least have called to say you weren't coming in. I expect to see you tomorrow, or at least get a call. 'Bye.'

We look at each other. 'She was up when I was this morning. I couldn't get into the bathroom.'

'Well, I don't know,' says Ben. 'I guess I was aware that there was someone else here, but I assumed it was Craig.'

'D'you think she's OK?'

'Probably just a hangover. She was out late last night, too.'

'Shall I go and see if she's OK?'

'Naah,' he says, 'I've got to get some clothes on anyway. I'll bang on her door.'

246

'Right. I'll get some plates. Tell her there's pizza.'

'Sure.' He goes back up the stairs. And how, as Gina Davies said about Brad Pitt in *Thelma and Louise*, I love to see him go.

By the time I'm back up in the corridor, I hear a rapping on the door upstairs, and Ben going, 'Donna? Are you OK?' The door opens, closes again, and I go into the living-room and switch on the telly, play with the remote. BBC1: cheery Cockneys duck, dive and share their double entendres with a tinned studio audience; BBC2: a man in a parka flirts with Baby Spice over the bonnet of a sports car; ITV: real-life amateur video footage of people being plucked from the jaws of death after they try to drive a Ford Sierra through a swollen river; Channel Four: a man with a wok drinks from the neck of a wine bottle; Channel Five: a 20-stone mother with a vest and tattooed arms complains that her two wet-look-perm daughters don't respect her. I settle for the jaws of death, curl round my pizza. Watch a fluffy puppy rescued from a drain, a woman cut from the remains of a car lodged beneath an articulated lorry, a teenager winched to safety down a cliff.

Two slices in, and the Bodyform woman starts celebrating the intense joys of menstruation while a young woman hops onto the back of a tandem in her tight white jeans. I realize that it's been at least ten minutes since Ben went into Donna's room, and no sign of either of them. Think about having another slice of pizza, decide I'd better see if the others want any.

When I open the door, I hear the oddest, muffled sound from upstairs. At first it sounds like sex, then I realize that there's no rhythm to it. A sliver of light shows beneath Donna's door. I head up the stairs, and the sound starts to take shape. It's some kind of keening. And, above it Ben, going over and over, 'It's OK, sweetheart, it's OK. OK. OK.' Jesus. Something's up. Something big, by the sound of it. I run the last few steps, tap and, when there's no reply, push the door open.

They're there on the bed, bundled up into a corner against the wall with the duvet over their legs. Donna, a livid red bruise closing her eye, her mouth scrawled across her face like a child's drawing, rocking back and forth. And Ben, arms wrapped round her head and shoulders, rocking with her.

Chapter Fifty

Bad Date

All I remember of the next 48 hours is that we all spend a good deal of it in tears. I'm quite calm the first night, when the whole thing's new, before we develop the weird feeling that this is something that has happened to us as well as to our friend. It's not until we've persuaded her that the police must be involved, which isn't until after lunch-time – the pizza has turned to Italian-cheese-toast in the living room – that I start to notice that I'm not feeling normal myself.

Down in the kitchen, putting on the kettle to make a cup of tea for the nice WPC who arrives to take Donna's statement, I drop the milk carton so it goes all over the floor, and it feels like the greatest calamity in the world. I stay kneeling on the tiles with the cloth in my hand for five minutes, crying stupidly and cursing my feebleness, while the milk soaks through the knees of my jeans and bleaches my trainers. Then I get up, make the tea, run the bag under the cold tap and hold it to each of my eyes for a couple of minutes in turn. This isn't my bad thing, and I won't be helping matters by lapsing into acopia.

Nice WPC accepts the tea with a brief smile, puts it down on the coffee-table and says absolutely nothing while Donna talks. Ben's been banished to the garden while this woman-stuff goes on, and is kicking a football against the wall over the dustbins. Every now and then there's a clang and a clatter as he aims too low. As Donna, clutching her snotty Kleenex, talks, I busy myself looking out of the window. I feel useless. Useless and powerless, and I want to howl at the injustice of it all, kick the walls, smash some glass, pick Donna up and take her to a place where things like this don't happen, where Mark Henleys don't exist. This is Donna, for God's sake: Donna who's never done anything to anybody; Donna who's always the first to speak out when things are wrong.

'I mean,' she croaks in a lifeless monotone, 'I know it was stupid to go back with him when I hardly knew him, I know it was. But he was just so . . . you wouldn't understand. You've not met him. He'd been the perfect gentleman all evening, so nice, so thoughtful, and then he just suddenly changed. 'We had a coffee and a brandy, and then I said I ought to get going. And one minute I'm putting my coat on, and saying sure, I'd love to see him again and thanks it's been great, and the next he's pulled the shoulders of my coat down over my back so my arms are trapped and he's tripped me up so I'm on the floor. I think I hit my face on the banisters. I don't know. It happened so quickly. I couldn't do anything.' She pauses, gulps, blows her nose and looks at nice WPC as though to get confirmation of her own helplessness.

'Don't rush,' says nice WPC, 'take your time.'

'And I was going "what are you doing, what are you doing?" I think I must have been in shock, or stunned, or something, because I knew exactly what he was doing. And he just kept going, "Come on, come on," and, "You know you want it," and I was going, "No, I don't, stop it," but he wouldn't.' Her face crumples for a moment, then she reins back and continues. 'And then he started hitting me.

Punches from close up. Just kept doing it, and he had his hand on my throat to hold my head still. I thought he was going to kill me. He kept banging the back of my head against the banisters. It's weird. I can sort of see it all happening in slow motion, like I wasn't in my body at all. He shoved his hand between my legs and pulled my knickers down and . . .' There's a long pause.

Donna lights one of my cigarettes from the packet I've left on the coffee-table by her. I long to get one for myself, but don't want to disturb the flow. I've got my face pressed into the curtain now, though I'd rather be safe under the duvet. 'And then he started undoing his trousers. He had his knee on my chest and I could hardly breathe, and it felt like my arms were being ripped out at the sockets . . .'

She takes a puff, closes her eyes, rubs the back of her hand across them. There's no mascara left there to streak. Donna's usually so scrupulous about putting her make-up on before she shows her face to the world. ' . . . And I realized I wasn't going to be able to stop him. And the way he was talking, slag this, slag that, I thought maybe he'd do something worse if I fought any more. So I said please can you use a condom, and he laughed, and said what did I think? He was going to − ' a sharp breath '− fuck a thing like me without a condom? He called me a *thing*.'

The room falls silent. The sound of Ben's football − thud, slap, bounce, thud, slap, bounce − leaks in from outside. Nice WPC takes a sip from her tea, sits forward quietly.

'So then he put a condom on, and he . . .'

Donna gulps a lungful of air, puts her hands over her face, goes quiet again. I press my index finger across my lips because I'm scared I'm going to make a noise. My eyes seem to have started leaking again. I surreptitiously wipe them on my cuffs.

She blows her nose, finishes her cigarette, stubs it out. 'He just went ahead.' She waits for a few seconds, gathering her composure, and when she continues, her voice is calm.

'I don't think it took very long,' she says, 'but it felt like hours. He had his elbow digging into my neck, and that really hurt, and he was crushing me so I couldn't breathe. I just – I don't know, I just gritted my teeth and waited for it to be over. He was dribbling, I remember that. And pulling my hair. Look, there's a couple of plaits gone. I'll have to get them redone now. It takes bloody hours. And he was calling me a bitch and a slag and saying, 'You like that, don't you? You want some more, you little bitch?' and I was just lying there, waiting for it to stop.

'And then he just stopped, and pushed himself up and went into the bathroom. I could hear him splashing around in the sink, and flushing the loo. I tried to get up, but I was feeling groggy, and my arms were still trapped, and I couldn't get the coat up them. So I was still on the floor when he came out, and he stood over me and went, 'You still here?' I couldn't say anything. So he said, 'You can fuck off, now,' and kicked me a couple of times in the side while I was getting up. Shoved my bag into my hands and pushed me out of the front door. I think he might have used his foot, actually, because my back is really hurting. I didn't know where I was, except that it was somewhere in Barons Court, so I started walking around. I remember I had my keys in my hand. I was crying, and people kept walking past, looking at me, but no-one did anything. Eventually I got to the Cromwell Road, and found a taxi . . .'

'And this was?'

'Thursday night.'

'OK,' nice WPC gulps at her tea, scribbles something in

her notepad. 'And you've had a shower since you came home?'

Donna nods, miserably. 'Three.'

'It's a common reaction,' says nice WPC. 'It can't be helped. We're going to have to get you examined, though. Are you ready to come now? I can take you down to St George's in the car.'

Donna looks up at me. 'Of course, silly,' I say, and come over and take her hand.

'I need my bag,' says Donna. 'I don't know where my bag is,' and suddenly she's in tears again.

'I'll get it, sweetie,' I hurriedly offer, find it in the kitchen and take the opportunity to go into the garden to tell Ben what's going on.

He has given up with the football, and is ferociously pruning the clematis. No-one's touched the garden in a year, since lack of funds forced him to give up the firm that designed and theoretically maintained it, and the clematis has tied itself in knots. He hears me come out, and drops the secateurs to his side. Looks balefully up at me, and I see that his eyes are rimmed with red and his cheeks look like they've been left out in the rain and gone rusty.

'We're going to the hospital.'

'OK,' says Ben. 'Do you want me to come too?'

'Probably not. It's probably best if you hold the fort here.'

He turns and gazes down at the shed at bottom of the garden. 'Right. There's stuff I should be doing, anyway.'

I give him a hug and he hugs me back, so hard I think my ribs will break.

'What can I do?'

'Nothing.'

'Great,' he starts hacking at the clematis again. 'Super.'

In the car Donna leans her head against the window and

gazes out at the Clapham Road. People wander around on their Saturday mundanities, nursing hangovers, going to the launderette, heading for the Bread and Roses for a late lunch, and none of them has the first idea what happened on Thursday night.

Nice WPC runs us through what's going to happen at the hospital. 'You're very kind,' says Donna.

'It's my job,' she says. She's not much older than us. What a thing to do for a living.

A Saturday afternoon in Casualty, and the place is full of sporting injuries. Men with swollen knees, men with swollen ankles, men with cuts over their eyes. Donna hunches on a chair and nice WPC speaks quietly to the receptionist. They've been expecting us: a white-coated woman with Deirdre Barlow specs comes out and beckons Donna and WPC. I make to go with them, and WPC says, 'I'm sorry. If you wouldn't mind waiting?'

So I'm alone with a dozen sweaty, groaning men, and all I can see is a dozen pigs. I try to reason with myself, remember how shocked Ben has been, think about how kind Craig can be when he's not being tactless, remind myself that this is one man, not all of them, that these are probably kindly fathers-of-three who've bashed themselves on their weekly football game, but it makes no difference. I don't want to be around them. I tell the receptionist that I'm going to wait outside, leave through the sliding doors. It's drizzling. A couple of empty wheelchairs decorate the pavement, along with a middle-aged man, weeping into his chest and being patted by a young girl. I squat down on the kerb just beyond the doors, still under the canopy but not where I'll get in the way of an ambulance. Feel in my pockets for a cigarette, and find the jar of chilli peppers, which I never remembered to take out last night.

Chapter Fifty-one

Slow Motion

And all our petty little concerns fade into their true perspective, because now something Real has happened, something that chills you to the quick, something that makes you understand, at least for now, that all our nitty little middle-class squabbles are just a way of passing the time. Mark Henley turns out to have done this sort of thing before. Twice before, in fact, women have spent an evening with him, had a lovely dinner, got on like a house on fire and come away bleeding from the experience. Twice, a jury has found him so plausible, so respectable with his well-cut suits, his classical good looks, his good job looking after other people's money, that they've reasoned that the complaints were the revenge of a rejected slut, and let him off without a blemish to his name. The police know who Mark Henley is, the social services know who Mark Henley is, but the magistrates give him bail because they think it's unlikely that he will re-offend – after all, he's only done it three times now – and he's back at work while Donna stays in the house and waits for her bruises to heal.

All we can do is wait for the trial and hope that this time things will come out the way they should. It feels like struggling in amber. The wheels of justice grind very, very slowly, and while you wait for something to happen there's very little else to think about. I go to work each day, sit surrounded by strangers, and time edges forward so slowly that I think I'm going to scream. Donna doesn't have a contract with Sandro's, and they do away with her services at the end of the first week, while she's still sitting in her bathrobe on the sofa watching daytime television with Craig and refusing cups of tea and offers of food. Ben quietly drops the mention of bills and rent when she's in earshot, goes off to the set each day, comes back exhausted and falls asleep.

One night he's so tired he forgets that he's changed bedrooms with me since Matthew and Tania copped out, and I find him crashed out in my bed. And I can't be bothered to wake him, just crawl in beside him and take comfort from the warmth of another human being next to me. We wake up the next morning with the first of the traffic, Ben's arm thrown over my breast, and look sheepishly at each other before Ben gets up and makes us both a cup of tea. After that one of us ends up curled up with the other most nights, Ben in his trackies and T-shirt and me in knickers and an old dress-shirt my father wore to downy softness before he threw it out. We don't talk about it at all, just stay together for warmth. Ben and I used to sleep like this a lot before Matthew arrived on the scene; sleeping with Ben is like sleeping with your old wolfhound: bony, smelly, warm and safe. Sometimes I'll wake up in the night and lie there, listening to him breathing, and wondering what the hell to do about Donna.

Donna doesn't want to talk about what's happened, and what's going to happen, aside from the practicalities. She may not want to, but it's all anyone else wants to talk about. Everywhere I go, that's all they can say: how's Donna? Is she

OK? What happened? Tell me all. And I say why don't you come and ask her yourself, and they blench and say ooh, no, I don't want to bother her, just send her my love. They're afraid, I think, that it's catching, that they might come away from contact soiled in some way. Matthew and Tania come to see her while I'm out, and Marina spends hours with her, keeping her company if the rest of us have to be out of the house, but that's it apart from Carey, who arrived on the doorstep half an hour after I told him on the phone, armed with phone numbers of counsellors, bottles of wine and hugs.

But we can't move on until it's all finished. Donna can gradually start remembering to get dressed every day and begin to eat again when someone's cooked, but we're all frozen in time while the prospect of the court case is still hanging over her head. We speak all these buzz-words like 'moving on' amongst ourselves, but how can you move on while you're waiting for a procedure that depends upon you reliving the past? Donna is a resilient person, someone I've always admired for her ability to assimilate and shrug off, but she has no alternative but to sit, isolated in her amber prison, until she's been studied and her interlocutors have done their own moving on.

Sometimes, while we're being quite normal, when we've spent an evening playing cards or watching telly, she will suddenly drift away and stare into space. I don't know if she's remembering or imagining, and she's dry-eyed these days, but her face has lost its bounce. It no longer plumps up easily with merriment, wobbles in consternation, flashes with her bitchy grin; nowadays Donna has to remember to show amusement.

'Look,' she says one night while we're toying with McCartney bangers and peas at the kitchen table, 'I'm not sure how this is going to turn out, you know. Maybe I should just let it go now.'

And I say, 'What? Donna, you can't!'

'Why not? He probably won't get done anyway.'

'But he has to,' I cry, 'he has to! Everyone knows he's done it.'

'Yes,' she says, 'but look at how it'll look. I pick him up in a shop, make a date without knowing a blind thing about him, go back to his place all by myself. At the very least they're going to think I'm stupid. I mean, it's not like we haven't all been warned a million times about doing what I did.'

'Donna, we haven't got a law yet that says you deserve to be punished for naïvety.'

'Yeah, but I know what it'll look like. Silly tart on the make, thinks she'll get a rich boyfriend with a BMW. We all know we shouldn't go places with strangers. We learn that practically before we learn the alphabet.'

'Yes, and tens of thousands of people do it every day and nothing happens to them. You were unlucky, Donna, you weren't the one at fault.'

She shakes her head, pouts. 'Yeah, but maybe I ought to let it drop. Put it down to experience. Get on with my life.'

'And let him do it to someone else? Donna, if you don't stop him now, you know he won't stop himself. He'll carry on doing it.'

She blinks. 'I know. I know. I know that if I don't go through with this, I'll open the paper one day and see that he's killed someone, and I'll never be able to live with it. But I don't know if I'm strong enough for this. Everyone thinks I'm strong, but they don't have to go to court and get every detail of their past raked over. Think about it. I'm hardly Snow White. I've slept with loads of people. Do you think they'll just ignore that?'

'This is the 1990s, not the 1950s.'

'Yeah,' she says, 'and a slag's still a slag and asking for trouble. I don't know if I'm up for this.'

'You will be,' I say, 'you know you will. You have to be. And I promise you, we'll all be behind you. We'll all look after you. We'll make sure he doesn't get away with it.'

'Will you?' Her eyes suddenly mist up and she looks scared.

'Yes, Donna, yes. Me, Ben: all of us. We're your friends and we'll help you see this through to the end.'

'Yes,' she says, 'but none of us knows what the end's going to be.'

Chapter Fifty-two

Blackfriars

A simple rule of office politics: don't have conversations in the loo you don't want overheard, as the chances are that the person behind the closed cubicle door will be the person you're talking about. Either that, or they'll be a nosy temp picking up the gen on the place she's landed up in this week.

Outside my cubicle, where I'm taking a screen break, two women are talking, and what they are saying is not nice.

'Have you heard?' says a deep voice. 'Kat's gone. Resigned this morning.'

'Jesus,' replies a squeaky one, 'she'll have every one of us out before spring.'

'Shaft the competition. Make room for the boys.'

'Yes. And make room for herself with the boys.'

The click of a lipstick top. 'What do you mean?' deep voice asks, only it comes out 'Ok oo ea?' as she's obviously doing her mouth.

'You must have noticed,' says squeaky. 'You mean you haven't noticed? She's been picking off the attractive ones one by one. Everyone who might take attention away from her for a minute. Think about it. First it was Jean, then it was Susannah, then Kirstie, then Poppy.'

'Uh huh?'

'The blondes. There's not a blonde left. Then it was Carrie, Sharon, Daisy, Monica . . .'

'I remember. All really good, then suddenly their promotions get blocked, they can't get through her door, men half their ages get put into the jobs they should have had.'

'Exactly. And they all had bodies to die for.'

'Ooh, yes. I hadn't thought about it, but you're right.'

'Well, now she's picking off the good dressers. That and, of course, anyone who might make her look less than perfect.'

I can't believe what I'm hearing. Bridget Brougham? The famous Bridget Brougham, who I've been so excited about working for? Bridget Brougham, feminist: author, parliamentary lobbyist, authority on women's rights, TV pundit? Bridget Brougham, role model? The woman we've all grown up striving to emulate, who fought her way up through a man's world without sacrificing femininity, family or fun?

'I'll tell you what,' says deep voice, and what she says sends shivers down my spine, 'Bridget Brougham's no sister.'

'Yeah, well,' says squeaky voice, 'she's far too busy with the brothers to spare a thought for us.'

Damn. And here was I thinking that I might at last have fallen on my feet, reached a place where, even if I didn't get a break, I might get some sound advice. Bridget Brougham is always on the telly spouting about caring employment policies, the provision of childcare, the advantages of jobshares, open-door policies, brainstorming, employee consultation, flexible working, multiple tasking. Surely this can't be true?

'So why did Kat go, then?' asks deep voice.

'Couldn't handle the hours,' squeaks squeaky. 'Ever since

she had the baby, Bridget's been on her back. She's not got out of the office before seven since she came back from maternity leave. And she never got to work from home even though everyone else does. Every time there's a job that involves going away overnight, she got sent. This is a business, not a charitable institution, apparently.'

'You mean she talked to her?'

'Well, eventually. On the thirtieth attempt.'

'So much for the open-door policy,' says deep voice. 'You know what her secretary was telling me?'

'No?'

'Well, apparently whenever someone she doesn't want to talk to arrives, she grabs the phone and pretends to be engrossed in conversation.'

I can't really stay in the cubicle any longer; Bridget will have noted my absence by now. I flush the loo and, by the time I emerge, the room is empty: they obviously scurried out when they realized they were not alone.

Walking back across the floor, it all looks very different from how it looked when I came in. There are, indeed, more men working here than women, and the women all seem to have moleskin hair, taupe skin and checked flannel shirts. On one of the chairs outside Bridget's room, a woman five-odd years older than me waits.

'Have you come to see Bridget?' I ask.

'Yes,' she replies, 'but I don't want to disturb her while she's talking.'

'Sure.'

I go back to my screen, secretly observing the great feminist from the corner of my eye. Bridget puts her finger over the clicker, peers out at the chairs and, when she sees that the waiter is still there, lifts it off and turns her back, receiver pressed firmly to her ear.

Chapter Fifty-three

Council of War

What starts as a mourning party quickly turns into a council of war. Marina arrives promptly, arms full of vodka bottles and chocolate Hobnobs. Hugs me in the hall, says, 'Where is she?' and I point to the kitchen stairs. She drops her bag and coat on the hall floor, rushes down the stairs calling 'Donna?'

I follow, to find Marina stuck to Donna like a limpet, and Donna, who's been stoical in the extreme to this point, in floods of tears. Craig is sitting at the table smoking furiously, and Carey, ever the motherly one, is making tea.

'I'm so sorry,' Marina's saying, 'I'm so sorry.'

And Donna is sobbing, 'It's like no-one believes me. Why don't they believe me?'

'We believe you,' coos Marina. 'Everyone believes you. It's not that. You know it's not that.'

I prise the bottles and biscuits from Marina's fingers, put them on the worktop and resume my seat beside Craig. Eventually Donna and Marina let go of each other, wipe their noses with kitchen paper, and Donna sits down again.

'So what happened?'

Donna puts an elbow on the table and her head in her hand, as though it weighs too much to be supported merely by her neck.

'That nice policewoman came round and told me.'

'When?'

'An hour, two hours ago. I don't know. This afternoon. Craig was here, thank God. I don't know what I'd have done otherwise.'

'We were down at the deli getting stuff for a barbecue,' explains Carey helpfully. 'She'd gone by the time we got back.'

'And what did she say?'

'The Crown Prosecution Service have dropped the case for lack of evidence.'

Marina swears. 'They do that. All the time.'

'That was what she said. But I don't understand. Do they think I'm making it up?'

'No. I'm sure they don't.'

There's clomping on the stairs, and Ben's in the room with his mobile in his hand, make-up still on, and, following him, Matthew and Tania. Tania has a big bunch of flowers in her hand and a plastic bag hanging from her wrist. I feel distinctly weird seeing them, even though I knew they would be coming, as it was me that rang them in the first place. There's a tingly, itchy feeling in my spine, like having vertigo. I say nothing and grip the table as I get used to it.

'What the hell happened?' Tania starts, and Donna tells her.

'Lack of evidence?' she says. ''How much evidence do they need? You were *covered* in bruises. So they think you got those for fun? I don't know what the police think they're playing at.'

Carey hands Donna her mug of tea. She looks at it like it's landed from outer space and Matthew says, 'Do you want anything in that?'

Donna nods. We open Marina's vodka, and everyone

takes a slug, except Tania, who waves it away. 'I've got a big meeting in the morning. I'd better stick to the soft stuff.' Donna chews her nails and drains her cup in a couple of minutes. Carey, saying nothing, brings her a refill.

The ashtrays fill up, and a cloud of cigarette smoke hangs in the air. Tania repeats what she's just said. 'I don't understand. How can the police just drop the charges like that? It's not like it's shoplifting or something. Don't they have the first sense of priorities?'

She's looking peaky, Tania, and Matthew keeps stealing concerned glances at her. I'm not really sure how I feel about being in a room with the two of them after all this time. I knew it would have to happen sooner or later, but I'd always imagined I'd bump into them at some party and simply cut the both of them, make it clear that, though I'd moved on, I didn't want any truck with them. And instead, we're all sitting and standing around like nothing has happened, like Tania was always the one and I was always the flatmate.

'It's not the police,' says Donna, 'it's the Crown Prosecution Service. The police are very upset about it, but there's nothing they can do if the CPS won't go ahead.'

'And the CPS,' says Craig, 'say there's not enough evidence. It's pretty much Donna's word against his, and he's denying everything. They don't want to go ahead with cases they can't be certain of winning. Don't want to waste taxpayers' money,' he finishes bitterly.

'Shit,' says Tania, 'I give enough money to the taxman, they could at least give us some of it back. Shit, I don't believe it.'

'But,' says Ben, 'it's not like it's the first time he's been charged with this. He makes a fucking habit of it, for Christ's sake. He's evil. Can't they see that?'

Marina shakes her head. 'Inadmissible. You can't bring previous charges, or even previous convictions, as evidence. It's tough, but it's true.'

'So he just gets away with it?' Tania's voice rises, a tearful edge to her anger. 'He can just carry on doing this to any poor woman he comes across, and despite the fact that everyone knows he does it, there's nothing anyone can do to stop him?'

Carey, who has heard all about my perfidious ex, is studying Matthew and Tania like they're zoo exhibits. Not unkindly, but with an edge of amusement that he's disguising very well because this isn't the time or place for laughter. That's the thing with Carey: he's such a grown-up. I don't just mean that he's a lot older than me, or that because he's been around for longer he's accumulated more experiences, because it's not experiences that make you grown-up. God knows, if accumulated experiences were anything to go by, then we'd all be queuing up to have the Duchess of York as our personal guru. What I mean is that Carey has, I think, been a real adult for most of his life. Real adults look at the world with clear eyes and understand the difference between truth and fiction. Real adults don't bolster their own egos by other people's failings. Real adults understand that all states pass, and see their function as being to help others through the bits when they feel they are caught in quicksand. Real adults can see more than one thing at a time, and know which one to be concentrating on. Beside Carey, I know I sound like a whining child; that we all do. But he's adult enough not to mind. And, suddenly, I see Matthew through his eyes and a weight lifts off my shoulders. Here they are, this slightly weak-chinned boy whose good looks are the looks of youth, inextricably bound up in the hair and the complexion, and his ponytailed concubine, a woman who thinks that the world begins and ends in Hermès. Matthew looks good with his well-cut suit and his well-cut hair; he's filling out, getting his adult form onto which, I can see now, layers of flesh will gradually affix themselves until the suits hang like loose covers on a chesterfield armchair. Money may divide us, but age has a way of levelling us all. I glance at Carey and smile quietly at him: my new friend who has shown me things I never knew before.

I notice that Donna is once again in tears, hand across her face, hunched up in the corner of the sofa. Put my own hand on her thigh, find myself having to gulp back my own emotions.

'Are you OK, Dons?' Matthew says.

She heaves a heavy sigh, puts her hand down into mine and says, 'Yes. I have to be. It's over now, isn't it? There's nothing else I can do. I've just got to get on with stuff.'

'We've got to do *something*.' Whatever I think of Tania, I have to hand it to her that she's a fighter. She's like a pit-bull terrier when she gets going: once she's sunk her teeth into something, death is the only thing that will make her let go.

'Can't we bring a private prosecution?' says Craig. We've given up on the tea now; he makes the rounds of the room, pouring neat vodka into our empty mugs.

'Do you know how much that costs?' says Marina. 'Even I couldn't afford to do that. It'd take for ever and eat up everything we have, and we probably wouldn't win in the end anyway.'

'But he can't be allowed to just get away with it. This man raped my friend. Sorry, Donna.' Tania looks worried for a moment. The R word is one that's not been spoken much amongst us. It's as though we feel that if we use it, we become part of the act. Donna covers her eyes again for a moment, waving her other hand to say that it's OK, and I can hear my own pulse going thump-thump-thump behind my ears.

'No-one seems to want to do people for date rape: they're terrified it'll open the floodgates.' Marina looks sardonic as she says this; even lawyers don't always like the law.

'But there must be something we can do. We can't just leave the bastard. Can't we put up posters or something? Let the rest of the world know what he's like?'

'Not if you don't want to be done for libel,' Marina sighs. 'He's not done anything as far as the law is concerned. He's an upstanding member of society. A trusted celebrity accountant and pride of Crichton, Francis and Fraser.'

Carey sits forward. 'Where?'

'Crichton, Francis and Fraser.' Ben explains, 'They're a huge accountancy firm in the City. They used to do our band's accounts.'

'I know,' says Carey. 'I used to work there. Bloody hell. I don't remember him. He must be after my time.'

'Well, he works there now,' says Craig. 'Company car, trusting clients. A proper little pillar of society, Mark Henley. Works the system, charms the world, sleeps at night.'

'Yeah,' says Ben, 'and smashes up people with less power than himself.'

Silence. My pulse is still going thump-thump-thump. I'm so angry I know my hands would be shaking if I let go of the table edge. Anger and despair combined: there aren't many combinations more unpleasant.

'I don't accept that.' Tania digs in the fridge, finds some orange juice and pours herself one. 'There's got to be something we can do.'

'There isn't anything,' Marina reaches for the vodka

bottle. 'It's hopeless. I'm sorry, Donna. I really am.'

''Snot your fault,' Donna's voice is quiet, comes out on a monotone. 'At least we all know where we stand now.'

'I want to fucking destroy him.' Tania grips her fingernails into her palm and makes a fist. 'I want to make sure he never works again. I want to make sure that everyone knows what he's like and no-one ever allows him to be alone with them.'

'Me, too,' I say.

'Oh, God, what I'd give for that,' says Marina.

We all fall silent, contemplating our loathing and our powerlessness. I don't know if you've ever felt like this – maybe a bullying teacher or boss could have given you this feeling – but it burns like fire, makes you sick to your stomach, hurts right through your jaw. I look round the room, and the same expression of internalized savagery is etched across each face: grim, pale, defeated. I don't think any of us will be quite the same after this. Whatever else had let us down, we'd all believed in justice.

Then Carey says, suddenly, 'You know, there could be something.'

We all turn to look at him.

'I know how we could do it,' he tells us.

No-one says a thing. Eventually I say, 'What, Carey?' and he begins to speak. And we all listen, Donna sitting upright in her seat, each of us slowly starting to feel a glimmer of hope. After a short while people chip in with ideas of their own, expanding the plan until our vengeance is fully rounded, alive and kicking. And after a few minutes I suddenly realize that I'm smiling and so, I notice, is everyone else.

'Yes,' I say. 'Yes.'

'You'd do this?' asks Donna, shakily.

'It won't be a case of just me doing it.' Carey looks around us all, solemnly. 'Every one of you would have to be involved. I can do the hacking, but you're all going to have to play a part. And you must all swear, on your graves, that nothing of this will ever leave this room. We'd be breaking the law and we could all end up in serious shit. Do you understand?'

We all nod. 'Yeah,' Ben speaks for all of us, 'we understand.'

'And you can get the necessary?'

Ben nods. 'Of course. Lenny London. Don't you remember? He was even prosecuted for it a few years ago. Got off on a technicality, but it's an open secret that that's the sort of stuff he's into. I'll set up a meeting.'

Carey looks at Tania. 'Sure,' she nods. 'I can find that out easily enough. Give me a couple of days.'

Donna turns to me. 'You don't have to do this,' she says. 'You're the one who's going to be running all the risk. You don't have to do this for me. It's my battle.'

Maybe it's the vodka talking, but I'm certain that this is the only way I can go. This is where our lives change: take a stand now, or remain a passive target for whatever comes our way for the rest of our days.

'No,' I say, 'I want to do it.' And as I speak, I know that every fibre in my body means what I say.

Chapter Fifty-four

On Your Marks

'Brrrr.   Bip-bip-bip-bop-bip-bip-bop-bop-bip-bip-bip. Klung. Booop. Beeep. Grrr. B'dng b'dng. Tch-kkkkkkkkkkkkkk,' says the modem, and falls quiet.

The screen flashes, goes dark, reactivates itself: the logo of Crichton, Francis and Fraser; plain, reliable, grey-on-black, sans-serif lettering, no squirls or little pictures to relieve the tedium: just the sort of logo you would want your accountant to have. It says, while saying nothing, 'No surprises here. You can trust us, because we're not creative.' Must have cost thousands in design and focus groups.

Carey bangs his fingers down on Control, Alt and Del, and on top of the logo a panel demanding login details flashes up. 'BJohns2,' types Carey, and a password that comes up on screen as a line of asterisks. Satisfied, he hits the return key.

Chug, chug, goes the computer.

'Whose logon are you using?' I ask.

'Head of personnel,' he replies. 'Tania checked that it was still the same person when she rang in yesterday.'

'And how do you know her password?'

'She drinks,' he says cryptically.

I pick up the wine bottle, make to replenish his half-full glass, but he waves me away. 'Bad idea. I'll have a huge drink when I'm done.'

'OK.' I refill my own glass, take a big slug. Carey swears that no alarm bells are going to go off, no Hacking Police are going to come crashing through the door of his flat, but I'm still nervous.

'Right,' he fiddles with the mouse, whizzing through screen after screen and shaking his head. 'Sorry. It's been a while. For some reason they're not a department in their own right on the system. You have to go into Secretariat and then into them. Ah! Bingo!'

A pretty little spreadsheet is sitting in front of us. 'Personnel records,' it reads. 'Strictly Confidential. Information must not be disclosed without express permission of Secretariat.'

And below, in little boxes divided by faint horizontal lines, the names, job titles and dates of birth of every member of the 300-odd staff of Crichton, Francis and Fraser. Carey starts to scroll. Abernethy, Ackland, Alibadi, Amin, Armon, Bedford, Beddow, Bunbury, Burton, Burton, Chappell. He puts the cursor on the right-hand margin between the arrows, clicks. The screen jumps, reappears halfway through the Macs. 'Toilet Duck,' says Carey, who rarely swears, even with provocation. Clicks a couple of centimetres further back up, and we're in the I's. Ismail, Irvin, Ingram, Iddles ('Iddles?' I say. 'Mmm. I know. He's very downtrodden,' says Carey), Hussey ('she's not'), Hurley ('no relation'), Holroyd, Hines, Hill, Hill, Henley.

Just the sight of his name brings me up in goosebumps. Carey double-clicks on the name, and all of Mark Henley's life – well, the public stuff – is before us in black and white.

He's 32, not 28 like he told Donna, born South Africa, British Citizen, graduated Exeter University 1989, Economics, 2:1. Arthur Anderson (Graduate Trainee) 1989–1992, Price Waterhouse 1992–1996, joined CFF July

1996. Above-inflation pay increments Sept. 1997, Feb. 1999; Papers: Institute of Chartered Accountants, 1997 (x2), 1998, 1999, specialization loss-leader investments, expatriate travel implications. Flat 3, 47 Disraeli Terrace, W6 (0171-458 9618).

'Right,' says Carey, 'write this lot down. Current account for salary transfers: Hamlyn's Bank 66-23-25, account number 0778914, Name M. B. Henley. Deposit account for bonuses – this is probably the one you – Brick Lane BS 72-33-02, Account number 0882364, Name Mr M. B. Henley.' I scribble.

'Blimey,' says Carey, 'look at this.'

He's scrolled on, come to the personal notes.

STRICTLY CONFIDENTIAL: PERSONNEL USE ONLY it says at the top, and underneath:

'Mark Henley is popular with his male colleagues, who regard him as friendly, though sometimes a little aggressive and occasionally somewhat overcertain of his own knowledge. Female colleagues are less enthusiastic; to date, two have made unofficial complaints about his attitude, as a primary registering of concern rather than a demand that something be done. He has also been twice charged with sexual offences relating to women. While neither charge resulted in conviction, and no work-related incident has gone as far as official reprimand, we would recommend that his contact with female colleagues be kept to a minimum and that his client base should be, as far as we can manage, male.'

'Nice fella,' says Carey.

'We know that already.'

Carey backs out of Personnel. Double-clicks out of Secretariat, returns to the initial menu. Double-clicks on

Accounts Payable, swears as the system blocks him out. 'Damn, Janet doesn't have access.'

'What are you doing?'

'I'm going to go into Accounts Payable,' he says. 'Most of the clients have direct debit accounts to cover initial costs and then pay the rest by cheque or transfer. We should be able to pick up some details from there.'

'How are you going to get in?'

He smirks. 'Fortunately, I know the password of Geoff in Systems,' he says. Logs on as Geoff, goes into Systems. Runs a search on the word 'Password'.

'Bums,' he says, when nothing comes up apart from a memo from Personnel reminding everyone to let their secretaries know what theirs is in case they go on holiday, 'I suppose it would be too much to ask. Let's try "Henley".'

Chug, goes the computer, chug, chug.

A couple of hundred filenames appear on screen. Carey runs through them, dismissing files like 'C. Murray, Taxation 98–99', flicking into the odd memo, flicking out again. Chug. Then his eye lights on something called 'Error Log'.

'Of course,' he says. 'That's just Geoff's style.'

He pulls it up, and we find ourselves staring at a list of every logon and _password in the company. It hasn't appeared in the 'Password' search, because Geoff has listed the passwords under the heading 'Real Name'. Mark Henley's, I notice, is 'Monster'. Carey finds the logon of the Head of Accounts. ('Always go as high up as you can,' he says, 'it saves trouble in the long run.') It is 'Jessica'. 'Aah,' he says, 'sweet. That's his daughter. They're nearly always wives and husbands and children. Or the name of their childhood dog.' Logs out, logs on as the accountants' accountant, breaks into the bank details of a good quarter of the country's show-business luminaries.

'They're like lambs to the slaughter,' he says. 'You could bring Marlow and Bray to their knees without any trouble at all. The minute they buy the big spread on the river, first thing they do is ask their famous neighbours who the smart accountant is. It doesn't matter to them if they do their job properly, as long as they get sucked up to. That's why you always get fifteen pop stars being milked by a crooked financial person rather than just the one.'

We write down the details of a couple of heavy-metal outfits, a Cockney actor with an American wife who is always falling out of China White with her diamonds dangling and, to my joy, those of Candice Murray. That'll put the wind up her, I think: she'll think for a few hours that her cocaine habit's got out of control. Carey points out that Lenny London is also on the list. Lenny made half a million pounds last year from game shows, personal appearances and something called 'LL Incorporated'. Carey looks at me, eyebrows raised, and I say, 'No. Let's leave Lenny alone. He may be a scumbag, but he's helping us out, even if he doesn't know it.'

Carey nods. Pulls the plug on the modem. It clicks and the lights along the side die out.

He swivels in his chair, reaches for the wine bottle. 'Phew,' he says, 'I don't believe how easy that was. They can't have reviewed their security procedures since I left.'

He fills my glass and we clink them together.

'So you know what you need to do, then?'

He's told me the procedures three times already. I repeat them back to him and he nods. 'And how much time will it take, do you think?'

'I'll need a week or so to get used to the computer system. After that, I could probably do each one in a few minutes. How long will it take to get on to the internet?'

'No time at all. A minute, tops; it's a speedy system. Once you're in, the first one will take about three minutes to access and save, and after that it's roughly thirty seconds a pop.'

I nod.

'How are you feeling?'

'Nervous.'

'You should be. This is a dodgy thing you're doing. You can't afford to be confident.'

'I know.'

'So Tania's come up with the goods?'

'Yup. She was brilliant. Rang and spoke to Personnel, and said she was fed up with the agency they were using and was calling round other firms to find out if they were happy with theirs. They were pleased as anything to tell her.'

'And?'

'It's a small firm on Cheapside. About half their work comes through CFF. I've called them and I'm going in for an interview tomorrow. My name's Christa Malone, and I live in Mill Hill. All I have to do is pass the typing tests.'

'And your pay?'

'Kilburn, love. There are about three shops that pay out two-thirds on crossed cheques – it's an old and well-established scam. Don't worry. I won't starve.'

'Good.'

He drains his glass, goes to the fridge to get another bottle. 'So when do you start?'

'I can get registered tomorrow. It's a fast turnaround in this business. I can be working for them next week, and after that it's just a matter of time.'

Chapter Fifty-five

A Pregnant Pause

It takes until mid-July to finally get assigned to CFF after I've signed up with their habitual agency; I have nearly a month to stew on the plan, practise stuff in my head and get ready for action. A month, also, to calm down, turn into a creature of resolve rather than an animal driven wholly by anger. No-one can maintain indefinitely the sort of strangling rage that filled those early weeks, and I can now look at the world without wanting to slap it in the face. But strangely, as my emotions slide back down to manageable levels, so the edge of my resolve becomes colder, and harder. Now our revenge is born out of other things than knee-jerk fury; now it's something splendid, calculating, unstoppable. There is no chance that I will lose my nerve, back out and fail to act: like a hunting cat, I bide my time before pouncing. And Mark Henley, smugly thinking that he is untouchable, that he has got away with it again, will never see me coming.

A lot of things have contributed to this state of calm, but the foremost of them is Donna. Donna is magnificent, and I can't let her down. She's been having counselling once a week with Carey's friend Sarah and it's done her the world of good: after the first few weeks they stopped talking about the night in question and started talking about how she got there in the first place. A few days after the CPS dropped her case, Donna took a deep breath and decided that she wasn't going to be beaten.

'Look,' she says, 'I've got a choice in this. Either this becomes something in the past that I've had to get used to, or I let it be the thing the rest of my life is based on. Either I come out of this older and wiser, or I come out of it too scared to do anything. And if I let Mark Henley constrict what I do with myself in the future, then he's fucked me twice over. And that's not going to happen. We remember him, we get him, and then we move on, all of us.'

So I nod in agreement and the two of us take up kick-boxing down at the Fitness Centre, spending a couple of hours twice a week bashing the hell out of each other in a gymnasium that hasn't been painted in thirty years. When I wake up on the fourth Saturday with a hangover and decide that bed is a better place to be, Donna has a quick sneer, then takes her gym bag and her towel and goes by herself. And after a few weeks of bashing and thrashing, which she practises in the garden for an hour every evening, I notice that she's developing some seriously impressive muscles, which ripple sleekly beneath the gloss of her skin.

'I think I might turn into a big hairy lesbian,' she says. 'And rent myself out as a bodyguard.'

'Get big and hairy, babe,' I say, 'but you're no lesbian.'

'Well,' she gives me a fierce look, 'I don't think I want much to do with *men* for a while.'

And talking of men, the doorbell rings one Saturday in early August and Matthew is there on the doorstep when I go down in my dressing-gown. He's dressed in city-boy casual: Levi 501s, brown brogues and a striped shirt with the collar open, Ray-ban Aviator sunglasses. Where on earth did he *get* all these clothes? He must have spent a fortune since we split up, wandering up and down the King's Road avoiding the T-shirt shops. 'Hi,' he says.

'Hello. Have you come to see Donna?'

'No, actually. I've come to see you.'

'Oh. Why?'

'I need to tell you something.'

'What?'

'Can I come in?'

I realize that I've been standing across the door like you do with the Jehovah's Witnesses. Stand back and let him through. 'I'll just go and get some clothes on.' Funny how you can never be in front of your ex in a dressing-gown, even though he must have seen your pimply bottom a zillion times. I trot upstairs and collect a black jersey dress from the bedroom floor, drop it over my head, run my fingers through my hair to get rid of the worst of the tangles, wonder what on earth he wants. Catch myself in front of the mirror with the mascara and stop myself.

He's down in the kitchen helping himself to coffee. 'Want one?'

I shake my head, sit down at the table. 'So what did you want to see me about?' I can't resist a dig. 'Forget to take something with you? Telly? CDs?'

'Oh, look.' He sits opposite me. 'Please can we not fight?'

I shrug. 'So what do you want?'

'Um, well, I've got something to tell you, and I thought I should tell you to your face.'

'Fire ahead.'

'Well,' he looks nervous, and not a little sheepish, 'it seems Tania's pregnant.'

Gulp. 'What do you mean, seems?'

'Oh, well, is. It's just that we're not sure how it happened.'

'D'you want me to give you a clue?'

'No. Look, please don't be nasty.'

'I'm not being nasty, I—' I realize that I am being nasty, think, well, what the heck. 'OK. Sorry. So what do you want? Congratulations?'

'No. Well, yes, maybe, I suppose. Not from you, obviously.'

'So you're going to keep it?'

He nods. Sips his coffee, recoils as it burns his tongue.

'And when's it due?'

'Six months.'

'Blimey.'

Matthew looks miserable.

'And you're not sure?'

'I – well – we're terribly young. And it was an accident. I don't know. No, I'm not sure. I think maybe I'm not mature enough to be a father.'

And I think, great. Come on, Matthew. You can't go on expecting your womenfolk to sort everything out for ever.

'Lucky old Tania,' I say.

'Sorry?'

'Never mind.'

He lights a cigarette. 'I'm not allowed to do this at home any more. I'm not allowed to do anything any more.'

Diddums, I think.

'Thing is,' he pauses, exhales, and fixes my eye with what I think is intended to be a knowing, this-is-between-you-and-me smirk, 'I can't help wondering if I haven't made a terrible mistake.'

God, men. 'What exactly do you mean, Matthew?' I ask, though I know exactly what he's going on about.

He waggles his head, which I think is meant to look arch. 'You know what I mean. You and me.'

I stub out my fag, stand up and cross the kitchen to get out of harm's way.

'What about you and me?'

'Well, you know.'

'Uh-uh.'

'I think we really had something. An understanding. You understood me far better than Tania does.'

Yes, but you didn't understand me. Then again, relationships aren't meant to be two-way in your world. If I understand you and support you and admire you enough, you might just give me the honour of your attention. Nice.

'What you mean,' I say, 'is that Tania's being sick all the time and doesn't have the energy to dance attendance on you.'

'Of course not,' he huffs. Then, 'Well, obviously, the being sick is a bit revolting . . . '

'No it's not. It's normal. It's what happens when your hormone levels go haywire and your innards are being shoved out of shape. Grow up, Matthew.'

'Grow up?'

'Yes. Grow up. Take some bloody responsibility and grow up. It's too late to be whingeing about how you don't feel ready, and it's too late to be criticizing Tania. If you didn't think you were ready, you shouldn't have got her pregnant. You've got a kid on the way. You can't be a kid yourself when it arrives.'

Matthew looks surprised, sits while this sinks in. Then he says, 'I take it that's a no, then?'

'Too right it's a no. What did you think? That I'd say thank you, thank you, I've been longing for this day? Grow up and go home.'

'Oh, well,' he gathers up his cigs and leaves his half-drunk coffee on the table for me to wash up, 'it was worth a try.'

Chapter Fifty-six

Get Set

Craig's coming back from some arty-philosophical thing on Brick Lane full of people in baseball caps, so he stops off in the City for a drink. What with the police issuing yellow baseball caps to their plain-clothes people now that the moustache and bomber jacket look is so far out of fashion, I'm surprised half the arty people in the East End aren't being regularly beaten up by the gangsters, but perhaps that's because all the gangsters have gone out and bought yellow baseball caps in order to look like plain-clothes coppers. Eventually the whole world will be wearing yellow baseball caps, and the plod will have to find some other way of standing out so that no-one conducts forged-money deals in front of them.

We go to one of the new-style wine bars with bits of old corporate architecture forming part of the décor: tellers' windows at the coat-check, pharmacists' drawers for snacks. Craig and I nurse bottles of lager at four pounds a throw, waiting for the rush hour to die down, and Craig keeps up a running commentary on post-modernism and yuppie décor, and I feel slightly dazed from my day of typing and listening. And suddenly the hairs on the back of my neck stand on end when I realize that Mark Henley, of all the bars in all the world, has walked into ours. Goes up to someone I don't recognize, slaps him on the shoulder, says, 'Allo, mate, how yer doing?'

Mark Henley's voice is burned indelibly onto my synapses by now; after two weeks at CCF, constantly listening out for it, I would recognize it in my sleep. And every time I hear it, it feels the same as when Ivana was sneaking up behind me.

'Evening, Mark,' says his companion.

I pinch Craig's leg under the table, stopping him in mid-flow. 'Ow! What did you do that for?'

I breathe on the varnished surface of the table, scribble with my finger: 'MH.'

'Christ, no,' says Craig, 'where?'

'Four o'clock. Don't look.'

Craig looks. 'So that's what—'

I kick him and he shuts up. We both make like an old married couple, sitting in silence and gazing vaguely about us as though trying to think up something to say.

'What did you get up to at the weekend?' Henley continues. 'Anything good?'

'Not much. We had a barbecue on Saturday, and Sheila made me spend the whole day in Ikea on Sunday choosing a garden shed.'

'Phwooh. You don't want to let them get away with that sort of thing,' says Henley. 'Give them an inch and they'll take a mile.'

'Oh, I don't know. One has to do one's bit.'

'Not me, mate. Any woman tries to push me around, she soon finds out.'

Certainly does, I think. Even when she's not pushing you around.

'So what did you get up to?'

'Magic,' says Mark Henley. 'Went clubbing Saturday night.'

'Clubbing? You still go clubbing?'

'I'm not like you, mate. I won't get old before my time. Picked up this right slag in the Hippodrome. Monstered her up a treat. I'll tell you, I could hardly walk on Sunday.'

'Hmm,' says his companion. 'Sounds like your usual weekend, then. Seeing her again?'

Mark Henley laughs. 'You're kidding. Women like that are only good for one thing. No, I'm going out on Thursday night and seeing what I can score,' he says, 'No point going back when you can go forward.'

Mark Henley. For two weeks I've been quietly typing away and observing him, and he's no idea that I'm there. Hasn't even acknowledged me: he's one of those people who just points, when you come in with stuff for him, and says, 'Leave it over there,' without even looking up. Mark Henley: thousand-pound suits, hundred-pound haircuts, silk ties and a nasty attitude. I know this so far: he spends his spare time roaming the West End clubs in search of women, and he refers to sex as 'monstering'. There's one thing he cares about in the world, and that's his brand-new corporate BMW with the convertible roof and the leather seats. He calls it a pussy magnet. Mark Henley spends an hour a day in the gym, working on his body while he gazes at himself in the floor-to-ceiling windows. And when he walks down the street – I've followed him a couple of times, to see where he goes – he glances in every window he passes (and in the City, with all the smoked glass they put in in the Eighties, that's practically every ten seconds) and shoots his cuffs.

I sit, and I type, and I think about what we're going to do. This job is boring, boring, boring, but it gives me plenty of time, while I've got my headphones on, to think and scheme. Mark Henley struts up and down the corridor, boasting and preening, and I hear him and shiver. I hate Mark Henley: his greed and his violence, his pride and the small gold sleeper in his right ear. I hate him in my sleep, I hate him when I wake in the morning, I hate him last thing at night. And now that I see him each day, know what the arrogant, muscle-bound reality of him is like, I hate him even more.

And he knows nothing of it. Mark Henley thinks he's got away with it again, thinks he's going to spend the rest of his life picking on people from the safety of his professional position, putting his hands up and going, 'Wot, me, guv? A nice chap like me? You can't believe *that*,' and being believed.

His fellow drinker looks at his watch. 'Talking of taking advantage,' he says, 'Sheila will kill me if I'm not home in time to see the kids before bedtime. Want to walk down to the tube together?'

'Naah,' says Henley. 'I'm not under the thumb. I think I'll stay here and see what I can pick up.'

His companion departs and, shooting his cuffs, Mark Henley pats the back of his hair, settles back against the bar, and scopes the room for women on their own: there are never many of them in the City, and they tend to stand out like sore thumbs. Craig is desperately trying not to look like he's looking and, if our specimen were any less intent on his mission, I'm sure he would notice.

As it is, his eyes light on a woman sitting next to us, sugar-pink suit and too much lipstick, buried in a book with that self-conscious concentration of someone whose date is very, very late.

His eyes narrow and a small smile plays briefly on his lips. I don't think I'd be in the least bit surprised if his tongue flicked over them like that of a snake watching its prey. Mark Henley, every woman's nightmare, dressed up as the answer to her dreams.

Henley buys a bottle of Chardonnay – nothing flash like champagne: sets off too many alarm bells – and two glasses, pretends to be looking for a spare seat, gradually makes his way over to her. Hovers with just the right degree of humble uncertainty until she looks up. 'D'you mind . . . ?' he gestures to the two stools on the other side of her table.

She gives him one of those 'well, I can't stop you' shrugs, returns to her book.

'Thanks.' He shoots her a grateful, apologetic, harmless-but-handsome smile, shoots his cuffs, sits. Takes from his briefcase – believe it – a copy of *Fat is a Feminist Issue*, well-thumbed, I note, and pretends to bury himself in it.

I watch as she glances sideways at him, notes those extreme, small-featured, dark-haired, blue-eyed good looks and registers the title of his book. Looks surprised, then interested, then ducks her head back to her Georgette Heyer. Romantic meets stalker: I can almost feel his internal grin of triumph.

Nothing happens for ten minutes. Craig and I try to make desultory conversation so as not to seem too obvious, but we don't make a good job of it, just look like we should be locked up. But Mark Henley is too busy surreptitiously studying her as he turns his pages, minutely mirroring her gestures to put her at her ease, to notice us. And when her glass is almost empty, he pounces.

'Excuse me,' he says. 'Sorry to bother you, but you haven't got the time, have you?'

Girl in pink suit looks up, sighs. The time obviously weighs heavily on her mind. 'Ten past six,' she replies.

Mark Henley sighs in return, again takes up the same position as hers, says, 'Oh, dear.'

Then: 'Sorry, but you haven't seen a woman in a dark suit who looked like she might be waiting for someone in here before I arrived, have you?'

Pink suit shakes her head, tries to return to her book, but he says, 'Only, I have a horrible feeling that I might have got the time wrong. Either that, or – ' a self-deprecating laugh '– I've been stood up.'

'I know that feeling.' Pink suit laughs back, the same self-deprecation, played like a fish: get them intrigued, make them sorry for you, find something in common, make them laugh. Oh, you bastard, you've got it all worked out, haven't you? Craig squirms beside me, the same thought running through his head.

Henley pulls out his mobile, dials a number, waits. Speaks. 'Hello. It's me. Are you all right?' Pretends to listen for a few seconds, says, in a voice full of compassion, concern, 'Oh, poor you. How awful. Shall I come and find you? What can I do? No, really, are you sure? You know all you have to do is ask . . . . ' and sugar girl pretends not to listen, taking in every word. 'Well, just let me know,' he finishes, 'any time. You know you can rely on me. Yes. Of course. I'll be thinking of you. 'Bye.' He folds down his mouthpiece and drains his glass.

'Is everything all right?' Sugar girl tumbles headlong into the honey trap.

Mark Henley sighs, concerned all over. 'I don't know what to do. She's mixed up with a right no-hoper. What can you do? Until she decides it's time to get out, all I can do is support her and hope for the best.'

She sits forward. 'He's not – '

He shakes his head, replenishes his glass. 'Well, she says not. But I don't know.'

'Oh, how awful.'

A sigh, a nod, a furrowing of that elegant brow. 'What would you do?'

'I don't know. It sounds like you're doing the best you can.'

He shrugs modestly. 'I don't know. I can't help but feel like – look, I hope you don't think this is a cheek, but I've bought this bottle now and I'll never finish it myself . . .'

'Well, thanks.' She pushes forward her glass, accepts a share, and within five minutes they have forgotten about his putative friend and are, instead, discussing children's TV programmes they used to love.

'I was in love with Penelope Pitstop,' he laughs, and she, finding this endearing, laughs with him. From children's TV they move on to what they expected from adult life, what they thought they'd be when they grew up. She wanted to be an actress. 'Well, at the very least you could have been a model,' he says, and she blushes. 'No, really. Sorry, but it's true.' He leans forward, refills her glass and she doesn't even seem to notice.

'I was going to be a doctor,' he says, 'go out and solve the problems of the Third World.'

'What happened?'

'Life got in the way. My parents died and I had to get my younger brother through school. Still, life's not over just because you're thirty, is it?' he says.

'No,' she laughs gaily.

Craig goes back up to the bar, spends a tenth of his fortnight's dole on another round. By the time he gets back, Mark Henley has moved in for the kill. 'Listen, I don't usually do this,' he drains the last of the wine into her glass, 'but given that it looks like neither of us has anything to do this evening, why don't we go and have a bite to eat together?'

We watch in horror as she goes through the thought process: I don't pick men up in bars . . . yes, but this one's different, I didn't pick him up, we just started talking . . . but you know nothing about him: you can't just . . . if I don't go along with this, take a chance once in my life . . . and look at him, he's so good-looking, think how jealous everyone'll be . . . but . . . . ' 'OK,' she says. 'I wouldn't usually, but . . . '

'Don't worry. Nor would I.'

'Where shall we go?'

'Into town, maybe? Find somewhere in Soho?'

She nods again. 'OK.'

'Hold on,' he says, 'I'll just go to the cashpoint. I'll be five minutes.'

He goes to the bar, settles the bill, and departs, waving behind him. She sits back, smiling, but nervous. Another woman in the great metropolis, taking the chance that usually works out fine, unaware that this time, the time she makes an exception, lets her guard down, it won't work out fine at all.

Beside me, Craig stands up, goes to the bar. A minute later a waiter appears at the woman's table, bearing a glass of champagne and a note. 'A gentleman asked me to send you this with his compliments, madam.'

'Oh.' She blushes prettily, accepts it, sips. Craig comes back and sits next to me, not looking in her direction. She sets her glass down, reads the note. Goes rigid, the flush on her cheeks turning to ugly blotches on her neck. Tears it into tiny pieces, grabs her bag and her coat and stalks from the premises.

A minute later, before Henley has time to reappear, we follow suit.

'What did you write?' I ask, as we head towards Bank tube.

'I was really horrible. She'll probably cry herself to sleep tonight, but I had to think of something in a hurry.'

'What did you say?'

'Oh God. I wanted to make her just leave, then, not get into a discussion with him. I wrote: "You didn't think I meant it, did you? Sucker." You don't think that was too nasty, do you?'

'No, Craig. You're a fucking genius.'

'Well,' he says as we plunge down the Lombard Street escalator, 'as long as I stopped it in its tracks.'

Tomorrow I'm going back into work and in a few weeks, if everything goes right, Mark Henley will never hit on another woman, if not for ever, at least for a good while to come. Plausible, handsome, charming, evil: Mark Henley, I'm going to get you. You don't see it coming, but like the Furies, it will come screaming out of nowhere and, when it arrives, there will be nothing you can do.

Chapter Fifty-seven

Go

Two weeks and three days into my stay at Crichton, Francis and Fraser, and no-one has noticed that I'm there. Mrs Mouse, that's me: mousy hair, mousy clothes, no make-up, little round wire-rimmed specs, downtrodden demeanour. I'm two divisions up the floor from Mark Henley, but I can hear him all day: boasting, preening, waiting for the fall. And two weeks and three days into my stay, on a day when I know from hacking the diary that he has no appointments, no reason to leave the building, I pounce. Scary. I'm sweating all morning under my cardi, peering around to see if anyone's noticed anything different about me. But no, of course they haven't: in a firm where anonymous efficiency is the order of the day, I'm the most anonymous of all. That's why, a few days after I leave, no-one will ever remember that I was here. The waters will close over my head and I'll be gone.

Half eleven is when we've decided to do it. From the small corner of window next to my desk I can see down into the street below, one of those city streets where the buildings cut out the daylight and few passers-by choose to go. At half past eleven on a Wednesday morning it is deserted, just as we expected. Mark Henley's Beemer, his pride and joy, is parked down below, just out of the range of my vision. Mark Henley is in his office, hidden behind shoulder-high screens so that only someone who actually makes an effort to look through the gap can see that he's there. Open-plan it may be, but this office has been designed for discretion: a client can be in with his accountant, and no-one but the informed will be any the wiser.

Against my thigh Ben's mobile vibrates because I've got the ringer turned off. I dive into my pocket, flip the phone open, say, 'Yes?' and Craig says, 'OK? Ready?'

I gulp, nod, remember to say that I am.

'Is he there?' he asks.

'Yes. He's in. By the window. He'll hear.'

'OK,' says Craig, 'get set.'

I hang up. Strain to see down into the street and catch sight of Craig as he rounds the corner. He's wearing one of Ben's Urban Anoraks: it's collar turns up to ear height and zips all the way up. In his hand he is swinging a piece of metal: one of those big hooks with the bolt that they use to clip sections of scaffolding together. He crosses the road and disappears. I sit back, count under my breath: one caterpillar, two caterpillar, three caterpillar, until on the fifth caterpillar there's a resounding crash and the whoop of a car alarm. Craig bolts back up the street, his hand empty, disappears round the corner.

And behind me I hear Mark Henley shout, 'Shit! Shit! Shit!' and pound up the corridor. People pop their heads out, say, 'What?' and he shouts, 'Some bastard's just vandalized my car!' and runs on. Hits the button for the lift, pauses a second and then runs into the stairwell. I can hear voices mumbling in surprise, going, 'Well! Would you believe it!' but no-one follows him. He's not popular enough for anyone to bother themselves too much. I sit, and wait. Gradually people drift back to their work and the floor once again falls quiet.

Vvvv, goes the phone.

'He's there,' says Marina from the shelter of a fire exit four buildings away. 'And Matthew's there too.'

Matthew, dressed in his bond-trader best, the city uniform that says, 'I am someone you'll never spot in a line-up,' runs up the street, gesticulating in the opposite direction to the one in which Craig has taken off. Mark Henley stops for a moment, waves fists impotently in the air over the wreckage of his top-of-the-range electronic window, then the two of them take to their heels in pursuit of a vandal who is by now comfortably sitting in Starbucks with a vanilla latte and a copy of *Loaded*.

'You're clear,' says Marina.

I hang up, creep to the edge of my cubicle, look up and down. No-one in sight, a few voices murmuring into telephones, the rattle of keyboards, the rumble of filing drawers.

Taking a manila folder of completed correspondence for cover, I tiptoe silently up the corridor, the carpet soaking up the sound of my advance. Marina will call me if it looks like he'll be back, but Matthew should keep him busy for a while.

As I hoped, his computer is still on, in the middle of a spreadsheet: come between a yuppie and his car and he'll drop his grandmother if he has to. His jacket is still draped over the back of his seat, a cup of half-drunk coffee beside the mouse mat. I sit in the chair, which is too high for me, minimize the window and double-click accounts. Think, Christ, madam, you're so cool you'd chill a martini, and realize that I've been holding my breath for the last thirty seconds. Let it out, breathe in deeply, click into money transfers.

Most of the firm's clients, because of the large amounts of money involved in their tax affairs, keep deposits where their money people can get at them quickly and appease Her Majesty while everything's being sorted out. It's the ABS numbers for these that Carey and I have accessed already: all I need to do is pull up the requisite transfer forms, fill them in and press return.

And, in this instance, Mark Henley's deposit account is going to get a good deal healthier while his clients' suddenly curl up for want of sustenance. All I need is time and speed: I'm already logged in, and on his passwords. Thank God, all these weeks of number-pad entry has made me as fast as a pensioner with half a dozen bingo cards.

Transfer funds: From Account 70-52-33, 7781232, Metal Killers Inc. (Band taxation account); password: axeman; sum: £13,200; To Account: 72-33-02, Account number 0882364, Name Mr M. B. Henley; password: monster; return. Transfer funds: From Account 98-93-63, 4097118, Luvver Boyz Ltd (taxation account); password: bromide; sum: £7,600; To Account: 72-33-02, Account number 0882364, Name Mr M. B. Henley; password: monster; return. Transfer funds: From Account 22-17-98, 03469215, Ricky Carver (taxation account); password: Stepney; sum: £8,000; To Account: 72-33-02, Account number 0882364, Name Mr M. B. Henley; password: monster; return. Transfer funds: From Account 45-77-13, 6564729, Candice Murray (taxation account); password: sexpot; sum: I pause. I'm so caught up in my work I've forgotten to be nervous. Check my watch. Eight minutes have passed since my target linked up with my ex-boyfriend. Type in £3,800 as Candice's contribution to the Henley fortunes, then pause, think sod it, give the cow a shock, and add a two to the front of the figure. Send.

We've arranged that Marina will call if it looks like Henley's on his way back up. I quickly dial her anyway, just to check. Say nothing, because I don't want to give away the fact that I'm in here, but she's read my number on her display and says, 'They've just got back. Matthew's got his mobile out. I think he's offering to call the police for him. I'll go over. You've got at least another five minutes.'

Godgodgod: five minutes; so little time, but it can feel like an hour when you're up to no good. I pop my head out into the corridor and still nothing stirs. Go back to the screen and start to shake, because this is the important bit. The money transfers are just there to alert the world: it's the time bomb that we want them to find.

Turn the volume off, cover the modem with my cardigan and go into Internet Explorer. The noise of the modem, muffled though it is by layers of cloth, sounds like Bow bells to my ears as I dig in my pocket for the list of websites that Ben has charmed Lenny London into giving him. Bleep, bip, b'dng, chkkkkkk and in. Put my cardi back on ready for a fast getaway, hit STOP on the home page before it spends the next five minutes chugging a load of adverts onscreen.

Reading from the paper, I type hurriedly into the address domain: http://wwww.kiddyporn.com. Well, of course that's not the actual address, but if you want to find that sort of thing, find your own fading game-show host to bother. As a matter of fact, I've already expunged the addresses from my memory. A pity I'll never be able to forget the rest of it. There's stuff in the world no-one should have to think about. Nasty stuff: really ugly stuff; stuff that makes you gag once you realize what you're seeing. And children somewhere on this god-forsaken planet who have lived – or maybe they haven't – through it. I can feel my eyes turn into soup plates as I scan the pictures that come up on the screen before me: old men, hairy men, dirty men, men in string vests, men in leather, and little kids, their faces screwed up in fear or limp with the resignation of exhaustion. I look for the worst examples I can find. It would make me weep to see it, make me howl with rage and go in search of a gun, only I'm too busy; I can't afford the time, nor the luxury of emotion, if I'm going to avoid being caught red-handed, wallowing in some sick bastard's vicious acts. Pornography touches everyone who has anything to do with it. Later on I'll have to face the fact that by using these images I have, in my way, taken part in their production, but right now all I have to do is get on with the act and leave the conscience for later.

The hard disk will already have made a cache of the web address, but caches wipe themselves eventually, and we have to make sure that what we're doing is permanent. I double-click on the first picture. It has a little girl in it, and she's trussed against a wall, her face a mask of misery and fear. The computer grunts, asks for a filename and I call her Naomi, send her to the templates folder. One of those striped candy bars you see outside barbers' shops starts building up across the middle of the screen, signifying that the saving is in progress. It takes the best part of a minute. I've been here thirteen already: thirteen minutes to destroy a reputation. When Naomi's indelibly saved as a template, I move on: make a Peter, a Michael, a Joe, a Candy and a Rachel. And make one more, for luck: call her Lolita, poor baby, and lay her to rest with the others. Sixteen minutes. My sweat has turned icy on my forehead and my stomach is lurching.

The phone rattles again and it's Marina. 'He's on his way back in,' she says. 'I'm sorry. We tried to slow him down as much as we could but he's gone.' Jitters. Hanging up, I grab the mouse once more and miss twice as I attempt to click on the top left of the screen. I can actually hear myself panting as my trembling fingers force themselves to give it another go. The modem clicks offline. Computer chugs as it disappears the home page, freezes for a second as Program Manager reinstates itself. Inside, I'm screaming, but I wait, standing by the chair now to give it a chance to cool down from the heat of my body. The lift pings and he's back on the floor. Oh, God, God, God. I look around, check everything is back in place, glance at the screen and realize that it's not. Leap back onto the mouse and maximize the original spreadsheet. Snatch my manila folder and race to the gap in the screens just in time for Mark Henley, face red with distress, to run slap into me.

'Yes?' he says. 'Were you looking for me?'

'Oh, no, sorry,' I stutter, and look as insignificant as I can. 'I thought this was Bernard's office. I've got some letters for him.'

'No,' he dismisses me without a thought. 'He's two up.' Brushes past, sits down and picks up the telephone.

I pop into Bernard's office and hand him his file. He looks up and smiles appreciatively. 'That was quick,' he says, 'I wasn't expecting these until after lunch.'

I don't find it hard to look scared and mousy now; every inch of my body feels like it's about to melt. I totter back to my cubicle, sit down for a moment to catch my breath, then dash to the lavatory to throw up the breakfast I never had. Stay there, clutching the bowl and shaking while Mark Henley, blissfully unaware, calls a garage to mend his pride and joy. It's not yet midday, but I can't stay in the building any longer. I must work out the rest of the week here normally before I do my disappearing act; we can't do anything to attract attention, suggest that I was anything but another disposable, invisible office ant ready to be chewed up and spat out. But for now I have to move.

I go back to my desk, get my coat, put it on and walk slowly to the lift with my purse conspicuously in my hand like someone going to the basement in search of sandwiches. Plunge down to the ground floor, smile harmlessly at the old blokes in white hats at the front desk, push my way out into the open air.

The street is empty. The BMW stands in a pool of glass; Craig has done a good job for a hit-and-run. I crunch past it, hands in pockets, trying all the while to look like another dull little passer-by to a dull little street crime. Marina pops out of her doorway, smiles and falls into step beside me. Saying nothing, we walk together on to Poultry, traverse King William Street and, once we're well away from the building, in the safety of Clement's Lane, I throw my head back and yell out my triumph.

Chapter Fifty-eight

Festival

After that, things seem to suddenly speed up again. It's as if we've somehow found out the Great Secret – that nothing is irreparable if you take action and that, if you wait for things to happen, the good things will most likely whizz by without you noticing them. Nothing is going to stop us. It's as if, after a long period asleep, we've woken up to remember that we're still young, summer's almost over and we've got to make the most of it while we can.

Marina throws in the towel on her sinecure at Kalamaris and Kalamaris and starts looking for a traineeship with a firm of criminal solicitors; she says that if she's going to be an accessory to breaking the law, she might as well get involved in the sharp end of the dirty bit of it. 'Just think,' she says, 'I can help you out next time you decide to commit a white-collar crime and get caught, which you undoubtedly will if you keep this up.' Craig, fired up by the thrill of life as an outlaw, decides that he's going to be a maverick academic and enrols on a doctoral course at the University of Sussex, so that he gets a qualification in boring on about Derrida rather than simply subjecting the rest of us to it between bouts of Jerry. Matthew decides that being a daddy is the best thing that's ever happened to him, starts showing everyone who doesn't run away fast enough photos of Tania's womb and going, 'Look, there's his little todger,' as we nod in mystification.

Ben, now the film's wrapped, is getting raves off the rushes — partly, of course, because they've hired excellent publicists who are hardly going to claim that he's only average, but partly because he has actually proved to have a screen presence that no-one had noticed while he was body-popping in a singlet and hair gel — and everyone's calling him the find of the decade. 'Ben's the guy who's made psychos sexy again,' Marty O'Byrne tells a credulous journalist during a pre-publicity interview, and every other journalist in the country has lifted this quote off the wires while preparing their exclusive reports, and we've actually had to get a second phone line put in just to cope with the business calls.

And me? I've decided that, as a master criminal, I should stop fretting about the future and relearn how to enjoy the present. So I've whooped it up, and caned it, and spent some time giving it welly with my hips, and in the course of that I've somehow sort of accidentally slept with my best friend.

All of us built the ship, but it was Donna who got to launch it. Three weeks after I sloped out of CFF without a single ripple closing over my head, we gather for the inaugural celebrations in the living-room, with the telephone on the floor between us. Donna, confident in her new lean, mean, fighting-machine frame, sits beside it in bell-bottoms and crop-top and no bra, and dials 141 before she dials the rest of the four numbers she has to ring. And she gets through to four different showbiz managers, and then, in her best lawyer's voice, coached by Marina, she says:

Good afternoon. This is Josephine Smith of Smith,

Smith and Salmon, and I'm a solicitor representing a client whose name I'm not at liberty to divulge at present. I'm afraid that my duty to confidentiality prevents me from letting you know who it is. I think, however, that you should know that my client shares your accountants, CFF. My client has asked me to call you and let you know about a matter that may well be of some concern to you. He has recently discovered that certain funds have disappeared from his tax account, and no-one seems to be able to account for the discrepancy. He has reason to believe that he may have stumbled across an incidence of embezzlement. He is, naturally, concerned that the same thing might be happening to other clients of the firm, and has asked me to warn you, confidentially and off the record, to check your clients' accounts as soon as possible in case of discrepancies. And, as she hangs up to the sound of alarmed squawks at the other end of the line, she lies back like a starfish on the carpet, and laughs and laughs until she has to clutch her tummy and groan.

And that weekend, once Craig's gone south and Marina's gone north and Matthew and Tania have gone to Fulham, and there's just the three of us left, Ben looks out of the window at the Indian summer and says, 'Let's not waste the weather,' and the three of us pile into the jeep which he bought with his first big royalty cheque and still keeps like a talisman in the garage though he rarely drives it, and go into the deep west. It's the last weekend of August, and the last of the festivals in witching country is going down: three nights of mud and New Age nonsense and dancing. By Friday night the downs have been indelibly scarred by a million tent-pegs, the loos are overflowing and queues are forming round the water-carriers. While Ben is having his photo taken with some hairy blokes whose three-chord ability on the guitar has already earned them over a million pounds, most of which they've been sharing out among the low-profile blokes called Scottish Fred and Italian Jake who hang around on the sidelines at these things wearing sweatshirts with hoods and well-trimmed goatees, Donna and I take off and get our tarots read by Madam Susie, whose business cards say that she comes from Swindon.

'Ooh,' she says to Donna, 'you've had a hard time, haven't you?'

Donna nods, shrugs, says, 'Yes. I s'pose so.'

'Well,' says Madam Susie, 'you don't need to worry any more. You're very lucky to have such loyal friends. And things have changed recently. I can see that a lot of your unhappiness has lifted, but you're still unsure about what you're going to do next.'

Donna nods again, enthusiastically this time.

Madam Susie stabs at the ten of wands. 'You're going to break away soon. You'll be offered a chance to go to a completely different place, and I think it would be wise to accept. There's very little left to hold you where you are at the moment, but much that is green and gold at the other end of your journey.'

'I'm not going to bloody Jamaica,' says Donna. 'There are limits,' and hands over to me.

Madam Susie lays out a Celtic cross, looks at it and says, 'Oh. Oh, dear.'

'What?' Fantasies of horrible deaths dance through my brain.

'Well,' she says, 'you've got a choice coming up. It's been a very frustrating period for you, and all that is going to change soon. But it's not going to be straightforward.'

'How do you mean?'

She looks at me speculatively. 'There are two things that

you've wanted for a long time now,' she says. 'One you've always known you wanted, the other you've been keeping secret, even from yourself. But you're going to find that both of them are given to you, at the same time, and the bad news is that someone's going to have to make a big choice.'

'I can't have both?'

'Sorry,' she says breezily. 'Life very rarely gives you everything you want all at once.'

'So which should I choose? What are the choices?'

'That,' says Madam Susie firmly, 'is up to you to find out. All I can tell you is that the choice may not end up being as difficult as you will think at first. You must look for alternative solutions, and something will come to you. You've wanted both things for a long time; don't let your emotions blind you to your options. You're at a crossroads, my dear. Choose carefully.'

And with that she dismisses me, her eagle eye flitting on to the next person in the line behind me: £15 for a ten-minute consultation. Donna and I walk away through the beginnings of the mud and Donna says, 'Well, that was bollocks. My mum swears by that sort of thing. I always said she was mad.'

'Choices,' I say. 'As if. I've never had to make a choice in my life other than what to eat for dinner.'

'Well, here's a choice,' says Donna. 'Shall we go and join in the conch-playing workshop, take part in the naked didgeridoo session in the stone circle, eat an energy ball, take part in the Goddess Studies discussion group, or get our noses pierced? Or shall we,' she adds, 'go and find Ben and get totally headfucked?'

We go and find Ben.

★

Saturday morning, and I wake up in the back of the jeep with the sound of a conch playing somewhere on the inside of my skull. Slowly realize that it's just my ears ringing from standing next to the speakers punching my fists in the air on either side of my head for four hours, roll over and clout Ben in the face. He moans, mutters something about wanting someone to turn the bloody light off, and assumes the foetal position. All I can see of Donna is one little plait sticking up from the top of her sleeping-bag.

I'm wide awake. My head is hurting, but I'm wide awake. I check my watch, see that it's only just gone noon; nothing's going to start up again until three, when the first band, a trance outfit called something like Eat the Blue or Heisenberg's Uncertainty Principle, will start going doingdy-doing on a single note for two hours. I shift out from between the others, slide between the front seats and decide to go for a walk.

First things first: I let myself into an eco-friendly earth lavatory, squat with my trousers around my ankles and my bum daintily poised four inches above the seat. On the back of the door is a poster proclaiming that these facilities were supplied by Todhunter's Travelling Toilets, and a phone number. I pocket a couple of business cards, thinking well, at least there's somewhere I haven't worked yet, close the door and have a quick Pits-Tits-Pussy scrub at the tractor-pulled water tank while everyone else is still moaning in their tents. Look in a mirror I find dangling from a reclaimed goods-wind sculpture, and see that I look remarkably healthy for someone who drank two bottles of wine and half a dozen rum-and-Cokes the night before. This is Donna's Certainty Principle: drink a single glass of wine at lunch-time on a working day and you will be asleep at your desk by three. Drink a skinful on holiday, and you will be up at six for a swim before breakfast. I tie my hair back with a rubber band, head off to find some breakfast. There's not much going, apart from sourdough-bread-and-alfalfa sandwiches, but eventually I track down a couple of girls in shalwar kameez who are selling free-range organic egg and dairy products at massively inflated prices. Buy a plate of scrambled eggs and toast, go and sit in the sunshine. You can't get better than this: sitting in comfort on a white plastic chair knowing that, all around you, twenty thousand people are waking up to a day of soyburgers and cesspits. The coffee's still disgusting, though.

'Mind if I join you?'

I look up. Of all people, Candice Murray is standing over me with a pair of sunglasses and a croissant. I didn't know that Candice ate, actually: there was a rumour, once, that someone saw her pick the raisin out of someone's Danish pastry and swallow it, but I never believed it. 'Sure.'

She sits, pulls a tiny corner of pastry off, slips it into her mouth, chews hard and, eventually, swallows. Now, there's something to tell Ben.

'What are you doing here?' I ask. 'I didn't know this was your sort of thing.'

'Oh, yeah,' replies Candice, 'I like coming to events like this. They sort of, like, help me centre my Chi.' I nod; I know all about how it feels to have your Chi centred these days.

'Anyway,' says Candice, 'I hear, that our Ben's going to be a megastar again.'

I shrug.

'Well, do remind him,' she says, 'who his friends used to be. I've always been fond of Ben. Very talented, and so handsome. Are you two an item still?'

'We never were, Candice.'

Candice drops her specs down onto the bridge of her nose. 'No?'

I shake my head.

'Well, well, well. And here was me thinking you were quite the loyal little childhood sweetheart, putting up with him shagging everything that moved and sticking with him through his troubles. I had you pegged for a marvellous career as a politician's wife.' To my astonishment, she pulls off another flake, chews and swallows. 'So what's the deal between you two, then? You a beard, or something?'

'We're friends. Old friends. We grew up together. He's like my brother.'

'Some brother.' Candice looks away, tears off another piece of croissant and absently rolls it between her fingers.

'So how are you, Candice?'

'Dreadful, actually,' she says.

'Why, what's happened?'

'Well, my bastard ex-husband is suing me for maintenance, and it turns out that my bastard accountant has been milking my bank account for months now.'

'No! Really?'

'Yes! Can you believe it?'

'How much did he get? Have you got it back?'

'Well, no. Well, some. He's been doing it with almost all his clients apparently, skimming off a thousand here, a thousand there so nobody noticed. Anyway, a few weeks ago he got greedy and took – can you believe it? – very nearly £25,000 just from me. Unbelievable. I mean, did he think I wouldn't notice something like that? Blatant as anything. No attempt to cover it up. The money was still sitting there in his deposit account, bold as brass.'

'How awful, Candice.'

'Well, that's just the half of it. He's had the same amount again over the last year, and my manager never noticed. And it turned out, when the police took his computer away, that not only had he been robbing half his clients blind, but his hard disk was completely stuffed with child porn taken off the internet. Completely. Can you believe it?'

'No, I can't,' I lie, 'that's unbelievable.'

'Of course, he's denying the lot. Says it's nothing to do with him and it's all been planted, but I don't think anyone's going to believe *that*, are they?'

'No.' I can't wait to get back and tell the others. 'Poor you.'

'And he's been doing it to everyone. If I hadn't been smart enough to keep an eye on my finances, he would have got away with the lot. There's a few people owe me a favour around here, I can tell you.'

Candice drops her pummelled bullet of croissant on the floor by her feet, and leaves the rest on the table. 'Anyway. I'm off to powder my nose. Don't suppose you fancy joining me, do you?'

'Thanks,' I say, 'it's a bit early for me.'

'Fair enough.'

I watch her bony hips wiggle their way across the field, patting myself silently on the back, and wondering where she'll find a flat surface to lay out on, finish my eggs and go back in search of the others.

Donna is groaning in the back of the jeep. 'Dead,' she goes, 'dead. I will never drink again.'

Ben is sitting up in the front seat with his top off, scratching his armpit. 'Jesus,' he grunts. 'Don't tell me you're all right?'

'I'm fine.' I climb in behind the steering-wheel, settle down. 'I'm great, actually. I've just heard something amazing—'

Donna interrupts me, sitting up. 'Who were those Irish chicks I was dancing with?'

'Which ones?'

'The ones with the shaved heads. Look like Sinead O'Connor, only no spots.'

'Oh, those ones. They're the Scary Sisters. Indy dyke punk with lipstick and skirts. They were playing at eight o'clock, while you were in the Crap Seventies Disco tent with the speakers that run on a dynamo.'

'Oh, right. Do you remember any of their names?'

'There's Siobhan and Mary Grace and Maeve,' says Ben. 'I can't remember the other one, but I can't spell it either.'

Donna nods. 'Siobhan. That was the one,' and doesn't elaborate.

'Listen,' I say impatiently, 'I've got something to tell you.'

'What?' asks Donna. 'You've met someone at a drumming workshop and you're going travelling?'

'No. Something serious.' I tell them about Candice.

To my surprise both of them react by saying nothing at all to begin with, just pass the water bottle and look out of the window. Then Ben says, 'You mean Candice eats?'

And Donna says, 'So he'd had his fingers in the till all along?'

And I reply, 'Looks like it. All we did was attract attention to the fact,' and, 'Well, if you call half a croissant eating.'

Donna wraps her arms round her knees and says, 'So it's done, then,' and Ben reaches out a hand and scratches the back of her neck. She shrugs the gesture off, puts her head on her knee and stares off into the distance.

'I think this might be a girl moment,' says Ben. Reaches into the back and pulls on a black V-necked pully. 'There. Do I look OK?'

'Good enough to eat,' I reply.

'Better not get near Candice, then. I'll see you over by the hospitality tent.'

'Yeah,' says Donna, 'Thanks, Ben.'

'It's cool. I'll see you later.' He jumps out of the jeep and marches off across the grass.

Donna and I curl up under the duvet, and she says, 'He's a good friend, Ben. He understands stuff.'

'He does. He's the best. And he loves you very much.'

She sighs, and I say, 'How do you feel?'

'I guess I feel good,' she says, and sighs again. 'I guess. At least we've done something.'

'Yes.'

Donna curls a plait round her index finger, pouts at the car roof. I don't have the first idea what she might be feeling, so I leave it and wait for her to speak.

Outside things are starting to get going. The Goddess-worshippers have got on their bike, literally, to fire up their speakers, and some faux-druidic chanting is accompanied by the sound of a portentous – and, oddly enough, male – voice reciting: 'She is where we come from, where we are going, the sun, the moon, the harvest, the spring, the Goddess . . .' Someone stops outside the jeep and goes, 'Well, Willow, you can have one energy ball for breakfast, but we've got to save room for lunch. Zak's cooking lentils.'

And Donna, eventually, says, 'You know what I really wish?'

I say nothing.

'I wish none of this had happened in the first place. I wish I was still the idiot slut I was before it happened. That's all.'

'Yes.' There's nothing else for me to contribute. Revenge is only compensation: it can never put things back to how they were before.

'I'm sorry,' she says. 'I hope I haven't cheated you out of your celebration.'

I shake my head. 'I don't think a celebration is what any of us want. It's just done.'

'Yeah.' Donna rolls over to face me, puts her hand on my shoulder. 'You know, there is one thing that's more precious to me than I ever knew.'

'What?'

'How lucky I am to have friends. The ones I've got. All of you, you've been, well – ' she wanders off again, thinks a bit more. 'I know not everyone is as lucky as I am. I know that.'

'Me, too.'

And we look, solemnly, deep into each other's eyes, and touch each other's faces, palms flat on each other's cheeks. My friend Donna, the star: you can't find a finer thing in the world.

Then she blinks, grins, sits up and starts lacing up her boots. 'Ah, well,' she says. 'S'pose we ought to get on with it. No rest for the wicked. Have we got any more water?'

I sit up, too, and crack my knuckles. 'In the back. Under the case of beer.'

Chapter Fifty-nine

I Laarve You Too

And then that sort of accidental thing happens that I told you about before. Maybe it's something to do with the conversation I had with Candice at breakfast, maybe it's just overexcitement, maybe it's because we had to do it sometime to get it out of the way. Or maybe it's got something to do with the half E that one of the Scary Sisters gives me at half past eight, when I'm already tipsy enough to stop being such a prig. I know half an E's not much, but because I don't do this sort of thing more than once in a blue moon, it's enough to have me running around in circles telling everyone I love them, that I'm never going to bother taking any other kind of drug again as long as I live, and developing a gorgeous, rushy, muscular urge to find the nearest warm body and wrap my arms and legs round it. I'm only lucky I don't run into Candice, or I'd be suing her for maintenance myself by Tuesday.

The heavens have opened during the afternoon, and we're all covered in mud. Out in the main arena people are wading about, and the earth privies overflow, resulting in a busy Sunday for the St John Ambulance. I think this is hilarious, and so does Ben, who seems to be as happy as I am despite the fact that his tolerance for wild living is about three times what mine is. We haven't eaten since the morning, but I don't care. Donna is sitting on a piece of tarpaulin with Siobhan, playing scissors–paper–stone, a game that seems to involve a lot of hand-slapping and arm-wrestling.

'Donna,' I say, 'I laarve you.'

'I love you too,' she replies. 'Have you met Siobhan?'

Siobhan waves.

'About fifteen times.'

Ben comes up behind me, wraps his arms round me and snuggles his chin into the crook of my neck. 'How you doing?'

'I'm great. How are you?'

'Good. Great. Honey?'

'What?'

'Do you fancy going for a walk?'

'A walk? Where? Why?'

'I don't know. I just thought, you know, we haven't been out in the country for years. I wanted to go somewhere where it's dark and there isn't all this noise.'

It must be about three hours since I last noticed the noise. The thumpathumpathumpa of the bass has tuned in so perfectly with the rush of my heart that it's been more like swimming in it than hearing it. But now that he mentions it, I think, yes, what a good idea: somewhere cool and quiet to look at the stars. Then again, he could probably have suggested we go to the local conservative club and I'd have thought it was a good idea.

I turn round. 'OK.'

Ben looks over my shoulder. 'Donna?'

'What?'

'We're going for a walk.'

'Good. Have fun.'

'Do you want to come with us?'

Siobhan laughs loudly at this. 'Of course she doesn't.

She's having a good time.'

'Only, we might go back to London tonight.'

'Cool. That's fine.'

'Sure?'

Donna drops Siobhan's hand, gets to her feet. Puts her arms round the two of us. 'Look,' she says, 'you promised you would stop worrying about me. I'm twenty-three years old and I've been looking after myself for seven of those years. Go. I'm having a good time. I love you.'

'I love you too,' I shout. And she pushes my arm off and splats back down on the tarpaulin next to Siobhan.

So Ben and I wade through the car park, change into dry clothes and set off. God knows, the angels must be on our side tonight. I've been with Ben all afternoon, and I know that what he's taken into his body has way exceeded what I've managed. But we make it out of the car park without mishap, and the copper on the gate waves us through with a friendly cap-tipping.

'Hear your new film's great, Ben!' he shouts. 'Good luck to you, mate!'

'Thanks!' shouts Ben, looking serious and sober, and the next thing we know we're speeding through darkened, empty roads.

Maybe it's not the angels. Maybe it's just that none of the locals want to be driving around while all these crazed hippies are in the area, and the police aren't bothering to look for miscreants until the last band leaves the stage. Either way, Ben drives along going, 'God, I shouldn't be doing this. There are two sets of white lines,' and the only people we pass are a knot of half a dozen thirteen-year-olds who are standing on the edge of a village, headbanging to the distant sound of the music drifting down the hill. Everything drops quite quickly behind us, and within minutes the only evidence that there are thousands of people dancing round some standing stones made of expanded polystyrene and queuing up for henna tattoos is an eerie glow of light hanging over the hill. 'Weird,' says Ben. 'I thought it would take hours.'

'The gods are on our side tonight,' I reply, and Ben grins and changes up a gear. 'So where shall we go?'

'I don't know. I haven't the first idea where I am.'

'Me neither. But we'd better get off the main road soon. We can't expect this luck to last for ever.'

'Ben?'

'Yes, sweets?'

'I think I might be completely wasted.'

'I know you're completely wasted. You just changed your clothes in the car park without even looking round.'

'Do you mind?'

'Do I mind what?'

'That I'm totally wasted.'

He shakes his head. 'Everything you do is all right by me. You couldn't do anything wrong if you tried.'

I snuggle down in my seat, feeling warm and rushy and loved. 'Why do you feel that way?'

'Why? Lots of reasons. You're my best friend. I've known you since you were a vicious little brat with a tractor in your hand and you've been making me laugh since about two minutes after you first bashed me. You're my lucky star. I don't feel like anything would have gone right for me if I didn't know you. You're stroppy, and a bit mad, and you can't deal with drugs at all. You—'

'Look!' I sit up and point at a road sign. 'Chipping Soddenham! It's a sign!'

'Yes,' he says mildly, 'The councils put them up.' But he swings the wheel and we find ourselves trickling up a winding road overhung with old beech trees. The headlights pick out the moss on the drystone walls and flick over rabbits fleeing for their lives. 'Spooky.'

'Atmospheric.'

On our left a bridle-path sign looms out of the dark. Ben hits the brakes, backs up, turns. 'This will do fine,' he says, and we bump through the trees for a hundred yards before coming out on the downs.

At the crest of the hill he pulls up, and we pile out into the starlight. The moon has gone down, but the horizon seems to be lit up, startling white against the shadow of the earth. I breathe deeply, listen to the sigh of wind over grass.

'Quiet,' I say.

'Mmm.'

Down in the valley, a lone howl rises into the night air. 'Wolf!' I hiss. The lone voice is joined by a dozen others, then another dozen, until the air rings with barking, yipping and yells.

'There must be a kennels down there,' says Ben.

'But what are they howling at?'

'They're howling at us.'

And up in the night sky I see a shooting star begin its descent. I grab Ben's forearm, point up to it. 'Quick! Make a wish!'

We both close our eyes, mutter under our breaths. When we look again, it's gone. We sit down on the grass and listen to the night air: rustles, small creeping things, the hush of leaves brushing against each other. I realize that we haven't been alone together out in the country like this since we were fourteen or fifteen: before the fame thing happened, back when Ben was still a crofter's son and I was still a virgin, and everyone thought I would grow out of my village boy and marry a nice doctor.

Ben throws his head back and laughs with the joy of it, setting off another round of howling in the valley. 'It's so good,' he says, 'this is the best night,' and leans over and kisses me.

And then he says 'Sorry,' and I say 'No, don't be,' and kiss him back.

And then we're a bit subdued for a moment as we take in the fact that we've just crossed the line, and then we're all crushed up against each other, and our hands are touching bits we've always carefully avoided, and Ben's going, 'Christ, I've always wanted to do this,' and I'm going, 'Don't talk about it, stupid.' And then there are clothes all over the place and my skin is getting rasped by rough old downland grass, and Ben is locked inside me and it feels so good. It's like coming home and stretching out on an empty beach and closing your eyes when the sun falls on your face and sinking into a hot bath, but most of all, it's like that secret part of me always knew that fucking Ben would be.

All this time, and we've never even kissed before, but we know everything about each other and nothing, nothing gets in the way. It's chocolate and silk and steel. And we're cheering each other on, going yes, yes, oh, that's good, oh, do that, oh yes, go *on*. We make so much racket that the dogs start up again down in the valley, howling encouragement, and it's so good I feel like I'm going to burst, feel like if I die now, I won't care.

And when we're consumed and happy, we roll over and over in the grass like puppies and hug. Neither of us wants to let go. And Ben says, 'I love you. I really love you. You're my best friend and you'll never be anything else,' and I say, 'I know. I know, my darling. I always will be.' And we kiss all night, and talk and giggle, and lie face to face, limbs tangled like old knitting. And we finally fall asleep at dawn, waking hours later, covered in midge bites and bruises, slashes of Indian-summer sunburn striping our thighs.

Chapter Sixty

Russell Square

And now we're back in London, and I'm a still a temporary secretary, even if I am one with a criminal past. Ben is doing the chat shows, and giving interviews to people who wouldn't have been seen dead associating with him six months ago. And the two of us have never said a word about this change in our lives, but his stuff has started not going back from my bedroom to his, and I've silently made room in the drawers to accommodate it.

Tania has announced that she's going to give up work when the baby's born. 'You don't understand,' she says, 'how important it is to spend time with little ones when they're tiny. And anyway, you're all so obsessed with careers and money. There's more to life than all that, you know.' She's taken to wearing pink lipstick, and is doing a cordon bleu course in the evenings. And I don't mind, one little bit; it all seems so distant to me now: more of a running joke than an open wound.

Donna announces that she's going to live in Dublin and be a personal assistant to the shaven girl band, at least until she's decided what she actually does want to do. 'It'll be great in Dublin,' she says. 'I always feel at home with the Irish. They're the blacks of Europe, you know,' and I give her a peculiar look and ask how come, then, they all went to America to be cops and kick the life out of black motorists, but she just laughs and pushes me in the small of my back.

Craig has settled happily in a student house in Brighton. 'It's no good just sitting around on the dole waiting for things to happen to you,' he tells me sagely, and I, sweetly, agree.

And I've decided that, if I can't make an immediate impact on the way my career's going, I can at least make the most of it: stop resenting every minute and see what I can learn. And if I see an opportunity to move forward, I'll jump on it instead of sitting in the background feeling passed over without even trying. After all, if I can get away with an audacious white-collar crime, I must be able to persuade someone to give me a try in the end.

Tracie places me in the world of oil, where I'm to take over from Jackie in the reprographics department of one of the North Sea projects. After the hiatus, the petrol producers are starting to build again out there where the wind is big and the men are brawny, and there's work aplenty for engineers and architects, designers and safety people, for typists and people who are willing to spend their days reducing great big blueprints down to matchbox-sized negatives and blowing them up again. Jackie is an angry woman. You can tell by the way she holds herself. I wonder at first if she's angry because she's been sacked, but realize that she would be unlikely to be staying to show me the ropes if this was the case. But Jackie is quitting halfway through the project, and she makes it very clear that she has her Reasons.

This is a dull job, but the money's good and reliable, because most of the temps here end up working for months, if not years. It mostly consists of glorified filing:

logging things, assigning numbers, checking work in and work out in rigid chronological order, opening the boss's post and – my career has always, it seems, worked backwards – photocopying. If I keep this up, I'll be turning up after hours with a trolley full of cleaning products before the year's out. Apart from me, this basement room holds five wisecracking lads, two men with beards who sit at tables silently moving bits of paper, the boss and his deputy. The boss is called Mike. He goes to meetings a lot. I haven't met the deputy, Alec, yet.

'That's about it,' says Jackie, slamming shut the drawer where the date-stamps live. 'Got the basic idea, do you think?'

'Yeah, I guess.'

'Great. Well, I reckon I'm out of here, then.' She almost smiles, glances at her watch and says, 'It's nearly lunch-time. I don't suppose you fancy going for a drink to celebrate my freedom? No-one else has time.' I'm a bit surprised, but can't think of a reason not to go.

We end up in one of those olde-worlde-themed pubs with sawdust on the floor, plastic beams and a couple of highly polished spittoons at either end of the bar, and sit in a corner with spritzers and packets of pork scratchings. Jackie raises her glass and finally manages the full-on smile. 'Cheers,' she says.

'Cheers. What are you moving on to, then?'

'Oh,' she says, 'I haven't got anything.'

'No?'

'No.'

Blimey. She doesn't seem like the sort to take risks with her mortgage. 'Why are you leaving, then?'

She shakes her head, looks sour again. 'I couldn't stick it any more.'

'Oh.' I feel my stomach turn.

'Don't worry,' she says. 'You'll be OK for a month. I just feel sorry for the poor girl who signs up to do it permanently.'

'What's wrong? They all seem OK to me.'

'Oh, yeah,' says Jackie. 'It's not the guys you work with that are the problem.'

'Well, what is? You might as well tell me. I've got to deal with it, after all.'

Jackie makes a face like she's just seen a bulldog licking its bum. 'Alec,' she says, and the word comes out like a purgative. 'You probably noticed he wasn't there this morning.'

'Well, I didn't think about it, really.'

'He wasn't there on purpose. It's always the same. He deliberately absented himself so he didn't have to say goodbye to me.'

I think about this for a while. The usual reasons why people duck situations are either arrogance or fear. Neither seems particularly promising. 'Oh,' I say.

'Yeah,' says Jackie, 'oh.'

'So what's the problem?'

Jackie drinks half her spritzer in one gulp. 'It's more a question of what's right,' she says. 'I don't even know where to start. He's the worst boss I've ever come across. I genuinely think I hate him. We all do.'

'Why?'

She shakes her head again, makes a sort of 'Khaagh' in the back of her throat. Bursts out. 'He used to be an army sergeant. Thinks he knows about man management from six years bossing people who are trained to click their heels and shout, "Yes SIR!" without question. He's got rules for everything. Everything. How you dress, how you speak to people from upstairs, who can go to lunch when. You practically have to ask permission to go to the loo,' she says, flushing appropriately. 'He throws himself around the place barking orders, and he never listens to anyone. Just shouts things like, "I don't want excuses, I want solutions!" and, "The buck stops here!" and "Not next week, now!" and "When I tell you to do something, I expect you to do it immediately!" It doesn't matter if you're in the middle of some really tricky bit of copying with loads of A3 detail inserts and blueprint folders; it doesn't matter that if you drop what you're doing and leave it in a state where you can pick it up again without throwing the whole lot away and starting again from scratch, then the machines you've been using are going to be tied up so no-one else can use them, and then you get backlogs. It doesn't matter that we have a first-in-first-out rota. If one of the big cheeses he wants to suck up to needs something done, he yells at you until you drop everything to suit his priorities.' She runs out of breath, takes another gulp of spritzer. 'I can't stand it.'

'Crikey,' I say.

'I've stood it for three months, but not another day. I'm the fourth person to leave since he got here.'

'Oh.'

She drains her drink, looks spiteful. 'And another thing,' she says, 'he's revolting. Tattoos and no legs. And a hair transplant. I know it sounds stupid, but there's nothing worse than being talked down to by a man with a hair transplant. How can you take someone seriously when they've had that done to them?'

I laugh.

'No,' she says, 'you'll see.' Points at my empty spritzer glass. 'Do you want another one of those?'

My watch says I've only been gone twenty minutes. 'Yeah, OK.'

At half one I return. Down in my new basement home, machines hum and rumble, rollers squeak, five lads in Ben Sherman shirts scoot around pressing buttons, standing on foot pedals, conning order sheets with furrowed brows.

And standing with his back to me is Popeye's twin brother: legs a couple of feet long, upper arm muscles so overdeveloped he can't get his elbows to his sides, a peculiarly distorted picture of a young woman in her birthday suit on the left biceps, her ample bosom heaving as the owner of the offending muscle flexes and relaxes. He turns, approaches, and I see that his scalp is pocked with tufts of hair a centimetre apart, like a cheap doll. Stops in front of me, hands on hips so that the young woman looks fit to burst. 'Alec Hurst,' he says. 'You're The Temp.'

'Yes,' I say, 'how do you do?'

'I don't remember anyone saying you could go to lunch,' he says. 'Who gave you permission?'

'Oh,' I reply meekly, 'I didn't realize I needed permission to go to lunch.'

'Check with me from now on,' grunts Alec as he walks away. Behind him, Phil, the red-haired lad who works the big 3M blueprint camera, rolls his eyes and grins.

Chapter Sixty-one

Some Hairy Moments

I can't say that this is the toughest job I've ever done, but it's killing brain cells by the day. Mostly what I do is sit at my desk and wait for people to bring down things for copying. This firm is about two months off the design end of a massive construction project, and there are a lot of things that need reproducing for lots of people to read.

Part of my job is to explain that the word 'urgent' can't be stamped on everything that comes down, as if everything was urgent nothing would be given priority. Then I fill in a little yellow form with the time in, name of the person it's for and a job number. Then I write the same things in a book. Then I put the job in the in-tray. When it comes back, I tick it off in the book and put it in the out tray. Twice a day the post comes and I sort bills from direct mail shots from companies hoping to sell Mike their latest shiny new copying gadgets.

Not difficult, but there is at least one fly in every bouillabaisse. The two here are the heat – despite the fact that we preside over a dozen enormous machines, we live in an air-conditioningless basement, and the temperature reaches 80 degrees by 9 a.m. – and Alec. The heat comes from the fact that this basement is full of giant humming machinery: machinery that chugs out A1 prints, blueprints, microfiches, photographs massive drawings and turns them into two-inch-square negatives, guillotines that whoosh a blade along a strip of wire, copiers that sort 200-page documents in batches of twenty. Like a factory, it's fascinating as long as you don't have to spend the rest of your life working in it.

Alec is everything that Jackie described, and more; a walking cliché with a neck like an Aberdeen Angus. He has stored for regular abuse every phrase read in a management manual. The other day I overheard him saying, 'You should treat every problem like an opportunity,' to Dave. Dave replied that he couldn't see how complete meltdown in the feeder system of the big copier could be seen as an opportunity, and Alec just marched off shouting, 'Solutions, not excuses,' while Dave muttered that the solution had already been booked to come and replace the buckled parts that afternoon.

Mike, fortunately, possibly because he doesn't have the natural ventilation system on the top of his head that Alec has, takes our overheated situation a bit more seriously. 'I don't think,' he says, 'that I can get air-conditioning put in at this late stage, but would a few big fans help? They would at least keep the air moving down here.' We all agree enthusiastically – anything is better than nothing – and Mike throws me an office-equipment catalogue to go through. 'Find the cheapest thing you think will be effective,' he says. 'Nothing too paltry, or they won't do any good, but remember we have a budget.' So I pore over the pretty pictures and the specifications, and pick out a copse of fans on stands that we can move around to blow over the machines we are most chained to on a day. They cost £107.95 each. You don't get nothing for nothing these days.

I show them to Mike. 'Isn't there anything cheaper?' he asks.

'Not that will do any good,' I reply.

Mike sighs. 'OK, I'll see what I can do.' This is when I discover the drawbacks of working in a huge organization with a civil-service-style management. Because ordering a fan is like setting up a cash till and ringing up. Being nosy, I've already found out that Mike is working on a contractor's day-rate of £350, which, taking off holidays, weekends, bank holidays and so forth, means that he is earning just a smidge under eighty grand a year, or, put another way, £43.75 an hour. Despite this, he has no authority to sign for any purchase over the value of £99. This is obviously an attempt by the management to minimize fraud, but I don't think they can have made any inflation-related increases in a decade: reprographics departments across the world have a spend limit of £99 and that's the bottom line.

So Mike sits down and writes out in longhand a memo requesting that the people upstairs consider buying the fans and his reasons for making the request. It takes him an hour. Ching: £43.75. Then I spend thirty minutes (at the £19 an hour that the agency charges for me) typing it up and printing it off, and making five copies in different colours and putting them into orange internal envelopes and looking up the names of the people I have to scribble into the bottom window. Ching: £9.50.

The memo goes upstairs to be read and considered by six people who, assuming that they're superior to Mike, must be on, say, upwards of £400 a day. At ten minutes a pop, that's an hour. Ching: £50. They then put the request on the agenda for the weekly budget meeting, spend twenty minutes discussing it. Ching: £100. The upshot of the budget meeting is a decision to refer the request to central office. Temp secretary to type up memo, copy it and send it off: £9.50. Central office, whose executives must be superior to the people down here but are probably on salaries, so, say, only on £300 a day (apart from directors who will be on £400) discuss it in their weekly budget meeting for twenty minutes. Eight executives on £300 plus two directors on £400 for a combined total of 200 minutes; ching: £133.33.

By now it's two weeks since Mike initiated the request, and we are slowly melting: Alec's scalp looks as though it's been got at by Indians at the end of the day. Executive committee decides to send a time-and-motion person down for a day to check out whether our claims are true. Ching: £150, plus report-writing, two hours, ching: £37.50. Executive committee have another meeting for another twenty minutes; ching: £133.33. Salaried secretary to type up their agreement and send it back to our executives: ching: £3.50. Project executives meet for ten minutes to sign it off; ching: £50. Mike fills in order form, plus payment request for accounts; ching: £14.58. Accounts process payment; ching: £5.30. Total cost of fans before executive protocols: £539.75. Total cost of fans after executive protocols: £1279.96. Total use for fans after executive protocols: three weeks, though the project will probably run late, as they always do, so more like six.

But no-one seems to feel that there is anything odd about this. Alec, in fact, seems to revel in it, firing off memos at the drop of a paper-clip. But then Alec likes management strategies. He's the man who buys all those books you see in airports: *Selling for Success*; *The Techniques of the Great Managers*; *How I Made My first Million Bucks*; *Secrets of the Snake-pit*. And in one of them – probably *Dress for Success!* – he must have read that statistic about people taking bald people less seriously, and decided that the hair transplant was the only answer.

This is funny, because what it actually is is a distraction. I'm not sure when he had it done, but it's either recently or it's not taken too well. His scalp is an unhappy puce, and the hair pokes out in corn-rows of a different texture from the rest, like oats that have suddenly found themselves planted in a field of wheat. Dave reckons they have used his pubic hair. Phil calls him Elton behind his back. Whatever, the dome of his head looks like a Mason Pearson hairbrush and is mesmerizing. Whenever he bends over, everyone nearby cranes to get a better look. But Alec obviously believes that he is the dominant male around here, and what he says has to be accepted with the grateful humility of plantation workers, or there's hell to pay. While the Great Fan Race is going on, he calls us round his desk for a meeting. Employs the classic dominance technique of remaining seated while we all stand around. I'm not going to put up with this sort of nonsense any more, so I sit down on the floor. After a few seconds the others follow suit, which means that we all disappear below the desk and the boss has to come forward and perch on one corner to see us.

Alec, polyester short-sleeved shirt, tie and mono-grammed pen in his top pocket, puts his hands behind his ears and starts. 'It's time we sorted out our act around here,' he announces. Bemused silence. 'We've got a problem,' says Alec, 'and it's called lack of professionalism.' More bemusement. I don't think any of the boys have thought about their button-pressing as more than a job before.

'I've got plenty of ideas,' says Alec. 'You're going to see a lot of changes around here, and the first one starts tomorrow. I want everyone to smarten up their dress. You can't take a job seriously unless you're seen to take it seriously.'

Dave looks down at his toner-stained T-shirt. 'What do you mean, Alec?'

'As of tomorrow, everyone's in jacket and tie. And you –' he nods at me, '– I want you in a suit.'

A stunned silence. 'Alec,' says Phil, 'you do know what we do, don't you?'

'Of course I do,' says Alec, 'in case you hadn't noticed, I'm the boss.'

'Look,' says Phil, 'we cart reams of A1 paper and tubs of dirty stuff around in 85-degree heat. We can't dress like account executives.'

Alec's scalp takes on a dangerous thundery quality. 'Don't argue with me!' he shouts. 'You don't make the rules around here, I do! And what I say goes!' I, meanwhile, am trying to work out who I can borrow a suit from. I'm certainly not getting the interview suit anywhere near that dyeline machine. Alec continues. 'You,' he fires at Phil, 'have an attitude problem. Don't think I haven't noticed. I've got my eye on you, lad. One more word out of you and there'll be real trouble.'

Chapter Sixty-two

The Smoker's Revenge

It's a tribal thing. Offices as much as any other community break down into tribes; the bigger the office, the more tribes. An office of up to, say, eight people will generally work as a single tribe and, unless a new member is a leader type, in which case a power struggle ensues, he or she will generally slip into the speech patterns and behaviour of the group. Once a room gets large enough to prevent colleagues communicating without walking, tribes start to split off, showing differing group characteristics. People, on the whole, have a need to belong, to define the space that defines them; it's comforting in an overlarge world.

In the wider world, this tribalism shapes the way we all think all the time. We belong to the big tribe of Europe (threatened by America, Asia, the Pacific Rim and less so by Eastern Europe, pals with Canada and Australia, patronizing to Africa and South America). More emotively, we're British patriots, and more emotively still, members
of the sub-British tribes (feel superior to Northerners, Southerners, the English, the Welsh; everyone has someone else to feel superior to). After that, we're employed or unemployed.

And within the workplace the tribal thing gets really

heavy. Most people stick more or less within their own stratum of seniority, and after that more or less within their common task group: creatives with creatives, accounts with accounts, IT with IT, secretaries with secretaries, editors with editors. Funnily enough, these tribal groupings often seem to break down those of race – many people's first friend of a different colour is made through the workplace – but not of gender: women and men still gang up on each other, the gay people in a building will always find each other and make pals. Think about it: why do wine bars exist? So women can go somewhere for pasta and mineral water rather than beer, chips and beans.

So which tribe do you belong to? Remember, you can belong to more than one. The fourth-floor tribe? The tribe that takes lunch every day, or the tribe that makes a virtue of never doing so? The bulls or the bears? Suits or smart-casual? Young, middle-aged or nearing retirement? Married (call the kids to say goodnight) or single (call your mates to plan the night)?

And which of these two relatively new tribes do you belong to: smoker or non-smoker? This is an interesting one, because there is always friction between the two and, though the non-smokers were the ones to create the tribal thing, ganging up together to ban the smokers, it seems to have backfired. Non-smokers don't recognize themselves as a tribe, because it's hard for tribes to cohere around a negative ('anti'-smoking). Smokers, meanwhile, however hard it is for non-smokers to understand, have a powerful positive in common: their love of the weed. The exclusion of smokers has done two things: created the embattled circumstances within which group unity thrives, and invented the smoking-room.

The smoking-room, or stairwell, or front steps, depending on how far the non-smokers have pushed it, is the place where all other tribal differences break down, where executives and post-room operatives ask each other how they are, where people become privy to information they would never have known if they'd stuck to their personal striation. Ever had that experience where you've come bouncing in with some gossip hot off the presses only to have a colleague say, 'Oh, didn't you know about *that*?' There's a 2-1 chance that they smoke. Ever asked someone how they know the art director only to have them say something like, 'Oh, I've just met her around'? Same thing.

The threat of tribalism, of course, is tribal wars. This us-and-them-ness resulted in the unions-vs-management wars of the Seventies and its very bloody resolution in the Eighties. And the antis are beginning to catch on at last; hence the rumbles in the past year about people having Too Much Fun in the smoking-room, the widespread refusal to install telephones or computers there so that no-one can both smoke and work concurrently. Where's it going to end? Bloodshed? Probably. But remember: the full-frontal attack of the last decade has honed the minority's guerilla tactics, and, as anybody with experience of Palestine, Afghanistan or South Africa knows, guerillas may often take a long time about it, but they usually win.

So after four weeks of labouring under the burden of Alec I decide to nip off one afternoon, while I'm taking a rush job up to the department that designs little round doodjamaflips that stop liquids going backwards, onto the back fire escape for a crafty fag. A stand-up yelling match has erupted between Alec and Phil because the big Xerox machine keeps clogging up, probably because of the sub-standard paper they're using to save money, and I don't feel like going back in a hurry.

The back fire escape leads out to a car park which mostly lies empty, because not enough people here are on the statutory level that qualifies them for a parking space. Never mind that there's all this room that the company is paying through the nose for: rules is rules, and only executives, level three, get parking spaces. I settle down on the landing bit on the third floor, light up and sit back. Bliss. This is the best bit of the day, so far.

The door opens below me, and two thrusting young execs emerge, Bensons in hand. You can always tell oil-company execs from your average freelance-engineer types, because they have haircuts that look like their wives did them at home with a tape-measure, a pudding basin and the kitchen scissors. Maybe it's a standard-issue haircut. Maybe it's some sort of secret code by which oil-company execs recognize other potential oil-company execs at the interview stage. Whatever, you can always tell them. I can spot them on the tube these days.

They are in the middle of talking, stop to light up and carry on their conversation. Brown-haired Exec says, 'Well, obviously it makes sense to employ people on contract and temp bases, but it's a real pest when something like this happens. I wonder if we could put the temp agencies on some sort of notice contract? We can't have people walking out in the middle of the day, especially not with things getting so close to deadline.'

'I know,' says Blond Exec. 'It's a bummer, isn't it? Do you know why she went?'

'Well, you know these girls,' says Brown. 'Always getting

big ideas. She said something about not liking being patronized, put down her notebook in the middle of the meeting and just walked.'

'So now,' says Blond, 'Adrian's got no secretary and we've got no minutes.'

'Oh, no, the minutes are OK. We got Bill's secretary to come and do those. But it's going to be at least a week before Adrian's got a PA, and you know what it's like with the agencies. They'll probably send someone with two GCSEs and a lot of experience at filing first off.'

'Doesn't personnel have any sort of pool?'

'You'd have thought so, wouldn't you? But no. They say their two pool people have taken off for the Gambia and they've not had a chance to find anyone else.'

'Damn,' says Blond. 'So where the hell are we going to get someone who's not going to be completely hopeless?'

'Dunno,' says Brown, pushing open the fire door, and they disappear back inside.

I think for about five seconds, then dig in my bag for a mirror and start patching up where my eye-liner has streaked in the heat. Rearrange a few hairgrips to make my bun look professional rather than like something that's just come out from a stint in the rain forest. Sniff my armpits and decide that they will have to do, slick on a bit of browny lipstick, tuck my shirt in where it's come undone at the back, take a deep breath and trot up the fire escape to the sixth floor.

I push the door open and come out in another world. It's lovely up here where the toffs hang out. Carpet that doesn't give you electric shocks when you touch something made of metal, wonderful views over the rooftops and garden squares, solid dividers between offices, the lot. I duck into the loo, have a quick nerves pee, then wander down the hushed corridor until I find the door of personnel. Knock, push it open and smile at the horse-faced Sloane who sits behind the reception desk.

'Can I help you?' she asks.

'Yah,' I say, speaking in the voice my parents always wanted me to use, 'I was wondering if I could talk to you for a moment.'

An hour later, back down in the basement, Phil and Alec are still at it while the other lads seem mysteriously to have colonized the machines closest to them, where they can hear what is said better. Dave winks at me and Paul looks away to suppress his smile. Red-haired Phil is living up to his colouring, tendons on his neck standing out as he yells from the depths of the Xerox machine's innards. 'I told you, I'm getting it!' he shouts. 'But it's going to keep jamming while you expect to use lightweight paper. It's not built to handle this sort of paper. Look! You just have to touch it for it to tear, and it folds up when it brushes against anything!'

Mike, as usual, has his nose buried in an A4 ring-binder up at the far end of the room. I've realized over the last couple of weeks that Mike is one of the more hopeless managers I've come across: so weak and afraid of confrontation that he will simply bury his head in the sand at the first sign of trouble. This, of course, is why he has employed Alec as his 2-i-c: I've found that weaklings often mistake the bully's swagger for a sign of strength.

'And I told you,' yells Alec, 'that I don't want to hear any more excuses! We all know about bad workmen and tools, and I don't want any bad workmen on my team!'

'I'm not a bad workman!' howls Phil. 'I know more about the insides of these machines than you will ever know! That's why I'm telling you!'

'If you're not part of the solution, you're part of the problem!' barks Alec. I think, Christ, in a minute he's going to say that if he can't stand the heat he should get out of the kitchen. Instead, he says, 'If the boots don't fit, then get to walking!' and rounds on me as I try to sneak past to get to my desk and start packing up. I thought the best thing to do about my sudden promotion was to tell Mike, who wouldn't have the gumption to get annoyed, but it looks like I'm not going to get the opportunity.

'Where have you been?' Alec shouts. I notice, suddenly, that though he has very little natural hair on his scalp, the hair in his ears has decided to make up for it, and sprouts in satyr-like tufts from the depths. Phil returns, muttering imprecations under his breath, to rattling levers in search of the elusive corner of paper that has jammed in a roller.

'Upstairs.'

'Upstairs?' The improbable woman on his arm is hopping about like a belly-dancer. 'I didn't give you permission to go upstairs.'

'Mike sent me.'

'Oh.' He's temporarily flummoxed, then starts again. 'It's been over an hour! Where have you been?'

'I dropped in on personnel.'

'Personnel,' he snarls contemptuously at the girly sound of the word. 'Can't stand the heat, then?'

'No,' I say, 'to be honest, I can't.'

'Well, get out of the kitchen! I don't want people who can't hack it in my platoon.'

I can't help it. I burst out laughing. Alec has obviously forgotten that we're on civvy street now. Belly-dancer starts jumping about; I think she might come off his arm altogether in a minute.

'Well, don't bother whining to personnel,' he shouts, 'because you can leave right now! Plenty more where you come from!'

'Are you sure?' I can't believe how smoothly this is going.

'Yes! You can have your money to the end of the week, but you can get out now!'

'Thanks,' I say, 'but I don't need the money. I'm starting upstairs tomorrow. I'm going to be Adrian Malone's personal assistant.'

I pick up my coat, get my fags out and head off for an early night. As I leave, the humming of the machines is the only sound I hear.

Chapter Sixty-three

How do You Like It?

One thing I've learned from working for everybody from the bottom to the top is that, the further up the ladder they get, the more difficult it is to work out what someone actually *does*. Take me, for instance. I've gone from £6.50 an hour to £10.50 – I'm a contractor now, which means that I have no more job security, but the company is paying roughly half what it would have done for my services – and instead of rushing around slicked with sweat, I sit behind a desk and do invisible things.

Adrian is the furthest up the ladder – a director of Prissyco (the company was named after the wife of the Texan dirt-farmer who discovered that the black stuff ruining his crops was actually worth a great deal of money) – and, although I do everything for him, I still haven't worked out what his function is. People ask his permission to do things, I know that. And he has some function of liaison between the people building the top side of the rig, known as topsiders, and those building the bottom· – believe it or not, the bottom-siders – who have been conducting their own version of the cold war since about six weeks after the start of the project. And I schedule him into lots of meetings with people from other oil companies and other engineering firms, and send them letters afterwards saying how pleasant it was to do business with them and any further questions, please do not hesitate etc., but that's it.

The rest of what I do is answer the two telephone lines, which rarely ring concurrently, and say, 'I'm sorry, he's in a meeting right now, Can I take a message for you?' Four or five times a day, in the brief periods when Adrian is in the office, I look up from my desk and say to the queues of pudding-basin haircuts as they troop up to my desk, 'Good morning/afternoon. Can I get you anything to drink? Tea? Coffee?'

Coffee. If only it was like it is in the ads: interior-designed jet-setting silk-shirt lifestyles and sophisticated *frissons* available even to the instant-drinking classes. Humorous, confident, kindly bosses like Cherie Lunghi putting bumptious men in their places without losing business/promotion/being labelled ball-breakers. Exiting oceans at night with neither jellyfish stings nor goosebumps, to be towelled down by a sensitively ill-shaven muscleman who nuzzles your ear as you inhale the orgasmic aroma of arabica.

Most of the people I make coffee for bear more resemblance to PG Tips monkeys than lovely shiny half-smiling Cherie Lunghis. I would never dream of complaining, because burning my fingers on those plastic cups so thin they might as well call them membranes, that companies install in their machines in the hope of saving £35 a year, is part of my job remit. And you can learn a lot about boss character through the ritual. Like the rude ones. No-one has ever surpassed the guy who, when I introduced myself as his secretary, merely said, 'Right. I take milk-no-sugar and I expect one on my desk on the hour every hour', but they are an odd lot. I think maybe many people feel uncomfortable about having servants, but I can never get over that 'pretend the waitress isn't there' thing.

You know how it is: No. 1 boss and No. 2 boss have a meeting with some outside honchos. You empty the mouldering sludge from the filter compartment because no-one ever feels washing-up is any business of theirs, go down to the corner shop to buy filter papers and milk, dig out the set of white china with the wiggly ridges on the top, decant milk into jug, scrape the worst of the limescale off the teaspoons, improvise a sugar bowl out of the clear Perspex lid of a box of pens, carry the whole lot through on a tray, best smile, knock on door and make your way in with your bum because it never occurs to anyone to hold the door for someone whose hands are occupied. All conversation stops; four pairs of eyes stare balefully at you as you set the cups, one by one, in front of them. Smile plastered on, you ask if anyone needs anything else, and No. 1 boss grunts a negative. As you close the door, a voice says, 'So you don't run to biscuits down here, then?' and someone else laughs.

The rudes are simply rude; the indecisives, those people who are so lost without their regular secretary to make decisions for them that they become paralysed when asked a simple question, are exhausting. They are the sort of people who say, 'Do I like these?' to their partners before biting into a profiterole. You can take ten minutes worming out of them what their preferences are. 'Milk and sugar?' 'Oh, gosh, Jenny usually makes my coffee.'

This trying tendency, though, seems like an endearing quirk when you're up against an anal retentive. Not only are anal retentives picky, they're also usually mean as all-get-out: take days off to avoid contributing to leaving-present collections, accept with alacrity when someone's

340

making a canteen run but never leave their desks themselves ('I'm always so busy I never notice the time'). And if their drink isn't exactly as it should be, there is hell to pay.

I've worked for them all, you know. Ms 'Whose mug is this? What's happened to my Love Is mug? I can't drink out of a Snoopy mug'. Mr 'When I said a drop of milk, I meant a drop, not a splash'. Mrs 'Don't you know the difference between a spoonful-and-a-quarter of sugar and a spoonful and a half?' and Dr 'These sweeteners seem to be made of saccharine'. A girl can go all day without time for a cup of Earl Grey, with all this rushing about.

Most of the people here for whom I get coffee have it white, two sugars and a custard cream. They love their custard creams. I think it's part of the oil-company hierarchy: down at the bottom, while you're still perfecting your haircut, you only get to drink machine coffee, black, because the creamer has run out. Then, once you've moved up a rung, they put pints of milk by the machines. Higher than that, they get a secretary to work the filter machine and a tin of assorted plain biscuits. Once they're at assistant VP level, the biccies have toppings and fillings. No wonder they're so thrilled when they get to play with the Big Boys. You'd have thought, when I offered them a choice between chocolate Hob-Nob and Bourbon, that I'd presented them with a company car and keys to the management loo.

The only spare cup I can find up on this floor for myself is actually a milk jug; everything else is earmarked. I'll have to bring one in for myself from home, but in the meantime this will do. People give me looks, but it works fine if you sip from the lip. We even have a proper filter machine up here, with two jugs, both of which everyone leaves on the hotplate with a quarter-inch of liquid in the bottom so that, by the time the next person comes along, all there is is a caramelized crust that needs scrubbing. But of course, because Adrian is such a Very Important Person, he doesn't have any truck with the company filter. For Adrian I have, two or three times a day, to put on a coat, go out to Starbucks and spend over £2 on a double-decaff latte. When I get back upstairs, I decant it into a mug with 'Oxford University' written on the side in gold with a load of bogus crests, in case anyone should think Adrian went to a redbrick, and sprinkle chocolate on the top from the little shaker in the top drawer of my desk. Yes, it's a tough life being a top-flight PA.

Chapter Sixty-four

Fly on the Wall

And just as I think I'm going to die of boredom, when I'm thinking, hey, maybe I should just be grateful that I have plenty of money to go and blow on a Saturday afternoon, Dan Cassell enters my little world and things start getting interesting. It should, really, be obvious Dan Cassell is going to make a change, because he refuses biscuits and coffee and asks for tea, black, and as weak as I can make it. 'Just dip the bag in for, like, a second,' he says. 'Sorry to be a pain.'

At this, I blink. No-one's ever apologized to me before, at least, not in the work sphere. I take a quick look at him, wondering if he's some sort of ecological interloper come to blow up the building to protect the whales or something, but he looks mild enough, and smiles pleasantly when he catches my eye. He's an odd-looking one, it's true; he's wearing a big jumper rather than a suit, and his haircut, which is well up above the ears, seems to bear traces of gel. Adrian is still out at a meeting somewhere, so I smile, settle him in a squashy waiting-for-the-boss chair and trot out to the kitchenette to get him sorted.

When I come back my little outer office is full of people. There's a man with a camera and a large black metal box, a man with a big boom microphone covered in the sort of fur you find in the lining of those coats people wear for trainspotting and never wash from one decade's end to the next, a woman about my age with a ring through her nose and a square light-box thingy tucked under her arm. And there's a lawyer-type fellow from oil country, the press officer, smiling with all the might that her newly stretched facial skin will allow, and Adrian, who has taken off his specs and is polishing them frantically.

'Ah, there you are,' says Adrian. 'Can you get these people whatever they need and bring it through, please?' and I politely concur, getting two milk-and-sugars, one black and two more just-dip-the-bags. It seems a waste to use a whole new tea bag, so, after checking that no-one's about to catch me at it, I fish the old one out from the bin, sloosh off the coffee grounds and recycle it. Dig out the china-for-guests (white, unbreakable and dull), put it all on a tray and bring it into Adrian's office.

Everyone is seated about the place, press lady with one notebook in her lap, lawyer with another in his, sound, camera and lighting peering about them while Mr Cassell talks. Adrian is behind his desk, steepling his fingers and attempting to look fierce and knowing. Dan is sitting forward, speaking.

'What we're looking for, of course,' he is saying, 'what Channel Four are looking for, is the drama of these weeks. The excitement and anticipation. The highs, the lows. The tension and the moments when it exerts itself. We're aware that this is a very exciting time, being on the edge of bringing a huge project like this to fruition, and we want the viewers to understand just how it feels.'

Handing round the cups and biscuits, I look at Adrian and think, how on earth are they going to get this guy to show any signs of being anything other than asleep?

'Well,' says Adrian, bites into a garibaldi and mulches it

very slowly round his mouth, 'obviously I could hardly refuse head office when they said they were sending you down here . . .'

'And,' says press woman, 'obviously, it's an excellent public relations exercise. The Green lobby is scoring all the points at the moment. It would be a good thing for the public to see the human face of the oil industry.'

And I think, now hang on, did I just gather that these people are making a fly-on-the-wall documentary for Channel Four? Have any of you *seen* a Channel Four fly-on-the-wall documentary?

'But,' continues Adrian, ignoring her as he tends to ignore most people, 'we're hardly showbiz here. But I'm sure everyone will be happy to help your team understand the engineering side of things. Mud injection is a fascinating subject, and one that I've never felt has been properly done justice by the media.'

'Mud injection?' asks cameraman, 'I thought you were pumping oil?'

Adrian sighs. 'Not pumping in the way that you would understand it. In simple terms,' the four simple media folk sit forward for their lesson, 'we drill, essentially, two holes, one an inlet and the other an outlet, the inlet going into the aquifer below the oil, the outlet into the very top of the deposit. Then we suck liquid mud up from the bottom of the ocean and pump it into the aquifer. Eventually the pressure that builds up is enough to force – ' Adrian becomes almost animated as he says this, throwing his hand upward in a gesture that is obviously intended to indicate a liquid travelling at great speed' – the oil up into the drilling pipe. It's far more economical than pumping, especially when it's being done from a floating vessel.'

I've not heard Adrian talk so much in one go before. We all stop for a moment to contemplate the whoosh of the world's energy as it shoots up a pipe, then Adrian blinks a couple of times and continues.

'As you can see, there's a lot more to this than tension and excitement, though certainly our engineers will be working flat out from now until the project's finished.'

'And we can have access to everything?' asks Dan Cassell.

'Well, yes, within reason. Of course, there are aspects of design that are still sensitive, but otherwise I dare say we can allow you general access.'

I can't stay in there any longer without it becoming blindingly obvious that I'm earwigging. I quietly remove myself, sit at my desk and begin typing up the morning's pile of correspondence. Someone wants to order in ten gross of Rotring pens before the rush starts; the supplies committee has authorized five. Mike, I see, is seeking permission to buy a higher quality of paper for the machines downstairs; permission granted. Personnel think it would be good for morale to hold a cheese and wine reception the day after the committee have met to finally approve the initial plans; wine, beer and soft drinks are OK, but only crisps and light snack foods.

As I type, I think, blimey, this is going to put a few cats among the pigeons. There are going to be people competing to get on camera, this media lot are going to be looking for every sign of discord and incompetence and making the absolute most of them. And I think, I can't wait to see this when it comes out: the plonking structures, the levels of perks, the inflexibility, the arrogant young men who elbow their way past as one tries to get into the lift with a big pile of folders, the engineers on topside who refuse to speak to the engineers on bottom side in case anyone claims credit for their ideas, the sweat, rage and custard creams. This will be fun. The door to the inner sanctum opens, and Adrian appears. 'Can you come in here for a moment?' he beckons.

I trot obligingly through, stand in the doorway awaiting instruction. Adrian indicates the TV crew. 'These people,' he says, 'are going to be making a four-part documentary about this project. I am far too busy to nanny them, though obviously they will be wanting to consult with me, and Andrea – ' he waves vaguely at press woman – 'will be extremely busy helping them with information and so forth. So we've decided to put you at their disposal. You can work for me the majority of the time, and get switchboard to put calls through to John Giddes's PA when you're needed. Get them what they need; schedule times for them to visit departments, fill them in on what you know, see they've got whatever backup is required.'

'Fine,' I say, 'cool.'

Adrian peers at me over his specs. He doesn't like his staff speaking in colloquialisms. 'Well,' he says, 'I just hope you're up to the job.'

Four pairs of eyes are studying me, speculatively. I nod. 'I'm sure I will be,' I say.

My new charges follow me out of the room, carting their gear, and I take them to the lift. As we wait for it to come they all smile at me, and stick out their hands, one by one, as Dan introduces them. 'I'm Dan Cassell,' says Dan, 'and I'm directing this thing.' We shake. The cameraman is called Liam. Sound bloke is Dave. Shona, with the body-piercing, turns out to be an assistant producer-cum-researcher. They all solemnly shake me by the hand, say how nice it is to meet me.

'So when do you start?' I ask, holding the door open as Dave and Liam hump their stuff into the lift.

'Monday, God willing,' says Shona. 'We're just getting the final contracts signed, but I think that's all going ahead smoothly.'

'Fine,' I say. 'Just call me if you want anything ahead of then, and I'll be ready and waiting for whatever it is you need on Monday.'

'Great,' they all say together. And then Shona says, 'Actually, that's a point. No-one told us what your name is.'

'Alexandra,' I say, 'Sasha for short. Sasha Lindsay.'

'Nice name,' says Dan. 'Well, Sasha Lindsay, we'll look forward to seeing you next week.'

Chapter Sixty-five

The Power of Television

I used to notice this around Ben when he was in the band – well, not Ben exactly, who was the one, obviously, on whom the cameras were trained anyway, but the people who surrounded him: the publicists, the make-up people, the print hacks, the little girls who would have laid down their lives to get into his drawers – but it still strikes me as odd how people change whenever there's a camera around. The genuinely shy ones become even shyer, practically throwing themselves into cupboards to avoid getting their face on screen, but the vast majority will act up to any extent you could predict and then probably more so when they see their chance to be filmed. It's weird. You see people who are otherwise the most balanced, upright members of society practically break into tap dances at the approach of a camera. You see them perform handstands, knickers in the air, against walls, jump up and down behind whoever's speaking, preen their hair, pull playground faces that would have their mothers cringing.

This is a culture of thrusting execs, and they have all become that much more thrusting in the week since the cameras arrived. The lifts ring with phrases like 'up to my arse in alligators' and 'yes, but we're talking the bottom line here'. Ties have got brighter, suit buttons have been replaced with little sartorial details, the pudding basins have been out in force over the weekend. People slap each other on the back, prance around each other, feinting boxing moves, boast about how much they drank in Quag's the night before, and always with tiny glances into mirrors, into the reflections in windows, over the corners of rooms to see if the camera is on them.

The engineers, meanwhile, lumpy, bearded teddy bears of men with a blokeish demeanour and a team-driven distrust of authority, have become more blokeish, more beardy, more cynical. They crack jokes about the execs and their play-acting, but they, themselves, are walking around with big signs around their necks saying 'Natural man. Film me.' Each seems to have worked out a stock of asides and bad jokes which they swap, constantly, over their drawing boards. They would never do anything as undignified as slap each other's shoulders, but they gather in knots in the hallways and jiggle the change in their trouser pockets.

The women, meanwhile, are wearing conspicuously more make-up. I would love to say that this wasn't true of me, but I found myself getting up a quarter of an hour earlier on the first Monday to fit in time for foundation disasters along with the rest of them. And I suddenly understand why everyone always seems to be so tall on telly: it's because they're all wearing stilettos. The average female height went up by three inches over the weekend when the news got round that there was a documentary team due in the building, and the first aiders have reported a surge in sprains and falling injuries of late. I hear them out in the corridors and can't stop myself smiling behind my mask of make-up: tinkling laughs have replaced surly snarls, enquiries after colleagues' health abound. The younger the employee, the more extreme the dress, but everyone is looking alarmingly smart around me. Thank God I've still got Tania's old suits on loan. And all this for an audience that couldn't be more uninterested if they were trying. These TV people are hard nuts to crack. Dan has a certain charm, which he employs when he's persuading someone to perform for the camera, repeat a telephone conversation, explain what they're doing and where the drawbacks are, but it switches off the second they've wrapped on a shot. I guess it comes with the territory, that after a while of being bombarded by the self-appointed class joker, the acid-tongued queen, the girl who wants to be a model, the man with the gravitas, the toxic vixen, you tend to shut yourself off, learn to concentrate doggedly on holding your boom just so, getting the light pointed in the right direction. But it's weird nonetheless, for, if they were involving themselves with their subjects more, they would probably have a better idea of where to look for a bit of drama. Then again, if they were involved with their subjects, they probably wouldn't feel so free to be ruthless if they found anything to be ruthless about. As it is, they remain aloof and things aren't going so well.

They're pretty nice to me, on the whole, though I don't fool myself that they would give me the time of day if I wasn't useful. But this is more interesting than sitting in Adrian's vestibule typing, so I'm content to tag along with my list of names, show them the after-work pubs where everybody drinks, trot up and down to personnel and the press officer to check things, and watch how they work. I wouldn't mind doing something like this myself: it must be a gas to go into other people's lives without responsibility, observe them and report your viewpoint to the world.

But they keep finding nothing. The fact is, though these people are making something terribly exciting, dangerous, controversial, the way they go about it is absolutely boring. Watching them hunched over their drawing-boards, comparing notes on the holding properties of different types of widget, is like watching paint dry. Most jobs that involve responsibility for other people's lives are like that. Apparently life on the minefields when there are no celebrities around is deathly, too: just rows of blokes poking inch by inch over the ground with sticks for months on end. After ten days my new colleagues are in despair: they've used over twenty hours' stock and got less than ten usable minutes.

So they do what everyone does when they're in despair, and go to the pub, and take me, because I'm almost a part of the team now, with them. We end up in the same place, at the same table, where Jackie and I sat all those weeks ago, only it's vodka and cranberry and dry-roasted peanuts with this lot. And they all, apart from Dave, smoke as though there was going to be a blanket ban on the activity from tomorrow. The ashtray fills up like the ones at home, and Dan starts grumbling.

'I had no idea that so little happened,' he says. 'I was under the impression that the tail-ends of these projects were complete mayhem, people working round the clock, loads of dramas.'

'Oh, they're all working frightfully hard,' I say. 'But when what you do is draw things and think about things, it doesn't show much.'

'But don't they have disagreements? Don't they get into states? Don't things go wrong?'

'Of course they do. But problems don't show all that much, because all they have to do is recalculate things on the computers and get them right.'

Shona lights another cigarette. 'So no-one's at loggerheads with anyone else? There are no rows going on?'

'Well, yes,' I tell her, 'You must have noticed that topside and bottom side aren't talking to each other at all?'

Dan sits up. 'No! No-one said anything about that to me!'

'No, well I suppose they wouldn't.'

'And when did that start?'

'As far as I can gather, a couple of months after the project did. Topside, who are this lot, accused bottom side, who are another firm of heavy engineers contracted in from the outside, of interfering with their work. And then someone on bottom side leaked some secret about what they were doing to topside, who tried to get out of paying that part of the contract because they claimed that they'd thought of it first. So then there was an almighty row, and the doors that link the two sides of the building were sealed up, and only Adrian and about five other people are allowed to have any contact with the other lot.'

Shona has taken out her notebook and is scribbling. 'So when they meet to put the two together, it will effectively be the first time they've done it?'

'Mmm.' Well, Adrian did tell me to give them whatever they needed.

'And who signs off the other side's expenses?'

'Adrian. Via head office.' I tell them the story of the fans, and they start to smile.

'So,' Liam asks, 'is that what they have to go through every time they want something?'

I nod.

'And how long does it take?'

'The fans took three weeks. But I've heard that things can take months if they get caught at the committee stage.'

'How do we find out about who's trying to order something?'

I consider: how do I maintain discretion while helping them out?

'Just ask the heads of department. Everything has to go through them.'

There's a pause.

'Oliver Jones is usually helpful,' I finish. Oliver Jones is, it's true, unusually garrulous; and the graphics department has just put in an order for another copy of PowerPoint to keep up with the impending rush.

Shona scribbles. Dan goes and gets in another round.

'Do you like working here?' asks Shona. 'How long have you been doing it?'

'Me? I'm a temp. I've been there about five weeks now.'

'A temp? But you behave like you know everything that goes on. I thought you must have been there years.'

I shrug. 'You get good at finding things out if you do this for any length of time. Otherwise you're floundering all the time and it's really miserable.'

'A temp, huh?' Shona licks the end of her finger, turns it round the corners of the empty peanut packet. 'I did that for over a year. Shitty, isn't it?'

'Mmm,' I say, then I think, yeah, but I haven't been hating it the same way for a while. Once I stopped feeling I'd been cheated out of my real career, it's not been so bad. 'But you learn a lot of stuff. People, their motivations, what really goes on under the patina of business, who hates who, who loves who. It's not so bad once you get used to not having a home.'

Liam laughs. 'Sounds a bit like my job,' he says. 'Load of strangers, in, bosh, do the job, go back to my real life for a few days.'

'I hadn't thought about it before,' says Shona. 'But you're right. We never stay anywhere long enough to make friends either.'

'Well,' says Dan, putting down the drinks in front of us, 'it's not so bad now. Now we're established as our own production company, at least we know each other. And you two,' he nods at Dave and Liam, 'are working with us at least a third of your time now.'

Dave sniggers. 'Yeah. Proper little team we are these days.'

'So,' says Shona, 'is there anyone who really does hate anyone there? Any really showy tyrants? All we're getting is a load of blokes in suits trying to impress. We need something a lot funnier. You know. Blood, sweat, frustration and shouting.'

I look round them, and I think, well, what have I got to lose apart from my boredom? That's what you get when you insist on employing half your workforce off the agencies. You may save a ton on National Insurance, but you can't expect people to stay loyal when they know you'll sack them whenever it's convenient.

'Well,' I say. 'You haven't been down to the reprographics department yet, have you?'

Chapter Sixty-six

Bolognese

'It was brilliant,' I say, waving the chopping-knife in the air, 'they couldn't have got better if they'd rehearsed it.'

Ben takes the knife and carries on with the onion while I go to the sink and splash water over my eyes to clear the stinging. I've never managed to get used to onions; always have to rely on Ben to cut them up in the end.

'You mean,' says Ben, 'he head-butted him, just like that?'

'Mmm.' I slop some olive oil into the pan, put it on the heat, chuck in the onions. 'They'd been down there filming all morning, and you know how people get all exaggerated in front of the camera. So Phil had got even more don't-bovver-me-I'm-from-Stevenage, and Alec had come completely true to form. I think he's the sort of bloke who thinks that if the world were to see his management techniques on celluloid—'

'Video,' says Ben. 'They're probably shooting on video.'

'Don't be a wanker. Jesus, are you sure you've got enough garlic there?' Ben's chopping up a full half-bulb.

'It's good for you,' he says. 'Cleans the blood. And, it's not like we're going to be breathing over anyone else much.'

I shrug. 'Anyway, I think he's under the impression that he'll get headhunted if he shows off enough. So he's marching around like a cockerel on heat, barking out orders and actually *snapping his fingers* at people to get their attention.'

'I saw Candice Murray do that in the Ivy once,' says Ben. 'I wouldn't have liked to eat her soup. Definitely looked a bit gobby. Then again, it was vichyssoise.'

'Vichyssoise shouldn't look gobby. It should look creamy, with a few nice herbs floating in the top.'

'Well.' Ben throws in the garlic and the room fills with lovely smells you never encountered in our northern homes.

'So Phil was showing them round his machines, opening the doors to show what they looked like inside, that sort of thing, and he took off his jacket and rolled up his sleeves. To look more butch, I think, and maybe to show off the Tottenham crest on his forearm. Anyway. Alec notices that he's done it, and comes bustling over to get himself on camera again, goes, "If I've told you once I've told you a thousand times, I will not tolerate sloppy presentation in this department."'

'Have we got any chillis?' asks Ben, chucking a handful of herbs into the pot.

'Not fresh, no, but there's a jar of little dried ones.'

'D'you mind if we chuck a couple in? I know it's Bolognese, but it'd be nice to spice it up a bit.'

'Fine by me. Anyway, Phil folds his arms, juts his jaw and says, "And I've told you a thousand times, it's not possible to do manual work in toffs' clothing." And before we know it, and all with Liam soaking up every moment, they're yelling at each other. Alec's stabbing his finger into Phil's face and going on about insubordination and Phil riding close to the edge, and Phil's going on about orders having to be reasonable. And then Alec suddenly goes: "Right! That's it! You've had your chances, sonny Jim, and this is the last time! Get your things and get out! You're sacked!"'

Ben throws in chicken livers, starts them off browning. 'You're kidding. On camera?'

'Yeah. These people are fools to themselves. I don't think they have the first idea how they're going to look.'

'So then?'

'Well, Phil goes, "I'm sacked, am I?" and Alec goes, "Yeah. I don't want a workshy tosser like you in my department," and Phil looks at him, and then he goes "Well, that's fine, because I don't want to work for a *wanker* with a hair transplant!" and whacks him one between the eyes. Breaks his nose, blood everywhere, Alec yelling blue murder, going, "You boge by dose you badard!" Mike burying himself behind some catalogue pretending it's not happened, and the next thing we know not only Phil's gone, but Paul and Dave and Steve have got their coats and walked as well. So now they've got no-one to work the machines and Alec's walking around looking like a cockatoo. It was brilliant. Brilliant.'

I chuck in the mince, open a can of tomatoes.

'Ah, testosterone,' says Ben. 'Makes you proud. Bet the TV people were pleased.'

'I've never seen them so happy. They were out the front door and back to base to make sure the film was out of harm's way before you could blink.'

'Fabulous,' says Ben, finishes stirring the meat, chucks in mushrooms and a handful of olives. 'This is going to be brilliant. Do we have any anchovies?'

I check in the store cupboard. 'Yes.'

'Great,' says Ben. 'Hand them over.'

'Tell me about your day?'

'It was good. *The Times* want an interview for their arts

pages, and – get this – the *Face* were on the phone to my agent wanting to do a piece on reinventing myself. "Emerging from the Ashes", they want to call it. Bloody cheek.' Of course Ben's got a new agent. You didn't think someone could survive in the whacky world of showbiz without one, did you? Only this agent is called Hilary, and she's young and hungry, just like us. He goes out for drinks with her in China White and comes home singing these days, because everyone wants to talk to him again. Amir's been on the phone to get him to take part in some charity gig in March, Candice wants an exclusive for the teen-movie promo slot she's fronting between *Buffy the Vampire Slayer* and *EastEnders* on Thursday nights. Suddenly, every boxer in the country is queuing to put their arm round him and give the thumbs-up.

'So are you going to do it, then?'

'Of course.' He laughs, chucks in the tomatoes and half a tube of tomato paste. Ben's calm these days; all the rage seems to have evaporated, and what's left is this sunny, laughing skinhead who tells jokes in the day and can't wait to come home and cuddle me at night. But, you know, we haven't talked about it at all. I think maybe both of us are scared that, if we ever used a phrase like 'going out', the whole thing would crumble to dust in our hands.

Ben goes over to the wine rack and pulls out a bottle of red. Opens it, slings a glassful into the sauce, pours us each a glass. And says, 'Hey, I've just thought of something. This is really nice, isn't it?'

'What?'

'Being able to come home and find that things are where you left them. Not having to go to the offy every night because someone's polished off your drink and won't admit that they did it.'

He puts his glass down, turns back to the sauce. 'I mean, obviously I'd have Donna back tomorrow if she wanted to come. Donna's cool. But it's kind of nice just having the two of us around.'

I think that this is a declaration of happiness. That's Ben all over. The passionate articulacy of a footballer.

'Yes, it's good,' I say in response. 'I'm happy if you are.'

'Och,' says Ben, 'I'm more than happy. I've got all the company I need.' He takes another slug, tops us both up. 'So how's the PowerPoint requisition coming along?'

'Fantastic. They're thrilled. They've filmed six committee meetings so far and they still haven't come to a decision. Graphics are going mad, queuing up to get at the one screen when they're meant to be turning out fifty charts a day.'

He shakes his head. 'Babes in arms. When do you think they'll get it, if they do?'

I blow a bit of fringe out of my eyes. 'It's only three weeks 'till the first stage is meant to be done and dusted. Even if they get it next week, they'll only have use of it for a fortnight.'

'Great.' Ben leans forward, tastes the grub and swears that he's the best cook in London. 'I could always get a job on the Carlton Food Network.'

'I don't think you're going to have to, sweets.'

'D'you know what?' I'm watching the curve of his cheek, the fine stubble dotted across his jaw, the bright green of his eyes as he considers his future, and thinking, God, I'm proud of you. 'I don't think I am, either. The film's not even out yet, and Hilary's had three scripts in already this week.'

'What sort of stuff?'

'The usual. Grainy minority-channel underworld dramas. Oh, and one for ITV where I get to be a toyboy.

They're after Francesca Annis for that one.'

'Nice.'

Ben grins. 'Yeah. Yeah, it is.'

'I'm very proud of you, you know.'

'Don't get soppy.'

Ben salts the sauce. Tastes again, hands me a spoonful to taste as well. 'Good, eh?'

I nod vigorously. It's true. Somewhere along the line, Ben learned to cook.

'Right,' he says, turns down the heat, puts a lid on the pan, picks up the bottle and heads for the door. 'Leave that for an hour and a half and it'll be magic.'

He turns, smiles at me and says, 'Hey, Sasha?'

'Yes?'

'While we're waiting for supper, d'you fancy a bath?'

How nice. 'OK. Sure.'

'Good,' says Ben. 'Because you bloody need one.'

I grab the J-cloth from the draining-board and fling it at his head.

Chapter Sixty-seven

Bored Meeting

The differences between topside and bottom side are a distant memory as of today. For today the two sides meet to put their blueprints together and slap backs. This is the moment they've all been waiting for, the moment when, after three long years of planning, in-fighting, receipt-checking, copying, printing and drawing, everyone can sit back and say, 'Gentlemen, we have an oil rig.'

So momentous is this occasion that Adrian has actually authorized sandwiches for everyone, even though half of them are only at executive level. I've called the sandwich shop and ordered cheese and pickle, prawn with Marie Rose sauce, beef and horseradish, and roasted vegetable with sun-dried tomato, which have turned up covered in cling film on stainless-steel platters with bits of parsley all round the sides. Debbie, John Giddes's PA, and I have arranged bottles of mineral water down the middle of the boardroom table, surrounded by Arcoroc glasses just like we used to have at school, and brought the coffee-machine through and plugged it in. So now all that remains is for the engineers of Prissyco to face the engineers of Michaelson, Bowles and Willis, shake hands and parlay. And for me to scribble furiously in the background as the minute-taker.

Of course, Adrian has invited the TV crew in to witness his day of triumph. He's been working on his closing speech for a week now, and a very fine speech it is too, now that I've tacitly tidied up the grammar and he's not noticed the changes. Dan and Shona have been pumping me for information: are there going to be any shocks? Do I think that there'll be much evidence of the tension between the two teams? Does everybody get gypsy creams? I don't have a lot to impart, however. This is my first time at such a momentous occasion myself.

And of course, the truth of the matter is that it's just as boring as every other meeting I've ever been to. Two solid hours of injection pumps, gas caps, shale, anticlines, flare stacks, drilling cables and self-congratulation. I crouch at a corner of the board table, breaking protocol for the sake of having somewhere to lean, scribbling frantically until my wrist hurts and my fingers start cramping, hoping to hell that I've been taking the figures down correctly, as I only understand about a third of what's being said. Appropriately enough, my faux-shorthand looks increasingly like Greek as the morning wears on. Liam circles the table, homing in on individuals as they expound on mud quality, doing close-ups of youthful pudding basins as their hands slide across the table to snaffle another chocolate homewheat. Including Shona and me, there are four women in the room among the twenty present.

Blueprints slide round the table, though everyone has a carefully collated set of their own, put together on overtime by Paul, persuaded back from the dole queue with promises of air-con and casual clothing, and his new helper, Derek. They start with Adrian, on my left, and pass, portwise, round the table until the whole pile ends up in front of me. I suppose that this means that I'll have to clear them up later. As new gas valves are unveiled, gasps of admiration rise from the throng, murmurs of appreciation ripple across the table at the sight of special bolts, super-duper hawsers. And I scribble and scribble, and the sweat beads my brow.

After two hours Adrian gets to his feet and everyone falls quiet to hear his words.

'Gentlemen,' he says, and adds as an afterthought and with a courtly bow in the direction of the two female engineers, 'and ladies. I just want to thank everyone for their sterling work on this project. As we know, things have occasionally got a bit tense between us all, but now that the day has finally come, I think we can all accept that we have ultimately shown what great teamwork can produce. It's teamwork that Prissyco is famous for, and teamwork that has brought us to this point.'

From the pile in front of me he pulls out the two primary blueprints: the pictures, one made by Prissyco and one made by Michaelson, Bowles and Willis, of what the fabled topside and the fabled bottom side will look like when they are finally joined and bobbing about in the great North Sea. Ceremoniously he lays them out so that the two parts link together and the whole is there for all of us – and the camera – to digest.

'Teamwork,' says Adrian. 'Teamwork, communication and scrupulous attention to detail. It is these qualities that have pushed back the frontiers of exploration, made our great companies the bywords they are in the industry for innovation, courage and reliability. Here, at last, is the Raptor platform. Phase one of the Raptor Project is finally at an end. I think we all deserve to give each other a round of applause.'

There is a moment of quiet, then clapping breaks out,

swells in a crescendo and dies away as Prissyco executives and MBW executives rise to their feet and, like the congregation of a church in the decade of evangelism, start shaking hands with the person next to them, slapping backs and even, here and there, exchanging manly hugs. Eyes are damp, though not a tear is shed: this is, truly, a heroic occasion.

When it's all over, Adrian, who is still on his feet and rubbing his hands together, says, 'Well. I hope you will all have time to stay for a spot of lunch. Debbie is about to come in with some champagne for us all to toast our achievement. Congratulations.'

The door opens and Debbie enters, wheeling a hostess trolley that I had no idea the company owned. Corks pop, laughter rings out as glasses overflow, and Liam chases about the room capturing middle-aged faces etched with the satisfaction of a job well done.

Adrian pats me on the shoulder. 'I hope you'll stay for a glass,' he says. He's still not mastered my name, but I don't mind so much any more. I accept gratefully and find my-self, as usual at things like this, standing around feeling conspicuous as I remember that I don't really know any-one, that I'm not really part of the team.

To pass the time I start to read the blueprints that Adrian has laid out so stylishly on the table. I've always been a bit obsessed with maps, spending hours staring at them, attempting to translate squiggles and lines into hills and valleys, rivers and roads. This holds a similar fascination: Alec was constantly shouting at me downstairs for getting so interested in what was on the drawings that I would forget to hand them over for copying.

It looks magnificent, this metal giant, this surfaced kraken; part monster truck, part cathedral, with soaring gantries, spires and steeples. I put my glass down, lean my elbows on the table and gaze. Try to imagine what it will look like when it's twice the size of this building, when it's working, when the pumps are pumping and tiny ant-sized people are running about on its ladders and surfaces. I look at the figures, trying to imagine what 1,000 tonnes actually *looks* like, what sort of swimming pool 5,000,000 cubic metres would fill. It's amazing. I only wish I understood more of what I'm looking at. I start having another of those career fantasies: the one where I go back to school, take maths and physics and geology A levels, go back to university, train as an engineer, learn to build things rather than sit around in an office fantasizing about it. The numbers look really odd to me: really odd; I only wish I understood how they worked.

Adrian breaks into my reverie. 'What do you think, then?' he asks in his little-woman voice, the one that he uses for asking me to go down to Starbucks.

'It's amazing,' I reply, quite genuinely. 'Breathtaking.'

'Good,' he says complacently, though why anyone should be gratified by the opinion of an ignorant secretary is beyond my ability to hazard. 'Understand it, roughly, do you?'

'Well, I suppose so. There's just one thing, though. I don't know. I'm probably being stupid . . .'

'Oh, I'm sure you aren't,' he says in a voice that assures me that he knows that I am. 'Ask anyway. You'll never learn if you don't ask.'

'OK.' I point at the figures in the top right-hand corner of the Prissyco diagram, and the figures in the top right-hand corner of the MBW one. 'Look, I know I'm being dumb, but I don't understand how come, if the top half's half as heavy again as the bottom half, and it's going to be floating, it won't just turn upside down when you get it in the water.'

'Oh, no, no, no,' says Adrian, laughing heartily. 'You're reading it all wrong. It's—'

He stops mid-flow, bends closer as if being nearer at hand will somehow make the figures undergo a miraculous change. 'What the—' he says. Looks at me, looks back at them, looks up to call his *alter ego* from the MBW side over and finds himself staring directly into Liam's hovering lens.

Chapter Sixty-eight

One Door Closes

What do you do when you get a piece of bad news? Shoot the messenger, of course. I know, the moment the words leave my lips, or at least in the three seconds after that, as Adrian turns from benevolent patron to man in fear for his salary, that my days at Prissyco are numbered. I just don't realize how tight the numbering is. By mid-morning the next day, in fact, I am a free woman. I've been terrified of coming face to face with Adrian all night, wondering what on earth I'm going to say. I mean, seriously, this wasn't a deliberate boo-boo. I've learned my lesson, I will never be curious about something that I don't understand again, I swear. I'll sit tight, keep my mouth shut and never, ever put someone powerful in an embarrassing position.

When I arrive there is no sign of my boss, but the little sofa in my vestibule is occupied. Jill, the horse-faced Sloane from personnel, has a folder in her hand. 'Good morning,' I say, 'Were you waiting for Adrian?'

'No,' says Jill, 'I was wanting to have a word with you, actually.'

Oh, bugger, I think, here it comes.

'OK. Would you like a cup of coffee or shall we get straight down to it?'

'No, thank you. We might as well get straight down to it.'

I sit in my desk chair, clamp my hands together.

'There's no easy way to say this,' says Jill, 'so I might as well just tell you the truth,' which I've learned from experience is what people say when they're just about to tell you a whopping porky. I say nothing; take a small pleasure, at least, in making her work for her cushty salary and the space in the car park for her air-conditioned Vectra.

She shuffles her papers, blinks. 'The thing is, we've been reviewing our staffing costs, and it's been decided that we are spending too much on temporary staff.'

'Uh-huh?'

Another blink, another rustle. 'So I'm afraid we're going to have to let you go.'

'I see.'

I'm buggered if I'm going to say anything else. Actually, though I've seen this coming, I'm furiously angry under my composure. It's not my bloody fault that the whole project's been run like a school playground and the result of everybody putting everybody else in Coventry is that they've built their bloody oil rig upside down. I put my elbows on the desk and give her a stony look.

'Uurk, ark,' says Jill, whose training hasn't prepared her for this reaction. 'We want you to understand that this doesn't reflect in any way on your work. You've been super – ' Super. Super. I've saved them from going belly-up and glug glug glug to the bottom of the sea, and I'm super like a member of a hockey team. 'A real help. Adrian's been full of praise for you.'

I continue to stay stumm, because quite a lot of phrases like, 'Fuck off, you cow,' are bubbling around the inside of my lips.

Jill waits for me to react, gulps a few times, looks around

like a trapped animal. Finally I say, 'So when do I leave, then?'

She sifts through her papers again and produces an envelope.

'Today, if you don't mind.'

I raise my eyebrows.

She continues. 'We understand, of course, that this is going to be an inconvenience for you. So the management has approved an *ex gratia* payment for you. As you know, you don't have a notice period, so this is purely a gesture of goodwill on the company's part.'

I take the envelope. Inside is a cheque for £2,000. I've never seen this much money all in one go.

'And what do you want in exchange for this?'

'Obviously, we need you to sign this waiver form.'

She hands me a couple of sheets of paper. I skim them. They're not a waiver form, they're a secrecy agreement. I'm to agree not to discuss the firm's business outside the building. Which is a joke, really, as Dan, Shona, Liam and Dave have the whole lot on film.

'Have you got a pen?'

She hands me a Mont Blanc Meisterstuck: British racing green with gold details; the kind of pen people give to personnel staff for their birthdays because they can't think of anything else.

I sign on the dotted line. Tuck the cheque into my purse. Pick up my bag, shake her hand, walk down the silent corridor, drum my feet in the empty lift, bid a fond farewell to Stan on the front desk, a lovely old soldier working twelve-hour days for minimum wage, and find myself out on the streets of Bloomsbury at a point when everybody else is hunched over their desks. And that's the end of my career in the petrochemical business.

Chapter Sixty-nine

Another One Opens

With two grand in my pocket and a serious dose of the sod-its, I turn into Craig. Sleep in till lunch-time, lie about on the floor in my jim-jams watching Jerry, pop up to the offy for a bottle of red (I can't quite sink as low as Red Stripe, though given time I'm sure it could happen) at five o'clock. I'll get my act together in a bit, but for now I feel like I've done enough struggling. Everyone else struggles and gets somewhere; I struggle and end up where I started. Even Marina can't annoy me into taking action now; she arrives one evening to give me a lecture, and I tell her to shut up. And to my amazement, she smiles and says, 'Don't worry, Sash. Something will turn up,' and goes to the offy herself.

Ten days after Prissyco wave me goodbye, I'm lying on the sofa while two enormous chicks in hot pants and fright wigs jab fingers through the air and shout, 'You tink you aw dat 'n' a bag o' fries bu' arm hearda tell *you* duh yew *ate* aw dat!' at each other, when Ben's phone rings. The phone is by my head, but I can't be arsed to pick it up. I dip into a giant bag of Kettle chips and turn Ricki up a couple of notches.

The answerphone goes off, and Ben's voice competes with someone shouting, 'Don't *go* there! Don't even *go* there!'

'Hello,' says Ben. 'This is Ben Cameron's office. Please leave a message and we will contact you as soon as possible. This machine is checked regularly.' And it beeps.

The hiss of someone calling on a mobile phone. Then: 'Er, hi, yes, I'm sorry to bother you. My name's Dan Cassell and I'm trying to get in touch with Sasha Lindsay. I didn't know any other way of—'

I flip the mute button on the telly, pick up the phone. 'Dan?'

Hiss. Then a surprised voice is going, 'Sasha?'

'Yes.'

'Hi,' says Dan.

'Hi. How did you get hold of me here?'

'I remembered that you'd said you were Ben Cameron's flatmate. So I rang *Spotlight* and got the number of his agent, only it turned out to be some guy who was extremely sniffy and said that he no longer represented him because he was going to hell in a handbasket and he didn't want to be associated with failure. So then I had to ring up the production company that made this film he's in, and after I'd persuaded them that I wasn't trying to blag tickets to the première – did you know they're like gold dust, by the way? Are you going? Presumably you are? – they gave me the number of his current agent, and after I'd spent about half an hour explaining that I was trying to get hold of you, and who you are and that I wasn't trying to bypass her to give him some work, she gave me this number and here I am.'

Dan takes a deep breath after all this completely unnecessary detail.

'Oh,' I say.

'How are you?'

'I'm fine. Watching Ricki and eating crisps.'

'How nice,' says Dan. 'I'm on a train between Bristol and Bath.'

'Oh, yeah? What are you doing there?'

'Coming back down from London. I've just been watching the edits and they're hilarious. The fight among the photocopiers is some of the best telly I've ever done.'

'Oh, good.'

'Oh, Christ,' says Dan, as the roaring sound in the background gets louder, 'I'm just about to go through a—'

The line goes dead. I dial 1471, scribble down his number for luck, turn the sound back up on Ricki. The chicks in hot pants are by now haranguing a member of the audience, their own fight a thing of the past.

'Sit down!' shouts one, dabbing her palm face down in the air like Adolf Hitler. 'Sit down. You dote know nuttin aboudit!'

'You got low sel-vesdeem,' yells audience member. 'Ditch the zero, get a hero!'

'Sel-vesdeem!' shouts hotpants No. 2, 'I'll show you sel-vesdeem!' and standing up and turning round, bends over and wiggles her cellulite in the direction of her heckler.

The phone rings again. I pick it up and it's Ben, sounding annoyed, on his mobile. 'I was trying to access my messages. Do you always pick up when you're in the house?'

'No. But I just had Dan on the line.'

'Dan?'

'The guy who was making the fly-on-the-wall at Prissyco.'

'Weird. What a coincidence. What does he want?'

'No, he wasn't calling you, he was calling me.'

'Why was he calling you on my phone?'

'Because he couldn't find out my phone number. Oh, never mind.'

The call-waiting bleep starts. 'Ben, there's someone trying to come through. Shall I get it?'

'OK. Tell them I'm not there.'

'Yes, I was going to. Shall I tell them you're on the other line?'

'Depends who it is.' A typically Ben answer.

'Hold on.' I hit recall-2 and it's Dan back again.

'Hang on, Dan. I've got Ben on the other line.'

'Oh, right. Shall I go away?'

'No. I'll get rid of him.'

'Oh. OK.'

Recall. 'Ben?'

'I'm still here.'

'Dan's on the phone.'

'Ah.'

'He wants to talk to me.'

'Oh, right. Have I got any messages?'

I check the answerphone, which is silly, because I've been sitting next to it all day and the phone's not gone once except in the last ten minutes. 'No.'

'Oh, OK. I'll go then, shall I?'

'Yes.'

'Righty-ho,' says Ben, 'see you later.'

'Yes. Later.' I hit recall and there's no-one there. Dan's obviously going through another—

It rings again. As I have the handset already primed, I pick up halfway through the first ring, to find static. 'Hello?' I say again.

'Oh, hi,' says Dan. 'That was quick. I hadn't even finished dialling.'

'Speed queen Sasha. Anyway. What can I do for you?'

'Oh, well,' says Dan, 'we were all wondering how you were. We felt really shitty about what happened to you. By the time we arrived the next day, you'd already gone, and no-one would even tell us what agency you'd come through. I wanted to check that you were OK, and say that we're really sorry you lost your job because of us.'

'Don't worry about it. I've got a feeling it would have happened whether there were cameras there or not.'

'Well, anyway,' Dan continues, 'I wanted to say sorry. You were brilliant, and we all really enjoyed your company. I honestly don't think we'd have got anything worth filming if it wasn't for you.'

'It's fine. It was fun. And it's probably the best revenge I could have, isn't it?'

He laughs. 'Yes. I guess so. Look. I wanted to talk to you.'

'Talk away.'

'We were wondering – you know we're doing really well at the moment? We've got three things in development, and Shona's completely run off her feet. We all are.'

'Congratulations.'

'Well, I think it's about time that Shona moved up and became a producer full-time. She's really good, you know, and she'll go off elsewhere if I don't appreciate her properly.'

'Great,' I say, wondering, why are you telling me all this?

'So it's like this. We're going to need to take someone on to fill up what she was doing. Well, obviously not every-thing she was doing, but all the research stuff and the gofering and organisation things. You know. Quite a lot of it's what you were doing while we were at Prissyco, only it would be for us and you wouldn't be able to go home at five o'clock.'

'Uh-huh?'

There's a pause. I wait for Dan to continue, but it seems like he's waiting for me to do the same.

'So what do you think?' he says.

'What do I think what?'

'Well, do you want the job or not?'

I sit up bolt upright, spilling the crisps off my tummy onto the carpet. 'You're offering me a JOB??'

'Yes. Sorry. Didn't I make that clear? It's a pretty humble job, of course, but it's probably more interesting than what you're doing at the moment. And we wouldn't be able to pay you much, but it would be enough to live on, and it's a start, isn't it? And you'd probably like Bristol, once you'd settled in. One of Shona's friends has a room going in her house in Clifton, so you'd at least know a few people from the off. I don't know. Maybe you've got things to keep you in London. Maybe you're happy with what you're doing. We just thought, well . . . ' He trails off.

'Are you serious, Dan?'

'Yes. Totally. We'd love to have you, and we've practically given you a dry run as it is.'

A job. Not just a job, but the first rung of a career. Something really interesting; something to get out of bed and look forward to the day about. A salary. A place in the world. Christ.

'Of course I'd like to,' I say. 'Jesus God yes, I'd love to. Thank you.'

'You don't have to decide straight away. Think about it and call me back.'

'No. No. I don't need to think about it.' You don't get opportunities just dropped in your lap like this very often; if I've learned one thing over the last year, I've learned that. 'I'll take it. When do you want me to start?'

'Whenever you can. Straight away, if you can. Whatever. So can I take it that that's a yes?'

'Yes,' I shout. 'Yes, yes, YES!'

'Well, that's fab,' shouts Dan, 'I'm thrilled and I know Shona will be too. We'll talk about details when—'

And the phone goes dead again. I look at it, hold it gingerly in my hand like it's a magic wand, a source of miracles. Ricki's finished her little homily, and a tiny fluffy kitten is being hand-fed to heart-wrenching backing music on *Animal Hospital*. Oh, God: the moment I've been waiting for. Here, at last: my place in society, my function, the thing that lets me hold my head high at parties and say, 'This is what I am.' I kiss the telephone, hug a cushion, and, because I'm a girl and it's what girls do, burst into tears. And then I grab the phone again, and call Ben.

Chapter Seventy

A Spanner in the Works

Magnus looks around the living-room approvingly. Ben looks at Magnus half-approvingly. I look at Magnus and wish, please, God, let Ben say that this one's OK. We've done twenty of these interviews now, and he's turned everyone down flat. I mean, you don't expect to hit paydirt first time when you're hunting for lodgers, but you can't afford to be too fussy. I swear, if Ben's difficult about this one, I'll clock him. It's slowly dawned on me that he's being deliberately perverse, that he's turning people down for the sake of it, but he can't find anything to object to about Magnus. The guy's clean, and well-mannered, and friendly, and has a cool name. OK, he's not on the surface of it the most inspiring person in the world, but there's not actually anything there to object to, either.

I close my eyes and will Ben: like this one, you bastard. Just accept this one, please.

'Well,' says Magnus, 'I think I could be very happy here. It's a lovely house, and my bedroom would be just fine.'

'Good,' says Ben, and I'm about to whoop with joy because this is the most enthusiastic he's been all night, when Magnus continues.

'And my Bible-study group will be thrilled with this lounge,' he finishes.

Ben stops short, just as he's about to speak. Looks with narrowed eyes at Magnus and says, 'Bible-study?'

'Yes,' Magnus leans a clean hand on a clean knee and smiles enthusiastically. 'I'm sure I mentioned it. We meet twice a week, on Mondays and Thursdays. Just the usual sort of thing: tea, cakes, biscuits, lots of chat. It's a social thing, really, as much as a religious one. An opportunity to get to know each other better and share our faith in an informal fashion. You'd enjoy it.'

Ben looks poleaxed. 'Do you have a group of your own?' enquires Magnus. 'Because you'd be more than welcome to join ours. You'd have a lot to contribute, I'm sure, with all your rather unusual life experience. Some awfully nice people. Lots to say for themselves. It can get quite lively, there are so many opinions flying about!'

'Right,' says Ben.

'So when could I move in?'

'Um. Well, I'll have to let you know. Obviously, we've got a load more people to see.'

Magnus, crestfallen, says, 'Oh. I was under the impression . . .'

'No.' Ben stands up, offers him his hand. 'I can't just let all these people who've got appointments tomorrow down now, can I?'

'Well, yes, but . . .'

'Thank you,' says Ben, 'for coming to see us. We'll let you know.'

I show Magnus to the hall, hand him his coat, shake his hand. Wave him off into the night, come back into the living-room.

'I am not,' Ben starts as I enter, 'having a bloody God-botherer in my house.'

'No, I know.'

'You can't make me.'

'I'm not trying to.'

'Well, you can't.'

Ben brushes past me. 'I'm going to make dinner.'

'OK.' I follow him down the stairs to the kitchen.

'I don't believe,' he slams open the fridge, 'that on top of everything else, you're trying to make me live with a God-botherer.'

'Ben, I'm not. It's fine. You don't have to live with him. But you're going to have to make your mind up soon, or you'll have to do the whole thing on your own. I'm leaving in two weeks, and you'll have no-one in the house at all.'

A couple of chicken breasts have only just passed their sell-by dates. Ben slaps them down on the counter, finds the piri-piri and shakes it over the top. 'You want potatoes with this, or rice?'

'Whatever.' I wave my hands in the air, hopelessly.

'Whatever,' he repeats in a playground boy-imitates-girl voice.

'Ben, you've got to stop being so picky. You've found something to hold against every single person we've talked to. Someone's got to live up to your expectations. For God's sake, you lived with Craig for long enough.'

'Every single person has been awful,' he says sulkily, fumbling around in the store cupboard. 'We'll just have baked potatoes.'

'They weren't. There was nothing wrong with Rosanna.'

'What, with that voice? You want me to share a house with Minnie Mouse?'

'OK. Mike.'

'Filthy. Did you see the state of his fingernails?'

'He's a painter.'

'I'm not having those hands near my food.'

'All right. Joanne.'

'Stuck-up cow. Daddy owns a sweatshop and she thinks she rules the world. I suppose,' he continues evilly, 'that you'll be wanting me to live with Babs next.'

Babs very nearly fainted when she walked in through the door and realized that the landlord was Ben. Asked him for his autograph about fifteen times and announced that her friends would all want to come round and meet him when she told them who she was living with.

'No.' I try to sound very, very patient. 'Of course not. But what was wrong with Richard?'

'Richard?' He puts two spuds in the microwave, turns it on. '*Richard*? Did you see that guy's eyes? He was obviously hearing voices.'

'No, darling, I think that that was the fact that you had the stereo turned up so loud he couldn't hear a word you were saying.'

'Ah, bollocks.'

'OK. Mindy.'

He rounds on me, puts his hands on his hips and rolls his eyes. 'I am *not* living with someone called Mindy. Not. *Mindy*.' He spits the name out with a grimace.

I'm so tired of this. Ben is bloody impossible and I never noticed it before. An impossible, bad-tempered, small-minded snob. 'Bollocks,' I snarl back, and bang the chicken onto the grill pan. 'Then you can just bloody sort it out yourself.'

'All right, I will.' Ben gets out the Scotch bottle and pours himself a glass. I notice that he doesn't even offer me one. 'I don't need your help anyway.'

'Fine. Can I have one of those?'

'Do what you want. It's not up to me, is it?'

I help myself to a drink, try to calm down. Say, 'Ben, I'm sorry. I'm only trying to help. I didn't realize you'd think I was interfering. If that's what this is all about, then—'

But Ben interrupts me by banging his hand down on the counter. 'Just shut up,' he cries. 'Shut up, Sasha. I don't want to live with anyone, do you understand?'

Taken aback, I start again. 'Well, why didn't you say? I thought you said you'd be lonely once I'd gone . . .'

'Ohh, God, woman,' his voice rises like a cartoon character about to explode, 'don't you understand anything?'

'Understand what?'

He whirls round and grasps my elbows, his fingers digging in so it hurts. For some reason, he seems to be absolutely furious, his mouth drawn back in a snarl, all the tendons in his neck standing out like hawsers.

'Ben! Stop it! What are you on about?'

'Don't you understand, you obtuse, idiot, blind bloody woman, that the only person I want to live with is you?'

Abruptly he lets go, turns his back on me, shoulders drooping. I search around, find my jaw on the floor and click it back into place. Can't find a thing to say, so wobble there behind him, looking at the floor.

'Well, say something,' he mutters.

'I don't know what to say.'

'Oh. Well, there's my answer, I guess.' His voice is deep with despair.

'No, Ben, it's not that. Why didn't you say anything before?'

'I didn't – I – you were so happy about your job, and – I don't know. Maybe I hoped you'd say something to me. Maybe I just thought something would happen so I didn't have to say anything at all.'

'Oh, God. Ben, why didn't you tell me?'

'I didn't want to spoil things. Look. I've gone and spoiled them now. There you were, so happy, and I've spoiled it all.'

'No. Yes. I don't know.'

'If you'd known before,' he asks, turning round so he can look at me sideways on, glancing through his eyelashes, 'would it have made any difference?'

Ben, I've loved you for years. I've sat through all the shit times and all the good times, the times when you were so bigheaded no-one could talk to you, the times when you were so miserable you couldn't talk to me. I've followed you wherever you went. There's no-one else in the world who means as much to me as you do, and no-one ever will.

'Well, of course it would have. I had no idea. You never said anything. I thought you were just – I don't know. I thought it was just convenient for you, comforting, or something.'

Ben puts his hands over his eyes. Speaks slowly, quietly. 'But I said, Sasha. I told you I loved you, that first night. Didn't you hear me?'

'Ben—'

'I love you. I always have. I've loved you since the first day I met you, but I never thought you'd be up for it. I didn't think you saw me that way. And these last few weeks, they've been the best in my life, being with you, being with you all the time, being able to go to sleep with you and wake up with you, and tell you about my day and listen about yours, and eat with you and lie around on the sofa together. I don't think I'll ever sleep again once you've gone. I love you.'

I've got tears in my eyes. God, Ben, why did you have to leave it till now?

And then he steps forward, and once again holds onto

my elbows, only gently this time, and says the worst thing he could say. The worst, and the best: the thing I've secretly wanted all my life, deep down in that quiet place that has always known the truth about my best friend, that no-one else will ever take his place, that life without each other will be a life without meaning.

'Don't go,' says Ben. 'Please don't go. You can stay here, we can stay together. I know I should have said this before, but it's not too late. You're my luck, and I'm yours. You know that. I know that. We can't walk away from each other now. We could be together for the rest of our lives.'

I look at him. My darling, my best, my only. And I'm thinking: what do I do now? What in the hell do I do now?

And Ben is standing there, hands on my arms, bending down to see if he can read the answer in my face.

'What do you think, Sasha?' he is saying, in a voice full of hope and despair. 'What do you think?'

Chapter Seventy-one

Première

It's not that I want to leave, but I know better than most that dream jobs don't fall in your lap very often. As the time for leaving rushes towards me I find myself thinking more and more about my reasons for staying, and get strange moments of vertigo at the prospect of being parted from them. But all my friends – all my reasons for wanting to be here – are encouraging me, congratulating me, getting excited on my behalf, and of course I know that they're right.

Obviously, I can't go anywhere until after the launch of the movie. We've all sworn that the opening was something none of us would miss for the world. We all owe Ben a lot, one way or another, and the least we can do is all be together on his big night. Donna comes back from Dublin, Craig comes up from Brighton, even Matt and Tania drag themselves from the safety of Fulham up to the West End for the night. Carey discovers that he actually does have a suit without cigarette burns, Marina slips out of an evening at the Savoy celebrating the engagement of one of her cousins to another of her cousins. Tania, Donna, Marina and I wear black – Donna a bundly traditional thing that accentuates her breasts and her bum, a crazy turquoise turban and huge gilt earrings, Tania a hugely expensive maternity tent with a label hanging out at the back, Marina a severe Callas-style suit, dark glasses and a bob as sleek as a Pamela Anderson catsuit and me in something floaty from Ghost that, if they had but known it, I have Prissyco to thank for – and the eight of us squeeze into the ghastly white stretch limo with pink neon strips along the side that pulls up outside the house in Stockwell and attracts the attention of every little boy within a square mile.

For the first time in history Tania leaves the chauffeur to find his own way to Leicester Square, because she has discovered that the cocktail cabinet contains three bottles of free champagne. 'It's only Veuve,' she says, 'but I guess I can have the one glass. I could get used to living like this,' and caresses the cream leather covering the seats.

'I thought you already did,' says Craig, and Tania laughs and squeezes Matthew's hand.

'I think we're more Gloucestershire-rectory people than stretch limo,' she replies, and Matthew, looking content with his projected future, pats her bump with pride. Ben puts an arm round me from one side, Carey from the other; each, for some reason, succumbs to an urge to tickle me as he does so.

To our astonishment Leicester Square is not only roped off to allow a straight path to the front of the cinema, but is heaving with photographers on ladders, gogglers and shrieking young women. The publicity people have done their job, although the only 'stars' involved are one washed-up teen-throb and a footballer who was always more famous for his scoring off the field than his scoring on it. When Ben emerges from the limo, first, as is his right, the shrieking girls go up an octave, break into song:

'We love Ben Cam'ron, we do. We love Ben Cam'ron, we do. We love Ben Cam'ron, we do-oo. Be-en Cam'ron *we* love *you*!'

All the twelve-to-fifteen-year-olds who were in love with Ben back then are hovering around the twenty-year mark now, just ripe for their first arts-cinema crushes and with a few quid in the back pocket. The seven of us follow Ben at a respectful distance as he runs the gauntlet, smiling shyly as only he knows how, awkwardly putting his hands in his pockets and shuffling about as he pooh-poohs any suggestion that he is a star. Damn, Ben's good at this stuff. If anyone was ever good at British modesty, it's him: Hollywood will lap him up. As usual, as Ben passes the bank of print photographers, a zillion flashes light up the dusk air. As Carey, Tania, Matthew, Marina, Donna, Craig and I reach their patch, we hear a whisper go round – *who are they? Who are they? Are they anybody? No, they're nobody* – and suck in the sigh of frustrated boredom as we pass. An elbow digs into my ribs and I step aside as Diana Pepper, dressed only in chain-mail, pushes forward and tucks her arm into Ben's. And we drift on into the lobby as, sheepish but proud, he squires the greatest bosom of the Seventies about the pavement.

The film gets the statutory ovation at the beginning, and a genuine one at the end. Sitting next to Ben in the dark as he laughs quietly at his own frenetic performance is the weirdest thing: Ben may think he's funny, but no-one else does. I understand now why *Empire* has been calling him (along, of course, with everyone else in the last ten years) the biggest discovery of the millennium, why the *Sun* has been on his case for some topless work. Ben is magnificent: scary, angry, gentle and beautiful. Without the flush of alcohol that usually accompanies these qualities when he's with us, I can see those noble-savage qualities as others see them. Ben is a beauty: Ben is fine. And Ben's driving me down to Bristol tomorrow afternoon.

So after the applause has died away and Ben has made his way through the throng in the hallways and receptions, who slap him on the back until I can see him wince in pain, pump his hand and press their business cards into his top pocket. Surreptitiously, we make a dash for the limo. 'Eeeee!' scream the girlies. 'Eeeee! Ben! Over here! Eeee!' It's like the old days, those scary nights when he'd have to be surrounded on all sides by a bank of giants with walkie-talkies, when you wondered, sometimes, if he'd have any clothes left by the time he reached the safety of the bus. 'Ben! Me! Look at meee!'

He chucks himself in through the door and slams it shut, locking the doors and laughing like a maniac.

'My God,' says Carey, 'is this what it was always like?'

Ben shrugs. 'God, no. It was *much* worse.'

Carey sits back and looks at him. 'And you want to go back to it?'

Ben pulls a face, half grimace, half sorrow. 'I don't know anything else, Carey. That's all I've known since I was sixteen.'

'I would hate it.' Carey looks through the window at the bodies pressed up against the smoked glass as the limo inches its way forward towards Piccadilly. 'How can you want to be unable to go anywhere without anyone recognizing you? Not to be able to go for a quiet drink in the pub without some stranger thinking they know you?'

Ben looks serious, then cross, then just calm. 'Carey, mate,' he says, 'for the last three years I've had people come up to me and ask if I used to be Ben Cameron. I've had people take the piss out of me in public places for being a failure, for having been someone they all once wanted to know. I've had people laugh at me and patronize me and say things like, "Not so mighty now, eh?" I've got a face that everyone recognizes. I would have spent the next twenty years living with that until I grew out of my face and they let me be a suburban nonentity with a past, living in fear of documentary cameras popping up to make jokes about the balding obscurity of my life. What do you expect me to prefer? That, or this?' The limo picks up speed, heading over to Kensington, where there's an all-night party with cameras and canapés set up to celebrate the film.

'This is your last night, though,' says Marina, 'when you'll be able to be out like a normal person. Doesn't it scare you?'

'Of course it scares me. It scares me stupid. I think maybe you'll all stop being my friends, that I'll spend the rest of my life hanging around with fickle, name-dropping, painted people who do therapy in order to confess about it and think that they're doing their bit to support the Third World by spending a third of their disposable income on cocaine. But you know, I got chosen by this life when I was sixteen years old, and it's as much part of what I am as any of the bits that you lot have seen me through.'

We fall quiet, watching the bridge-and-tunnel people wander up the Haymarket in search of hamburgers and turn to stare as we glide past in our armour-plated microclimate. And, as we turn into Piccadilly, Ben says, 'But I'll tell you what. I'm not going to start tonight.'

He puts his finger on the intercom button and asks the driver to take us over the river to Gabriel's Wharf. 'Oooh,' whines Tania, 'I was looking forward to going to the paaarteee.'

Ben's eyebrows draw so close together that they almost combine. 'Tania. You can get out now if you like, or you can come with your friends and spend the last evening you're likely to spend with all of us for a long, long time.'

Tania, startled, cringes and then curls round in her seat. 'Ah, well.' She drops the flap down on the minibar, pulls out another bottle of fizz, shakes her head and exchanges it for the bottle of Highland Spring. 'I might as well make the most of the luxury while it lasts. It'll be nappies and hamburgers before we know it.'

Chapter Seventy-two

Gabriel's Wharf

There's a definite nip in the air, but we sit outside at a long bench-cum-table outside the pub on Gabriel's Wharf that no-one's ever known the name of because the ads for Hoegaarden beer are so large they hide everything else about it. Inside, the place heaves with South London hearties ordering jugs of cocktails, but outside it's just the eight of us, elbows on the table, extremities rubbing against each other, competing to be heard as our voices rise with each extra injection of red wine.

Carey's on great form, keeping Donna in fits as he imitates, one by one, every drag queen that's ever been through the Two Brewers. Marina finally takes off her sunglasses, and starts telling stories about the sex lives of the Eurotrash. Every time I tune in, I hear phrases like 'With a Dobermann, my dear . . . I always worry about the security guards catching something on that yacht.' Matthew keeps up a constant stream of jokes that have come into the dealing room on the internet within minutes of any notable dying in unfortunate circumstances.

Tania, still sticking nobly to the mineral water and waving our fag smoke away, says things like, 'Of course, he's going to have to give up swearing. I simply won't have swearing in the house. We were thinking of getting a couple of horses. We could keep them at livery in Richmond and ride at weekends. What do you think? Or should we just bite the bullet and buy a cottage somewhere? Oh, but the driving . . .'

Craig laughs at her. 'Tania,' he says, 'I really don't know why I like you, but I do. It must be pheromones or something.'

'Nonsense,' says Tania, 'you like me because I'm the only person you know who's got her life together.'

'*Together*?' shrieks Donna. 'Excuse me, but who's the one who's having an illegitimate child in a two-bed flat in three months' time? *Baby*-mother.'

Tania waves her left hand, on which we all see a diamond of grotesque proportions nestling among the gore-red nail varnish. 'I'm not getting married,' she says, 'until I can fit into my Azzedine Alaïa suit. Call me old-fashioned, but I want to look nice at my wedding.'

And I think, God, look at these people. Everyone who walks past and sees our little group in the dark, showing off and shouting, must think: Damn, I'm glad I'm not one of them. Tiresome, spoilt, opinionated, irritating, big-mouthed children playing at being grown-ups and only occasionally succeeding, but they're my friends. They're part of me. I get a drunken rush of affection, unhook my legs from around Carey and Ben's ankles and get to my feet. Tap on a bottle with my glass until everyone shuts up.

'A toast.' I'm not entirely steady on my pins, but what the hell. 'A toast to Ben for tonight and the future. A toast to the baby, poor little bastard, may he survive his parents. And a toast to all of us. I may be sodding off to the West Country and out of your lives for ever, but I just want you to know that I love you all.'

A second's quiet, and Donna bursts out in a cackle.

'Sasha's off.'

'Dozy tart,' says Craig. 'Never could keep her sentimentality under control.'

'Aah, bugger it. You're all bastards, but I love you anyway.'

'And we love you,' Carey mutters, turning back to Marina and her tale of a German prince, a crossbow and half a dozen naked prostitutes.

'I'm drunk,' I say. 'I'm going for a walk.'

Ben extricates himself from the mass. 'I'll come with you.'

We take a bottle of wine and a couple of glasses down to the river, walk out onto the pier to look at the lights of the Oxo tower reflected in the water. The sound of the others dies away as we round the corner, and by the time we're leaning our elbows on the railings at the end of the pier, all we can hear is our own voices and the hum of the traffic working its way along the northern embankment. I lean over, watch as an old wooden orange-crate – funny how you only ever see those in the river, never in the street where you could use them for a coffee-table or something – drifts past below us on the tide.

'Feeling OK?' asks Ben.

I nod. 'Yeah. I'm fine. Just nerves, I guess.'

'Are you scared? You're not having second thoughts, are you?'

'No. No, no, no. You're not, are you?'

Ben leans across and smiles into my face. 'Never in a million years. Never in my lifetime. It'll be fine, you'll see. And the job will be great.'

I nod again, visions of myself carting that Klieg light around over my arm dancing before my eyes.

'It'll be brilliant.'

Ben puts an arm round my shoulders, kisses me on the

cheek. 'I'm really proud of you, you know. It's plain sailing from now on. Everything you've got, you've made for yourself and you deserve it.'

I put an arm round his waist and squeeze back. 'And I'm proud of you, my darling. You've won at last, and I couldn't be gladder.'

'You know, we should go home,' he says, 'if we're to have a last night at all. You're going to have the world's worst hangover, and we'll have to get going early if we're going to get to Bristol before dark.'

'What time's Magnus coming in the morning?'

Ben grimaces. 'Bloody bible-basher: eight o'clock. Doesn't have any concept of a civilized hour.'

'Still. He'll be a perfect tenant. Clean, tidy, no drunken parties and totally honest.'

He shakes his head. 'I worry about the tea stains on my carpet, though.'

We linger a moment to take a last look at the lights of London. I always thought that London was where I was going to stay, my future, my career. I still have trouble grasping that as of tomorrow I'll be a Bristol chick.

I turn and look at him: my lovely man, my messy, clomp-footed, clumsy oaf, and think, Ben, none of this would mean a thing without you.

And I say, for the millionth time, 'Ben? You're sure you want to do this? You don't mind?'

And he kisses me, and nuzzles my cheek, and says, 'I've told you a million times. Bristol's great. It's a good city. We can be as happy there as anywhere else, as long as we're together. I can live anywhere now; I can go wherever I need to be. And the only place I need to be is with you.'

And I kiss him back, bury my nose in the smell of his neck, and think, God, life can be good when it's permanent.